Big Damn Magic

Big Damn Magic

KEVIN PETTWAY

Cursed Dragon Ship
PUBLISHING

<u>Anthology</u>

Last Night at the Jolly Chicken

<u>Misplaced Mercenaries</u> by Kevin Pettway

A Good Running Away

Blow Out the Candle When You Leave

Big Damn Magic

Illusions of Decency

Heroes Kill Everyone

<u>Hettie Stormheart series</u> by Jen Bair

One Good Eye

Ruthless Alchemy

<u>Huntress and Harvester series</u> by Jessica Raney

A Seed Once Sown

<u>Wrong Way series</u> by Kevin Pettway

Wrong Way to Heaven

Wrong Way Home

<u>Invasion of the Chromium</u> by William LJ Galaini

Chromium Rise

<u>Pick's Pocket</u> by C.M. McGuire

Beer For My Corpses

If You've Got the Money, I've Got the Crime

<u>The Kin</u> by Ethan A. Cooper

All Hail the Kin

Gullhome
Oldam's Temple
Norrik
Raiders Sea
Icebite
Spirit Oyster River
Summervatn
Vikkan
Krysuvik
Badiron
Majloc
Disn
Tyrran
Knarrax
Summer Trades
Gradron
Mirrik
Piping
Green
Brimland River
Shoaf
Low Wood
Rousea
Walchport
Rousland
The Arlean
Dalut
Arlea
N
W
E
S
Steed
Sejent
Sedrios
Southfen
Wheue
The Paradisals
Bangut
Runfish
Port Placid
Puff
Lan

Full-color map at KevinPettway.com

CONTENTS

I dedicate this book to Covid 19.
For forcing me to stay in the house where I can write,
for introducing me to grocery delivery services,
and for showing off an ability to be locked
in a house for a year with one person...
and still love her more than anything.

1

KEANE LOSES A KINGDOM
KEANE

Oldam's—something. Ah, fuck it." Keane blinked against what sunlight filtered in between the tree trunks. He groaned as his muddled vision cleared.

The man in front of him, cutlass in his hand and wide-brimmed leather hat on his head, raised a brow.

Keane rubbed at his eyes and smeared blood across his forehead. "This isn't . . . You're dead. I killed you. It was the best day ever."

The trees of Three Sisters Wood rustled in the chill breeze. Broad oak trees mixed with birches and elm. Tall yellow grass dreamed of sunlight from the floor of this tiny round patch, roofed as it was by powerful leaf-covered limbs that reached out and up.

Pain from being clubbed in the head with a sword hilt blurred his vision. As he became able, Keane blinked out at the murderers surrounding him. Where in all of Oldam's sand-chafed underclothes was he?

Now he remembered.

Keane had led his wife Megan and her mother-in-law Loffa here last night while the wicked Duke Regent Songham Hubrane overran Treaty Hill and crowned himself as the new ruler.

It had not been a good day to be king in Greenshade.

Mercenaries surrounded Keane in the small clearing. Queen Megan and Loffa were nowhere in sight.

Keane lurched to his feet. With two awkward pulls, he drew his blade free of its scabbard. "Harden, you miserable bastard, where is my wife?" He staggered and turned in a clumsy circle, his blade pointed out at the half dozen grinning mercenaries. Keane hurt, the ache in his back tolerable only because the pain that screamed in his skull drowned it out. The trees tilted to one side, and Keane tilted to the other. Megan appeared under one arm and held him up.

"I've got you," his young wife and queen said. "You look terrible, by the way."

She smiled, and the throb in his head lessened. Even in the uniform of the Duke Regent's infantry, Megan shamed every other woman he had ever met. She was small with pale Andosh skin, long brown curls, and a smile that set off fireworks in Keane's brain. He, on the other hand, was on the tall side, with a rangy, warrior's build, and wearing the same uniform she was. His normally light brown Pavinn skin was gray and blotchy, and dirt and leaves covered his clothes.

Not exactly the picture of a king.

He pointed to his head. "I think someone hit me again." No, he corrected himself. Not just someone. "Harden."

"Here, boy. Right in front of you."

Keane yanked his head upright, and grasped Megan's shoulder to stay on his feet. About the same height, Harden looked Keane dead in the eye. Gray and dusty, Harden was slimmer than Keane and all gristle. He claimed Pavinn heritage, though no one could tell it. Thin gray hair hung to his shoulders, and he managed a balance between comfortable and menacing, beneath his gray hat that used to be brown and a long leather coat that used to be purple.

The cutlass he pointed at Keane's face shone bright enough though.

"You wanting to settle some scores?" Harden shrugged. "I could kill another king of Greenshade." He gave Keane a slow, cold-blooded smile. "That would give me a place in history for sure. Everyone in the Thirteen Kingdoms would know my name. I can't even *imagine* how much I could charge for mercenary work."

Laughter sounded from the men around the clearing's edge.

Keane was technically even with Harden in regicide, having just put a bloody end to *King* Songham himself but did not mention it. Harden might want to put another point on the scorecard.

"Welcome to the Free Hand, Keane my boy. There's only seven of us, but a man has to start somewhere. Especially after you blew Wallace's Company to hell."

By degrees, Keane's blade fell until the tip rested on the grass. He couldn't beat Harden's dear, dead grandmother in the shape he was in now. Better to play for time and look for opportunity later. Maybe find a way to get Megan out of here first.

Megan spoke up. "So, you killed my father and sacked my city. My father was an ass—and Songham's just like him. Looks like your page in history has already been torn out."

Harden frowned and scabbarded his cutlass. The fancy gold basket hilt gleamed in the morning sun. "Eli," he said over his shoulder, "bring his majesty some water. He looks like shit."

An older man, bald, Andosh-white, with an iron-gray beard and wide shoulders over his paunch, stepped away from the encircling trees and walked to Keane. He handed him a waterskin and swatted him on the back. "Good to see you again, lad," he said.

Keane rather doubted it, but he kept his thoughts to himself and washed the sour taste out of his mouth with a swig of water. He felt just good enough to stand on his own. Keane gazed around the camp slowly so as not to make himself dizzy again.

They stood in a hollow along the edge of a broader clearing in the woods, all of it filled with tall yellow grass. Not at all where he had been knocked out. He couldn't see the Middle Peaks so they hadn't gone too far north, but neither could he smell the ocean anymore.

Keane spied Queen Mother Loffa who sat upright on a fallen log and stared at its knobby surface. His worry for Megan had erased the queen mother from his thoughts. Happily, she seemed no worse for wear.

Loffa radiated feminine perfection with flawless posture and proportion. Her shining flaxen hair fell in a gentle blaze over the wine-colored tabard of Songham's duchy. She had been a gift to Megan's father, King Rance, from the Sahansah of Oulan, a specially trained slave with every spark of creativity and intelligence beaten out of her and replaced with a pliant blandness that made her a perpetual innocent. The old king decided that Loffa was an easier wife than Megan's mother, so he disposed of the first queen and crowned his slave as the new one. After Harden and Wallace's Company of mercenaries killed King Rance, Loffa abdicated and made Megan the queen. Soon after, the new queen married the hero that drove Harden and his mercenaries from the city.

That hero was Keane.

"So"—Keane held his head in one hand and tried to look nonchalant about it—"we're heading away from Duke Regent Songham, who I expect would have paid a good deal for my return. Could it be that you've changed your mind about working for Tyrraneans?" There was no chance Harden already knew Keane killed Songham, and Keane intended to keep it that way. The fewer complications, the better.

Harden spat on the ground, making a foul face. "Bugger the Tyrraneans. They couldn't pay me enough."

"Now you know that's a lie," Eli said with a chuckle.

"I do." Harden favored Eli with a tight nod. "I do at that. Anyway, Songham isn't duke regent anymore. He's already kinged himself and denounced the real duke, Branch's boy, as illegitimate. So now he's king *and* duke."

"The catfucker didn't lose any time. And Branch's kid is *not* illegitimate." Keane clasped his arms together over his head to try and get his blood flowing. Was Branch's son, Reid, the legal king now that Songham was dead? Keane had met Reid's mother, Sigga, before, but he had no notion of her ability to keep the country running until Reid grew up. With so many aggressors pressed in from every side, could a child and mother be kept safe?

He looked at Megan and swallowed his fear.

Keane needed to recover fast before Harden thought to take his sword from him. "Huh. So why in the shining stone sphincter of Oldam Almighty am I out here then? Are you looking for a wagon to tie my guts to?"

Harden walked up to him. He got close enough for Keane to smell the pipe smoke on his clothes and the wine on his breath. "Tell me why I shouldn't."

"Because he's the *real* king." Megan shoved her way between the two men. "Even a villain like you should—"

"I think we've already established my record with kings. Especially kings of Greenshade. But I want Keane to tell me why he deserves to live. After all, he was my boy long before he was yours."

A short time ago, Keane had served under Harden Grayspring with Wallace's Company. He and his best friend Sarah worked side by side, threatening villages and looting small towns—even fighting when there was no way to avoid it.

Life had taken some dramatic turns since then.

"All right. I'll tell you why you should keep me alive." Keane held up a finger. "First, if you really do hate the Tyrraneans—"

"Provisionally," Eli said. "King Brannok owes us fer a job. He could pay up."

"That self-righteous prick isn't ever going to pony," Harden said with a sideways scowl at Eli. "He's an evil jackass, and he likes it that way." He returned his attention to Keane.

"Sorry. You were saying?"

"To begin with," Keane said, "everyone knows I'm not Prince Despin of Tyrrane, the poor sap that King Brannok sent to Greenshade to marry Princess Megan. I came clean to everyone in Treaty Hill, and I'm still the king."

Eli's mouth dropped open. "You told everyone in the capital city that you wasn't really Despin and they just said, 'That's cherry?' You expect us to believe that?"

A man Keane did not recognize came forward. He was average height, with ginger hair and beard, and thin. He wore faded green leather armor and a kind smile.

"Maybe he had the pretty little princess flash 'em her titties while he told them."

Keane reassessed the smile.

"That's a queen, Holt." An even thinner woman in black leather meandered to the man's side and leaned against him. Her pale face was beautiful, her black hair unkempt, and her half-lidded eyes made her appear as if she had just rolled out of—probably not a bed—maybe a pile of leaves.

"You should be polite." She bowed her head to Keane. "His name's Morholt. I'm his sister Raven." Raven smiled from beneath her disheveled black hair and whispered, "I don't really give a shit for kings. Don't go getting any ideas."

"Sorry, Majesty." Morholt waved his hand in front of himself in a vague approximation of a bow. "Didn't mean to be crass. I should've said boobies."

Raven slapped Morholt on the side of the head.

"Harden." Keane resisted the reflexive urge to call the man "sir." Kings didn't say sir to mercenaries, and Keane wasn't Harden's man anymore. "Duke Songham is working for Tyrrane. If he's paying you, then you're—"

A crash from the brush interrupted Keane, and a huge man ran through the wood from the west. His curly brown hair waved out behind him, and his big feet pounded the turf. His name was Burgen, and Keane knew him as one of Harden's mercenaries and a bully.

"They followed us," Burgen said, out of breath. "They's—" An arrow from the opposite side of the grass whizzed by his head from behind and stuck in a tree next to Loffa.

Burgen shrugged. "They's here."

2
———

AN ARROW FOR YOUR THOUGHTS

KEANE

Everyone dove behind trees and shrubs to disappear from sight. Eli grabbed Loffa and went to ground with her behind a huge oak. Two large Darrish mercenaries, one tall and ropy and the other shorter and broad-shouldered, who both wore honey-colored leather armor, vanished into the grass ahead of Keane.

Burgen ran through the trees along the south edge of the clearing back the way he came.

"Run for it, my brothers!" he shouted. "Get ye to safety while I hold off the brutes!"

Keane raised a brow. "What?"

Burgen was a thug, plain and simple. He could dash your skull in with a draft horse, but he was a coward at heart. Running interference wasn't his strength.

To one side, Keane saw Burgen laid prone on the ground, propped up on his elbows, while he sniggered in the direction of . . . himself.

"There are two Burgens," Keane whispered. "Why are there two Burgens?"

The giant man looked at Keane and grinned. "Ain't I tha hero?"

"This is your world," Megan said from the ground at Keane's left. "Just tell me what to do."

"Are you all right?" Keane asked her.

Megan's hand went down to her belly and cupped the slight swell there. She nodded.

"Then just hang on. Stay in the grass, and let the idiots do the fighting."

He pushed himself up on his fingertips until he could see over the top of the grass. Further to the left, there were the sounds of men running away through the brush. Across the clearing, Songham's men ran out of the trees, their wine-red tabards stained with dirt and sweat. A few had bows and shot away to the right toward the improbable boom of Burgen's voice.

"Ha, ha! You missed again, you rat-faced tosspot," the deep voice rattled from the trees. "If you spent less time with your fingers up your mother's twat and more on your shooting, perhaps you could hit something smaller than the ground."

"What the stone fuck is this?" Keane's head hurt.

Next to Keane, Burgen laughed and clapped his hand over his mouth. From behind, he could hear the black-haired Raven giggle.

"Burgen, Raven," hissed Harden's voice from somewhere. "Shut it now. I swear you two are the biggest children."

Keane counted fifteen of the wine-colored tabards. Harden's bowmen, the two Darrishmen that crept out into the same grassy field as Songham's men, were nowhere in sight.

The archers, led by a man who did indeed resemble a rat in an unflattering fashion, drew their swords and stomped off toward the other Burgen. The remaining ten men, blades still sheathed, ran toward the sounds of frantic people through the trees to Keane's left, the source of which he never actually saw.

The extra Burgen led half Songham's men on a merry chase while what sounded like a small army of invisible men in flight somewhere in the woods distracted the rest.

Honestly, Keane had no idea what was going on.

"Get ready, lads," Harden said. "Wait for the arrows."

"Stay out of sight," Keane whispered again to Megan.

"Not going to be a problem." She gave him a quick peck on the cheek.

Songham's men were three-quarters of the way across the field, when behind them the two Darrish warriors stood up out of the grass. They raised their longbows and filled the air with death.

The squad spun and yanked their blades free in the yellow sunlight which left them unprepared for Harden, Eli, Burgen and, to his own surprise, Keane who charged into their backsides.

He seemed to be one of the idiots, too.

Keane stabbed the first soldier in the back with a dagger, but the blade stuck in the man's spine, and he had to leave it. He shoved aside a clumsy attack by a red-cheeked man with a round nose and elbowed him in the side of the head.

Red Cheeks stumbled sideways and received a quick sword chop through the neck from Eli. The old mercenary captain took another swipe at the soldier's head as he fell, then moved on.

Keane jumped backward to avoid an overhand blow from a muscular soldier who jumped right after him. Keane reached forward and snaked a hand onto his attacker's wrist, shoved the next blow well outside, and instead caught a rock-hard fist in the ribs. He cried out and stumbled, and the black-haired Raven swung in fast and liquid, like a striking serpent.

She crept beneath and around the soldier's blows, rewarding each one with a stab into his handsome torso, all without apparent effort. He bled from four fatal wounds in as many seconds, not yet realizing he was dead.

Raven stood away from him, expressionless.

The man Raven killed was the last of the ten soldiers in the tiny field. He raised his sword and dropped it.

"I . . . yield." He crumpled into the grass.

She walked to him and put one foot on his dead face. "Yeah, you do."

A horrifying roar burst from the far side of the clearing. Keane yelped and jumped backward to face the sound.

Songham's archers bolted back out of the trees. They threw their blades to the ground and fumbled their bows once more off their backs in panicked terror.

The biggest bear Keane had ever seen, at least eight feet at the shoulder, smashed its way out of the foliage after them. Rat Face ordered the draw and fire, and the animal roared again as their shafts tore into it. It stood up on its hind legs and screamed fury at the sky, at the morning sun, and at the new arrows piercing its underside.

Though he stood to run, Keane stared, transfixed, not at the huge bear, but at the two Darrish mercenaries who, with slow and careful precision, shot down Songham's archers from behind one by one.

Within ten seconds, only Rat Face remained between themselves and the gigantic, enraged bear.

The bear looked down at Rat Face, winked, and said in Morholt's voice, "I know you're tempted to be self-conscious right now, but I wouldn't be. I'm sure loads of mighty warriors piss themselves all the time."

Rat Face spared a glance down the front of his red tabard and grimaced at the spreading stain below his crotch. He half pulled another arrow in his bow and broke out in sobs.

"Wow," said the bear. "I was not expecting that. This is embarrassing. Can, uh, can someone put this guy out of my misery?"

If the rest of the mercenaries had not been mooning about as if the gigantic bear had been someone's slightly attractive cousin, Keane reckoned he would have run a half mile away by now.

The taller of the two Darrish men shot Rat Face through the back of the skull.

"Thanks, Sabni. He's pissing himself, and I'm the one getting red-faced about it. Is that all of them?" the bear asked.

"Burgen?" Harden said.

"Oh, uh, yeah. That's all of 'em," the apparently actual Burgen said.

The bear nodded, satisfied, and blew away in the morning breeze like so much bear-colored smoke. From the trees behind it, Morholt stepped out, packing his pipe as he walked. "That went pretty good," he said.

3

WHERE DID THAT BEAR GO?

KEANE

"Can someone tell me what just happened?" Keane asked. "Where did that bear come from? And where did that bear go? How can Burgen suddenly make two of himself, and why does one of them not sound like an idiot?"

"That was great." Burgen waved a beefy fist in the air. "Did you see me? 'Rat-nosed mommafucker.' Hah! That's fuckin' brilliant, that is."

Raven slinked up to Burgen and wrapped her arms around him. "You're a poet," she said and pulled herself up to kiss him.

"Aw, come on, Raven." Morholt squeezed his eyes shut while he lit his pipe. "Isn't it bad enough that I have to listen to you two humping all night? Now I gotta watch it happen too?"

"Arrows for everyone," the lanky Darrishman said and raised five quivers taken from the fallen. He stood six and a half feet tall with dark black skin and an infectious smile. Oiled braids fell loosely behind his head, and a short trimmed beard glistened in the spotty light. Long rope-muscled arms gleamed in the morning sun. "Would anyone like a bow? Not the best quality, but they'd kill even the deadliest of pheasants."

"I'd like a bow," said Megan.

Keane spun around, still confused about what had happened. He saw his wife help Loffa up from her position next to Eli and lead her out of the hollow.

"I don't, uh . . ." Keane said.

"Certainly, little Queen," the big Darrishman said and handed her a bow and quiver. "Do you know how to shoot it?"

"I have competed in the ladies' archery competition since I was eight," Megan responded. She took the bow and fit the quiver to her back. "I can handle myself."

"I have no doubt that you can," the tall warrior said. "Still, as we know from the story of the *Immortal Queen Nefret and the Fallow Orchard*, even the greatest of warriors can benefit from practice and the observations of others. It would be my most delightful honor to instruct the great Queen of Greenshade in the use of the noble bow, if she would consent to my humble tutelage."

"Please say yes," the shorter of the two Darrishmen said. "If you don't, he'll just keep talking about it."

"Yes?"

If he and Megan and Loffa were captives, why would this big Darrishman hand Megan a bow? For that matter, why did Keane still have his stolen sword? Was Harden simply that contemptuous of any harm Keane might deliver?

What an *asshole*.

"Marvelous," shouted the taller man, and he clapped his hands together. "My name is Sabni, and this sour excuse for a warrior is my companion, Mahu. Mahu, tell the little queen hello."

"Hello."

Where Sabni stretched long and lean, Mahu hunkered thick with broad heavy muscles. His hair and beard were both cropped close, and like Sabni, he wore beautifully maintained leather armor the color of deep honey, with shining metal plates on the shoulders, forearms, and shins.

"I asked a goddamn question." Keane frowned his fiercest frown and placed his hands on his hips. "I expect a goddamn answer. I'm not one of your soldiers anymore, Harden. Eli. I said, can someone tell me what just fucking happened here?"

Their faces still pasted together, Raven and Burgen laughed into each other's mouths. Morholt rolled his eyes and returned to the camp.

Eli reached behind the oak and lifted Loffa's hand to guide her into the center of the camp. "You done met Morholt. He'd be the Free Hand's official runecrafter." As if that explained everything.

This was seven coats of batshit fuckery, but Keane just shook his head and tried to get past it. "So, I guess this means you aren't working with Songham?"

Harden laughed. "Nope. Sure was funny watching you squirm though. We've been in Songham's army for a while, but we were working for the Barons' Conclave."

"What?" Keane said, eyes intent. "The conclave is working against Songham?"

"Mayhap. They asked us to keep an eye on the squirrely little shit. But when we found you, we figured a king's carcass might be worth a fair penny more."

That brought up another question in Keane's mind. "How *did* you find me? Or even know that I'd made it out of Treaty Hill alive?"

"Morholt's got this magic painting he talks to. Tells him things sometimes. This time, it told him where and when to find you."

"Thank you for explaining my magical secrets to any asshole who asks." Morholt looked up from his pack with the frown of a man who had just discovered his bag of pirate candies were made of cow turds instead of apples.

"I'm not any asshole," said Keane. "I'm King Asshole of the country you are standing—sitting—in right now."

"Whatever." Morholt returned to rummaging through his belongings.

"Be that as it may," Harden said, "those men were after you, not us. More will come when those ones don't make it home. We oughtta get gone while we can. Gotta rendezvous to get to anyway."

Maybe more would come, Keane thought. Maybe none would. Or

maybe a lot more would soon charge through the woods howling for his blood. The murder of their ersatz king could alter their priorities.

They broke camp with practiced speed and made their way into the woodlands. Keane followed along, easily falling back into his old rhythms and gait. He held Megan's hand. The two of them would have a lot to talk about soon. She held herself stoically in the face of unfamiliar adversity and misfortune, but she had lost her home and her people only yesterday, and that could crush the hardiest of souls. He looked at her as they walked. At nineteen, she didn't look like a girl to him. She looked like a determined and dangerous woman. He couldn't remember a moment when he had been prouder or loved her more.

Burgen carried Raven in front of him while she ground her leather pants against his.

Morholt walked past, his thin face averted and eyes downcast. "You've ruined sex for me. I hope you know that."

4

THE ROYAL TITLE WRITER

KEANE

I f you mention it again, I'm going to have you bound, gagged, and dragged the rest of the way in the dirt," Harden said. "No one has offered me payment to rescue war prisoners. Therefore, *I* am not going back to Treaty Hill and rescuing any war prisoners. I do expect to be paid for handing over a king to the Barons' Conclave. Therefore, *you* are not going back and rescuing any war prisoners. Give it up, King Keane. King Keane. Has anyone mentioned how stupid that sounds?"

Harden and Keane followed the trail Raven blazed for them through the wood. The rest of the group came up behind them. It was late afternoon, and the woods were full of light. Game trails and the occasional wagon track crisscrossed their path.

"It's been discussed. But as you've mentioned, I am the king. I can pay you myself." A while ago, he and Sarah buried a pillowcase full of stolen loot from the castle somewhere in these woods, somewhere nowhere near where they were right now and much closer to the castle they were fleeing.

Oldam's muddy sharts.

Harden rolled his eyes. "Even if you had more than what's in your pocket, I don't trust kings, and I *never* trusted you. Only times I ever got stiffed, there was a king or two involved. Besides, I have a schedule to keep. Bustin' a bunch of toothless peasants outta some prison camp ain't on it. You know how this works. How long ago was it now—six months?—since you were one of us?"

"Did you ever really consider me one of you?"

Harden flashed a grin. "Nope. You were just Sarah's baggage. She was the prize."

"If some historian ever decides to write a book of my memoirs"—Keane blew out a sigh—"I think *Sarah's Baggage* would be a perfect title."

Privately, he wished Sarah were here right now to chop Harden's head from his dirty gray neck. She'd have the whole lot of them laid out like a platter of luck biscuits on the Days of Oromamus. Except that she probably wouldn't. She was a better person than he was.

He missed Sarah *so* much.

"What do you know? Maybe I missed my calling," Harden said. "I should have been a title writer for royal memoirs."

Keane glanced behind and saw Sabni hold his huge bow out to Megan. She listened intently to whatever instructions he gave. Keane hated the idea of his newly pregnant wife being in a position to need to draw on a stranger, but here they were. Sabni appeared to be a capable teacher and more than respectful enough.

Keane knew his way around a bow, though he was not close to being in Megan's class. Based on the few snatches of conversation he heard between Sabni and Megan over the past couple of hours, the tall Darrishman knew more about archery, stealth, and warfare in general than anyone he knew.

Except maybe Sarah.

Sigh.

"So, you've been a part of Songham's revolt since the beginning?" Keane asked in an effort to move the subject in a less depressing direction.

"Conclave sent us to March Castle three months ago," Harden said. "King Duke Songham Hubrane's childhood home. We joined up then to come back here and crash your party."

"Must have been fun for you," Keane observed.

"A little," Harden admitted, "though truthfully we never intended to do any fighting. That wasn't what we were getting paid for."

A thought occurred to Keane. "How did Songham get the walls down so fast? We were listening for sappers and we never heard a thing. And when the walls came down—"

"Dead men come up out of the holes, except they come up angry and swinging." Harden grimaced. "Songham had himself a demon. Evil monster named Valafar. Every time we'd lose a man to bowshot from the wall, Valafar would bring him back up. He'd still be dead, just like, walking-around dead. Sent 'em up into the city at night close to the wall and set 'em to digging. They dug by hand, so they barely made any noise at all. Also, they never got tired or needed food. Perfect sappers."

"Ugh." Chancellor Finnagel, a sorcerer and advisor who lived in the Forest Castle, told Keane the same thing, but he hadn't wanted to believe it. The confirmation stung.

"Yeah. Man dies, he oughtta be left be."

"Wait just a fucking minute." A piece of Harden's conversation drifted back up to Keane's attention. "You said the conclave sent you to March Castle three months ago?"

"Yeah. So?"

"And they knew then that Songham was planning an attack on the capital?"

"That's why they sent us," Harden answered. "Oh. You didn't know?"

"I was still listening to that creepy little fucker blowing bullshit in my council chambers three months ago." Keane smacked a fist into his palm. *Should have killed the scrawny shit a long time ago.*

"Just to let you know, I don't know why the conclave didn't tell you about Songham, and I don't know what they might want with you when I hand you over. But if you decide to kick up a fuss about coming along, I'll be happy to truss you and the missus up like pigs to market."

Keane stared at Harden for a moment. "They aren't demons."

"What?"

"They aren't demons," Keane said. "This Valafar is a sorcerer. A human that uses magic. Like your Morholt. He works for Angrim, the worst sorcerer of the lot, who lives in Dismon."

"How do you know so much about sorcerers and demons living in the capital of Tyrrane?"

"Because Sarah is a sorceress too," Keane replied. "She's apprenticed to a master sorcerer in the capital." That master sorcerer was Finnagel, but since most people believed as Harden did that sorcerers were demons, Finnagel's identity was kind of a secret. Used to be, anyway. Keane was past giving a shit about *that* old poop weasel's problems.

Keane watched Harden's shocked reaction through the corner of his eye. It almost made the whole trip worthwhile. Sarah represented something special to Harden, something like a favorite daughter. The old mercenary tried to kill Keane just because he was friends with her, and Harden thought Keane might be holding Sarah back.

It felt good to crush a few of the bastard's illusions.

"Well, whatever you want to call them," Harden said, shaken, "this particular demon, Valafar, jumped on his big black horse the instant the outer wall fell and headed north. Rumor was he was riding for Dismon. We'd heard he was supposed to meet up with the Ebon Host and guide them into Greenshade. Looks like that may have been more than a rumor."

This was terrible news. Songham's army already occupied Treaty Hill, and now the Ebon Host of Tyrrane marched to join them against the rest of Greenshade. And Keane had what? A stolen sword at his hip, a dagger in his sleeve, and a wife with a longbow that was too big for her.

No, that was all pretty typical.

"Cheer up, Your Majesty," Harden said, his wolflike grin back in place. "It'll be someone else's problem if the Barons' Conclave kills you."

Which brought up another question in Keane's mind. "So why aren't *you* killing me?"

"Money. I expect to get paid. That's all."

Keane smiled. He wasn't great at a lot, but he was pretty good at knowing when people were lying to him. "That's a lie. I don't believe it, and neither do you. I'm still wearing a sword, and your man is teaching Megan to be even deadlier with that bow than she already was. What's your game here?"

Harden's grin drew down into a cold line, and the old man's eyes went dark. "I have my reasons, boy. Reasons I don't have to tell you, and I'm not gonna. Now if it'll make you happier for me to take your weapon, tie a rope your feet, and have Burgen drag your scrawny ass through the woods, I'll do it. Your pretty little queen, too. Tell me if I'm lying now."

He wasn't.

5

JUST PUT THE DAMN CROWN ON
HULDA HUBRANE

Hulda Hubrane, duchess of the Western Marches, swept into the Forest Castle's Great Council chamber, a magnanimous smile on her pretty young face. The morning was full of sunlight and potential.

Who should she kill first?

As Songham's widow, Hulda was now also Queen of Greenshade. Her husband had been murdered during the mercenary king's escape, likely at his hands. But she knew the bastard would have had help. Whoever helped Keane break free of the castle dungeon would help *her* next.

After all, on top of everything else, Hulda was still the head of the Hubrane Merchant House, the farthest-reaching criminal/shipping enterprise in Greenshade. She knew a little murder on the first day could go a long way toward establishing the right relationship with all the survivors.

Her ducal guard stood in front of the assembled council—mostly tired old men with frightened faces and shaking hands—and kept them pressed against the high-windowed walls. This room soared hundreds of feet above the cobbles below in the midst of one of the famed Flying Halls that reached between castle towers.

Hulda swayed her generous hips on her way to the throne at the far end of the room. Tynos, the Darrish assassin, and General Roen Kalkenndremm flanked her. She could practically feel the daggers the tall dark-skinned woman and the pale Andosh officer, stiff in his wine-red military uniform, shot at each other behind her back. Their recent and torrid affair had not ended well, and Hulda enjoyed their murderous glances far too much to demand they stop.

The throne itself was a gilt chair with thick legs and a wide seat that three Huldas could have shared. It must have been King Rance's before the mercenary took over. Why didn't he replace the thing? It was awful.

As she contemplated the chair, Hulda wondered if Songham ever found the opportunity to sit in it once before being murdered by the mercenary. Would he have remained standing after his coronation? Did her late husband's butt ever touch this vast expanse of cushion?

Well, hers would. The thought that all she had done was walk upstairs and her occupation of the castle had already outlasted her husband's, put a rosy glow in her cheeks.

Hulda sat straight backed in the middle of the throne and smiled out at the room. Her silver-white hair, all the more spectacular for her youth, shone in the sunlight through the windows.

"Hey, sweetie." Hulda gestured to a terrified page.

His skinny knees crowded together in his green and yellow hose. Despite his obvious discomfort, he approached the throne.

"What's your name, hon?"

"Loyal, Your Grace." His knees straightened, but his breath remained shallow and hitching.

"Loyal? Really?" She resumed her upright posture in the chair. "All right, Loyal, which one of these crusty old farts coronates me and makes me your new queen?"

From one arm of Hulda's throne, Tynos kept a gimlet eye on Loyal and one hand at the pommel of a curved dagger that rested on her hip. Of everyone in the room, Tynos dressed the least appropriately for the chill. Her breezy linen clothing, sleeveless and hemmed just above the knee, was made for freedom of movement, not warmth.

The stiff-backed General Roen, on the other side of the chair, watched Tynos with a thunderous expression one might have reserved for a servant who replaced your perfume bottles with rat pee. He dressed in full Hubrane military regalia, his dark mustaches waxed, and fully ready for the occasion.

The general did not like that Hulda called him by his first name which was why she did it. He had long since given up asking to be called General Kalkenndremm as was proper.

"Um," Loyal said, "as I understand it, ma'am, you're already queen. You been queen since King Song—that is—since your husband got turned into a king."

"You can say his name, Loyal." Hulda reached out and took one of the boy's hands, which set him shaking once more. "If Songham weren't dead, I shouldn't be here at all. It was a *good* thing."

Loyal did not respond.

"But that won't do." Hulda tapped the armrests. "We need a ceremony. Something to *celebrate*."

"If I might assist?" A woman in a practical and stately green dress, with a matching hat pinned atop her whitening red hair, raised a hand from the wall.

The Baroness Lady Roselle Tralgar. Hulda knew her by description and reputation. The leader of the Barons' Conclave, Lady Roselle was said to be a shrewd woman of power and intellect. Alone, that was neither good nor bad. She had been uncovered in a tavern posing as a serving wench and dragged back to the castle.

That was rather ghastly.

"Yes, dear?" Hulda disliked this woman on an unexplained and instinctive level. She needed to listen and understand what she represented before she threw her out the window. Reputation was not the same as experience, and Hulda was not the type to allow a resource to be defenestrated before being properly exploited.

"Thank you, Your Grace," Roselle said with a perfect curtsy. "Both of the people who might conduct a coronation ceremony are either dead or likely dead. Although we would normally wait an appropriate amount of time for the nation to grieve the loss of its king, I doubt most of our citizens were even aware King Songham had ascended the throne before he was dead."

"Do you know if he actually sat in it?"

Tynos, obviously paying little heed to the conversation, glanced up at General Roen in his martial finery, curled back a lip in disgust, and looked away.

"I honestly couldn't say," Lady Roselle answered. "I wasn't here."

"Right. And you don't think I'll execute you?" Hulda leaned her head forward and purred the words.

Lady Roselle took a moment before answering. "I am . . . not concerned about it. The former king was more malleable. I doubt anything I could do would serve to change your mind if you decided to have me killed, so why worry? Although I suspect I could be of more use to you than I could have been to King Songham. We have mutual experience with problematic husbands, after all."

That's right. Hulda recalled the story now about the baroness. Threatened by mercenary soldiers in the field of battle, she instead seduced the leader and escaped. And later left her worthless pig of a husband behind for a more indolent position in the castle.

Maybe she could learn to like this baroness.

"Very wise." Hulda crossed her legs. Poise was everything. "But we're off topic, sweetie. Who crowns me?"

"Your choice." Lady Roselle gave a small bow. "I would be honored to officiate, if you would have it."

"Will it take long?" Hulda asked. "We want a party, but this is going to be a pretty full day."

"Recent coronations have required an abbreviated schedule of events," Lady Roselle said. "I think we can take care of all the important bits in a few minutes."

Maybe Hulda could throw Lady Roselle out of the window tomorrow. She seemed to really know what was going on around here, and everyone else was too scared to speak up. Hulda would need someone like that when she cracked this city open across her shapely knee.

"Great. Let's do it."

SEVERAL MINUTES LATER, Queen Hulda held the Golden Wings of Promise, symbolic of her responsibility to the people of Greenshade, the Scroll of Fealty, to demonstrate the obedience of her new subjects, and wore the crystal Crown of Purity, to show her virtue and clarity of thought.

The last one threatened to make Hulda break into laughter.

She returned the ceremonial items to Lady Roselle, who passed them off to the doddering old chamberlain. Hulda would have to replace *that* useless fool.

"My queen, if I may?" General Roen stepped forward and bowed. His lips pursed tight beneath the waxed mustache, and his eyes danced merrily. The general had a secret.

"My dear general"—Hulda put a soft hand on his epauletted shoulder and let it trail down his arm—"have you done something to curry my favor over your competition?"

Tynos had too much self-control to let anyone see her anger, but Hulda could feel the heat radiate from her. These two were so much fun. She would be sad whenever one of them finally killed the other.

General Roen stood and clapped his hands, and from the entrance a pair of ducal guards dragged in an Andosh woman in her late forties, beaten, black hair disheveled, and filthy. Bruises stood out on her pale cheek and neck, and her once fine dress was torn in great rents.

Despite all this, she moved with unerring elegance and command. The men who held her flinched away when her gaze flashed on them.

Lady Aerith Ravenstok, the thrice-damned lady of Crosshouse and Hulda's only true criminal adversary and rival. Here. Entirely under her power.

Hulda jumped out of her seat and kissed General Roen on the lips.

"Oh, Roen, I *love* my present!" She bounced up and down and ran to Lady Ravenstok. Abruptly, Hulda remembered her all-important poise and smoothed her tightly fitted red-and-black gown against her torso.

"Hi darling," Hulda said, bright and happy. "I bet you're glad to see *me* here."

Lady Ravenstok took a slow look up and down Hulda, her bloody and swollen face passive. "Do I know you?"

"Know me?" Hulda was confused. Had her guard beaten the woman too severely? "We've known each other for years. Hulda Hubrane. The Hubrane Merchant House?"

Lady Ravenstok stared, and a glimmer of recognition showed in a single raised eyebrow. How did the woman convey so much with so little?

"Hulda Hubrane. That *is* you." Lady Ravenstok leaned back to get a clearer view through a rapidly closing eye. I see it now. I'm sorry, my dear, I thought someone had dressed a donkey in a horrid tablecloth and let it loose in the council chambers."

Hulda's delight let out of her in a low hiss.

Lady Ravenstok continued, "For a moment I was thinking, *I suppose they really will let anyone rule in Greenshade*, and then I realized you weren't a donkey. Now I see the situation is so much worse."

"Great Council of Greenshade," Hulda shouted. "I have just conceived of a new game. In four days, everyone present will enter their idea for the most *creative* way to kill good Lady Ravenstok here. The winner will receive right and title to her township of Crosshouse and all that entails."

An excited murmur whipped through the council members.

"And do your best." Hulda wanted to be encouraging. "Last place forfeits lands, titles, and wealth to the crown. It'll be fun!" That would keep the pinched-up old shits at each other's throats for a while. Long enough for Hulda to set her plans in motion.

The mood in the room died faster than a commoner with a horse standing on his neck. Like that as well, it was fun, but over too fast.

"Boys," Hulda addressed the two ducal guards who held Lady Ravenstok, "please take the lady to the most miserable cesspit of a dungeon cell available in this stupid green castle. And keep an eye on her. I know she's likely to trip, fall into doors, and get kicked in the face on the way."

"Ta," she said to her stone-faced rival.

6

FIGHT LIKE A GIRL

EMPEROR BRANNOK OF TYRRANE (THE BAD GUY)

Black-tabarded Capital Guard soldiers shifted nervously to make room for the emperor and his daughter as they clattered along the cobblestone streets of Dismon, grim principal city of the Second Tyrranean Empire. One of three wagons, they traveled to smash a cell of rebel agitators in the tanneries and flew through packed lanes of citizens with spine-shattering speed.

The horses pulling the wagon bashed aside yet another commoner unable to leap to safety in time. Brannok observed his only daughter's lack of compassion with pride. Why could Jason not have her sense?

"Not at all, my emperor, I understand the utility of proficiency with arms." Jasmayre's dark red braid flew up in the air as the wagon jounced painfully on the stones, and she braced herself with thin arms on the box board behind her. "Isn't that what all the soldiers are for?"

"You are the head of the Capital Guard, Daughter." Brannok had to concentrate to keep from biting his tongue while he talked. "The only woman *ever* to hold that position. You need to know what real fighting looks like. What it *feels* like. This is your operation."

The Ebon Host was the best trained army in the Thirteen Kingdoms, and the Capital Guard were the elite of these. The men in these three wagons were the deadliest soldiers anywhere.

The mission, on the other hand, was a routine rout and burn, which was why the captain of the Capital Guard had recommended it, and Brannok had chosen it for the outing. Jasmayre was the most cunning of his brood, but she had little in the way of personal experience in combat maneuvers. She had to see real fighting for herself: the dirt, the blood, and most of all, the unpredictability.

Everyone bounced a good six inches out of their seats, and Jasmayre landed with a hand down to keep her dark green dress skirt from flying over her head. "At the moment, I'd say it felt like a sore ass, but I look forward to my continued education."

Brannok gripped the box board with one powerful hand and held the pommel of his sword with the other. A cool wind blew through his fiery hair and beard. He was not intended to be anywhere near any actual fighting. After all, he was an emperor, not an infantryman. But his blood was singing with the thought of further violence to come, and he couldn't help the laughter that boiled out of him.

He had a stressful job, after all. He was due some relaxation.

Black stone homes and businesses gave way to broad wooden buildings, and the stink of old food and animal droppings gave way to the stench of rotted urine and carcasses. Men with long knives and double-tined pitchforks shouted and waved their weapons in between wide tubs, four feet tall and filled with filth and skin.

The wagon clacked to a halt, and the rebels pulled together in a knot of about fifty grungy men in the center of a broad and muddy field of the huge tubs. Tannery buildings surrounded them, and more screaming people, well over two hundred of them, waved their fists from the shadows of the watery morning light.

Together, there were perhaps thirty Host here.

Bolstered by their superior numbers, the rebels advanced in halting steps toward Brannok and the three wagons. They were still scared at the sight of real soldiers, but they were getting over it. Over half wore the floppy black felt hats of the Tyrranean commoner, faded by the sun but warm and cheap. Each had a wide daub of red paint on the side to show their purpose. It gave them a look of solidarity, as if the simple garment were a uniform of a fighting regiment.

It really wasn't.

"Half down, string, and nock, and pull." In very little more time than it took for the Host sergeant to shout the orders, half of the fighting men, still clean in their gray-and-black tabards, jumped out of the wagons while the rest stood. With practiced speed, they bent their half bows against the ground and strung them. When they lifted the bows, they already had arrows in their other hands, nocked and drawn all in a single motion.

The rebels stopped their advance, open horror on their dirty faces.

Brannok grinned.

"*Loose,*" the sergeant shouted.

Three rebels went down beneath the Host's arrows. The rest dove behind the big tubs—as if they were ready for exactly this kind of attack. By reflex, Brannok scanned the area around him for ambushers.

Before he spotted them, Jasmayre hit him from the side and bore him to the wagon bed. Above them men cried out and fell both in and out of the wagon, pierced from behind by short, thick crossbow bolts. Over the side of the wagon, Brannok saw a woman in a tannery window cranking her bow to reload.

"*Run,*" he whispered to his daughter.

Together, they clambered over the dead and wounded and ran back up the street.

"Follow the package," the sergeant shouted. To Brannok, the voice sounded wet and bloody.

A dozen Host ran in pursuit of Brannok and Jasmayre, eager to protect the imperial person with their lives. They came up on both sides to shield their royalty from the windows to either side of the narrow street.

Crossbow bolts continued to fly past from behind, but the fools were trying to shoot as they ran and could not hit anyone.

Brannok did not know this part of his own city, and at this point, he was not even certain in which direction the Fell Citadel lay. He did not stop to consider the possibility that he and his daughter might die out here. It was not in his nature.

Anger replaced his blood and turned his skin as red as his hair. Mail jingled beneath his bearskin cloak as he stomped up the cobblestones. Perhaps the agitators would prove more tractable toiling away in a tannery painted brown with their own fallow innards.

At the first crossing, Jasmayre turned right. "City Warden garrison!" she shouted over her shoulder and dashed up the street.

While the exact opposite end of the fighting spectrum from the Capital Guard—which was why they had not been invited to the party—a garrison of wardens would still provide a good sixty armed men to delay or kill the rebels while Brannok regrouped to smash them and Jasmayre was spirited away to safety.

They turned left again with the rebels still in pursuit, though out of loaded crossbows. That was wrong. They knew the area. Why would they follow the fleeing group to the doors of a—

"Soul of anger," Brannok whispered.

Behind a steady line of disheveled commoners with knives, hammers, and any other implements of pain they could pull to hand, lay the corpses of the City Wardens, snatched from the garrison and slaughtered in the square.

Brannok reconsidered the sinister connotations behind the red-painted hats.

The buildings this far out of Dismon's center were wattle and daub with thick timbers jutting and everything painted a dark gray. They created a uniform wall around the street and square and left the group surrounded on both ends by rebels. At least a hundred of them together.

This had been no routine call to insurrection. This was a trap.

In his first real instant of fear, Brannok noted that Jasmayre had pulled a thin dagger from her hip and stood ready to defend herself.

He drew his own blade, an average-looking sword with a bronze cross guard, and pointed at the face of the lead pursuer, who now stood still catching his breath. Dirty brown hair fell over his eyes, an out-of-place mustache, perfectly waxed, traced the smirk on his lips. The leader held a spear made from a plow claw tied to a pole.

That bastard would die first.

Jasmayre pulled at Brannok's shoulder toward one edge of the street. Always thinking, that one. They would fight side by side with their backs to the wall. He could think of worse deaths.

A few rebels crept forward, the rest held back by fear of being the first to come into sword range of the Capital Guard. A hundred against a dozen, and still they cowered. Even if Brannok went down, he did not think much of this rebellion's chances. Dismon was a big city, and a full third of the Ebon Host was permanently based here.

No more crossbows. They couldn't afford more than the two or three bolts they had apiece, and the bows themselves were undoubtedly stolen.

Brannok shook his head. He wouldn't be killed by the likes of these.

Then the fighting began.

"Unhand me, girl." Brannok rounded on his daughter, who continued to drag at him, now away from the boarded-up building behind them. "I can't protect you if you—oh."

Jasmayre kicked the rotted mortar at the mouth of a sewer drain, and a stone fell in with a distant splash. She had found a way out.

"Like to help?" she asked with a bewitching smile.

Brannok drove his sword point, ruining the edge but saving their lives, into the sandy mortar again and again, cracking it and separating the discolored stonework. He sheathed the blade and kicked at the stones, which gave way in a tumble.

The crowd threw themselves at the tiny knot of soldiers, who showed their color with astounding ferocity. They stabbed, slashed, and kicked, but mostly they utilized a teamwork born of countless hours of drills and exercises to keep the rabble back and each other safe.

There were but six Capital Guard left when Brannok slid into the filth beside his daughter, and he was sorry to see them go.

BRANNOK WAS FORCED to lean down in their flight through the sewer tunnel and used his hands to run almost as much as his feet. Though delayed by the remaining Capital Guard, the sounds of the hate-filled rebels were not far behind. Fortunately, there had been no rain in over a week, so there was little water in the system of underground tubes, though that meant an eyewatering quantity of human waste sat beneath every drain.

Among other, even less savory things.

"If we can find a tunnel going downhill," Jasmayre said, "we can go straight to the Blackwood River. There'll be another warden garrison at the docks with patrols. If those traitors follow us into the river, they won't stand a chance."

They passed beneath another storm drain, far too small to climb up out of. They would never make it as far as the river. Below a wide cut high on his daughter's thigh, the dark skirt ripped open, her leg was an almost solid crimson, bright in the slanted light. Her face was white.

"Damn." She stopped and leaned against one side of the tunnel, her hand to her head. "I think I'm going to . . ."

Brannok stepped forward and scooped her up as she fell. Stooped over with his back already beginning to complain, he ran as fast as he was able with his bleeding daughter in his arms.

Though all he wanted to do was turn around and murder every one of the treacherous cunts behind him.

The sounds of pursuit came louder.

Brannok stepped into a taller chamber, still round as the tunnel had been but a good seven feet high. His relief was short-lived as he realized it terminated after less than two full paces into a deep black shaft. Across the fifteen-foot hole, he could see another tunnel

continuing onwards and another to either side. The left one definitely had a downward grade to it.

But to his right, a ladder built into the stonework rose to a wide
grate in the street above. He could probably even escape—if he left
Jasmayre behind.

He would find the person responsible for this. The person who
organized the agitators and set them on this path to regicide.

And when that person was found, they would take years in the
dying.

Brannok set his daughter down in the center of the floor and
rested her head on her folded arm, in full view of the tunnel behind
them, and just before the yawning black drop. He withdrew to the
right and pulled his sword from its scabbard. In his other hand, he
held his daughter's dagger.

"Whuzzat?" came a voice from the tunnel, rough and uncultured.
"It's the girl."

"The bint?" This voice deeper, angrier. "It's a trap. She had a knife.
I saw it."

"Gimme the thing," said the rough voice again. A pause and some
shuffling.

"Last one," said a woman.

"Trap this, bitch." The first voice was punctuated by a snap and a
thud. A crossbow bolt now protruded from Jasmayre's thin shoulder.
Her eyes fluttered open, and she moaned but dropped away again.

The world turned red for Brannok. Inside his head, he raged and
screamed but held his body still and taut, while his grip on the blades
he held focused his limitless anger.

They would all pay.

A cautious head poked out of the pipe, intent on Jasmayre. The
gray and balding man grabbed the side of the opening and prodded
her with a foot. From the open hole behind her, the sound of dripping water echoed, hollow and distant.

In blackest shadow, Brannok waited.

The older man stepped fully out of the tunnel, and another
followed him. A straggly haired woman peered out behind these two

and turned toward Brannok. She squinted, her eyes flew wide, and her mouth opened to scream.

Brannok chopped into the back of the balding rebel's neck, nearly taking his head. The rebel tripped forward over Jasmayre and pitched into the dark.

A floppy black hat twirled out over the abyss, its red paint flashing in the tiny rays of sunlight it caught from the street grate before disappearing entirely.

The second man whirled with a long thin blade, but Brannok went beneath it and slid his daughter's dagger between his ribs and into his foul heart. He fell against the far side of the wider tube with an aborted scream.

Below him the straggly haired woman cried and beat at the boot that stamped on her other hand and held her pinned. Brannok grabbed a handful of her hair and lifted her out of the tube and into the air. He heard the bald man land somewhere in the black, and he flung the woman after him.

Brannok ducked into the tunnel and faced the surprised and terrified insurgents.

He released his rage.

Anger howled up out of his soul and into his limbs. The frustration of a king thwarted by a monster who lived in his basement, the anger of a man not permitted to be loved by the people around him for fear of showing weakness, and the desperate rage of a father trying to save the life of his only daughter.

Brannok climbed over their corpses. The remaining traitors wailed and fled, but they could not get away, not now that he had his boiling anger to push his arms and legs. By the time he reached the storm drain he and Jasmayre had kicked open, there was only one rebel left.

A dirty man, skinny—with a perfectly waxed mustache.

~

"The surgeon has ordered you to stay in your bed for two more days, and that's where you'll be if I have to strap you to the damn thing myself." Brannok scowled down at his daughter who glared right back at him, the arch in her neck cowing before no one. Though he pretended not to be, he was prouder at this moment than he had ever been of any of his children. "I thought you were dead, but apparently it all looked much worse than it was."

Her frown grew deeper. "There's work to be done, sire. We need to discover if there are any more cells in the city. This level of organization isn't a fluke. If enough of them struck at once—"

"The matter is handled." Brannok slid the single chair in his daughter's bedroom beside the bed and sat. His wife, Moru, had refused to visit once she'd discovered what had actually happened, which was fine by him. He never liked her much anyway.

Jasmayre's eyes narrowed. "How do you mean?"

"The leader was a subversive from Mirrik." Brannok hunched forward and clasped his hands together below his knees. The dressings from his wounds on his back, arms, and knees kept him from wearing his customary mail, and he felt naked without it. "Ten minutes under the afflicter's care and he was all too happy to reveal everything he knew. The Capital Guard has already wrapped up two other cells. King Wagnersen has been busy. He had men in the home of the Guard's captain and held his family ransom to lead us into the trap. It was on his recommendation that I picked this for you."

"You captured the man leading the traitors?" Her expression softened.

"Hardest thing I've ever done." Brannok gave an uncharacteristic smile. "I had his throat in my hands, and I did *not* strangle him to death."

She leaned back against the pillows piled behind her and relaxed. Black with gold trim, they matched the rest of the furniture in the room. "You're getting soft in your dotage, sire."

Brannok thought to take his daughter's hand but could not quite bring himself to do it. What if she withdrew? What if she despised his weakness toward her?

One thin brow arched on his daughter's narrow face. "You never said. Did I complete my mission? Am I now fit to send men into battle?"

"We would not have survived without you," Brannok said, his voice soft and rough at the same time. "I would have fought them in the street—and died there."

Jasmayre reached out with a long-fingered hand and patted her father on one broad shoulder. "I know. You just need someone to look out for you. That's why I'm still here."

7

BLACK AND WHITE,
PURPLE AND YELLOW

SARAH

Bizarre and beautiful, the landscape pressed against Sarah. She and her two companions rode their windibou west into glittering bands of white and black sand. Behind them, the sun crawled up a vast wall of bright gray. Its light caught crystals in the white sand and reflected back brilliant lines of prismatic colors.

She was far from home, whatever that was. Far from the people she loved, at any rate.

Far from Keane.

Sarah considered her two companions. One she trusted with her life—and the other one. The windibou they rode, similar to large horses in size and function but with curving horns and bigger shoulders that necessitated a forward-leaning saddle, did not seem to care who Sarah trusted.

Ill-favored Cassius Dare had seen better days. Normally, he commanded a room. Pale Andosh skin, a rakish smile from behind his icy blue eyes and sandy, perfectly arranged hair. Today he sat slumped over his saddle, the bruises on his face turned from purple to greenish-yellow, and his fine blue-and-silver coat and trousers torn and faded.

The biggest windibou went to Grohann. The troll stood eight feet tall and five feet wide at the shoulder. Sarah and her sorcerous teacher Finnagel had killed Grohann's father, Old Stone. The embittered elder troll had been possessed by a wicked sorcerer named Angrim, and Grohann had joined Sarah in both purpose and friendship in return for Old Stone's death.

"Looks like a painting," rumbled Grohann. "Only there is just two colors."

Dour mountains crowded the variegated field to the north, south, and the distant west. Cassius estimated at least a hundred miles from the southern range to the north. The ground alternated with black-and-white bands of sand that created irregular stripes resembling some vast beach without any water in sight. The black sands glittered in the early morning sun, and the white shone with millions of tiny rainbows. The effect was spectacular, and they rode into a world of color and shimmering light.

"Pretty, huh?" Cassius tied another strip of fabric to his mount's small curled horns.

Sarah couldn't decide if the windibou's head looked more like a Dorastros Moon-Day decoration or a laundry line.

"It's a good omen." The air smelled fresh and salty. She stretched and felt the tension in her upper back pull on her muscles, yanking her arms back down when she pulled on the stitches there. She didn't hate riding, but these windibou took some getting used to. High King Ivarr didn't keep horses.

Sarah reached up and refastened her hair behind her head. She was Pavinn, an island people with almost-black hair and dark, intense eyes. She stood taller than most men, slim-waisted and broad-shouldered, and could outfight, outrun, and outdrink most of them too. Sarah was a sorcerer, or so she had recently found out, and the magic that coursed through her, having had no other outlet, improved her physically. She hoped soon to learn to do more with it than blow out candles from across the room.

Two weeks ago, her instructor Finnagel, had been murdered by deadly magics at the command of his former apprentice, Mogh Kadir.

She still wasn't sure if that was a good or a bad thing.

Sarah also boasted an impressive set of wounds where one of Coldspine's big tundra cats had raked her face. Four claw marks ran from her right cheek up into her hairline, narrowly missing her eye. Ivarr's healers had stitched her up, but it still itched like hell.

"The warriors of Coldspine fancy themselves poets," Cassius said. "Many a brave man or woman has come here looking for inspiration for some grand epic or another."

Though Sarah still felt the anger just below the skin every time she heard Cassius speak, she had resolved not to let it out on their journey. That kind of rancor could be deadly out here in the wilderness. After all, he wasn't going to betray her to King Ivarr again, and she still needed Cassius to guide them.

"The varriors have made good poems?" Grohann asked. His own horns were similar to the windibou, but much larger. "Yoo know some?"

"I think they mostly went blind," Cassius answered the big troll. "Poetry can be tough."

A cold wind blew through the valley and sent a glittering cloud ahead of them that slightly rearranged the black-and-white stripes in the sand.

Grohann nodded his head. Sarah shook hers. She was no poet, but it didn't seem that blindness should be a prerequisite. Then again, this was the north, and people up here were different.

"Does it stay this bright all day?" Sarah asked. If it did, they were going to have to travel at night, when the real cold came.

"No," Cassius said. "Maybe another half hour. The reflection only happens like this at first dawn, when the sun is behind you."

"All right." Sarah slid off her tall mount to the crunchy sand. She turned the windibou away from the multicolored glare and sat. "We'll wait it out then. Grohann, can you hand me the red pouch from your saddlebag?"

Grohann swung a muscle-bound leg over the back of the huge windibou High King Ivarr of Coldspine had gifted him and dropped to the ground. The troll stood head and shoulders above Sarah, who was over six feet herself, and his olive-colored skin bore a detailed map of battle scars. On his head, scarred horns curved backward like those of a ram, and a massive sword hung over his mail-covered back.

The big troll sifted through his saddlebags and found the red leather pouch Sarah requested. He handed it to her and gave her a sharp-toothed grin along with it.

"Today is better for your carving, no? Today you vill be successful."

Sarah took the pouch from Grohann and smiled back up at him, which caused her to wince again at the stinging pain from her stitches. "Hope so. I don't think I'm really getting the hang of this so far."

She reached in and pulled out a yellowed cloth with a drawing of a walrus on it and spread it in front of her. Next she pulled out an oblong piece of aspen wood, twice the length of her hand and covered in pits and divots. Last, she withdrew a small, sharp knife. She inhaled, closed her eyes, and let out a long, controlled breath.

"If you were any more uptight about that thing, I think you'd crack in half." Cassius let himself down from his windibou. "You're terrible at carving walruses. Why do you care?"

Sarah cut her eyes at Cassius and favored him with a scowl. "I don't care. It's just . . . I'd like to be able to make something pretty. All the things I'm good at involve people screaming. And bleeding. And dying. It'd be nice to be good at something that made people happy instead."

She did not say that she made the carving as a present for Keane. It was stupid, and she knew she was never going to actually give it to him, but working on it made her feel closer to him. It was like a kind of conversation with him in her head, shaving away all the parts that did not look like a chunky blob of walrus.

And regardless, she did not want to hear about how inadequate her efforts were for a king.

"You made me happy." Cassius sat down in her shade.

"That's your one." Sarah's features hardened, and she pointed the small knife at Cassius's eye. "Thinking about that night makes me think about the way you treated me afterward, and that makes me want to carve open your lower half and force you to carry your entrails the rest of the way to the Tower of Chains. And that doesn't even begin to touch your working secretly for Tyrrane."

Cassius had been unforgivingly horrible when he thought he held all the cards. Now that Sarah was in control, he was all smiles and sincerity.

"Seems reasonable." Cassius leaned away from Sarah. "Thank you, by the way, for removing my chains. I don't think they were a good fit." He rubbed at the still-raw flesh around his wrists.

"Not really worried about you running off anymore," Sarah responded.

"Finally willing to accept my assurances of good faith?"

"Everyvere is all flat oot here," Grohann interjected. "And High King Ivarr, he gave me a troll bow. This is good, yes?" He held up the bow in question which was easily seven feet long and as big around as Cassius's biceps. Grohann ran a fingertip over the animals carved into the weapon's surface and raised his furry brows.

Conversation quieted for the next part of an hour while Sarah assaulted the chunk of wood with mounting irritation. At the end, it looked no more like a walrus than it had before, though it was somewhat shorter. Sarah sighed, replaced the items in the red bag, and handed it to Grohann.

They remounted and continued west.

8

THE BEST TRIP EVER

SARAH

A few hours of silent travel wore down the fascination with stark striations along the ground, and already Sarah could see them pass below her mount with her eyes closed.

A brilliant white and cold sun traced an unaltering path across the curve of blue sky. It glared down with disdain at Sarah and her traveling companions, who crept across the black-and-white stripes of sand—until they abruptly fell from their bucking mounts with screams and wails.

Sarah hit the ground with a shout, her face screwed against the pain and her hands clamped over her ears. At the same time, her mount reared and wheeled about, its hooves stomping to the left and right of Sarah as she rolled on the sand.

Grohann jumped off of his windibou and ran to her, but as he neared, he moaned, clamped his thick hands over his own ears, and danced on the cold black sand as if it burned.

Cassius sat still and watched.

Sarah crawled back. She grabbed Grohann by the ankle and pulled him along. When she reached just past the point where she'd first reacted, she stilled and fell face first into the sand. Grohann stepped up beside her and went down to his knees.

"What in Bizzith-non's underpants was that?" Sarah's voice was raw from her screams.

"It vas bugs." Grohann's wide eyes swiveled side to side. "Bugs so loud there is no room for thinking. But I do not see them."

"Our destination, the Tower of Chains, is known by a delightful array of colorful names," Cassius said from the back of his sedate windibou. "The Death in the North, the House of Folly . . . and the Wailing Prison. The legend is that when the god Hagrim imprisoned his wife in the tower for murdering their children, she went mad there. Her cries serve as a warning to all others that they encroach upon death." Cassius smiled, a swollen, bruised version of his easy old grin. "Or that's what they say, at any rate. The group I rode with didn't make it much further than we have now."

"So, you knew this was here?" Sarah pulled herself upright. A line of blood ran down from the stitching over her eye. "Tell me again about your assurance of good faith."

Cassius fidgeted on his mount, uncomfortable and silent.

"Cassioos says the noise is crying?" Grohann asked, his voice a deep rumble. He stood and brushed the sand from his leggings. "It does not sound like crying to me. It sounds like all the bugs in the vorld, clicking and chirping and everything more. So many noises. I cannot hear anything else. It fills my head to cracking."

"I didn't hear that," Sarah said. "Not bugs. I heard . . . it was sort of like battle except thousands and thousands of weapons clashing. People dying. It was maddening. And so *loud*."

"It varies for everyone." Cassius stared west over the sand. His face was drawn, bleak. "But it will be with us until the end. Anyway, the mounts won't go in. We can let them go or slaughter them for meat."

"Hooray," Sarah said. "No more boring silence and windibou riding. Just earsplitting racket and trudging through the sand—after we murder our faithful mounts, that is—or leave them here to starve to death." She wiped the blood from her face and started to scratch at the stitches, then stopped herself.

The sorcerer who stole the body of Grohann's father, Angrim, also called the Anger Under the Snow or Anger Under the Mountain, was by far and away the oldest and strongest sorcerer in the Thirteen Kingdoms. He somehow commanded the Swifthart family who ruled the militaristic and expansionist nation of Tyrrane. No force known could defeat Angrim, but Sarah's teacher Finnagel had intimated that a weapon might exist in the Tower of Chains that would. Somewhere ahead of them, too far over the torturous sand to even see, *might* be a means of rescuing everyone she loved and thereby herself as well.

Sarah stared ahead at the threatening sand. "This is the best trip ever."

"You can always turn back," Cassius offered. "This place, that noise, it affects people. Makes them act strangely."

"Yeah, let's forget about finding a weapon to turn the war against Tyrrane and take you back to Treaty Hill instead. I'm sure Keane won't feel the need to hang you for being a Tyrranean spy."

Without meaning to, Sarah chuckled at the thought. Keane probably *would* hang Cassius for getting Sarah drunk, screwing her, and then ignoring her to flirt with every serving girl he saw, even if that wasn't what really happened. She sighed. In truth that was all on her. Cassius had been a childhood crush, and she let herself believe he was the person a little girl once believed him to be. But he wasn't, and he really never was.

He was a traitor and a spy for the enemy.

She wondered what Keane was doing right now. Al-Dagos's eyes knew she missed him. Keane was her best friend, her family.

"Let's figure out what we need to take and what we can leave behind. I'll go get that one." Sarah gestured toward her windibou, who stood and shivered a few hundred yards away.

"Perhaps ve chop up Cassioos for food and carry his vindibou vith us for conversation?" Grohann tried to grin, but it came out as more of a frustrated scowl.

"I thought we were friends," Cassius said, eyes wide and back straight.

Sarah patted the troll on the chest and looked up into his face. "No killing Cass until I get back, all right?

"If yoo say so."

Sarah retrieved the wayward windibou and led it back to the others. Grohann and Cassius stacked two piles of goods on the dark sand, one to take and one to leave. Sarah surveyed the piles and removed the red leather pouch from the take pile to toss it on the other one.

"Necessities only."

The buckles clicked as Sarah unhooked her mount's saddlebags, and they dropped to the ground. She went through them and sorted their contents into the piles. Cold wind blew eastward across the sand, and grit blew over their stacks of food and water.

"That's it," Sarah said. "Time to, uh, you know."

The troll took his mount's head in his powerful hands. "It is not right for yoo to die here, friend. You are a good, strong vindibou. I am sorry."

Cassius stroked his windibou on the shoulder. "Hope you taste good."

"We need to do this all at once. We'll never catch any survivors." Sarah drew her thick-bladed broadsword and handed Cassius a slimmer long sword. "On three. One . . . two . . ."

9

STRIPES OR SPOTS?

SARAH

The noise was cacophonous. World-ending. Sarah tried to stuff cloth in her ears, but it was even more uncomfortable and didn't lessen the tumult at all, so she pulled it out and suffered. She tried to scream over the noise, but neither Cassius nor Grohann could understand her. The inability to escape, to just *get away,* drove her to distraction. Her heart pounded wild and fast, and she could not focus her gaze on anything for more than an instant.

She was in hell.

The punishing sound stopped on a band of black sand, perhaps twenty feet wide, but started again as soon as they attempted to move off it. So, for the moment, they halted.

The irregular stripe of dark lay littered with bones, people who could not face the abusive sound and would not continue, yet also found that they could not turn around and go back.

Sarah had always been the strongest, the fastest, and the most skilled. As a mercenary, she had existed side by side with hundreds of murderers and rapists, all of whom gave her a wide berth when she came walking through. It was true she was a different person now, one who had been afforded the luxury of morals. But out here, it was as if everything she had ever been was stripped bare. All that was left was bloody nerve and pain.

A wide black band lay just ahead. Sarah screamed when she reached it and the noise did not stop. It was a hundred-yard sprint to the next band of white sand and blessed silence. She fell into it and coated half her body in sharp powder.

Was Greenshade really worth this? This—unmaking of her soul? Every step sanded away another layer of herself. Soon there would be nothing left. Would Keane do this for her?

Of *course* he would. Greenshade be damned, she would continue for her friend. Her friends.

From that point on, wind and grit-scoured bones became a regular feature on the white-and-black sand.

After an unknown period that might have been seconds or years, they found another stripe, this one white, less than a foot wide, where blessed silence reigned. The three of them stood there, still and balanced, to keep their heads above the white.

It seemed an extra slap in the face that the colors were not consistent with the mind-shattering noise.

"I-I'm sorry," Cassius said to Sarah, his eyes red. "I don't expect you to forgive me, I wouldn't. But you should know that I'm sorry. For everything."

"Sorry?" Sarah tried to roll her eyes far enough to see Cassius. "Oh, is this supposed to be the crazy noises making you show me your true heart? Why would you think I care if you're sorry?"

She truly did not. If the mind-blasting noise made Cassius contrite, it pushed Sarah the opposite direction.

"It is quiet here." Grohann's rumble took on a threatening quality. "Yoo must be quiet too. Do not ruin my peacefulness, yes?"

A breeze whipped up, frigid and fast, and blew the tiny strip of white away, leaving only black behind. The cacophony resumed. Sarah fell to her knees, tears in her eyes, and screamed her frustration and suffering into the howling sandscape. She screamed until her voice went tattered and rasping.

No one heard.

A gentle hand gripped her shoulder. It was Cassius. He reached out to help her to her feet. She ignored him, pulled herself up, and stomped out ahead westward.

Sarah's thoughts burned in her head. This trek careened from disaster to disaster and had done so since Duke Branch, Keane's friend and advisor, and Chancellor Finnagel, his maybe enemy and advisor, sent her away. The mission was to contact Greenshade's allies, remind them of their obligations, and ensure they would be there for the coming war. Sarah hated leaving Keane and Megan, but she did what was necessary.

Now it was hard to think of anything else.

Her brain crashed among her memories, scored to the sounds of screams and the clash of weapons. Old Stone the troll as he tore the meat from her arm with his teeth, the death of Finnagel as his former apprentice Kadir magically flayed him to the bone, and the treacherousness of Cassius when he tried to turn King Ivarr against Greenshade and for their enemy, Tyrrane.

And now this. Swords crashed, men cried, and flesh tore. The sounds of a million battlefields pounded against her skull. All of it, everything she had done since leaving Treaty Hill and Keane a waste. She would die out here, miserable, scared, alone.

"Well, will you look at that," Cassius said into the sudden quiet.

AFTER A BIT of excavation on their hands and knees, Sarah and Cassius uncovered the remains of a campsite, complete with a large stock of firewood. The broad stretch of black sand that kept the noise at bay went on for several hundred feet, and looked in no danger of being blown away by the wind any time soon. Sarah learned fast that these reprieves only seemed like blessings. While being out of the horrifying racket was an immense relief, the stark decision from that point was to either re-enter it or starve on the tiny island of quiet. The decision was less easy to make each time.

Grohann sat a short distance away. His hands covered his wide face.

"Is good now. Not vanting to kill you if I cannot see you. All is good now, yes?" Since entering the noise, Grohann became more and more agitated, wanting to murder anything he saw. By a peculiar quirk of troll psychology, he discovered he could stem the bloodlust with closed eyes.

Sarah barked a high, shrill laugh. "Cass, would you make a blindfold for Grohann? I'd really like to not get killed because he forgot to cover his face while he scratched his butt. Make it comfortable." Her hand fluttered to the stiches in her cheek and away. She did not trust herself to scratch the itch there anymore. She leaned back against the firewood they dug up and moved her shoulders up and down. An itch had formed that fled every time she reached around to scratch it. Maybe it wouldn't see the logs and branches until it was too late.

"I'm sorry." Cassius flinched away. "I mean, yes, of course. I want to help. I'm sorry." He stood, hurried over to the troll, and fashioned a blindfold from a strip he tore from his shirt.

Cassius had become a problem. His sorrow turned to a desperate grief for his actions and made him unpredictable. Sarah might even enjoy it if she didn't know it for a falsehood induced by the mind-affecting noise. She knew men in his condition in her past. Mercenaries unable to cope with the realities of their deeds, who looked to end the pain. She thanked the quiet wisdom of Al-Dagos that Cassius's chains waited for him in her pack.

Sarah remained unaffected. If she had been affected, she would have thrown her worthless body down on her sword miles ago. How long did this emptiness go back? Miles? Days? Her whole life? But she thought only of Keane. She loved him, and he loved her. They were perfect friends, and friends came through for one another, no matter what.

If only she could remember why.

"Here, let me help," Cassius said.

Sarah sat back and dropped the pile of firewood she continued to bury and dig back up.

"Yes, good. You should do that." Sarah cast about. "Lots of bones."

"This was a Tyrranean scouting expedition," Cassius said as he worked. "They were looking to create a forward base to use against Coldspine. Prince Brannok the Second, the current king's eldest son, led them here."

"Huh? How do you know all that? They're just bones."

"Because I was with them," Cassius replied. "I watched them all die."

Sarah looked at the mountains all around them and, in particular, those to the west. The sun would soon drop behind them. It seemed unfamiliar. That couldn't be, though. They had been out here for a week at least. Could it have only been a few days? She looked at their supplies, still the same as when they'd killed the windibou. Al-Dagos's eyes, had they been in this hell for no more than *hours*?

"Is story time." Grohann smiled from beneath his blue blindfold. "Good. Is time for fire and meat and stories. This is good." The troll turned his head in Sarah's direction. He coughed up tiny laughing sobs, but he said nothing.

The firewood caught fast and burned faster, but the deep pile Cassius and Sarah uncovered would last a while. As he threw another slender log on, Cassius sat back and pulled out the package of windibou meat from his sacks. He separated the meat into precut strips with Sarah's dagger, and after digging holes in them, spitted them onto a lengthy stick. This he handed to Sarah and made another for himself.

"Sure," he said. "The 'everybody dies' story. That's a happy one. Well, I was in the citadel at Dismon on business when Prince Brannok recruited me for the expedition. He'd wanted to do it for months but lacked a suitable guide. I had some knowledge of northern Coldspine, so the decision was made, and off we went.

"The trip was fun. Prince Brannok is a dullard and a bully, but once you're on the inside with him, at least you're abusing other people." Cassius shrugged at Sarah's expression of disdain. "He's a good hunter, too. We took down all sorts of game along the way, and when we got to the plains, we hunted a few Coldspiners as well."

"That doesn't seem smart. What if the locals noticed their missing people and came looking for them in numbers?" Sarah found her attention arrested by Cassius's story. Anything to take her mind off of where they were.

The sun dropped behind the peaks to the west, and a new chill set in. Soon the evening wind would sweep from the warmer western end of the glittering sands where the sun still reached and toward the shaded mountains in the east. The winds blew hard and often shifted the banded sand out from under their feet.

"Yes, hunting Coldspiners in Coldspine with a small expeditionary force was quite stupid." Cassius's mouth smiled into the fire, but his eyes looked forlorn. "Of course, that was not the sort of thing you said to young Prince Brannok. All of King Brannok's evil, with none of the brains. By the time we rounded the southern spur of the Bitter Heights mountain range and turned into the glittering sands, there were well over a hundred men chasing our twenty." Cassius paused and stared at the fire. "They wouldn't enter the fields though. They just stood at the edge, laughing and waving goodbye to us. That really should have been a clue."

Grohann laughed. "Cassioos is no smarter than Prince Brannok. Pretending to be friends with trolls but vorking for Anger Under the Mountain. Pretending to be friends with Sarah but vorking for Tyrrane against her friends at home. Cassioos is stupid, shitty friend. Ha!"

Sarah couldn't remember seeing a face so bleak as Cassius's in that moment. He sat silent and collected his thoughts before returning to his tale.

"Everything went fine at first. We had food and water, and our rear guard reported that our pursuers rode off once we left their sight. The mood was good. Happy. Then we hit the sound."

"You never told us, Cass," Sarah said. "What does it sound like to you?"

"I hear her. The goddess Magda. She cries for her lost children. For her loneliness. The mistakes she's made." Cassius swallowed. "Like I would, if I were human enough."

"That's just what I was thinking," Sarah said. "So, what happened then?"

"First, all of the horses ran off. We killed a few—shot them down in frustration more than anything else—but the majority of them got away. They took our supplies with them, too. By happenstance, a few of the horses we killed had firewood on them." He indicated the stacks of wood. "One of our number, a boy I think, cut his own throat less than a minute in once he understood that the prince intended to keep walking into the noise. More followed him. Every time we hit a place where the noise stopped, we left men behind. The prince had them killed whenever they wouldn't continue."

This story no longer seemed just the thing to take Sarah's mind off of her trials. Still, she didn't want to interrupt for fear of making it take longer. It did not even occur to her to ask Cassius to stop talking. The punishment was eternal. Why try to fight it?

"By the time we got to this place, the only men left were fanatically loyal to the prince. It was a big swath of silence, like it is now. There must be rocks below holding a leeward gully. Anyway, Brannok was in a towering rage. We started to make camp, but he was having none of it. He ordered the men into a line.

"Now these were real warriors, understand? A few of them seriously hard men with big names on the battlefield." Cassius gestured with his meat-loaded stick. "He made them fight him, one at a time. Thrust-dead. Chop-dead. Cut-dead. One by one. Soon there was a pile of bodies as high as my waist.

"I always wondered why they just stood there. Why not attack all at once? Honor, I guess. It just looked like idiocy to me."

"How did you survive?" Sarah asked, intrigued despite herself.

Cassius shrugged again. "While Prince Brannok was busy chopping his noblemen in half, I hid amongst the dead. He never noticed, and if anyone else did, they didn't say anything."

"Cassioos is sure being big hero. Vy not shoot you the prince vith bow, save the varriors?"

"I thought about it. I had my hunting bow. But that night, everything was so crazy. What if I didn't kill him with the first shot? What if I did kill him, and the rest killed me for it?"

Grohann nodded. "Scared."

In Sarah's experience, men did not tend to live past one good bowshot. But Cassius and Grohann were pretty crazy right now. Perhaps some level of cowardice could be understood as part of that. She pulled off a piece of half-cooked meat and rubbed it on her face to keep away the thoughts of her imminent death and wondered why they had been affected so much more than she had. She rubbed in careful circles around her stitches. Couldn't get meat in the wounds. Not sanitary.

Cassius's eyes shone in the firelight. He stared right at Sarah. "Rii-ight. Anyway, after the prince finished the last of his friends off, he fell over and slept until dawn. I watched from the pile of dead until he finally woke and went back east."

"Did you follow him?" Sarah rolled the used-up strip of windibou into a ball and dropped it in the fire.

"Eventually. Once he'd gone far enough, when I could only sort of see him, I followed. This was when I discovered the salt-pools, and the slugs that live in them. It was a good thing, too. There was no more food and only a little water."

Sarah remembered that Cassius mentioned the slugs before they entered the fields, back in the tundra of Coldspine. Taste like chewy, he'd said.

"After—I don't know how long we wandered—I found him sitting in the sand. I was terrified to go to him but desperate to get away from the wailing. Desperation won out, and I ran the last hundred feet or so. He was sitting just outside the sound, laughing. I was so happy to be out of it for good, I fell to the ground and cried. He came over and held me to him, like a baby, until I stopped."

Grohann chuckled. "Heh. Prince is confused, eh? Kills varriors and leaves Cassioos alive. I bet he is feeling stoopid now."

Wind sprang up and sent the fire burning sideways. The light made strange hollows in Cassius's puffy and discolored face. He coughed. "Brannok said that the whole time we were in the sound, he could hear his father, the king, raging and beating his mother, who just screamed and cried. The whole time. For days. Once we were back in Coldspine, he looked over his shoulder and said, 'Nothing really there, I guess. Except maybe a good place to send family members on holiday.' He seemed to think that was extremely funny."

Sarah leaned away from the wind and put her hands under her, so she couldn't scratch at the scars over her eye. She might have let High King Ivarr be eaten by the tundra cats if she'd known how much the recuperation would itch.

"So, what have we learned, other than Prince Brannok is a murderous nutter just like his dad? Anything?"

"Alvays keep piles of dead varriors for hiding behind."

"Try not to be around when bigger people than you go mad," Cassius said.

Sarah rocked forward and back where she sat. "No and no. The lesson is never to let Cassius tell stories when you want to feel better. That was abysmal."

"I'm sorry."

10

NOT EXACTLY A BEAT YOU CAN DANCE TO

SARAH

Sarah held a chain stretched out behind her in her left hand. Sometimes it pulled against her; other times it did not. She forgot what it was for. A thick blue string hung from her right wrist, loose and comfortable. It reassured her, though she did not know why. The chain pulled again, and Sarah leaned forward to drag it taut behind her. The chain irritated her in the rare moments she was able to consider it.

It seemed as if some of the stripes in the sand had been safe, so very long ago. But she did not trust this. It was hope, and hope was only there to distract her. Destroy her. Kill her spirit. In any case it was no longer true, if it ever had been. Nowhere was safe.

So Sarah walked. Her world crashed in a horrible symphony of battlefield noise, the notes of steel and death-defying sense or rhythm. It deconstructed her ability to think in lines or, in time, to think at all.

Instead, she walked.

Sarah went away. She continued to go away, forever. There was someone, a friend. But she forgot what he looked like or if he was even real.

She knew that *she* wasn't.

Sarah walked. She cried, for a lifetime, and screamed for longer than that. She was silent. She was always silent, in the raging noise of—

"Ow." Sarah bumped her nose against a tall, wooden door. "Ow." She marveled at the sound of her own voice. "Ow! Owowowowow! OW!" An unbidden grin consumed her entire face. She had a voice. How was such a thing even possible?

Sarah stood on a terrace made of dark stone that angled out of the sand from a small rampway. In front of her, the stones made a wall. Set into that wall was the door she stumbled against. Behind her was too loud to see through.

A misshapen creature attached to a chain shambled off of the sand and onto the stone stoop beside Sarah. Bloody rags hung off of it, exposing ugly pink skin covered with scratches. The pathetic thing filled Sarah with disgust. She kicked it back into the sand and noise, reveling at the sound her boot made against it. Her eyes welled up with tears of happiness, and her legs dropped her to the stone, weeping.

Next came an enormous olive-skinned man wearing a blindfold, with backward-curving horns on his head and mail armor that jingled when he moved. Jingled! The blue string attached her to this man, and warmth flushed her face and chest to see him. Sarah crawled up his leg and body to hug him with fierce strength.

"Urk," Grohann said.

"Grohann. I'm so happy you're still here. I can hear you, Grohann. Grohann. Grohann. I can hear your name."

"Choking . . ." Grohann pulled at Sarah's arms.

She held fast a moment longer, not understanding, and then laughed and let go. She dropped to the ground and saw the mewling creature out on the sand.

"Cassius." Sarah pulled the chain and dragged the battered weapons merchant up onto the stoop. He looked awful. His spiraling state of mind had forced her to put the chains back on him at the last camp, for fear of him trying to harm himself. It now appeared that the effort was only half successful. Anywhere he could attack his flesh, he had. Bruises and fingernail scratches covered every bit of exposed skin on him. He held a red leather pouch tight to his chest. It meant something to Sarah, but she couldn't place exactly what. Something she had lost?

"What are you smiling at?" Cassius whispered, his voice a dry husk.

Sarah put a hand to her face and felt the wide grin still there.

"The quiet." She could not bring herself to speak above a hushed breath for fear of attracting the attention of the cacophony to her.

Behind her, the door within what was an enormous tower proved unlocked. The three of them opened it and sat in the entryway in apprehensive silence. Once Sarah realized that the sound, which had clouded her vision like a windstorm, truly could not touch her here, she relaxed and looked about.

The building jutted abruptly from the striped sand to soar over the cold desert. Smooth and gray and silent, it bided, considering. The place felt as if it knew something the rest of them did not.

A tiny amount of food and water remained of their stores, but Sarah lacked the energy to eat it. She drifted off to sleep, luxuriating on the bare, frigid, but soundless stone floor. A vague itching at her forehead threatened to distract her, but she could not hold the thought.

SARAH AWOKE BY GENTLE STAGES, awareness growing bit by tiny bit as she did. Her limbs felt leaden and warm, swaddled in softness. A hand, kind and soothing, ran over her forehead and through her hair, the way a mother's might. A feminine voice sang a quiet comforting song in a language Sarah did not recognize, at once calming and arousing.

Sarah stiffened in alarm. Her eyes popped open. She was somewhere inside the tower, though how she'd gotten there was a mystery she would have to address later. Of more immediate concern was the giantess in whose lap Sarah now found herself.

"You are awake, little button," the woman creature said. Behind her a tall, skinny window let in gray light, maybe a hundred feet away.

"Yes, I am," said Sarah, unmoving. "Who are you?"

The flawless woman must have been twelve or thirteen feet tall. That was where her resemblance to an actual giant ended. Where those people looked as if they had been smashed in the face with a shovel at birth, this woman glowed with an unearthly perfection. Also, she just glowed. Other than the watery light at the window, the room was dark, and Sarah couldn't make much out past her captor.

The giant's smile threatened to melt Sarah. This was sorcery. She ordered her mind and set the strange magnetism aside.

"You're Magda, goddess of beauty." Sarah did not say the full sobriquet; goddess of seductive beauty, insanity, and obsessiveness. Although Sarah's mind was numbed by her walk through the fields of sand, starved from lack of food and water, and now scrambled by her proximity to what she could only assume was an honest-to-god god, she had not yet been rendered entirely stupid.

"Good button," Magda replied. "*Magic* button."

"What language was that? The song, I mean."

"Metzoferran." Magda's eyes closed and her face grew distant. "It is the language the gods speak in their houses."

"Metzoferran." Sarah had heard of it. Metzoferran was the seventh language of magic, said either to be lost or mythical. "I thought that Dagoshi was the gods' tongue."

Magda's face darkened, and her eyes became angry slits. Storms raged behind those eyes. Despite herself, Sarah shivered in terror.

"Does my granddaughter bend a knee to a mute fish?" Magda demanded with a hiss.

Al Dagoshi, the Pavinn "wise dragon," gave the gods' language of Dagoshi to his people, that they might speak like men—or so Pavinn mythology taught. But those were Pavinn gods, not Andosh.

Were dragons a kind of fish?

"No?" The blankets cocooning Sarah prevented any sort of fast movement, and that included flight. How far up was that window?

The huge face darkened further. "Do not lie to me, little brown button."

"Really." Sarah's voice only squeaked a bit. "Religion isn't my . . . thing."

The scowl deepened, then vanished. Magda threw her head back and laughed. "Ho, ho! Good button. Excellent granddaughter." She stroked Sarah's head and hair again.

Sarah winced in anticipation when Magda's hand crossed the stitches, but no pain stabbed at her. The stitches were gone, and the wounds were too. She wiggled a hand up and out of the blankets and brushed over her own smooth forehead. She felt the faintest of lines where the stitches had been. Magda's wrist, by contrast, sported a garish wound where a cruel manacle dug into it. The chain drooped away into the dark. The sight provided a startling juxtaposition with the goddess's immaculate presence.

"You have brought a present, and you do not wail so, as the others have." Magda peered into Sarah's eyes.

The meaning of this statement seemed important, perhaps even vitally so. But in that embrace, in that moment, Sarah could not bring herself to question it. She hoped that Magda could not see her thoughts.

With a deep sigh that blew across all of Andos, Magda lifted Sarah up and placed her on her feet. The blanket rose away and ended somewhere close to the ceiling.

The room encompassed a full half of the tower's width and, from the view out the window, sat at least halfway up its height. Furniture fit for any queen rested about, white and gold, of normal human size. There was no bed.

Magda stood beside Sarah, perhaps seven feet tall now, and placed a hand on her shoulder. The goddess wore a dress of shifting greens and blues that went to the floor but left her arms bare. Sarah could not make up her mind if Magda was as ephemeral as a soap bubble or so real that the stone beneath her feet seemed little more than a gray dream.

"Am I awake?" asked Sarah.

Once again Sarah found herself bathed in the radiance of that otherworldly smile.

"You will wake the nations of Andos or burn them down. I wonder which it will be?"

11

KEANE MEETS AN OLD FRIEND

KEANE

After traveling with them several days through Three Sisters Wood, Keane understood the Free Hand's rhythms. A remarkable crew, they required little oversight from Harden or Eli. Except Burgen of course. He remained a damn idiot.

The thin girl named Raven, Morholt's sister, showed affection for Burgen to a publicly alarming degree, but Megan had observed to Keane that this seemed calculated to nettle her brother, Morholt. Keane wondered how much that might have bothered Burgen were he capable of understanding it.

Sabni and Mahu, the two inseparable warriors from the southern empire of Egren, did everything together; they even slept in the same small tent. Eli described it as some kind of elite warrior practice and encouraged Keane to go ask them about it, which Keane took to mean he should steer clear of the subject.

Morholt delighted in rubbing Keane the wrong way and often made comments about Megan that would turn a sailor red. Megan just laughed and went back to chatting with Sabni about archery.

Sabni's tutelage fanned the flames of Megan's tournament abilities, and that skill grew bright and hot. Keane hoped she would never need her growing talent, but his darker thoughts suggested the foolishness of that hope.

Keane's relationship with Harden had not been improved by the two of them stabbing each other near to death half a year ago, though necessity dictated that each barely tried to kill the other now. This looked to be the closest to progress they were apt to make.

And that was fine with Keane. If he ever wanted a best friend like Harden, he would just squat down and shove his own balls in a badger's mouth.

Now that winter had arrived, the sun set in the late afternoon and the moon already shone in the sky. The Free Hand crept through the woods and followed the blazes left by Raven. The bright moon made shining signposts of each place where she stripped away the bark to signal the way. Keane, intent on finding the next blaze, jumped when Raven stepped out of the dark beside him.

"Fuck it," he said, embarrassed. "Can you not do that?"

Raven looked to Harden. "Patrol ahead. Six. Wolf heads on their tabards."

"Tralgar's men. They're pretty far from home." Harden grinned at Keane. "More fans of yours?"

"Horace Tralgar?" At Harden's nod, Keane said, "We're acquainted. I liked him better when he used an oak tree on his banner. Back when Wallace's Company gave his army a hot knife up the ass."

"He changed it after that," Harden said, still grinning. "Pretentious prick wants everyone to call him 'The Wolf' now."

Keane nodded. "Yeah. As if that was ever gonna happen. I kicked him out of Treaty Hill along with Songham. Sent them both to go fight Norrikmen. I guess they found better things to do."

"Harden come up against Baron Tralgar twice now." Eli stepped up to Keane and Harden. "Kicked him good in the stones both times. The time you remember were the second one. Reckon if he's heard the Free Hand is about, might be *your* head, sir, and not the little king's he's after."

"Maybe," admitted Harden. "How's that change the landscape?"

"Don't reckon it does," Eli said. "Just makin' an observation, is all. Both those other times you had an army at your back. Now there's but ten of us, countin' the wimminfolk."

"Just when I think I have you figured out, Eli," Harden said, "you pop up with something new. Imagine that, Keane. Eli doing maths."

Raven sniggered. Burgen looked up and cast about, as if he hoped to see something funny.

"Yeah, yer a hoot, sir." Though Eli's expression spoke otherwise. "I'm just sayin' I know you like rubbin' folks' faces in how much smarter you are than them, but mebbe this time we oughtta be more careful."

"I shall be the soul of discretion, good Eli." Harden grabbed his second by the shoulder. "We'll play it safe this time and get him next go-round."

"Yer gonna completely ignore me, ain'tcha?"

"It seems likely."

Eli sighed, shrugged at Keane, and returned back to the mercenaries of the Hand.

"Orders?" asked Raven.

Harden cast a glance back at Eli and rolled his eyes. "Fine, whatever. Avoid the patrol, and get us to the meeting spot. We'll make Baron Tralgar squeal next time."

Megan knew the conclave, and she said that even if they found themselves at odds with the barons, they would still be likely to receive a decent meal and a bath before being locked away for Songham's retrieval. That wasn't enough to make him want to go there any more willingly, but if he were being honest with himself—something he did not appreciate being forced to do—he, Megan, and Loffa stood no chance of escaping from this crew.

Raven was a ghost in the woods. Mahu and Sabni were excellent trackers. Hell, even Eli knew more woods craft than Keane did. They'd be far more apt to get injured or killed in the attempt.

His hand tapped against his thigh while they picked their way through the trees and brush. Their lives were to be in the hands of strangers, but that was a better bet than the people he knew and was with now.

More than anything else, Keane hoped to find allies amongst the barons, people willing to fight with him against Songham. It was a shitty roll with lousy consequences if things went bad, but these were the only dice he had.

Megan took his hand and held it in both of hers.

"I know," she said. "I know."

A LIGHT DUSTING of snow fell on the treetops. Lone flakes made it through here and there to melt away on the woodland floor. The Free Hand rested among the moonlit trees where they whispered, grinned, and complained to each other. Raven materialized from the gloom, stepping from behind a tree next to Keane.

"Boo," Raven whispered. She grinned broadly when he startled. Again.

"Oldam's stinking stone sphincter, woman," Keane said. "Is scaring me the only game you know? Maybe Megan can teach you to play Squares."

"He's there," Raven said to Harden. "Alone."

Harden stood from his squat against a tree and stretched. "Come on then." He waved to Keane. "The rest of you wait here. I imagine we'll be back presently."

The mercenary and the king followed Raven's blazes through the wood and into a small rounded clearing. A white stone floor lay in the ground, obscured by leaves and dirt, barely visible in the moonlight. Behind it, a stone stair crawled north and up a tree-covered hill out of sight. A distant and continuous roar floated in through the hole in the tree canopy.

In the middle of the stone circle stood a tall, broad-shouldered man in a dark long coat and hat with fur trim. Even in the night,

Keane could make out piercing eyes, thick eyebrows, and trimmed beard.

"Baron Orrikson." Harden stepped forward and reached out a hand.

Orrikson clasped Harden's hand but kept his other at his belt, over his dagger. "Who do we have here?" he asked, voice a rich, deep baritone.

Keane sighed and shook his head. Why did no one in his kingdom recognize the king? He was even on the money now, wasn't he? Maybe that was supposed to start next year.

"I'm your king. Not that anyone seems to fucking know it."

"You must be the foulmouthed one." He frowned. "Whether or not you are our king remains to be seen." Orrikson indicated the stair. "Retrieve your comrades and follow the stairs. The path beyond leads to Fenrath Hall. The full conclave is in attendance tonight and will be eager to hear your report, Harden." He glanced at Keane, his expression unreadable. "I suspect they will be interested in meeting you as well, King Keane."

Though Keane revealed his true identity while Treaty Hill lay under siege and had only just escaped, he was unsurprised the barons already knew he would come here. Where else might he look for potential allies?

He wished he knew what Harden was up to. The old bastard clearly wasn't saying anything about it, except maybe to Eli. Keane was a captive being hauled off to the highest bidder, wasn't he? Except the conclave was the only place left Keane might find willing troops to fight on his behalf. But no. Tralgar was still the head of the Barons' Conclave, and *that* could only spell doom for Keane.

He looked again at Megan's bow, slung over one petite shoulder. Sabni was training her to be a dead shot, even more so than she had been before. How did that make sense? Harden detested Baron Tralgar. Was this part of some plot against the baron?

Of course, Keane and the two queens had not arrived here of their own free will, and the barons had no way of knowing in advance the

Free Hand would encounter him. Providence had led him where he was supposed to be.

Keane shrugged. He couldn't get away, and he was as prepared as he was going to be. If he didn't die here, this might be a useful journey.

The Free Hand reassembled and ascended the stone stairway. The slope turned into a foothill and from there a low mountain. The trail, also paved with the same ancient stone as the steps and the floor behind them, turned to the west and wound its way along the mountain's southern face. The roar grew louder, and all at once, the trees to the south and the clouds above gave way, and brilliant moonlight bathed them in blue-white radiance.

They climbed higher and further away from the close embrace of the woods. This far up the mountain, the sky vaulted above them, blue-black and shot through with cold pinpricks of white light. Keane felt as if he could reach up and pop one in a bottle, the way Sarah sang emberflies into her lamp.

The Baroness Lady Fenrath was, by Megan's account, a fair-minded but severe woman. That this meeting was happening in her home could be a good sign. But Baron Tralgar led the conclave, and that was most definitely not. Orrikson said the conclave was in full attendance, and that meant Tralgar was there too. Keane wouldn't be able to simply order the man out of the room as he had in the Great Council meeting.

So much depended on what the other barons thought of Songham.

Water spilled in a rush from the rocks above, pouring from a prominence that hung well away from the sheer face of mountain rock. Their trail headed beneath it, behind the fall, as Keane could see from the bright stone path. The left side of this path bordered a drop into darkness several thousand feet wide, into which the water spilled. Opposite Keane's position on the other side of the drop, stood the massive stone and redwood Fenrath Hall. The building's major wing extended back beneath the prominence behind the cascade of water. Firelight from its lamps and torches danced, lending the torrent a cheery glow. The scene took Keane's breath away.

Megan stared and smiled, her fingers tight around Keane's arm. "I know I've told you never to do this, but just be yourself. I think they might respond well to that. And these people will sniff you out if you're false with them."

Keane nodded, though his nerves mounted. Truthfulness was not really his thing.

Her grip on his hands squeezed his fingers together. "What?" he asked her.

Her bottom lip poked out. "My feet hurt."

"You're walking for two," he replied.

"I think I'd let them kill *you*, as long as they had comfy chairs." Megan stared dreamily into Keane's eyes. "Big chairs with huge cushions, so big your feet don't reach the floor."

"Will you visit my grave after you've had a nice sit-down?" Keane asked.

"No," she said. "But I'll have someone else visit you for me. Queens are busy people."

Beyond the hall, extending down and curling around the falls, lay the town of Fenrath. It glowed in blue moonlight, punctuated by its own orangey-yellow points of illumination. The town looked quaint and quiet from this vantage; a few taller buildings higher up the slope gave way to modest but sturdy homes further down. The waterfall dropped downward into darkness, and Keane could not tell if it pushed out into some stream or river or fell away beneath the earth.

"Now that is a magnificent sight," Sabni said, his grin so wide his face appeared to split in half. "As Queen Nefret is told by the soldier in the Parable of the Angry Wind, 'Though my sword and the arm that swings it belong to my king, my soul belongs to she who placed such wonders in the world.'"

"This from someone who won't look twice at a fine young woman's ass," said Morholt.

"I am looking at an ass right now." Sabni shook his head and frowned at Morholt. "The waterfall continues to be the more breathtaking."

"This really isn't my best light," Morholt replied.

The mercenaries and their guests traversed the stone path behind the fall, which led them to the east wing of Fenrath Hall and a pair of wide double doors. Two night-blue-liveried guards waited there for them beside a glass lantern. The hall made Keane feel small. Red timbers, ten feet on a side, soared upward and projected strength and power. All of this rested beneath a natural vault, hundreds of feet high of smoothly curving stone. The whole of it felt impressive, but crushing.

The water crashed too loud for conversation here, though it was not the earthshaking clamor Keane expected. This would be hell on a person's constitution, he thought with consideration for the guards. Could you ever get used to this much noise? With relief, Keane stepped into the lamplit doorway.

Inside the warm and smoke-scented hall, the rumble subsided to a muted thrum that Keane more felt in his feet than heard. It lulled him. Without thought, his hand found Megan's, and they followed the guards together down the long hallway.

Inside was a little different. Strength and size guided the architecture. Yellowed plaster and wide beams conveyed a sense of rustic authority. Those who strode these tall rooms and halls held mastery over this part of the world, and they wanted everyone to know it.

"Nice house," Raven observed.

"Hands off," snapped Eli. "These folks is payin' customers."

"Just saying." Raven raised her arms in mock surrender, then crossed them over her chest. "It's nice. Homey, if you're a giant anyways."

The two guards led them to a pair of tall double doors made of polished redwood. Keane could hear yelling on the other side. He gripped Megan's hand, though which of them most needed the reassurance was an open question.

"Don't forget," she whispered to him, "you're their king. They swore fealty to the crown, and that's you."

Keane squeezed her hand in reply. He should have been taking notes of all of Megan's advice.

"By the way, there's something you oughtta know, boy." Harden spoke to Keane in a hushed voice. "I don't hate you anymore." At Keane's incredulous expression, the old mercenary glowered and went on. "Don't mean I *like* you, just that everything from here on out really *is* about money. It ain't personal."

A dozen cutting responses flashed through Keane's head, but he settled on the most important to him. "Why is that? What's different now? And why should I trust you?"

"I don't care who you trust." Harden's expression collected gloom from the shadows between sconces and held it, hollow and black. "But as for what's different, I almost killed you back then. Figured I had. Stabbed you through the lung, as I recollect. And it lost me the one thing I thought I was doing it for."

"Sarah," Keane said.

Harden's eyes narrowed, and he nodded. "If there's to be any chance of ever getting back in her good graces, I reckon the *not* killing of you could only help. And maybe now you're a king and all, you're not holding her back as much as I thought."

"You're a fucking bucket of virtue," Keane said.

The two of them stopped behind their escort.

"The conclave is meeting," said the lead guard. "I'll announce you. Please wait here." He withdrew through the doors.

"Nobody's took our weapons," Eli said. "That seem odd to you?"

"We talked to a guy in the woods when they hired us. Maybe this is normal. Or maybe they just aren't afraid of us," Harden said. "I'll let you know when I decide if it's odd or scary." He turned to the group. "I shouldn't need to say this, but nobody talk unless someone asks you a direct question, and then say as little as possible. That goes double for"—he paused and scanned the faces before him—"all of you."

"I hope they have pickled fish again for breakfast," Loffa said.

Harden looked at her and started to speak, but a big door behind him opened wide, and the guard within made the announcement.

"Their majesties King Keane of Greenshade, and his wife, Queen Megan, accompanied by the Free Hand led by Marshal Harden Grayspring."

Everyone walked into the hall. The glossy wooden floor spread perhaps fifteen feet wide in front of them and twice that in length. Eight feet up, a gallery ran a circuit of the room, behind which sat the eight stone-faced barons of Greenshade. The walls reached up into a dark and smoky ceiling. Opposite the door Keane and the others entered through, with the short wall to himself, sat the leader of the Barons' Conclave.

"Baron Horace Tralgar," Keane said to the smug, smiling figure facing him. The baron appeared to have given up on sleeping in the month since Keane last saw him. Bags hung under his eyes in a round aging face, and he labored for each breath. The gray pelts of wolves hung from his shoulders, piled high to imitate muscle. "Were you able to find any Norrikmen to fight, or did you get lost on the way?" Take command of the room fast. Let everyone know the goddamn *king* was in charge.

Tralgar's smile rose on one side into a yellow-toothed leer. "Guards, put this lot of traitors and miscreants in irons." He rose from behind the wooden wall of the gallery to display a wide stomach covered in fur-trimmed brown velvet. "King Songham has asked for your safe return, false king, so you can be punished properly for your crimes. But he's not here, and I have a bit of punishment I'd like to hand out myself."

Once again, it seemed the wrong time to mention that Songham was dead.

Keane's hand moved to his sword, and he felt the mercenaries doing the same. Apparently Tralgar really was in charge here. A sense of foreordained calamity closed in on Keane, and his breathing constricted in his chest. Not allies, then. At least whatever fate Harden had set for Keane had caught him as well.

As the guards closed in with chains in hand, Megan stepped forward to speak.

"Stop."

The command froze everyone. To Tralgar's right, a tall straight-backed woman rose to her feet. She wore a long dress the same color blue as the guards' tabards, and her steel-gray hair rose in an artistic sweep above her head. Thin and regal, the older woman turned to Tralgar, looked down her nose, and said, "You presume too much, Tralgar. This conclave has yet to decide whether to follow the usurper king, Songham, the impersonator king, Keane, or to say bugger the both of them and install a king of our own." She raised an arch eyebrow. "Or have you forgotten the reason we are here today entirely?"

"That's Baroness Fenrath," Megan whispered over her shoulder to Keane. "She's smart and stubborn. She never got along with Dad, but maybe that's a good thing."

Sweat made the grip of Keane's borrowed sword slick in his hand. He had a sudden terror that should he draw the weapon, it would turn in his hand on its own, and he would forget what to do with it.

Battle jitters. Just breathe.

A red flush crept up Tralgar's spotty neck as he regarded Lady Fenrath. "Baroness, I am the head of this conclave, and I say we will give our fealty to the rightful monarch, King Songham of Greenshade!"

"Duke Regent Songham is a weedy little fuck better suited to scullery than leadership," came a cry from the left wall. An elderly baron stood, white haired and mustachioed, with keen eyes and weathered skin. "He's a sneak and a cheat, and I'd rather follow a viper down a hole than bend a knee to that spineless brigand."

"Baron Hapstan," Megan said into Keane's ear. "Uh, he's a hunter? I think."

"I like that old fucker," Keane whispered back, a touch high-pitched.

Chatter broke out around the room, most of it animated and loud. Keane couldn't tell if the room leaned toward him or not. He heard Harden give instructions to a quiet Free Hand. This had the potential to become a tremendous and violent mess.

The red reached the top of Tralgar's hairless and blotchy head as the volume of the bickering increased. He opened his mouth for what looked like was going to be a deafening bellow, and the rest of the room paused and held its breath. Into this momentary silence another voice spoke.

"I'd like to call for a vote, please. If there are no objections?" To Keane's immediate right, a man with a long face and a knowing smile winked down to Megan. He pushed a strand of black hair behind an ear and continued, "I think we have everyone here, do we not?" His white tunic and cloak, thickly trimmed in black, stood out amongst the more muted shades of the others.

Megan smiled back and whispered, "That's Baron Sins. He's funny and I think pretty sneaky. Dad liked him. He would bring me candies I wasn't supposed to have when no one was looking."

Sins cleared his throat. "Baron Tralgar?"

"I have instructed everyone here," Tralgar's voice grated as his head purpled, "to refer to me as 'The Wolf.' I will have your respect!"

"I thought you fancied horses," Harden broke in. "Those big red ones from Levale? Howzabout we all call you Horsewife instead? Seems more apt."

Keane whirled to glare at the mercenary leader. "You catfucking idiot. Why not just shove all of us up a boar's ass and roast it on a spit yourself?"

"Oh, they can all make fun of him and I can't? Read the room, boy," Harden replied and gestured to the barons to their right and left. "Our problem's about to take care of itself."

Around the room, the other barons laughed. An occasional "Horsewife" could be heard above the murmur. A beet-red Baron Tralgar fixed his gaze on Harden.

"I second the motion for a vote," Baroness Fenrath said.

As agreement sprang up around the room, Tralgar seemed to come to a decision. He turned and let himself out through a door behind him. Seconds later, he emerged directly below into the base of the hall, and stormed across the floor to Keane.

Above, the barons watched with grim narrow eyes.

"Songham is king now, renegade," he said with a snarl. "Come with me immediately, and I will see you safely to Treaty Hill. Stay here, and I will kill you and all of your friends."

"He's not my friend," said Burgen.

Well, shit. Harden was right. Tralgar had overplayed his hand, and the only thing left to do now was give him a little shove out the door. Flooded with relief, Keane knew just what to say.

Keane crossed his arms and opened his mouth, but Harden beat him to the punch.

"Hey, Horace," the wily mercenary said, eyes aglitter and teeth exposed in an evil grin, "remember that story about your wife? The one where she gets a visit from some mercenary in the night, and then she up and leaves you? You ever wonder who that was?"

"Don't you dare tell me it was you." Tralgar's voice vibrated on the edge of a scream.

Keane shot a glance over at Megan who watched with eyes wide, mouth a tiny circle.

"Me? Oh no." Harden leaned back, hands on hips. "I was too busy slaughtering your army. No, I'm afraid that was our boy the king here." He took Keane's shoulder in a firm grip.

One brow went up on the baron's face at an off angle, and a disquieting leer parted his lips. A blotchy red-and-yellow pattern finished its creep over his head, and Keane could hear the evil prick's breath rasp deep within his chest.

Baron Tralgar leaned forward to Harden and said, his voice a harsh croak, "I am going to kill you for *days*, you miserable old goat. Your torments will be—"

Keane yawned loudly and stretched, and his extended fist neatly punched the baron in the forehead.

"Whoops," Keane said. "Sorry."

Harden winked at Tralgar and said, "He got you again."

"*I'LL KILL YOU!*" Tralgar shrieked and aimed a clawed hand at Harden's cheek.

The old mercenary hopped back out of the way, and both Mahu and Eli stepped in and punched Tralgar on opposite sides of his head, which sent him skidding to the floor. Alarmed, several of the barons stood, though Lady Fenrath held out a hand to instruct her guards not to intervene.

Keane chuckled. This was as good an excuse for the Barons' Conclave to rid themselves of Tralgar as it was for Keane.

Horsewife the Wolf pushed himself up against the wall and tottered to his feet. He glared at Harden and Keane with naked hatred. In response, Harden turned his back and Keane raised a hand and waggled his fingers goodbye.

"You're excused." Keane let his gaze slip off the baron's face and onto a spot on the wall over the man's right shoulder.

Tralgar held his jaw and, eyes watering, let himself out of the hall's grand entrance. Outside the doors, the baron's outraged shrieks could be heard, as well as small objects smashing to the floor.

Nervous laughter came from above which stopped when Lady Fenrath raised her arms.

"That was unfortunate but necessary, I fear," the baroness said. "The arrival of our mercenary spies from Songham's army has revealed the usurper's agent in our own midst and confirmed our suspicions." She lowered her head for a moment and collected her thoughts. "Before we get further afield, I call the vote. Those for the support and rightful rule of King Keane and Queen Megan, let your voices be heard."

The vote began at Keane's left and ran around the room. Every baron gave their "Aye" to Keane and Megan. If there were any dissenters before, the display between Harden and Tralgar made it impossible for anyone to side with the now-absent baron.

Keane watched them, openmouthed, his face a slack-jawed grin by the end.

Finally, he stood a chance.

"I apologize for the subterfuge, sire," Baroness Fenrath said to Keane. "We have long suspected that Horace Tralgar did not share our priorities, and we have used you to flush him out. I do apologize."

"Happy to have been of service." Keane would have danced on a pack of flaming jungle cats for the show he had just seen. "But I do have a question. Where the hell were you people when Songham was storming Treaty Hill?" He felt Megan cringe. "It never had to come to this. Why are you suddenly supporting me now?" He did not trust everyone's new goodwill toward him.

"We could not move against Songham or his widow while Tralgar sat amongst us," Orrikson answered. "There would be no way to keep him from knowing our plans before we'd carried them out and nothing to prevent his attacking our baronies the instant our troops were on the march. At least now we know where he and his armies are, which primarily, are not here."

Keane did not like Orrikson's answer, but at least he understood it. *What was that about Songham's widow?* Was Orrikson saying that Hulda Hubrane was already in Treaty Hill?

"Now that's out of the way," the baroness said and settled herself in her seat behind the short gallery wall, "we have some things to discuss, my king." She smiled and nodded to Keane. "Would you do us the honor?" She indicated the empty seat Tralgar just vacated.

Keane started to agree but could he hold his ground with these people?

"Go." Megan shoved him. "You can't do worse than the last guy."

"Before I do"—Keane took in all the barons along the walls—"I'm afraid there's something I need to tell you."

"If it's that you killed King Songham, we found out yesterday." Baron Sins watched Keane absorb the news. "Our messenger used a road to get here. And a horse."

"Son of a bitch," Eli whispered.

So, Harden and Eli *were* capable of being surprised. This was not the reception Keane was expecting from the Barons' Conclave. Maybe it was not what Harden was expecting either?

"Did your messenger mention anyone else?" Keane worried over those left behind. "Lord Chancellor Finnagel?"

"The king's intelligence? No, sire. There was no mention." Sins shuffled through a stack of papers and withdrew one. "The Baroness Lady Tralgar is being well treated, however." A sly smile turned the corner of his mouth. "I think we can all be grateful for that."

Far more than an intelligence officer, Finnagel had served the crown of Greenshade for more than two centuries as both spymaster and sorcerer. Keane didn't understand it exactly—and didn't really want to given Finnagel's claims about the event—but the sorcerer had been attacked in Oulan and transported back to the Forest Castle. The event robbed him of his magic and left him no more than a normal man.

He would be a prize capture for Hulda Hubrane.

Feeling queasy, Keane crossed the floor to the still open door and went up the tiny stairs behind it. He emerged into the gallery where each baron sat at a wide desk behind the wooden wall. He took Tralgar's chair. Soft red velvet cushions, still warm from the previous occupant, contrasted with the heavy black wood.

The barons looked at him, expecting . . . something.

"While I am here, I demand you call me Wolfdick."

Megan's face fell into her hands, but the rest of the room exploded into laughter.

"Very good, Your Majesty," said Baron Orrikson, the man who had greeted the Free Hand earlier in the wood. "I believe we'll get along famously."

Megan shook her head. To her apparent consternation, she had been right about Keane being himself with these people.

Harden grinned and realization hit Keane right between the eyes. Lady Fenrath had said it. Harden and the Free Hand had been their spies in Songham's armies, as Harden himself told Keane when the journey here began. But that meant Harden had known all along that the barons were opposed to Songham—excepting Tralgar—and that he was delivering Keane, Megan, and Loffa into the arms of allies. Harden truly *had* rescued them.

Even if he spent the whole trip pretending otherwise.

"You're such a jackass," Keane said to Harden. The worst thing about it all was that Keane could not even bring himself to hate the old fucker anymore. While he appreciated that Harden and his Free Hand mercenaries had rescued *him*, their first priority had been to collect Megan and Loffa, a debt which rankled Keane. He had been so worried about them. And now he found himself *grateful* to Harden fucking Grayspring.

Harden only nodded and kept his grin in reply.

Baron Sins cleared his throat and the room quieted. "After your exit, Songham's wife, Hulda, announced that she would be assuming Greenshade's throne and that she would personally see to it that you died screaming for your crimes." He pushed the errant coil of black hair off his forehead again. "From all reports, she seemed rather giddy at the prospect. Were you two acquainted?"

"We've met," Keane replied. For some reason, his immediate sympathy went to Lady Ravenstok of Crosshouse. She and Hulda Hubrane had a long-standing feud that was about to come to an abrupt and unmerciful end now that Hulda was queen.

"Now, my liege," said an overweight baron in purple to the other side of Orrikson, "Baron Drake here . . . we need to begin planning. Together, Tralgar and Hubrane's numbers equal our own, and they have the advantage of position. They hold the Forest Castle, is that correct? Rollins?"

"Partially correct," answered a silver-haired man in a red leather jacket and gray shirt. He looked much more carefully put together than any of the other barons except perhaps Lady Fenrath. "We believe that Hulda has ordered Tralgar's men to the Forest Castle but that Tralgar has only sent a token force. He keeps the bulk of his men close to Castle Oak against the oncoming Ebon Host. Though Tyrrane and the Hubranes are purported to be allies, Tralgar is not a trusting man and does not wish to leave his lands unprotected. It appears to me that if we attack with haste, we may enjoy an opportunity to retake the capital that will not come around again."

"Not to bring a soggy prick to the orgy," Keane said, "but if you already knew that Tralgar was allied with Songham and that Songham was in bed with Tyrrane, why didn't you kick him out on his jewel sack before all this happened?"

Dark looks broke out among the barons, but Rollins treated the question as if it were no more than another item on a list.

"Horace had well earned his departure before your arrival, before we knew anything about him and Tyrrane." Baron Rollins leaned back and ran a hand over his silver hair. "But the man outnumbers any of us in the field *and* is a vindictive bastard. If we were to be any help to you—to Greenshade—we had to be absent of Tralgar first. Your arrival has precipitated this in a most useful fashion. Tralgar is now gone, and because of the Tyrranean troops in the field, he will not abandon his own land to attack us. This allows us a small window of opportunity to move against Hulda Hubrane in Treaty Hill. Do you see the symmetry?"

Great Oldam blow a wolf and call himself foxy. Keane nodded to the red-jacketed baron appreciatively. He liked Rollins, too. The man thought like a mercenary.

Across the hall, Megan smiled, and he flushed with pride. All in all, this was going *much* better than he had feared it would.

"When do we eat?" asked Burgen from the floor. Raven punched him in the shoulder.

Lady Fenrath smiled. "Immediately. Forgive our manners. Bhodi, please lead the Free Hand to the dining hall. We shall follow."

The baroness was older than she appeared from the floor. Her age and experience seemed both arms and armor on her, and Keane judged that she commanded the room as well as any hardened field sergeant.

The barons and mercenaries walked together through the huge passages of Fenrath Hall. Up ahead, Keane heard Loffa ask again about the pickled fish. The barons, sans Tralgar, were an unpretentious bunch. An entirely different sort of animal from the lords and merchants who lived in Treaty Hill. Or used to, anyway.

"That smells delicious." Sabni opened his arms to the sky. The smell of dinner carried into the hallway. "Just as in the tale of *Nefret and the Widow*: Feed my belly and I grow strong, but feed my soul and I grow happy, powerful, and wise."

"I'll be content to fill my stomach," said Mahu.

"You only say that because you've never been happy." Sabni shook a finger at Mahu. "And because you are, in the main, a sour grump."

Mahu frowned up at Sabni. Together they entered the dining hall.

Bigger than the conclave's meeting room, a pair of long tables ran two-thirds of the dining hall's length, with a buffet across the end. The almost-black glossy table bowed under the weight of roasted meats, baked fruit, bread, varied vegetables, and more. To his delight, Keane even spotted a platter of traveler's rolls.

Chatter and torchlight bounced from the dark wood floor that gleamed, smooth and polished, under Keane's feet. Windows high on the redwood walls peered into the unlit night, and thick beams crossed the ceiling every ten feet or so.

The aromas of the room punched Keane straight in the stomach, and he discovered a new depth of hunger. Megan clutched his hand, the only sign she felt as hungry as he did.

"You were great back there," she whispered into his ear. "Though it is worrisome to think what it means for us that the conclave are your sort of people."

Men and women stood beside the tables and waited for the barons. Lady Fenrath moved to the center of the room.

"Friends," she said, "the Barons' Conclave places value on equality and self-sufficiency. This extends throughout everything we do here, including dinner."

Keane doubted that equality and self-sufficiency were all that high on Tralgar's list of virtues.

"We all serve ourselves at dinner in Fenrath Hall," the baroness continued. "Be considerate. We have some extra mouths tonight, and they look like eaters."

Across the room, a cook beside the buffet rang a bell, and people moved toward the food.

"First!" Burgen ran through the crowd of people, most of whom only came to his chest, and grabbed a big wooden platter. He heaped food upon it, as much as any four others could eat. "Ha! This is great."

Lady Fenrath narrowed her eyes and tightened her lips at the thick-necked brute.

"He'd be one of those eaters," Raven said as she slunk past the baroness on her way to the food.

The inhabitants of the great hall left a respectful distance around

Keane and Megan at the buffet, though they jostled shoulder to shoulder with each other. Keane filled his own platter and saw the last of the food swept away on swift plates to leave the big buffet bare. He returned to Fenrath's table and sat across from Megan, already engaged in a fast-moving conversation with the baroness at the head of the table and another one of the barons to her left. Baron Sins, it was. The one in black and white that she said gave her candy.

The cooks at Fenrath Hall had prepared an excellent meal, in Keane's estimation anyway. He glanced up and saw Loffa, confused, standing in the entryway where the group of them walked in. Her basic understanding of court life in no way prepared her for the rustic customs of the Barons' Conclave. When the bell rang, Loffa simply stood in place and waited for a servant to lead her to her chair and bring her a plate.

Now she just stood.

Keane sighed and took a longing look at his platter of beautiful, delicious food. The mercenary he used to be went to bed with a hollow stomach on a regular basis, but the king that the man had become was no longer used to such privations. Still, Loffa required caring for, and he would do it.

He stood, thinking to grab a spare platter and divide his meal. When he looked up, however, Loffa no longer stood at the archway. Eli guided her across to the far table, where he sat her in front of his dinner. Loffa ate while Eli stood behind her and scowled over her shoulder at the other mercenaries, daring them to laugh.

With a shrug, Keane resumed his seat.

"I believe that mercenary is courting the queen mother," said Lady Fenrath with a wise smile. "That may be a situation that bears watching. I have witnessed more than one marriage begin in exactly such a fashion."

"Eli?" Keane asked. Eli had wasted more than a few paydays in whorehouses around Andos—along with Keane—but the man never showed any interest in trying to maintain a relationship. The old fucker was too set in his ways for that. "Heh, you wouldn't say that if you knew him better. I think we're safe."

"As you say, sire," the baroness said. "As for more pressing matters, I have discussed the situation extensively with Baron Rollins. You may have noted him in the meeting as our expert in strategic matters."

"Silver hair, red jacket," Megan said.

"Right, The tactics guy. I liked him. Please go on, Lady Fenrath."

"If we are to win this, we must have more men." The baroness dabbed her lips with a folded napkin and set it beside her plate. "Even if Baron Tralgar stays out of it entirely, which there is no guarantee he will do, Queen Hubrane still holds the defensive position."

"The Forest Castle can be taken," Keane said. "It was just taken from me, after all."

"Songham possessed greater numbers and magic," she replied. "But even if we were to defeat the queen, rumors have it that King Brannok is readying the Ebon Host for the march. Without allies, the best we could do would be to take the castle and then die there."

Six months ago, Keane had barely known who King Brannok of Tyrrane was. Since then, it seemed like the man's shadow stretched across every bad thing that happened to him. And that was a lot of things. When the two of them finally met, Keane intended to give him a good talking to—right after he ran the bastard through.

"We know that Oulan is for Tyrrane, but that's all we're certain about." Keane had lost track of Sarah in Oulan, owing to the treachery of the Oulani monarch and court sorcerer. "Brannok has apparently been pressuring all of Greenshade's allies to turn on us."

"After the meal, we will retire to the sitting room and discuss our plans," the baroness said. "Please come, and bring Harden along." At Keane's expression of distaste, she added, "He has been useful to us in the past; he may be so again."

"Yeah, fine," said Keane. "I suppose if all else fails, I can count on him to stab me in the back and kill me, so I don't have to do it myself."

Baroness Fenrath raised an eyebrow. "How would you stab yourself in the back? That seems an awkward position for a suicide."

"No, that's not what I . . ." Keane struggled to get the words out. This baroness intimidated him. "I-I didn't mean stab myself in the back; I just meant that all this has been miserable to go through, and no one is on our side. Not only is fighting this war impossibly hard, but it's obviously a fool's errand to try and"—he caught the tiny twitch in Lady Fenrath's cheek—"you're just fucking with me, aren't you?"

The baroness smiled for real. "Perhaps I am. A bit. This hall has not been a happy place of late. Still, do not be so eager to leave us for the dagger, sire. There is impossibly hard work to be done, and who else is foolish enough to do it?"

12

CEILING HEIGHT IS
NOT NECESSARILY
PENIS COMPENSATION

KEANE

As they followed the crowd of barons, Keane and Megan trailed further behind. Their fingers intertwined, and they stopped in the long library just outside the sitting room. Alone for the first time since their home fell to Songham, they stood in the dimly lit quiet and just looked at each other. Megan drifted behind a bookcase, just out of sight of the sitting room door, her hands in Keane's.

A fat tear rolled down Megan's cheek and more followed. Keane pulled her to him, and she sobbed noiselessly against his chest. He felt like crying too, but he wouldn't. He couldn't even if he tried. Between them Megan spent so much more time as his rock, his safe place to stand and hold him up. No force in the Thirteen Kingdoms would keep him from being that for her now.

She pulled back and daubed her eyes with the hem of her tabard. Keane smiled at the grimy uniforms of Songham's infantry that they escaped the Forest Castle in. The Barons' Conclave took a very different view of proprieties than the capital did, where visitors would clean and dress before being presented. But Keane couldn't help feeling the barons' direct and unpretentious ways were at least closer to his own, if not superior.

"We'll get the castle," he said. "I don't know how yet, but we'll win your home back from that snake."

"I know we will," Megan replied. "I have faith in us." She wiped the wet from her face and squared her shoulders. Only the red around her eyes betrayed her moment of vulnerability. "What? Why are you looking at me like that?"

"Because," Keane searched for the words to express himself, "I just . . ." He placed her hand over his heart. Now that she had regained her control, he threatened to lose his.

He spotted Harden in conversation with Eli through the sitting room door.

Oldam's weeping granite asscrack. If Harden saw him cry, Keane would have to murder the gray old fuck on the spot.

Megan pressed on his chest and looked him in the eye. "I know," she said. "Me too."

They slipped further in between the bookcases so as not to be visible to the gathering in the next room and held each other. When the moment passed, they walked together into the light of the sitting room.

This room, unlike everything else in Fenrath Hall, felt cozy and close. Warm oak covered the walls, and the ceiling stood a mere eight feet over Keane's head, half the towering height of the rest of the building. Through tall glass windows with scores of tiny panes, he could see the underside of the waterfall as it rushed past and the omnipresent thrum of that powerful cascade vibrated with even greater magnitude.

Most of the barons sat arranged in a loose circle by the ring of comfortable furniture in the room. Harden and Eli colluded next to a huge glowing fireplace, and Baron Rollins, the appointed strategic expert, stood in the middle and held forth. He looked up at Keane and Megan and waved them into the room.

"My king, my queen"—he indicated a well-upholstered love seat for them to sit in—"we were just bringing up the subject of Oulan. If they push straight west and traverse Three Sisters Wood at the northern tip, that would place their forces right where we stand. We could defend this pass over the Middle Peaks easily, but it divides our forces between here and the capital."

Keane and Megan sank down into the love seat's cushions. "As it happens, my baronites," Keane said, "I was personally told by someone who was actually there that Oulan won't be traveling anywhere near here. They're gonna take their new fleet of giant-ass ships all the way around to the Sedrian Channel so they can wall off the southern coast of Greenshade all down the Beacon Sea."

Rollins frowned. "Are you certain of this information, sire? That is a much longer route to attack from a much narrower vantage."

Keane had received the report straight from Finnagel's lips after the old sorcerer/spy's attack *in* Oulan. Keane tried again not to think about Finnagel's claim that he had actually been killed and reborn, which sounded crazy. But he could not ignore the military intelligence the sorcerer brought back with him.

"Sure as King Oldam's sandy stone pecker," Keane answered. "They'll own the Beacon Sea, and we won't get shit for reinforcements anywhere along the coast. Their notion is to catch all of Greenshade that won't suck Hulda Hubrane's lady dick between the Ebon Host from the north and the Oulani fleet from the south. Nowhere left to run."

"I know what I said," Megan whispered, "and obviously you should keep being yourself. But maybe just a little *less* yourself?"

"Perhaps," said Baron Rollins. "Although that does give us an advantage of time." Rollins ran a manicured hand over his silver hair. "We know that a third of the Host is stationed permanently in Dismon to defend the Fell Citadel from attack or revolt. Mostly revolt. Brannok is gathering the Host there to receive Angrim's blessings before marching to Treaty Hill. That means we have time to press our allies to the south before they get here."

"Who will help us against Tyrrane?" Baroness Fenrath asked. "Egren has a navy, and Verran has troops, but they consider anything that happens north of the Beacon Sea to be an Andosh affair. Sedrios has no military to speak of, Arlea has refused all diplomacy since the crisis began, and Rousland is just happy that someone else is on the end of the pike for a change."

"What of Kos?" Baron Orrikson asked. "They have yet to speak." The big-shouldered baron sat forward on his chair, as if ready to spring into action at any moment.

"King Larustines maintains a small fleet of ships for defense but nothing more." Rollins stared at the carpeted floor. "His people are fishers and farmers. They will not fight."

"No," Harden said to Eli from the far end of the room. The conclave went silent as the two mercenaries' discussion gained volume.

"It's money, sir." Eli pressed at Harden. He leaned in to meet his lord marshal's gaze.

Keane shifted in his chair to watch the old soldiers argue. Harden never tolerated dissent in the ranks, even from Eli. *But* Eli was his oldest friend and advisor and was not afraid to tell the Lord Marshall when he was being a dumbass.

Although he probably wouldn't phrase it that way.

"Stop that," Harden said at full voice. "Money isn't going to do you any good when I choke you on it."

"Just ask—" Eli broke off and gave Harden a stern glare.

"Don't you try pulling that shit with me," Harden said, now mere inches from Eli's face. "I taught you that shit. And I am *still* your commander."

Although he had been with Harden for years in Wallace's Company, Keane had no clue what Harden and Eli might be arguing about. Though mercenaries in general gossiped like fishwives, Harden stalked the Thirteen Kingdoms beneath a cloud of buzzing secrets, each less savory than the last.

"Ask what?" said Lady Fenrath, one eyebrow going up.

Harden, his back to the room, wilted. He turned around, still angry but resigned. "I may have a . . . relationship in the Paradisals that could help us. Maybe."

"The pirates?" asked Baron Rollins. "How could they help us? They're pirates."

"D'you remember fifteen years or so back, when Arlea was supposed to pull all the pirates outta the islands once and fer all," Eli asked, "but then no one never heard nothin' more about it?"

"I remember that well," said Baron Hapstan. He brushed his white mustache with a weathered hand. "I heard that the Arleans lost a few good men in that action."

Harden laughed, though it was not a happy sound. "A few men? Arlea was crushed. Orri Stoneprow, the name of the man you might know as the pirate king, called on every pirate vessel, from the biggest ships to the tiniest boats and all between, to band together and fight the Arlean navy. Those dumb bastards had no idea what was coming for 'em, and they never stood a chance against it."

Keane nodded along. He would not have known Orri Stoneprow from his elbow if not for Sarah's lifelong fascination with the Paradisal Islands. She often talked about them as they fell asleep in their dirty tents in their stinking mercenary encampment. Keane remembered the man was supposed to have been a raider from Norrik and was responsible for *merging* the pirates with the indigenous people of the islands—and their supposed ocean goddess, the Deep Witch.

"And you have a connection to this . . . Stoneprow?" Rollins asked.

Harden paused before answering. "Yes." He narrowed his eyes and stared at Eli, who stood to one side and would not meet Harden's gaze. "I won't make any promises, but I believe I might have some sway with the ruler there."

"He does, Your Baronship," Eli said. "That oughtta be worth a fair coin."

"*Eli Whister.*" Harden's normally gray face reddened, and his hand strayed dangerously close to the pommel of his dagger. "You may be my oldest friend in the whole damn world, but I swear by my own rotten soul if you open your damn mouth one more time to my private notions I'll cut out your tongue and hang you from these oversized, pretentious, couldn't-afford-a-real-goddamn-castle rafters!" He pointed up to the huge redwood beams over their head and gave Eli a scowl that would have sent a full-grown water dragon running home to its mommy.

Eli just shrugged and stared into the fire.

"If the employee negotiations are finished," said Baroness Fenrath, "then you shall leave for Port Placid in the morning. At your usual rate."

"No," Harden answered. "This is *way* more dangerous than the normal rate. I think three times what the Songham job paid. Half up front ought to cover it."

"I will be paying you to have a conversation," Lady Fenrath said, "not fight a war."

"Yes, but it is a conversation you desperately need me to have. Desperation costs triple."

"I will pay the conclave back if we win," Keane said. "If we lose . . . Well if we lose, it doesn't matter anyway, does it?" Except that Harden wouldn't get the other half of his payday. At least he'd have a reason to keep Keane alive.

"Now that's logic." Eli gave a stubbly grin and ignored Harden's black look.

"Very well," said Baron Rollins to Keane. "We'll keep the pressure up on Hulda in the capital, and you intercept the Oulani fleet with your pirates—and then get them to Treaty Hill before the Host arrives."

"Oh," said Keane. "Right. I guess I'm going along. Help to have a king there too, I guess."

"Correct," said Rollins. "We will keep the Queen and Queen Mother here, for safekeeping, while you undertake the journey. We will have horses and clothes made ready for you by morning."

"Nope," said Megan. "That isn't happening."

"Excuse me, your Grace?" said Baron Rollins. "Aren't you with child? You must stay—"

"The one thing we know for sure is that the Ebon Host is coming." Megan rose to her feet and commanded the room. "No point between Dismon and Treaty Hill can be considered remotely safe, including this one. Given the choice, I am staying with my husband. For safekeeping."

Keane roused at the sight of her, enflamed in both soul and crotch. Megan was, in this moment in front of this company, fierce, wily, imposing, and—against all odds—his. In a lifetime of improbable occurrences, her love for him was the most unlikely. Yet, here they were.

Oldam's molten heart.

Lady Fenrath smiled, rose, and crossed to the fireplace. She reached over it, removed a beautifully sculpted bow of ash and horn, and held it aloft in both her hands. She walked to Megan and held it out. The whole of it was covered with intricate etched depictions of woodland leaves.

"I understand you are an accomplished archer," said the baroness. "This bow belonged to my mother who was a formidable huntress herself."

"I'll say she was," agreed Baron Hapstan, to some laughter from the room.

Keane wanted to ask for the story behind the comment but, just this once, decided to be a little bit less himself and sit back and listen.

The baroness cut her eyes at the old hunter, then continued, "It is a storied weapon, with no small amount of fame attached to it. I give it to you now, with the expectation that you will distinguish yourself with it and bring honor to its name."

"You mean," said Keane, already defying his decision, "more distinguished than being Queen of Greenshade?"

Lady Fenrath glanced at Keane, then over at Queen Mother Loffa who appeared to be listening attentively to an inkwell.

"Quite," the baroness said.

"What is its name?" Megan still did not reach for the leaf-carved bow.

An uncharacteristically sheepish grin broke over Lady Fenrath's face. "You should understand that my mother was given this bow when she was still a child."

"And she named it what?" Megan said.

"Yes, well, my mother was always a very literal person."

"But what did she call it?" Megan tried again.

"This is the grand bow . . . Leafy," answered the baroness with an embarrassed smile. "It is deadly and true. It will save your life and the lives of your friends, if you would be its equal."

Megan stood and took the bow. "I accept Leafy as a gift of value, legend, and military support, from the Barons' Conclave to the Crown of Greenshade. We thank you." She curtsied to the baroness, who returned the gesture.

Across the room, Eli struggled to suppress his mirth. A hint of a smile broke through even Harden's dark mood.

Eli snorted, and Keane stared up into the rafters until he could look at Baroness Fenrath without grinning.

"At least she can use the damn thing," Harden said. "She oughtta be of more use than her husband. But Loffa—"

"I'll watch her," Eli interjected. "I mean to say, I'll keep the woman from harm and whatnot."

Harden's flinty glare narrowed, but he nodded and said nothing.

Keane stood. "It's late, and we have an early morning. If someone can show us to a bath and a bed, we'd thank them for it."

"Of course," Baroness Fenrath said. She went to the door and drew on the bellpull to summon a servant. "We will speak again at breakfast."

"Pickled fish?" asked Loffa.

"Yes, dear," answered Keane. "If there is any pickled fish to be had, you will have it. And you can eat it with the great and legendary weapons, Forky and Spoony."

Eli snorted again while Lady Fenrath and Megan both frowned at Keane. He held up his hands.

"Sorry," he said. "I'll just, uh, see myself out."

13

HOW NOT TO HAVE SEX

KEANE

I think this bedroom is taller than it is wide." Keane lay back on the overstuffed mattress. The thick sheets smelled clean and fresh, like the waterfall, and warmed his skin. He pulled one over himself.

Dark wood walls rose out of sight behind the unlit candelabra, much like the rest of Fenrath Hall. But unique to everything Keane had seen so far, a huge window dominated one entire side of the room, perhaps twenty feet high and twice as tall as those in the dining hall. The window split into a hundred panes of glass, and moonlight spilled onto the bed and far walls through the clear cataract outside, giving the impression that silvery water cascaded through the room. Keane lay on his back, mesmerized until his queen reentered the room.

Megan dropped the towel she put on after her bath and leaped onto the bed. She grabbed Keane's hand and held it to her breast. "We should take advantage of sleeping in a bed tonight," she said, a sly smile on her face. "It may not happen again for a while."

The breast felt smooth and young and vibrant in his hand, like Megan herself. But now that they were alone, he couldn't stop other thoughts from intruding.

"Hey, you." Megan waved a hand in the air. "Guy holding my boob. You with me here?"

"Huh?" said Keane. "I'm sorry. What did you say?"

"Am I interrupting something? What'cha thinking about?"

"Sarah."

Megan's eyes rolled heavenward. She detached Keane's hand from her breast and lay curled beside him, her head on his arm. She smiled at him and ran her fingertips over his chest before pulling a blanket over them both.

"Tell me about it."

Keane paused and tried to organize his thoughts. "When Finnagel returned to us, having been attacked I guess, he said that to the best of his knowledge, Sarah and Cass were safe."

"Right," Megan said. "He whooshed them away or something."

"Something. But he didn't really know where. He was aiming for Brittlepin, but it could have been anywhere north of where they were standing. It could have been the next room."

He placed his fingers on top of Megan's, feeling them from top and below. The touch of her skin soothed him. "But we don't know. We have no way of knowing if they ever made it to High King Ivarr and what kind of reception they might have gotten once they were there."

"Sarah can handle herself. That's why you chose her. And Finnagel. And Cassius."

"Branch and Finn chose her," Keane said. "And yes, Sarah is the best—the *only* person you want on your side in a tight spot—but that's not everything. I relied on her, constantly. But I think she relied on me too, just as much. And now, assuming she did get away and those stone-licking frost cocks in Coldspine didn't hurt her, now she'll be heading back home. Back to—"

"Hulda Hubrane." Megan finished his thought. "But certainly, Sarah would find out what happened before she got there."

"Maybe. But I can't stop thinking of a thousand reasons she might walk right into the castle without talking to a soul and bam, she's caught. And I've heard too many things about Cass since they left for me to trust that slippery butt snake. The whole thing is like standing tied up in a pit that's slowly filling with pigshit. You know you need to get untied, and you know you hafta get outta that hole before you drown. But all you can do is jump up and down and freak out because no matter *what* you do, you already smell like pigshit."

Megan hesitated, an expression of distaste on her face. "You worry about your friends because you are a good person, Keane." This elicited a snort from her husband. "You *are*. But we can only do so much, and our task is already difficult enough. I know you trust Sarah to take care of you, but you have to trust her to take care of herself too. It's easy to keep faith when nothing is going wrong. But she's doubly worth your faith now, when everything is upside-down."

"I suppose you're right," Keane said. "In my heart, I know it. I can't help from here, and here is the only place I can be. It's just . . ." He trailed off for a moment and made a fist of his other hand. "I just can't shake the feeling that something really terrible is about to happen to her."

14

WHEN YOUR ONLY TOOL IS
AN AXE, EVERY PROBLEM
LOOKS LIKE A NECK

HULDA HUBRANE

Queen Hulda lifted the hem of her red-and-black skirt and stepped over the freshly killed woman in the castle hall. Hulda tracked bright blood on the gray-green stone for a dozen feet before she stopped, turned, and looked back at the woman's face.

The wide stone hall curved out of sight at both ends with windows on the outside edge. Beneath the dark arch of the ceiling, staff, messengers, and functionaries gasped and recoiled as they came upon the savaged corpse.

Integrating the old King's Swords with Hulda's ducal guard was not going well. She assumed that friction would have been the source of any and all dead people in the halls—but not this one. "Roen, is that the woman I saw you dancing with last night?"

General Roen's mustache twitched. "Yes." He scowled at the corpse, as though anger alone might bring her back to life.

"Looks like Tynos noticed you two as well." Hulda patted General Roen on the shoulder. "There, there. Better luck next time. And you"—she waved at a horrified laundry maid, the terrified woman's hands full of bedclothes—"clean this up. That's a dear."

The pair, followed by two more guards, continued to one of the lesser-used reception halls in the main keep of the Forest Castle. They were to meet with a messenger from Tyrrane, and Hulda did not want anyone else listening in.

Along the way, Hulda noticed both glares and furtive glances cast her way by the castle staff. No doubt they planned some sort of insurrection in former Queen Megan's name. Hulda hoped she would get to show the deposed woman the corpses her love would inspire.

But daydreams were like soap bubbles. Beautiful, fragile, and bitter tasting when they vanished. Hulda had an opportunity to get back into King Wagnersen's court in Mirrik and out of Greenshade forever. And all it would cost would be one despicable country, one repulsive city, and one ridiculous green castle.

She would gladly step over the corpses of every citizen in Treaty Hill to do it.

When they got to the correct hall, Tynos was waiting by the iron-bound wooden door, aloof and silent. Her plaited black hair descended from her head in six neat rows and only deepened her stark look.

Before General Roen could say anything, Hulda spoke. "They already in there?"

Tynos nodded.

"Roen," Hulda said, "how likely is this to be a congratulatory mission?"

Without taking his enraged gaze off of Tynos, Roen answered. His voice glided, even and calm, at complete odds with his countenance. "You've continued King Songham's reign without disruption, which I imagine would have been King Brannok's primary concern. I expect that this is to reemphasize Tyrrane's arrangements with your husband. Ensure that you continue to work with their interests at heart. I would be wary of them trying to move that line, however, given that you were not there when those arrangements were made." He smiled ever so slightly. "And as long as they don't know your real plans here, they can believe they have the upper hand. It makes what we have to do easier."

Tynos nodded again. Very well.

"Oh, I almost forgot." Hulda beamed at Tynos and patted General Roen on the chest appreciatively. "I wanted to tell both of you how extraordinarily *pleased* I was with the disposal of Lord Chancellor Finnagel. That was absolutely inspired. Truly you should be proud of yourselves."

During Hulda's takeover after her husband's death, a routine check of the dungeon inhabitants uncovered the lord chancellor in an unusually shaped cell hidden well away from most of the rest. As a high-ranking member of the previous order that Hulda wasn't interested in, she had him executed.

She was surprised a few days later to discover him very much alive, locked once more in that same cell.

Tynos and General Roen, not yet at each other's throats, discovered by way of experimentation that Finnagel was a demon, and every time he was killed, he almost immediately reappeared in the cell, which had fortunately been locked.

They could have simply shut the old thing in the cell and been done with it, but the solution they came up with instead was *so* much better. And given that they came up with it together, the mere mention of it set them both growling at each other.

"Don't look so angry." Hulda delighted at their discomfiture. "Let's go annoy some Tyrraneans."

To set the tone for the meet, Hulda shoved the tall doors open with more force than was necessary. She knew Tyrraneans, and she knew the kind of meek docility they expected from a woman. But the scared girl that King Wagnersen sold to the Hubrane family in exchange for peace with Greenshade was long gone.

Long live the queen.

The door opened on a rectangular room just large enough to give easy access all the way around a glossy redwood table and chairs. Bright lamps showed the faces of three ornately attired Tyrraneans in their gray, black, and silver, and a painting of the Forest Castle dominated the wall behind them. The green of the castle ramparts was far too bright, and the Stone Tower wasn't even in it.

It made up in size what it lacked in talent.

The three men were of differing ages and ranks, but all had the same pale Andosh skin and dark hair of the central northern region. The one who looked to be in charge stood a few inches taller than his fellows, with broad shoulders and a bushy black beard.

The Tyrranean mission stood to attention, and Hulda breezed into the room, Tynos and General Roen in tow. Hulda winked at the tall man opposite who bore the most medals.

"Aren't *you* a cutie?" She twisted a coil of her shoulder-length white hair around one finger and let it slide off. "Now, what have you boys got for me?"

Momentarily confused, the man Hulda addressed turned to his fellow and cleared his throat. That fellow, an obvious subordinate with only a bit of silver on his head, smiled and spoke.

"Queen Hulda, Duchess of the Western Marches, we come bearing the good will and hopes of our Emperor, Brannok the First. Supreme General Lake speaks for Emperor Brannok in all matters pertaining to Greenshade, and we pray for your forbearance and attention."

Hulda studied the speaker. His uniform marked him as a retired major. His face spoke to her of hidden fear. Could be useful.

"That's right, I forgot Brannok was calling himself an emperor now," Hulda lied.

"Shall we begin?" Supreme General Lake extended a hand over the chairs, inviting all to sit. His voice was soft. Considered. Not a thought to rise to Hulda's bait. Military composure, all the way to the bone.

Much less useful.

Hulda sat at the head of the table, while General Roen glowered to her left and Tynos stood just behind on her right-hand side.

"Of course, sweetie." Hulda sat straight in her chair. "We're waiting on you."

"Very well." Supreme General Lake steepled his large hands in front of himself on the tabletop. Our arrangement with your husband was for him to rule Greenshade beneath the mantle of the Tyrranean Empire."

"That is an arrangement I am prepared to deliver on," Hulda said. "With a few minor inducements thrown in to show everyone's good-will." The actual inducements were irrelevant. This was only a ploy to display that *they* were courting *her* and that she was the true power in this room.

Supreme General Lake was having none of that.

"Emperor Brannok has no need of your commission of your husband's debts." Supreme General Lake held Hulda's gaze in his own. Steady. Calm. Implacable. "You may return to the March Castle in the west and assign a male relative to the duchy there, or you may await the arrival of our emperor's son Prince Brannok the Third and be wed to him."

"Ex*cuse* me?" Hulda's voice went flat.

"You are very ambitious," Supreme General Lake said as he spread his wide hands over the glossy table, "but you cannot escape being a woman. Tyrrane does not play games with its rulers by allowing them to be innately inferior, and Greenshade is now part of Tyrrane. You will therefore stand aside for a more qualified—and male—occupant to the throne."

"Yeah." Hulda lifted her right hand and hooked her forefinger toward Supreme General Lake. "That's what I thought you were saying."

Supreme General Lake's eyes widened, and his hands went to his chest, though by the time they got there, they no longer had the strength to pull the pair of knife blades free. One poked out just above his clavicle and went into his left lung at a downward angle, and the other protruded at a flatter angle from the side of his neck.

Tynos truly was an artist.

The only Tyrranean yet to speak stood and yanked his sword free of its scabbard as Supreme General Lake fell forward onto the table.

General Roen, on the same side of the table, shoved a chair with one leg and tripped the man. The general stood, drew his long-bladed cutlass, and stabbed it sideways through the Tyrranean's ribcage.

The general sat back down and cleaned the blood from his blade.

"Major." Hulda focused her attention on the remaining Tyrranean. "what's your name?"

The clean-shaven major swallowed and made a gulping noise. "Karel, Your Grace. Major Karel Talon. Retired."

"Well, Karel," Hulda said, voice full of airy light, "it looks like you're in charge of the mission now. Isn't *that* exciting?"

Major Talon did not reply, though his face drew ever paler.

"I'll give you a couple minutes to adjust." Hulda stood and faced Tynos. "I'm going to visit our friend in the dungeon. When I get back, I'll need to send an orven home to the March Castle. I want to arrange a visit for my nephew. I'll meet you in my sitting room."

Tynos nodded and left, quick to turn her back on General Roen.

This little bit of murder ought to make dear Emperor Brannok hopping mad, and Karel would make an excellent source of information to Tyrrane. Whatever information Hulda wanted Tyrrane to have, that was.

Men were so predictable.

She turned to General Roen. "Get Karel here fed and bathed. Make sure he gets a meal in him, and make yourself available this evening. I have an idea I want to run by you." She leaned across the corner of the table and whispered in the general's ear. "Oh, and Roen, Tynos is sleeping with a boy in the ducal guard named Tragg. Blond with freckles. You can't miss him."

One of these days Hulda would spring the secret on Roen that his wife back in the Western Marches made him look like a rank amateur when it came to infidelity—but not until it would *really* hurt.

General Roen's eyes gleamed as he finished cleaning his blade and slid it meaningfully back into its sheath.

It was all the reward Hulda could have asked for.

THE TORCH BURNED at the stink of the dungeon's lower levels a bit, but the scented cloth Hulda held over her nose and mouth did most of the work. The walls were black and dripped some kind of slime that simply would *not* come out of silk. Hulda wore a black cloak over her wine-red dress.

"You there, sweetheart?" Hulda lifted the torch to the barred window in the door.

"Just got back in," came the reply. "I was out picking stumpleberries. You should come next time. The weather is fabulous."

Hulda smiled to herself as she placed the torch in a sconce beside the door. She felt less guilty about keeping Lady Ravenstok locked away like this when the woman was so determined not to show her misery.

"I brought you something to go with your berries, if you like." She held out a hand to one of the two ducal guard who accompanied her, and the man handed her an opened bottle of wine and two wooden cups. Hulda filled both cups and handed one through the bars.

A thin and dirty hand accepted it from her.

"Ugh, is this March wine?" Lady Ravenstok asked. "Haven't I suffered enough?"

March wine came from the Western Marches and enjoyed a reputation for being very cheap, and for being wine. Not much more could be said about it.

Hulda rolled her eyes and grinned to herself beneath the scented handkerchief. "I forget, Aerith. Why haven't I killed you yet?"

"Because I'm the only one who has shared your experiences and understands what it means to be in your position," Lady Ravenstok answered through the door. "The rest of them are nodding monkeys. You might as well be talking to men. Now what have you brought me to eat today?"

The linen cloth Hulda took from her guard contained a small apple, a smaller wedge of cheese, and a thick slice of crusty bread. She handed the items through the door one at a time.

"Life's simplest pleasures," Lady Ravenstok said after a brief respite. "I don't know if I've said before, but you have assumed control of some first-class squalor and filth down here. More wine, please?"

Hulda refilled Lady Ravenstok's cup and passed it back. "Brannok is calling himself emperor now and wants to throw me off the throne because I don't keep all my brains in a penis."

"Hmm," Lady Ravenstok replied.

"Of course, that *is* part of the plan." Hulda leaned her back against the door and sighed. It would be satisfying to defeat Brannok herself, but given the forces in play, it would also be utterly impossible. The emperor's Ebon Host was a herd of oxen come to trample a tiny clutch of hen's eggs. If it weren't for the Beacon Sea, they might not even notice enough to stop their charge.

"I am still a little fuzzy on how you intend to survive your brilliant plan," Lady Ravenstok said. "Are you going to flee when Sigga Hubrane and Reid arrive? Leave them holding the bag?"

"No, sweetie." Hulda bit her lower lip. "I considered it, but Sigga's a pacifist. Too much chance she would surrender just to save everyone's lives. If this is going to work, both sides need to do as much damage to each other as possible."

Lady Ravenstok did not answer.

"You still there?"

"Trying to decide how you think you're going to escape with all the armies of Tyrrane surrounding you." Lady Ravenstok handed back her empty cup. "It's not like anyone could miss you bouncing along the roads. And my dear, you *do* bounce. And that *hair*."

Without meaning to, Hulda grinned at Lady Ravenstok's words. "Getting away from the castle will be the easy part. I know where the Host is and when they'll arrive. I have disguises and transportation being made ready." She waved away the notion with one hand before remembering that Lady Ravenstok couldn't see her.

"And if everything works out the way you think it will," Lady Ravenstok said, "your uncle will gratefully take you back under his wing before he marches out with all the armies of Mirrik to take what's left of both Greenshade *and* Tyrrane?"

"King Wagnersen is a shrewd man." Hulda leaned back against the wall. Her black cloak squelched and slid. "He'll recognize what I'm bringing him."

A sigh came through the small barred window. "What will keep this shrewd man from simply marrying you off to the next duke or jarl or . . . Issta's gates, what if he sells you to *Norrik*? No, no. Wait. I already know the answer to that. Quite clever, my dear. What foreign noble would be willing to marry you into their family when you've destroyed the last kingdom you were peddled off to and delivered it to Mirrik? Very clever indeed."

The praise settled on Hulda like a shroud. Yes, she was clever. And yes, the dead Supreme General Lake had been right to call her ambitious. But for no reason she could credit, those things did not seem like enough. They felt hollow.

"Do you miss Songham, Hulda?"

"What?" Hulda pushed off the wall and turned her face up toward the barred window.

"I miss Vikton," Lady Ravenstok said.

Lord Vikton Ravenstok. Hulda had forgotten about him.

"He was so sweet." Lady Ravenstok's disembodied voice was both sad and wistful. "He used to bring me sun blossoms in the spring and summertime. Pink and yellow ones from the hedge behind the house. They smelled like lemons."

This unwelcome swerve in the conversation caught Hulda by surprise. There had been no time to dwell since Songham's death, and she was not certain *how* she felt about it.

"Songham was a driven man." Hulda felt bleak, as if this cold place represented her heart, her feelings for her husband. "He wasn't around much. I feel like I lost him years ago." And even when he was, he was not a particularly pleasant husband. If Hulda had been married to someone loving like Vikton instead of a humiliating and violent man like Songham, would she be doing what she planned now? Or would she be manning the ramparts herself to defend her adopted home?

No. Don't think about it. *Fuck* this stupid green castle.

"Things were easier though," Lady Ravenstok said, "when they were around."

That much was true. A woman, even a duchess and, apparently, even a queen, were seen as prey if they were not possessions of another man. Prey for men who were not close to their equals. The thought angered Hulda even as it exhausted her.

A grimy hand extended through the barred window and stayed there, open.

Without a full understanding of what she was doing or even why, Hulda took Lady Ravenstok's hand and held it. It felt impossibly thin and light, as if the slightest pressure would crumble it to bits.

But strength flowed through that hand. Understanding and strength. Hulda felt something she had not experienced in years, possibly decades, from the touch of it. In the simple human contact.

She felt gratitude.

15

DON'T LOOK DOWN

SARAH

Sarah, Cassius, and Grohann sat cross-legged on top of an enormous stone dinner table in the Tower of Chains. The top half of the cavernous dining hall remained unseen in the dark, while tiny slits in the walls illuminated the bottom. The wind ran through the thin openings and made soft high-pitched voices around the edges of the dark. Walls, floors, even the furniture were all constructed of the same cold blue-gray stone. It held no heat, and the three of them continued to wear their furs.

Sarah at first thought it funny to eat their meal on top of the table, since they could not make use of the chairs, but now, in the light of their candlesticks, they seemed more like a meal waiting for a giant to eat them than witty and discriminating diners.

A sound from above echoed around the room, and Grohann's head gamboled about on his neck in an attempt to track it.

Cassius sighed and pushed his slice of slug meat to Sarah.

"You can have mine. I'm not hungry." He got up and climbed down onto the arm of a chair. He let himself to the floor and left the room.

The lone slice of slug vanished down Sarah's gullet before Cassius made the exit. The meat no longer tasted of nothing. It now boasted a gamey note of *decomposing* nothing. Either way, this represented the last of their food, and Sarah's stomach continued to rumble.

"Still starved." She leaned back and stretched out her legs on the tabletop. The main deck of the *Sword of Mercy* could fit on this table with a little room to spare at the ends.

"Yes. My stomach rumbles too."

She raised her flagging head and looked at the troll. "Oh! I'm sorry. I didn't even ask if you wanted that. I didn't mean to—"

"Is fine." Grohann waved his massive hand. "If ve get hungry enough, trolls can alvays eat the hoomans. Yes?"

Sarah's eyes went wide which caused Grohann to laugh.

"Yeah, you're funny." Sarah looked over her shoulder at the door Cassius left by. "Why d'you think he did that? Left his food. He can't be any less hungry than we are." Or could he? Maybe he kept a secret store of food somewhere. Maybe he'd found something in this dusty tomb worth eating.

"Cassioos is feeling guilty for treating yoo so bad," Grohann said. His voice rumbled like distant boulders rolling down a stone gulley. "Guilty for being a false friend, for sexing vith yoo, for betraying yoo to yoor enemies, for leading yoo to the noisy sands."

"Yup, those are pretty much all the reasons I hate him. Too bad a skinny slice of half-rotted slug doesn't make up for it."

"Vould make it up vith me." Grohann rubbed at his growling stomach.

"And that's why you are a better person than I am. But we need to figure out what we're going to eat while we're here. And even more, what we're going to drink. Magda's been here an eternity." Sarah glanced at the ceiling and hoped the goddess wasn't listening in. "Apparently, she doesn't need food or water."

"No food for guests. This is not good planning, I think."

Sarah tapped her fingertips against the stone. "Have you noticed that when Magda's in the room, you don't feel hungry?"

Grohann looked away. "Yes."

"I wonder why that is. I mean, is it just that distracting to be in the room with a goddess, or is her presence somehow nourishing to normal people?"

Grohann picked at the tabletop and said nothing.

"I'm wondering if we can use Magda's effect on us. Can we just go upstairs and say hello whenever we're hungry or thirsty? Does that sound mad to you?"

Grohann shook his head no.

"What is it? Is something wrong?"

Another shake.

"Are you scared of Magda?" Sarah asked.

"Not scared." Grohann's toothy mouth turned down. "Magda is . . ." He trailed off, helpless.

"What is it, big guy?" Sarah rolled to her feet, stepped to the troll, and sat beside him. "You can tell me. C'mon."

After a pause, Grohann spoke. "When I am in a room with Magda, there is no hungry, like yoo say. But, also"—he stopped again, and swallowed—"I cannot stop thinking about Magda's boobies. I vant to sex vith Magda. It is so hard to think at all." With the dam broken, the words flooded forth. "Magda is too skinny. She is ugly, like a human. Yes? But 'she makes the troll root into a tree' is the saying."

Without meaning to, Sarah peeked at Grohann's crotch. Her eyes widened in surprise, and she turned away. That did not look comfortable. If it were Keane, she might have made a wisecrack and laughed it off, but Grohann acted so embarrassed about his tree. Maybe he should find someplace private to take care of it?

"I am sorry." Grohann's misery was plain on his face. "Magda is a goddess. How are ve even being here vith her? Maybe ve are the ones who are crazy. Yes?"

"I'm the one who should be sorry, Grohann." Sarah leaned forward to put a supportive hand on his knee, then thought better of it. "First, this trip is my fault, so if you need anyone to blame for it, you can blame me. Second, I can't stop thinking of her tits either, and I don't even *like* girls. Not like that, anyway. It isn't us. It's just some effect she has on normal people. So, don't get upset about it."

"Yoo do?"

"Yeah, I do. But it was embarrassing, so I didn't say anything out loud. Like you." She stood again and patted Grohann on the shoulder. "And second—"

"Is third," the troll corrected.

Sarah set her jaw. "And third, you and I are a team. We are going to figure a way out of this. Plus, goddess upstairs, right? We came here looking for a weapon to use against Tyrrane. Could we do any better than that? She might be a little demented, but we've managed pretty well so far with Cass. This can't be much different."

Sarah walked around in front of Grohann and once more glanced downward by accident. She turned her head and stared up into the dark.

"I am going upstairs to talk to Magda. I want to come right out and ask her if she will help us and see if maybe she can god magic us up some food. I'll just leave you to deal with your . . . situation there." Sarah waved a hand in Grohann's direction.

"Yoo should have all the lucks."

"You too." She turned to leave and almost tripped over a small object on the table. Her red leather pouch, the one that contained her carving knife and "walrus" lay there on the cold stone surface. She picked it up and looked inside. The drawing of the walrus on the wrapping cloth peeked back at her.

How? Cassius? He had it when they entered the tower. He had carried it across the sand.

For her.

Sarah glared at the pouch and tried to sort through her feelings. "Son of a bitch."

She hopped down onto the chair arm.

16

GIVE YOUR GRAMMIE A HUG

SARAH

Human-sized stairs curled up into the darkness toward Magda's chambers. Sarah climbed and resolved to think no more about how the sixty-foot-high winding stair supported itself or how many bones she might break if the stair changed its mind about doing so. Since that first time she woke up in Magda's lap, she had set her path upon these stairs twice, and both times she'd chickened out before she gained the second level.

Magda occasionally came down to stand and creepily observe her uninvited guests. Whenever she came thusly to them, the goddess stood no taller than Sarah and spoke to none of them.

She seemed surprised each time to find them still there.

Sarah's head popped up through the round hole in the floor of Magda's chamber. She saw the white and gold furniture from her first visit, sized for human beings but this time lit by torches of various colored flame that were set into the walls. The anxiety of the stair left her, and her eyes turned as if of their own accord to the goddess.

Magda cut a forlorn figure, with her back to the room, silhouetted against a tall thin window. From her vantage point on the stair, Sarah saw the chains which dragged from the goddess's wrists trailed for fifteen or twenty feet before they became smoky and insubstantial and ended in mist on the floor. Sarah felt certain the chains did not end, however, and instead bound Magda to something unseen. Something *elsewhere*.

Out of nowhere the thought came to Sarah that this job was easier without Keane here. She felt a twinge of guilt for thinking it, but things were difficult enough without having to convince him to keep going every step of the way. She had no doubt that Keane would have been smart enough never to come here in the first place.

Don't suppose I could have thought of that before we hit the damned sands, could I?

"Have you come to visit, my button?" Magda did not look up. Sarah was not even certain the goddess's lips had moved.

"I, uh, yes," Sarah said, her head still the only part of her in the room. "I was, uh, I need your help"

A sigh escaped the goddess, and she turned her beautiful face to one side. Given her previous stillness, the motion shocked Sarah. "Ask, my button. I have had so little conversation"

"I . . ."

The instant Sarah saw Magda's face, she forgot all about her hunger and thirst, and her body thought of other, less appropriate things.

She shook it off and jumped in. "I'm sorry to ask, but are we going to die here? There's no food or water here, is there?"

Magda turned and leaned back against the window. A giantess once more, she wore a filmy gown that revealed her shape, backlit by the wan daylight behind her. Sarah understood Magda's reputation as the goddess of seduction and beauty.

"Does not my being sustain you?" The goddess opened her arms.

"Oh. Yeah. Absolutely. I was just making sure, you know, that we were getting sustained for real and not just in our heads."

"A mortal might live a thousand years in my shadow, without meat, nor fruit, nor wine passing his lips."

Sarah clapped her hands together and climbed the final rungs into the room. "Great. That's great. All settled then. So, can you come help us defeat Tyrrane?"

By way of answer, Magda raised her arms higher and displayed the chains that bit into her wrists. She smiled. "Clever button. Now we know the reason for the present you brought. But tell me, do you know why I am abandoned in this place?"

The tale Cassius told Sarah sprang forward in her mind. Where Magda murdered her children in a fit of jealous rage and was sentenced to spend eternity in this tower. Or possibly her husband convinced her to and later betrayed her. Some uncertainty surrounded the story, and neither seemed a good idea to confront a goddess with.

"No," Sarah answered with a straight face.

"Ages ago, when the world was green, I lived with my beloved Hagrim in our fine castle of stone. The mountains teemed with our children, and the sound of their happiness and play gorged my soul with the love of them. They were of us, magical, powerful, and special beyond all others.

"King Oldam, lord of the gods, asked that we in our turn make a gift to his creations, the humans of Andos. Hagrim and I could think of no greater gift than the children we made, that they might show the humans their magic and use it to care for them and nurture them."

Magda's face turned downcast, and Sarah felt her heart break.

"How wrong we were." A tear rolled down the goddess's cheek.

"The humans were fearful of our children's natures and jealous. They hated the magic we sent to help them because they possessed no measure of it. By their suffocating numbers, they murdered our children, their fear and insanity overcoming my babies one by one. There were many wars and incalculable bloodshed, for the children of Hagrim and Magda did not fall easily.

"Oldam returned to us in a fury, accusing us of poisoning his works with our gift. He demanded that we slay our precious offspring.

"Hagrim was inconsolable, and he made an oath against the humans so horrible that it shook down the walls of our treasured castle.

"I took that oath with him."

Magda paused in her tale. She strode from the window to the bed and sat upon it. Sarah watched her the entire time, and though she never saw the goddess change from giant to human size, it happened.

Magda patted the mattress beside her. "Come sit with me, my button."

At least seventy feet of cold stone floor separated Sarah from the bed, and she found herself in no hurry to get there. She no longer trusted what her senses told her about the world around her. But she went to the bed regardless and sat beside the goddess.

"Ours was no ordinary promise," Magda continued. "It was a god oath, and it reshaped the very natures of our few remaining children."

"You hid them," Sarah said. "You made them look like humans."

A sad smile flitted across the goddess's features. "Yes, clever button. We did not simply disguise them as humanity, we hid our children *inside* humanity. But that was not all. Whenever the time was ideal, a grandchild would be born of human parents, true to their bloodline. Within their essence, our oath placed a drive to control, to subjugate, to rule. We ensured that our grandchildren would realize their place above the humans and that they would conquer the inferior creations of Oldam. By this, our offspring would make Andos safe for more and more of their kind until humanity was finally, and utterly, stamped out."

Sarah found herself unable to respond, horrified by her own lineage. The details of the story brought her sorcerous teacher Finnagel into stark relief, and his casual bigotry toward humanity made sudden sense.

Toward Keane.

Was this where her destiny meant to lead her?

"Oldam returned a final time, his anger limitless. For now, he could not be certain of destroying our children without destroying his favorite creation, humanity itself. He demanded justice, and Hagrim, my dear, sweet, treacherous Hagrim, gave me over." No more tears came. Magda's voice was dry dust blowing over an unattended threshold into a dead home.

"Oldam imprisoned me in this tower, chained to its rapacious heart. It feeds upon my happiness. Or it should, were there any to consume."

"But sorcerers fight each other." Sarah strove to come to grips with the meaning of the tale. "How does that help their cause?"

Magda turned and pushed a strand of Sarah's hair behind her ear, as a mother might. "It does not matter. Eventually one will win out, and she will be the most powerful of all my grandchildren. The seed of sorcery lies within every human, though they do not know it. My grandchildren can never be vanquished. And for as many times as they are put down, they have to win but once."

Images of Keane, Finnagel, Kadir, of Grohann's father Old Stone possessed by the shard of Angrim, these and more flashed through Sarah's mind. Pieces slipped together that never seemed related. The fighting, the death—all of it because the people of the Thirteen King-doms existed as mere pieces on a board to the sorcerers. To people like . . .

Her.

And even the sorcerers merely acted on impulses molded into their beings, themselves no more free-willed than the humans they sought to subjugate.

"What if I don't want to conquer?" Sarah asked. "What if I want to live with the humans? Be one of them?"

The goddess took Sarah's hand between both of hers and met her eyes. "We are what we are, my button. And what we are does not care for our wants."

17

______

THE FREE HAND
DRINKS SOME NICE TEA

KEANE

"That's the Low Wood up there. We oughtta make it there by lunch." The steely stubble in Eli's beard matched the steely stubble on his head, and his voice sounded of dust and grass.

"I'll be happy to get out of the grassland." Harden made a sour face. He took off his wide-brimmed leather hat and ran a hand through his stringy gray hair. "We've been running around like targets on horseback for days now. It won't matter how stupid Tralgar's men are if they can spot us a mile off."

"Go choke yourself on Oldam's cock ring, Harden. Wasn't this direction your idea in the first place?" Keane was tired of listening to Harden poke holes in his plan. Old stringy bastard was used to giving orders, not taking them. And certainly not from Keane.

The Free Hand stretched out behind them on horses borrowed from Baroness Fenrath and followed a track of sorts through the brown waist-high grass. Intermittent snow and constant wind turned the mood surly for everyone but Sabni, who couldn't be unhappy if he tried, and Megan, who enjoyed learning more about her new bow than Keane could ever understand. Their talk turned esoteric days ago, speaking to the "soul" of the bow and whatnot.

"*Port Placid* was my idea," Harden said with a frown. "Heading through Baron Horsewife's territory is just stupid."

"Coulda caught a boat downriver," said Eli. "Sailed through the Beacon. Got caught by one o' Hubrane's boats 'twixt Greenshade and Kos."

Harden turned on his balding second, head back and eyes narrow. "Well that's even stupider than this. And since that's the option, this is the stupid direction for us. Unless of course we can all just agree that Greenshade isn't worth the trouble of keeping it from the Tyrraneans and move to an island somewhere. I know a nice one."

"Since I think I'm supposed to object to that"—Keane glanced behind himself at the Queen of Greenshade, who practiced bow-pulls on the off side of her horse—"I object to that."

She caught his glance and waved, smiling. Her dark curls bounced in the sunshine, and Keane's morning grew a little brighter. She talked of little these days other than bows and pregnancy, and the coming baby made him nervous. It was a dripping clock that loomed over everything he did.

"You better." Eli gave Keane a wicked grin. "I been watching that young girl learn to shoot. Pretty sure she could send an arrow up yer asshole and not even touch yer horse."

The same grin broke out on Keane's face. Despite the desperation of their cause, Megan was happy—and so was he. "You know, times like this make me glad her evil fuck of a dad is dead."

"You're welcome," answered Harden.

An hour later the Free Hand gained the tree line and, after a bit of searching, found a rutted track that led in a westerly direction. Raven went out ahead to scout, and her spear-thin frame vanished in the trees.

With dense trees and brush to either side, the group traveled by pairs on the wagon track through the wood. The late-morning sun kept the woods light, though the thickness of the trunks made it impossible to see far. The track itself ran up and down low slopes and around the really big trees, so even it afforded little in the way of distance of vision. Small animals rustled in the undergrowth as they passed, and the air smelled crisp and cold.

"Hi there, your honor." Morholt's horse clopped in the rut next to Keane's.

"It's Your Majesty." Keane didn't care for the ginger-haired sorcerer. The man smiled too much. Like now.

"Sure, it is. That's good." Teeth showed through the ginger beard. "Say, I got a question for you."

"Go away."

Morholt failed to go away. "That little queen you're married to. She's what, fifteen?"

"Nineteen. And she's very mature for her age."

Morholt's smile crept up into a grin. "'Course she is. 'Course. And you're what? Forty?"

His eyes wide and spine straight in the saddle, Keane said, "I am not forty! I am twenty . . ." He stopped, then whispered. "I am twenty-four years of age. Maybe younger, I don't know for sure. Probably younger."

"Really. Twenty-four? If you say so. I'm thinking that 'don't know for sure' part is the most accurate. You look older to me. To tell the truth, I'm wondering how an old man like you keeps up with a treat like her in the sack."

Keane stared at Morholt, who only grinned wider.

"'Cause I'm available if you need help."

Keane launched himself off of his horse's back to fly through the air at Morholt. As he connected, the grinning sorcerer burst like a bubble of smoke, horse included, and Keane fell into the bushes alongside the track.

From the rear of the procession, Burgen and the real Morholt brayed laughter and clung to their saddles. Loffa looked over to see what was funny, and Megan jumped down, bow in hand, concern written on her face.

Embarrassment competed with anger in Keane's brain, and both turned him a bright red. Eli smiled from the front while Harden frowned.

"If you idiots don't think you can make any more noise," the mercenary lord marshal said, "we could always set some signal-fires for Tralgar's scouts to find us by."

"Are you alright?" Megan asked. "What happened?"

"Boo." Raven poked Keane in the ribs from behind.

Keane screamed in Megan's face and jumped, whirling, blade in hand. Raven looked at him, and at the arrow Megan pointed at her eye, and gave a disarming grin. She had a big smile and used it infrequently enough that it always caught people by surprise.

Keane decided that he was going to cut off the head of the next person who smiled at him like that. The thought made him wish for Sarah again.

Morholt clutched his mount's neck and tried to breathe. Burgen gasped for breath and held his ribs.

Harden rolled his eyes and spoke to the black-haired woman over the two mercenaries' mirth. "Report. What did you find?"

"Scout patrol," Raven told him, at ease with the pair of weapons trained on her. "Six together, two more rangers out front. Mile west of here but headed this way."

"That sounds like an opportunity," Harden said. "They on this trail?"

"They are."

Megan put her arrow away and touched Keane on the shoulder. He looked at her, then back at his sword. His cheeks went pink, and he scabbarded the blade.

"Well then," said Harden, "let's set us up an ambush."

18

BABY'S FIRST MURDER

KEANE

They tied the horses off and left them with Loffa and Eli and crept forward along the track and into the wood. Keane wanted to insist that a different guard be left with the queen mother, but after his recent humiliation, he didn't need to paint another target on his back.

For that matter, he would have preferred she be left back at Fenrath Hall, but Megan had been completely correct about their lack of safety there. Out here they would be defended from whatever they might run across by the Free Hand. Anything they could not handle, they would simply run away from. But the town of Fenrath would be on the way to Treaty Hill for the Ebon Host, and if they decided to destroy it, there would be nowhere to run.

The Free Hand melted into the trees beside the trail and waited. Soon, a pair of men in leather armor and gray tabards with wolf heads on the breast moved into view. They were quiet and attentive.

"Mahu and I will take these men," Sabni whispered to Megan, just beside Keane. "Watch me, and tell me which of the parables we embody." Sabni locked eyes with Mahu across the track, and they nodded as one. Together, they rose, drew, and fired.

The scouts, each now with a feathered shaft through their necks, fell backward into the short grass of the trail. Burgen and Raven stepped out and stabbed the men through their wolf heads and dragged them to the side. In all, five or six seconds had elapsed.

"Well?" Sabni asked his student.

"*Nefret and the Donkey*," Megan answered. "The old man is deaf because of his life of debauchery in the city and can't hear the donkey making love to his wife in the next room."

With a broad grin, Sabni tousled Megan's hair. "You are, of course, correct, my queen. And what does the Immortal Queen Nefret do to help the situation?"

"She better shoot the next pack of scouts with her big fucking bow." Keane pointed further up the wooded track. Six more men in Tralgar's livery came around the distant bend, their voices audible to everyone.

"Wait until the last of them is even with the marshal," Sabni whispered and indicated Harden's hidden position alongside the road. "Shoot once at the second man on the left. After that, there will be close fighting. Too dangerous to shoot. You will wait here, yes?"

Megan nodded. She looked scared but resolute. Keane gripped his sword. A hint of clove oil rose from the blade. It should have been nice, but it always made him think of blood and death.

They waited for the soldier scouts to be exactly where Harden wanted them. The six men chatted. Keane overheard snatches of conversation about the new cook Baron Tralgar had hired and how much better the bread tasted now. The second man on the left spoke up to say that he was going to ask a serving girl to go on a picnic with him, which provoked laughter from his fellows. He began to protest when Sabni and Mahu stepped into the track and shot the men in front of him.

Megan put an arrow in his eye.

A flurry of activity followed. There were two screams, then quiet.

Burgen, white-faced, held his bleeding leg while Raven cared for him. Two of the remaining scouts lay dead in the trail while the third lay beneath Harden who removed the man's weapons.

"I'm gonna let you up now," Harden said, "and you're gonna be good so we don't have to kill you too. Got that?"

"Uh-huh," came the quavering reply.

Megan threw up into the bushes. Keane rushed over, pulled her long brown curls away from her face, and spoke in low, even tones.

"Just breathe, and let it go. It'll be over before you know it. Just breathe. You're going to be fine. There you are. All done. Feel better now? Oh, not quite done then . . . Don't hold your breath, it doesn't help."

After a moment, Megan stood, sniffled, and wiped her face. She turned and grabbed Keane tight. Sabni walked up behind her and placed a large dark hand on her shoulder.

"You are a warrior today, my queen," Sabni said. "Your grief is not for the enemy you kill but for the girl who has died here, though she is reborn a woman and defender of her kingdom. Mourn the girl, but celebrate the fighter who replaces her, for she is mighty and will save us all."

Keane almost hugged Sabni. The Darrishman's words were so much more comforting than Keane's own. Instead, he simply held his wife.

The hem of Keane's cloak served Megan as a handkerchief, and she turned to Sabni while she blotted tears with the sleeve of her dress. "That's *The Oak and the Stone*, right?"

"Queen Nefret's wisdom lights the path of all who would listen." Sabni smiled proudly at his student.

"Sabni," Keane asked the tall Darrishman, "why're you here? I mean, I guess you must be a mercenary—you're with Harden and all —but you're *better* than him. You know Darrish scripture and stuff. What gives?"

Sabni inhaled a deep breath and let it out, looking at the Free Hand over Keane's head. "All of us have our own reasons for being here, in this moment, in this place. Some of us are afraid, and some of us are lost." He put a big hand, warm and dark, on Keane's shoulder. "But all of us need the money."

"Here." Mahu tossed Megan an apple. "Hang on to that. Nefret's long on wisdom but short on knowing when a girl who just lost her lunch is going to be hungry again."

"Are you going to be alright?" Keane asked Megan.

"Yes. Go. We can talk later." Keane hugged Megan once more and walked to Harden and the prisoner. Morholt stood close-by.

"I really don't care," Harden said to the scout, a young man in his early twenties. There was a divot in his lower lip that zig-zagged all the way down his chin. "Don't talk. We'll just kill you and find another patrol with another scared kid just like you and ask him instead. Hey, Holt, show this kid the string we've made of our souvenirs so far this trip."

Morholt reached up under his cloak, his lips moving silently. He pulled out a rough cord from which hung several dozen objects. Keane turned his head, trying to understand what he looked at. Blood pattered off the pieces of flesh into the leaves. Keane and the scout both figured out which part of anatomy hung from the string at the same time, with similar reactions. The scout cried out, scrambling backward and falling on his butt, while Keane turned and walked several feet away, concentrating on not adding his lunch to Megan's in the bushes.

"Hagrim's eyes, Holt," Harden said, irritated. "We agreed on ears. What the fuck is that?"

"Seemed like a better motivator to me." Morholt shrugged. Keane looked back. The sorcerer stepped toward the cringing scout on the ground and held the string toward him. "What do you think? This make you more likely than a string of ears to tell us everything we want to know?"

"The Wolf . . . is sending patrols . . . every hour," the scout said between panicked breaths. "North, south . . . and east. If any patrol is late getting back . . . he sends everyone . . . to where they're supposed to be." He closed his eyes and breathed in and out. "Our patrol is due back in six hours. When we don't come back, two thousand soldiers will come looking for us. There's no way out. I'm sorry."

Harden frowned down at the young man. "You can get rid of

that," he said to Morholt. The sorcerer opened his hand, and the grisly cord fell away into nothingness.

The scout's mouth dropped open, and Harden hauled him to his feet. The mercenary pushed the boy back against a tree and unhooked a length of rope from his belt.

"Please don't kill me, sir." The scout's voice broke. "I got a sick mother. She needs me. She'd die without me."

Harden yanked the man's arms behind him, around the tree, and tied them together.

"If we didn't care about killing you, with whom we are having this friendly conversation," Morholt asked, his arms opened wide to take in the surroundings, "why would you assume we would care about some batty old lady—who is clearly a burden on society—that we haven't even met?"

The young scout sobbed. Keane figured he might have too.

"More to the point," Harden said from behind the tree, "why would I bother tying a man to a tree if I was just gonna cut his throat?"

"Re-really?"

"Shut up." Harden walked around the tree. He faced the Free Hand in the middle of the track, hands on his hips.

"All right," Harden said, a note of command in his tone, "in case you didn't hear, as soon as this little shit's squad fails to make it home, Baron Horsewife is gonna put two thousand violent-minded bastards in these woods to root us out. There is zero chance we get out of that alive. Now I don't mind risking your necks if I'm getting paid enough for it, but fortunately for you, I ain't. So, head back for the horses, and let's turn this little trip around. We're going back to Fenrath."

"Like hell we are," whispered Keane, low enough that the rest of the mercenaries could not hear. "That is not the plan, and that is certainly not all right with me. We go ahead until we find a path south, and we go around Castle Oak and Baron Tralgar. This may be no more than a sack of coins to you, but you're dealing with kingdoms and real people's lives. And a king who would lose *no* sleep seeing you at the end of a noose"

Harden pulled himself up onto the back of his horse and looked down at Keane. "Count the swords, boy," he said. "You lose this fight. Get over it, and follow us. Or don't. I don't give a shit. I'm sure you and the missus will do just fine against Baron Horsewife's two thousand troops."

Baron Tralgar may have loved his expensive horses more than his wife or lands, but Keane still thought that Horsewife was a dumb nickname. He'd have called him Horsefucker or . . .

That was all he had.

Megan whispered to Keane, "Let's follow him out, and we can find a path ourselves. We don't need him."

"We kinda do," Keane replied with a sigh. "Do you know any pirates?"

Keane and Megan fell in behind the mercenaries, and the Free Hand went back the way they came. Collecting Eli and Loffa, they rode east at a good clip. After ten minutes or so, Harden called a stop.

"Find an interesting tree to run away from?" Keane asked.

An expansive grin covered Harden's face. "Nice job back there, boy. All your whining really sold it."

"Sold? What are you talking about?"

"When Horsewife's men find that boy, every mother's son of 'em are gonna head straight east trying to catch us before we get back into Baroness Fenrath's land. They ain't gonna want to ride up on her with what looks like an invasion force. Without Hulda's men along for the ride, the conclave still outnumbers him."

"But isn't that where we're running to?" said Keane.

Behind Harden, Morholt rolled his eyes.

"You really didn't learn anything when you were with me, did you? No, Your Highness, we are taking this track right here"—Harden pointed to a game trail that led north—"and hot footing it past all of Tralgar's men. We'll walk through the town of Old Oak and right past his castle. Feh. No wonder Sarah had to take care of you."

Keane showed his teeth with a mirthless grin and shook his head. "I suppose if you're looking for something that will really surprise Baron Tralgar, being brave ought to do it."

Laughter erupted from first Harden, then Eli. Loffa joined in, though Keane judged little chance she knew why.

"That's funny," Harden said, "and also true. Burgen, how's that leg? You fine to ride?"

"He won't be winning any footraces," Raven said, "but he'll mend."

"All good, Marshal," Burgen added.

"Just a second." Keane rode over to Morholt, close enough that they bumped knees as the horses jostled one another. "I think I've figured out how you did that trick with the string."

"Oh, have you?" Morholt raised an eyebrow.

Keane's fist shot out like a bolt and smashed Morholt's cheek. The runecrafter's head snapped backward and his body followed. He slid out of the saddle and fell to the ground.

"Don't talk about my wife."

Silence held the Free Hand for a beat before Burgen guffawed at Morholt's prostrate form. One of the fallen sorcerer's arms described a feeble circle in the air.

Raven nudged her horse to where she could see her brother's face and clucked her tongue.

"You kinda deserved that," she said with a chuckle.

Morholt rolled to his knees, back covered in dead leaves and dirt. Squinting out of one eye, he smiled up at Keane. "Nice one."

"If we's all through punchin' each other inna face," Eli said, "I unnerstand there's some fairly life-threatenin' business on its way here that we need to be evadin'. So get back on yer damn horse an' let's go."

As Morholt clambered onto his horse and Harden led the Free Hand up the game trail, Megan moved her mount next to Keane's. Her eyes serious, she leaned over and drew him to her. She kissed him once and at length on the lips, then leaned back.

"Thank you," she said, and turned to follow the mercenaries.

Keane sat there stupefied for a moment until he realized they were leaving without him. Then he squeezed his heels and hurried after his wife.

"Now, you have to stop acting like that." The two of them were sufficiently behind the rest not to be heard.

After the intimate kiss, it took Keane a moment to catch up to what Megan meant. "Are you talking about what you *just* thanked me for?"

Megan nodded. "Yes. I appreciate you wanting to protect me. Really, I do. But this isn't a very stable situation, and you're making it worse."

"Hang on. How is teaching these goons not to be shitty to the Queen of Greenshade making things worse?" Keane felt his frustration—and his volume—rise. "There's no telling what they'll do if they don't respect you. And me."

Megan closed her eyes and took a deep breath. "Nothing is going to happen. You won't let it come to that. Not to mention Sabni and Mahu. But what you're doing causes resentment. Morholt makes a comment, you punch Morholt. What comes next?"

"I don't—"

"Shut up, and let me finish," Megan interrupted him. "It's all very manly to punch someone in the eye for talking about your wife. And I can't help but love it a little bit, especially after growing up with a father who was only all too happy to pile on with everyone else. But the stakes are too high for that kind of thinking. If this group falls apart because you're being a big tough man, then it's Greenshade who pays for it. I can't let that happen."

A spear fashioned of hardened green guilt ran Keane straight through the chest. The wound stank of selfishness and stupidity.

"But what am I supposed to do?" Being a mercenary was never this confusing before. Was he to stand by and do nothing when brutish men abused his wife? Even as he thought it, he knew that wasn't what Megan meant.

She smiled and took his hand.

"You've always had Sarah by your side. This was your world, the two of you. She covered your back while you watched hers, but you never had to actually be afraid for her. Sarah could take care of herself."

"And me too," Keane agreed.

A breeze ruffled Megan's waterfall of brown curls, and Keane thought of the scent of flowers. It made him sad to consider what he might personally lose in all this.

"Exactly. But now here you are, in a situation that you think ought to feel familiar, but it's not. Because instead of big strong Sarah beside you, you have a pregnant girl you feel like you need to watch over like a guard dog. And instead of the people around you being allies, now they're the ones you're watching out for."

"To be fair, other mercenaries have always been crappy allies."

"Shut up some more," Megan said, her smile wider now. "Everyone here is your ally for whatever reason they've chosen, even Harden. I said shut up." Her brows drew together to show she was serious. "I am not entirely incapable of defending myself, and yes, even Harden has a very real financial incentive to see me *and you* through this intact."

She released Keane's hand and sat up primly in her saddle. "So stop being such a *man* about everything that's irritating you, and start thinking like a *king*. Got it?"

Keane thought for a moment. "I can't promise never to punch Morholt again." He hurried the rest of his answer as Megan's mouth opened to speak. "But I'll try. I understand. Don't fuck up the whole orgy because one of the whores looks like your sister."

"Uh," Megan said. "I guess?"

Keane raised his arms and let them drop to his sides. "Well, why didn't you just say that to begin with?"

19

VILLAINS, SOME MORE TEA,
AND THE WRONG SARAH

KEANE

The tiny house in Old Oak barely accommodated the ten of them, plus the old man and woman who lived there. They crammed in and sat on the tables and bed while the woman tried to make tea for them all.

As a hideout, the home made a wonderful hatbox.

Everywhere Keane looked was packed with mementos of the couple's long life together. The corners were filled with brooms and shovels, walking sticks and fire pokers. The table held ceramic pots and stacks of clothes for mending, carved wooden representations of the Alir—three-inch high figurines used by old-timers to pray—and a plate with a small loaf of black bread that Burgen poured honey over before stuffing into his stubbly face. More items hung from the rafters: a stool, a fishing pole and throwing net, a lengthy bundle of sticks wrapped in cloth and bound in rope that Keane could not discern the purpose of, and much, much more. The hovel smelled of dust and sweat but in a comfortable way, like a well-broken-in shoe.

"You know you don't have to serve us drinks, ma'am," Keane said to the diminutive white-haired woman. "We're sort of invaders here. You can just sit down and wait for it all to be over."

"Listen to the man, Sarah," her husband, wrinkled, stooped, and squint-eyed, added. Keane felt certain he would have been bald too, under his gray-green cap. "These folks is villains. They's here to murder us sure as Mirrik's dingle."

Burgen laughed at that. It was an unpleasant sort of sound. Her arm slung casually around his neck as she sat on his knee, Raven smiled and nuzzled his ear.

"Language, Sammel," the old woman chastised. She wiped her hands on the front of her faded dress, and the flowers painted on it grew invisible. "What they is, is guests, and we ain't gonner be impolite ter no guests. We don't never get no guests, and you's why."

Her old husband grumbled an incoherent reply and sat back on his little three-legged stool. He continued to glower at his "guests."

"Excuse me," Keane asked the old woman, "your husband said . . . Is your name Sarah?"

"That it is, young'un. Sarah Cooper."

"I, uh," Keane felt awkward. He exchanged a glance with Megan, who nodded back to him.

"May I make the tea?" Keane asked. "I'd, that is, I would be honored to do something for you and your husband in return for your hospitality."

"Brigands," Sammel said from his stool.

Morholt rolled his eyes and removed a thick pasteboard card from its ratty green wrapping. He ignored the rest of the room and sat staring at it. From prior behavior, Keane knew that Morholt was consulting with his imp, a painting on the card named April. It seemed pretty outlandish to Keane, but then, his best friend *was* a sorceress.

Sarah looked up at Keane sidelong. He knew this woman could be in no conceivable fashion related to *his* Sarah, but the coincidence of the name made him feel close to her nevertheless. She nodded and sat next to her husband, keeping a falcon-like watch over what Keane did with her teapot.

Harden chose this particular home because it was less than a hundred feet from the front gate of Castle Oak, Baron Tralgar's home and headquarters. Like much of the town of Old Oak, the house's dilapidated condition made it easy to overlook, and it boasted the additional advantage of several glass windows to keep watch out of.

While he looked out one of these windows, Harden made his plans with Eli.

Even though he was a king now, Keane couldn't help but fall back into his old patterns of following Harden's lead. He tried to think of Megan's recent advice though and not get frustrated by the situation. After all, an uncomfortable metal ring on his head hadn't really made him any smarter.

"Castle's shit," Harden said. "Old motte and bailey. *Real* old. They haven't even built those for what, a hundred years?"

"Prob'ly," answered Eli. "Not since that hat of yours was in style."

"How do you make a castle out of wood?" Morholt looked up from the card. "What keeps attackers from just burning you out?"

"Not much," Harden replied. "That's why they don't do it anymore."

"They built the things outta wood because they had wood," Eli said. "If ya look at the keep up onna hill, you can see mosta the outside walls used to be covered in quicklime. That don't burn. Also, there's a stream runs through the southwest corner, so they's always got water to dump on anything what does. But that means we set a few o' them other buildings to light, an alla them in there's gonna come runnin' to put it out. That's a thing we can use."

Harden frowned out the window. "So the keep is on the hill in the back, and that's the stables, blacksmith's, barracks, and more barracks against the bailey walls. Big house is mayor, maybe? What's that long building on the right? The really low one with the flat roof."

The tiny windowpane held years of grime. Eli rubbed at it with dirty fingertips. "Not sure. Chickens?" He turned and gestured for the old man to come over to the window. "C'mere. You live next door. What's that building for?"

"I ain't no traitor. An' I ain't gonner help you fight the baron. So you kin fergit about that."

"You hate the baron," Sarah said.

"Shut up, woman. Gonner git us kilt."

"You have a beautiful home," Loffa observed from her perch behind the couple's bed. "It's very scary."

Keane couldn't help but notice Eli's chuckle.

"Hang on." Harden pressed his long nose against his own dirty window. "Well look at that. There's a good boy."

The windows were all taken by snooping mercenaries, so Keane peeked out the front door. Cracked and sharpened tree trunks lashed together stood at tired attention as a bailey wall, with allures around the inside top for guards to walk on. A group of soldiers ran into the front gate of the long palisade. In their midst ran the young scout that the Free Hand left behind in the woods.

"Now just give 'em a bit of time to think about what the boy's telling 'em." Harden's face showed amusement, but he held his body taut.

In his mind, Keane saw a wave of soldiers with wolf heads on their chests spill out of the palisade gate. It rolled over their hovel hideaway and destroyed them.

He swallowed and kept watching.

In less than a minute, horns blared within the castle walls. Officers rushed to-and-fro and shouted orders. Lightly armored scouts ran east into the Low Wood, but the bulk of the men took some extra time to get organized. A few groups rode off on horseback, but within thirty minutes, the main force moved north, directly past the house they hid in, and east down the woodland road.

None of them paid any attention to the tiny house, although two thousand men seemed a conservative estimate.

Keane shut the door and stepped back, a nervous smile on his face. He moved over to Megan and slid an arm around her, drawing comfort from the touch.

Everyone kept silent, though Harden wore a broad smirk. After the last of the troops left his sight, he whooped aloud. "Ha-ha! That worked perfectly. Told you I knew how that bastard Tralgar thinks. Damn, but I am one smart son of a—"

The front door of the tiny home cracked, and daylight shown through the middle with the force of the knocking from the other side. A deep voice bellowed, "Open this door in the name of the Wolf, or we chop it down and kill everyone inside!"

EIGHT SOLDIERS SHUFFLED in through the old castle gate. The two in the middle dragged Keane behind them. Blood and bruises punctuated their faces and their walk. Limping, with tabards torn and minus a few extra teeth, they hauled the King of Greenshade's bloody and drooping form to the front of the steps that led up to the creaky old castle keep. There they dropped him in the cold dust.

The wind picked up and brought an extra chill into the sunlit yard. Grit went up Keane's nose.

A thin man, with a disdainful expression to go with his pointed beard and dark orange coat, stepped out of the keep. His mouth turned down at the soldiers. "What is this? Why aren't you out looking for the false king?"

"Beggin' yer pardon, sir," said one of the soldiers, a grizzled old veteran, "but I reckon we done found him."

Despite the cold and the danger, laying in the dirt was the easiest thing Keane had done since leaving Treaty Hill. He could almost sleep.

"Idiots." The man climbed down the bending wooden steps for a closer look. "You'll be flogged for shirking your-your-no. Is that . . .?" All at once, the sneer vanished, replaced by a look of excited glee.

"Stay here," he said to the soldier who spoke before. "Stay right where you are. Hah!"

He turned and ran into the door.

Keane moaned. The soldiers looked around and nodded to their brethren on the walls.

The door of the keep banged open, and Baron Horace Tralgar, eyes runny and his beard smeared with beef fat and gravy, gave a triumphant laugh. "I've got you. I've got you. I've got you!" He ran and nearly tripped down the steps.

Behind him the orange-coated man followed with a scroll, quill, small inkwell in his hands, and a heavy-bladed sword under one arm.

Keane looked up and flinched away from Tralgar who danced from one foot to the other with delight. A strong smell of old wine and sour sweat rolled off of him.

"You overreaching mercenary trash," the baron shouted at Keane. "You think you could ever be a king? You think you could ever be more than a common thug? Maybe you think that fucking my wife makes you special. The wife of the mighty Wolf, Baron Horace Tralgar. Hm? Well, I've got news for you there, too, boy. You aren't the only wet-dicked splash of shit who gets hard for cows like Roselle, oh no. I'm afraid you've shared that rotted pleasure with every crap-stained cock she could fit under her tail."

Maybe this wasn't a good place to sleep.

A large silver pendant of a wolf head swung out from under the stained gray furs the baron wore over his shoulders. A fat drop of gravy fell off it and spattered in the dirt.

The baron held out his hand behind him. "Give me my sword, Ottig. It is time to end this sad chapter in Greenshade's noble history once and for all." Tralgar giggled. "And I get to be the one to kill you, pretender."

He took the blade from Ottig and shoved the point in the ground, leaning on the pommel. He wheezed for a moment, then collected himself. The manic energy left him, and he seemed almost dignified, though Keane thought he mostly looked tired. And stupid.

"Where are the others?" the baron asked the soldiers. "He would have been traveling with a pack of stinking mercenaries. Did you see them?"

"We did, m'lord Wolf," said one of the gray-tabarded men. This soldier was younger and more handsome than the others, and the only one not covered in blood and filth. "We killed them in the home of a local they commandeered. I made certain to leave the false king alive for you personally, but we would be honored to take you to the bodies when you are finished here."

"Hm. Good. I had hoped to be able to cut the great Marshal

Harden Grayspring's scabby throat as well, but I suppose I will have to content myself with slaying this rubbish king today." Tralgar looked down at Keane with a wicked leer. "Which one of you boys killed Harden?"

"Oh, that was me, m'lord," said the youthful soldier. "Truth be told, I was expecting more of a fight. I think the old man lost a step or two in his dotage."

Keane rolled his eyes, and one of the other soldiers scowled at the one who spoke.

"Well, you just earned yourself a promotion, son," Baron Tralgar said. "That was a service to Greenshade, no matter how slow the tired old buzzard was. Probably just too terrified to fight this close to my castle. Well, Pretender Keane, you rapist of queens and murderer of true kings, I guess it's time. You know, King Songham would have a fit if he knew I was about to kill you. He's even angrier at you than I am. He had his eye on the queen mother, and you went and ran off with her. I expect she and that little girl you've been befouling are at Fenrath Hall, aren't they? The Ebon Host will turn them out right and proper. Songham will have Loffa, and maybe I will have Queen Megan. Might have to beat that creature you put in her stomach out of her first though. Would that make you happy? It would me. There's a certain robust turnabout there, don't you think?"

Peering up, Keane whispered, "F-fuck . . . you."

Tralgar lifted the sword and put it on one shoulder. "Yes, that is more or less what I expected from you." He gripped the hilt in both hands and lifted the blade over his head.

"Goodbye, worm." A mad glee sparked in the baron's eyes. "You lived for a time in the asses of giants, but it was inevitable you would be yanked out and stepped on eventually."

Tralgar ran the blade through the back of Keane's head and six inches further into the dirt beneath.

Keane dissipated, a smudge of colored smoke in the frigid breeze. In his place, the now deceased captain of Tralgar's Home Company slid down his baron's sword blade into the dirt. Behind him, the real Keane yanked his sword from its scabbard and shouted, *"Now."*

The Free Hand, in the bloodied tabards of the Wolf but no longer covered by Morholt's illusion, leaped into action. Even before Mahu and Sabni raised their longbows to pick Tralgar's men off the outer walls, two of those guards fell from Megan's arrows, fired from the doorway of Sammel and Sarah's house. The rest, taken by surprise, went down fast to the Darrishmen's bows and Eli and Raven's thrown daggers. Well defended from outside assault, nothing protected them against attack from within.

Keane and Harden ran up the stairs to the door of the keep. As soldiers ran out the door, the mercenary and the king engaged and dispatched the soldiers with brutal speed while Burgen stood and looked menacing in front of the blacksmith's and mayor's houses.

A few people peeked, but no one ventured outside.

"I still think this was a fucking stupid idea," Keane said to Harden and grabbed his opponent's sword arm.

"Then why'd you agree to do it?" Harden danced aside, tripped the man he fought, and ran him through the back.

"I'm trying to get along." Keane shoved his man against the next swordsman behind him. "And I thought maybe you were right about leaving those dead soldiers behind in the old folk's house. Tralgar would know we gave him the slip and send more of these assholes after us." Keane kneed the man in the groin and shoved him off the stairway.

A shrill scream provided counterpoint to the mercenaries' attacks, and Baron Tralgar the Wolf fled across the courtyard and clambered up a ladder to the roof of a long, low outbuilding. Once there, he pushed the ladder over and lay as flat as his rounded form would allow.

"Well, I admit, I did think it'd be mighty funny to run that overblown twat to ground in his own castle. End his idiot feud once and for all." Harden made circles with the point of his cutlass in the next soldier's face. "You might have had a point in there somewhere."

Keane shrugged and centered his weight on his back foot, ready to put some power behind his next blow. "I'm not saying this wasn't dumb, I'm just saying I didn't come up with anything smarter."

Ottig, Baron Tralgar's scribe, flung himself to the ground and curled up into a dirty orange ball, crying out for someone to save him.

The keep's big wooden door slammed shut, which surprised the two remaining soldiers who fought Harden and Keane just outside. There would be no more allies from within.

Keane smacked his opponent's blade aside and whipped the point of his own sword up to the man's eye. "Do you yield?"

Keane's opponent dropped his blade.

Harden's adversary glanced over at his disarmed ally, and Harden chopped him in the throat. The disarmed soldier's eyes closed, and his fists clenched.

"Calm down," Keane said to his man. "That was fucking hard to see, I know. But the day doesn't have to be a total loss for you too, right?"

Harden shook his head and leaned forward, pulling down the brim of his grayed hat against the sun. "What's that bugger doing?" He looked back down the hill at Tralgar, who lay on top of the short outbuilding whose purpose the Free Hand had been unable to guess.

The Wolf leaned out over the edge of the low building's roof and reached for a pin that fitted into a large metal hasp. The door attached to the hasp shuddered as whatever hid behind it slammed against it, again and again. Tralgar overbalanced, windmilled one arm, recovered, and with a triumphant shriek, yanked the pin free. The door banged open and at least a dozen long-boned and rail-thin wolves tore out of what was now obviously a kennel.

A bolt of fear ran through Keane before he remembered Megan was still in Sarah and Sammel's house. A second jolt hit him when he realized *he* wasn't.

"RUN!" shouted Harden. The Free Hand made for the bailey gate as fast as they could go. Mahu yelled to Sabni in Darrish as they ran, and the two warriors turned outward just before the gate and launched themselves to the planking that served as the wall's allure.

"I was trying to train these miserable curs to be my personal murder dogs," shouted Baron Tralgar, who now stood on the kennel roof. "They're really unteachable. But it'll be worth the headache to watch them tear King Keane and Harden Grayspring limb from limb."

Burgen, still limping from the ambush on the trail, fell behind the others. The lead wolves jumped on his back and bore him to the ground. He fought back, gripped one beast by the throat, and punched at another. A third leaped in and tore at his stomach.

Keane turned away and concentrated on running.

"Go left," Morholt screamed as the rest of the mercenaries passed out of the old gate. As they turned, images of them shouted and continued to flee in a straight line down the center of the street.

The starving wolves shot out the gate and ran after the illusion. Behind them, Mahu shoved the gate closed and dropped the bar across it.

"Where's Burgen?" Raven asked.

Unwilling to make the already bad situation even worse, Keane did not answer.

A rope hit him in the head. Above, Sabni wrapped the rope around a pair of sharpened tree trunks and threw either end down to the mercenaries.

"Climb."

This seemed overly risky. Why had Mahu shut the gate with them on the wrong side of it? Why couldn't they have run back in once the wolves had gotten too far away to return in time?

Keane held the rope for Harden and Eli for Raven. Morholt looked down from beside Sabni, who shot arrow after arrow into the wolves that mauled Burgen.

"Shit," said Eli. "They're comin' back."

That was much faster than Keane thought it should have been.

"Go, you evil cowards," Keane yelled at Raven and Harden. Without waiting, Keane and Eli climbed the rope. Raven scampered to the top and leaned back over to help Eli. Seeing his sister safe, Morholt held out a hand for Harden, leaving Keane to dangle on the rope.

Keane pulled himself up as Harden's ass went over the top of the sharpened trunks and then let out a scream of his own.

"Oldam's slippery stone taint, I need some help down here!"

One of the wolves had his boot, and rock-hard teeth crushed into his heel. Eli, alarmed, swung his head back over and reached for him, but it was everything Keane could do just to hold the rope with both hands.

"Couldn't we have just run back in and shut the gate from the inside?" Keane yelled through gritted teeth.

"More climbin', less talkin'," Eli yelled back.

A second wolf snapped at his other leg, and Keane kicked at it. The first beast, its teeth dug into Keane's boot, pushed against the palisade and yanked him backward, into the air.

He felt his hold on the rope slip.

A *thunk* sounded from below. The wolf released Keane and howled in pain. Keane grabbed for Eli, and Sabni leaned over and grabbed his tabard and mail. The two of them hauled Keane over the palisade. He looked back and saw Megan shut herself inside the tiny house. Below, one wolf was pinned to the trunks with an arrow through the back leg, while the other hunger-maddened animals snapped at it.

Inside the wall, Raven ran to Burgen's side. Dead wolves pierced by arrows ringed him. She fell to her knees next to his bloody and unmoving body.

If they had run back in the gate like Keane wanted to, they would still have had those three wolves to contend with. By pulling everyone up over the wall and onto the allures, Mahu and Sabni had ensured everyone had the best chance to get out of this unscathed. Everyone except for Burgen, that was.

And Keane's boot. That was a waste.

On the ground in front of the gate, Mahu pulled and shot over Raven's head and into Baron Tralgar's thigh as he climbed the steps to the keep. He shouted and fell over backward.

In a fury, the black-clad Raven stalked to the whimpering Tralgar. Without speaking, she grabbed him by his thinning hair and dragged him across the courtyard. He shrieked in pain whenever the arrow through his leg scraped across the cold dirt. When she reached the middle of the yard, Raven dropped the baron beside Burgen's steaming corpse.

The Free Hand made a circle around the two figures on the ground. Burgen lay torn apart, his insides scattered about. Keane wanted to be upset about it, at least on Raven's behalf, but he still hated the degenerate lummox.

Tralgar, face white, pumped a steady stream of his own blood out the back of his leg.

"You really should have stuck with ponies you love so much, Horsewife," said Harden. "Those skinny dogs have gotten you into trouble."

Keane stepped into the circle of mercenaries. "Baron Horace Tralgar, you have been found guilty of treason against Greenshade, murder, attempted regicide, and"—he looked around—"uh, keeping wild animals in an unsafe manner. You are henceforth stripped of your lands and titles and are to be executed immediately. Your castle, such as it is, will be burned to the ground. It's a piece of crap and should be burned anyway, but mostly I just want you to know how much I dislike you."

"Wait, no, you can't," Tralgar pleaded. "This is a mistake. It's Songham! He forced me to turn against you. I never wanted to. I swear my allegiance to King Keane, the rightful monarch of Greenshade. You all heard me; I'm one of you."

Keane grinned wide, bloodless and predatory. "Can't blame him anymore. Songham is dead. I killed him."

The baron's face lost all color, and he mouthed a silent, "No." He pushed himself to a seated position and held his leg just above Mahu's arrow. "Good. He betrayed you, and you killed him, so that makes us allies, right?"

"Well I've certainly heard . . ." Harden shoved his cutlass at Tralgar's chest. But before the blade got there, Keane knocked the stroke down and pushed the cutlass into the dirt.

"Hey," Harden said. "Oh, I'm sorry. You weren't listening to that, were you?"

"Oldam's bushy boulders, Harden. Back off a second. I've got some kinging to do." Keane stood straight and cast about the yard. "Ottig, you still there?"

"Y-yes, Y-Your Majesty," Ottig replied. The orange-coated man looked up from the ground, his face half caked in dust and grime.

"You're a scribe, right?" said Keane. "Get over here."

With small hesitant movements, Ottig stood and picked up his supplies. He approached the angry mercenaries.

"Write what Horace here just told us." Keane said, "About Songham, and being forced, and renewing his fealty to me and all. We need a record if this is going to stick, right, Horace? Here, you can use my back as a table."

Tralgar nodded, a scheming smile on his face. Even terrified on his ass in the chilly dirt, he still managed to smirk. Behind the humiliated baron, Raven went rigid, her face white and fists balled, as if she might explode.

Keane winked at her.

Ottig smoothed the paper across Keane's back and transcribed the proceedings. He finished and held it out to Keane.

"That looks great," Keane said. "Horace, can you sign there?"

Ottig placed the paper on the ground in front of Tralgar, who signed in the middle of the page, below Ottig's writing.

"Really good, Ottig." Keane leaned back over the paper and pointed. "Just one more thing to add. I want you to write that King Keane, with the full support and approval of his good friend Horace Tralgar, orders all of the goods, livestock, moneys, and troops of the Barony of Old Oak to be held in trust by the Barons' Conclave for their use in the war against the usurper queen, Hulda Hubrane, and the forces of the nation of Tyrrane, until such time as more permanent arrangements can be made. Got all that?"

Ottig went down on his knees and mumbled as he wrote. He stopped to assess what he had written. "Yes, sire. I believe that's all of it."

"Good, now get up and you lean over so I can sign it . . .here. All good." Keane waved the page to dry the ink. "Should I assume all of the military commander types are in there?" He nodded toward the keep.

Ottig bobbed his head yes.

"Buncha white-haired old men in fancy uniforms?"

Ottig nodded again.

"Go get 'em," Keane said. "We need to chat."

He hunkered down in front of Tralgar. "I want you to know, while I *was* the mercenary in the tent with your wife that night and I *did* go in there with the intention of bedding her, I never did. She was too much of a lady, and I wasn't enough of a brute to force the issue."

"Then what . . . ?" began Tralgar.

"We just chatted."

"You . . . chatted." Tralgar's eyes darkened. "About what?"

"I convinced her to abandon her witless fucking thug of a husband." Keane clapped Tralgar on the shoulder. "Well really, all I did was help her figure out how to get her family's money out from underneath you when she went. She was already going to leave." Keane gave the speechless baron a pat on the head. "Of course, you screwed that up for her, so now I have to put things right myself." Keane inhaled deeply and blew out a long sigh.

"At any rate, I appoint the fair Lady Raven to be your executioner. Bye."

Keane walked toward the keep. Harden jogged to catch up. Over the screams from behind, Harden said, "Hey, I'm, um, sorry I tried to step on your show back there. That was a fair piece of kinging. I didn't think you had it in you."

Raising one brow, Keane appraised Harden. "Thank you?"

"No, really," Harden said. "I mean it. I never figured you for any more than a drunk and a thief."

Keane smiled and rubbed at the back of his neck. "Yeah. Thanks. So, when the commanders come out to talk, I'll send them off to Fenrath with their new orders. You take Eli inside and rob the dogfuckers blind, all right?"

"Of course." An appreciative smile stole across Harden's face, and he turned away to pursue his task.

20

THE GOOD SIDE OF BEING BAD

KEANE

After Tralgar's general, a tall Andosh man, skinny limbed with a pot belly and no chin, his white mustaches fluttering in the breeze, found himself turned out and sent to Fenrath Hall, Megan and Loffa entered the bailey, and Keane took his wife aside. Together, they walked to the leeward side of the keep and stood in the thin sunlight.

She shuddered with more than cold. Keane couldn't decide if she was angry or terrified. Either way, he knew this was a conversation he didn't want to have. Had not *wanted* to have, ever since the encounter with the scouts in the woods.

Which was why he dove right in with it anyway.

"With everything happening so fast, I wasn't able to talk to you before. Are you all right? I know it's one thing to shoot a target, but—"

"No, I am not all right. That man in the woods, I heard him talking before I shot him. He was going to ask some girl out. Now he won't. And that's because of me." Megan leaned against the side of the keep and picked dirt off the sleeve of her overcoat. "Then I killed two more. Bip, bip. Just like that. And all of these people Keane, they're mine. They're not from Tyrrane or Oulan or anywhere else. They're Greenshaders. Or they were, anyway."

Keane looked at her, silent. When he asked, he hoped she would respond that everything was fine and don't worry. Now that the answer came back differently, he was terrified.

"I thought . . ." He thought what? He had never dealt with her vulnerability before. She was always the strong one. What would she say to him?

"Keane, we're out here with our *baby*." She grabbed the front of his coat. "And I'm killing people. My own people. What kind of parents are we?" Megan sniffed and rubbed her nose with a sleeve. "What kind of *mother* am I?"

"You're a hero." It sounded lame, even to him. But that was how he saw her.

She let go of him and nodded to the dirt. "Yes, that's it. I'm a hero. Just like in the stories. *Murderers kill men, but heroes kill everyone.* I guess that's going to be me. I guess that's the world our child will be raised in, if we live long enough."

No army or onrushing horde of soldiers, not even the Demon of Gullhome terrified Keane as much as this talk did. Nothing he said could fail to make things worse. He wanted so desperately to make her feel better. To feel safe. But he didn't know how.

"You know I'll protect you," he said. "I'll protect the both of you."

"Oh yes, you'll protect me." Megan took a few steps away before rounding on him. "You'll protect me and my precious stomach, but you're the first one in line to stab one of our people in the face if he gets too close. King Headwound."

This was making less and less sense. Anywhere he went to be on her side, she flitted away to attack from another vantage. Maybe this wasn't the right approach.

"You're right."

"What?" Megan demanded. "Right about what?"

"I'll always protect you, no matter who gets in the way. I don't care who they are or where they're from. I'd stab my own mother in the face if she threatened you, and I wouldn't lose a goddamn wink of sleep over it." Keane's father had beaten his mother to death when Keane was six, but he was swept up in the moment and did not think the particulars really mattered. "Oldam's sandy shits, Megan, I have one job, and I'm gonna do it whether you like it or not. That's keeping you *alive*. That's what all of this is about." He waved his arms to encompass everything around them. "It's all about *you*."

There were tears on Megan's cheeks as she faced Keane. "You haven't listened to a word I've said. What makes you think I want this?"

"I've listened to *every* word that's come out of your face." He was yelling now, heedless of who might be listening. "I just don't understand any of it. I'm *doing* my job. If you wanna save everyone's lives while they try and murder you, make that *your* job."

"How?" Her face turned up to his, a heartbreaking picture of sadness.

It enraged him. "I don't know. *Shoot someone in the goddamn knee instead!*"

They stared at each other in the silence that followed. Cold, fragile, a skin of ice over a falling web of recriminations. Why was he so bad at this?

Megan closed her eyes and smiled. She chuckled and then laughed, gaining volume as her mirth poured out of her.

"Shoot them in the knee. Why didn't *I* think of that?"

Confused, Keane only stared until she opened her big brown eyes, still full of tears but now laughter as well, and they locked gazes. The corners of his mouth went up on their own, and he stepped in to grab her, hold her tight, and laugh with her.

He still didn't understand, and he suspected there would be a lot more talking in the travels ahead, but for now, for this instant, they were all right.

Hand in hand, they returned to the courtyard.

Everyone avoided looking at Keane or Megan.

Morholt had removed his wolf-headed tabard, his faded green leathers subdued in comparison. His hand rested on Raven's shoulder reassuringly, but her striking features held only grim intent.

Keane felt a chill run through him when he saw her. The pale-skinned woman was dangerous at the best of times.

A tarp covered Burgen, and drag marks in the dirt ran from where the wolves fell to their kennels. The animals outside the palisade lay dead in the streets or run off. Quiet held the moment.

Laughing, Harden and Eli came out of the keep doorway burdened by a small but heavy chest each and one large wine bottle under each arm.

"Ladies and gentlemen of the Free Hand," Harden said, a merry smile on his face, "this trip has just officially become worth it."

Keane saw Raven's black look at Harden's announcement, even if the old man did not.

Eli strode over to Loffa and gave her a hug. To Keane's dismay, she returned the gesture. The tough old mercenary handed her a ring which glinted red in the sun.

"That dirty old fuck." Keane started in Eli's direction, but Megan held him back.

"Loffa is one of the most tragic women I know," Megan said. "She's had no measure of happiness in her life, ever. But Eli makes her laugh. Can't we let her have that?"

His hands balled into fists, and Keane turned on her. "With him? No."

"Let me put this a different way then," Megan said, her voice sweet and lips smiling. "Let her have that." Her face was still wet, and her voice smelled like tears. But Keane had known Eli for far too long.

"But—"

"Look," Megan dragged Keane in the other direction, "we have loot."

The mercenaries gathered around Harden as he counted gold and silver coins into their hands. "None for you, boy," Harden said to Keane, a wide grin showing teeth. "Get along. This is for fighters."

"We fought just as hard as anyone else here," Megan said. "And we have just as much right to that money as any of you."

"Oh, I didn't mean you, my queen." Harden's wolfish grin grew by degrees. "There is always room in the Free Hand for an excellent archer such as yourself. If you want to be one of us, just come up here and take your pay."

"Really? Me?"

Nodding, Harden held out the coins.

"You're not really going to fall for that, are you?" asked Keane.

Megan frowned over her shoulder at Keane. "Get along you." She made shooing motions with one hand. "This money is for fighters."

The coins clinked into Megan's outstretched hand while Keane shook his head. He turned and walked to the stables. Baroness Fenrath's horses had run fast and hard, but they had also run long. Fresh mounts would be a welcome spoil.

Keane's whistle brought Sabni and Eli to the door of the stable.

"Now that is some fine-lookin' horseflesh," Eli said.

"Mother Love provides for those who love her," Sabni said. "And today, she provides miracles."

Unlike the rest of Castle Oak, or even the surrounding township of Old Oak, the inside of the stables gleamed as if built this morning. Every board ran straight, every door hung true, and not as much as a stirrup dangled out of place from the wooden pegs on the far wall. Even the dirt floor showed fresh rake lines. The smell of newly cut hay wafted out and into their nostrils. The building's central run stretched twice as wide as the royal stables in Treaty Hill, and every bit of planking shone brightly, the polished white oak reflected ample light from numerous windows.

The stables placed a distant second to the occupants, however. Big Levale chargers stamped and snorted from within eight of the twelve stalls. Red-coated and golden-maned, each one was worth a fortune.

Here lived Tralgar's true treasure.

Trained from birth for endurance travel, the beasts from Levale outran any ordinary horse and went as far in a day as any two others combined. The Free Hand would cross the grasslands between Old Oak and the port town of Dahnt in half the time Keane planned for. These huge muscular animals were a miraculous treasure indeed.

"Someone will have to double up," Sabni said. "Perhaps two of the women can—"

"I'll take Loffa with me," Eli interrupted and stalked through the stable doors. "We'll take that fine fella." He pointed to the biggest gelding in the building. "Where's the blankets?"

After a brief wait for Morholt to confer with April, which to Keane's eyes was no more than a rectangle of pasteboard with an ugly red and gray dog painted on it, the group departed. Keane asked Eli about it as they rode.

"He says the painted side's an imp or some such." Eli shrugged. "No one else can hear it but him. I'da said he'd lost his damn mind, but I seen the results. It tells him the future. How we found your ass out in Three Sisters, wasn't it? Runecraft. That's what Holt calls it. All demonshit to me." Eli turned and spat. "But at least it's *our* demonshit this time."

They rode west and ranged slightly north of the tree line to avoid the rest of the Low Wood altogether. The powerful horses flew over the grasslands, and Harden no longer worried about being spotted in the open. Even if they were, there was no pursuit that could keep up with them.

They made camp that night at the edge of the wood, where they drank to Burgen and told stories of his brutish exploits around a cheery fire. Both big bottles of wine vanished in an eyeblink, and Harden felt obliged to break out the whiskey as well.

Raven was reserved, but she did not cry for her lost lover again.

"So Burgen and seven or eight of his most giantest buddies are in this tiny little jail cell," Keane said, scrunching his shoulders to show his audience Burgen's discomfiture, "and I'm all up in his face. *Whatcha gonna do about it*? And then, just like that," Keane snapped his fingers, "big bastard's got me around the throat in one hand, and I'm seeing spots."

The mercenaries laughed at this, and even Raven gave a bleak little smile.

"So Burgen's waving me around in the air like I'm a fucking flag— or maybe a skinny chicken—and he's trying to snap my neck for suppertime, and then Sarah steps in." Keane paused for a few *ooos* and chuckles from his audience. Everyone knew what was coming next. "Snaps that goddamn tree trunk of an arm like it was a matchstick."

Keane hung one arm at an awkward angle to illustrate.

"Well, that sets all the other brutes in the cell off like a bagful of cats in a stewpot. They're all screaming and yelling like they been set on fire, and Burgen's had enough. His arm's broken near off, and he's understandably cranky about it. He sort of wriggles around—those fuckers are squished in there *tight*—until he's choked every one of the bastards unconscious with his *other* arm. Then he looks up at me, tells me to fuck right off, and goes to sleep on top of the rest."

As the laughter and storytelling died down, Morholt crossed the clearing to sit next to Keane and Megan. Somehow, he had ended up with Harden's whiskey bottle, and he passed it to Keane.

"You know, for a king, you make an almost passable mercenary."

"Well," Keane responded, taking a swig and handing the bottle to Megan, "as a mercenary, you make an appalling lady's maid."

Megan rolled her eyes and handed the bottle back to Morholt without drinking from it. She pinched Keane on the arm. "You lout. Why would you give an expectant mother a bottle of whiskey? Don't you know it's bad luck? I could give birth to a turnip."

Keane, more than a little drunk, shrugged. "Sorry," he said. "No whiskey. What do turnips like to drink?"

With a sigh, Megan dropped her head in her hands and laughed. "Water, you moron."

Keane clapped his hands together and reached over to his pack. He pulled the waterskin free and handed it to Megan.

"Thank you." As Megan drank, Raven stalked over and sat down next to her. She said nothing and stared at the fire.

"Morholt," Keane said, eager for diverting conversation, "who did you learn your sorcery from?"

The ginger-haired mercenary snorted and turned down his mouth. "I am no sorcerer. I am a runecrafter."

"Sorcerer, rooncrapper. What's the difference?"

"Oh fuck," Raven said from across the fire. "Don't get him started on his *art*. He will *never* shut up."

"You just don't like any kind of art that doesn't involve knives." Though Morholt's tone was pure snark, his eyes held kindness for his sister. They had a complicated relationship.

"Asking for a public demonstration?" Raven withdrew a curved dagger and sighted along the blade edge, looking for imperfections.

Keane had watched her do it a dozen times since he met her.

"I'm more a fan of Paturgalia's red phase," she said, "but you seem more of an early Arlean canvas."

"I don't think she's over Burgen yet," Keane whispered to Morholt. "It hasn't even been a whole day. Maybe we shouldn't antagonize her."

Morholt cast his eyes upward with a sigh and returned his attention to Keane. "Right. So, only blood sorcerers can produce sorcery. They're just born with it. It's hardly special. You wouldn't give a medal to a turtle for being able to shit outside of its shell, would you?"

"I dunno. Maybe. Are turtles sorcerers?" Keane was a little drunk.

"They might as well be," answered Morholt with another snort. "Sure, they have the raw power, but they have no style. And any jackass can get power if they know where to look."

"So, you're like a stylish turtle. You need a hat."

Lady Roselle was the most stylish woman Keane knew, and she always wore hats.

"What I do is *real* magic," Morholt went on, oblivious to Keane's comment. "I learned it from study and tutors and books. What's more, I can teach it to anyone. You don't have to have special blood. Hell, you don't even have to be all that smart."

"As present company demonstrates," said Raven, breaking her silence.

"Sorcery separates people." Morholt cast a scowl at his sister. "Only certain people get to do it. Runecrafting isn't like that. Because anyone can do it, it brings people together. People with different strengths that—"

"You've never taught it to anyone you weren't fucking," Raven declared over Morholt's speech. "Sounds like 'certain people' to me. Not sure how that's any different."

Before Morholt could respond, Megan released a loud yawn and hijacked Keane's blurry thoughts to warm blankets and soft curves.

"What I mean is—" Morholt tried again.

"Gotta go." Keane hopped up and helped Megan to her feet. "We gotta get some sleep if we're gonna ride all the way to—where the fuck are we going?"

"To bed." Megan led her inebriated husband to the bedrolls. "Goodnight, everyone."

21

SOME PEOPLE DON'T LIKE SURPRISES

HULDA HUBRANE

Hulda entered the Royal Castle Library in a delighted mood. General Roen inspected and inventoried the food stores, and Tynos had been called away by a security emergency in the Peasant's Hall.

The King's Swords and the ducal guard were engaged in another altercation.

Her only escort was a single guard who Hulda was confident would not survive the upcoming encounter, though she was concerned that she had not taken the opportunity to remove the carpet first.

A letter had arrived in her waiting hall this morning. It promised a visit from an unidentified member of the Tyrranean nobility—sent by the emperor himself—in the interest of smoothing over relations and formalizing her rule as a part of the empire. They were to meet, in secret, here in the library.

As traps went, Hulda thought this one had style. Someone with secret knowledge and the brains to use it had come up with this. Baroness Roselle, perhaps.

The royal library was reserved for the use of the queen and her family. It was one large room surrounded by bookshelves, with comfortable furniture, desks, and artwork arranged on a beautiful oversized rug. To prevent accidentally setting fire to the vast trove of knowledge housed here, the only light allowed was from emberfly lanterns hung by long slender chains from the ceiling. A walkway ringed the outer walls fifteen feet up, to provide further access to even more shelves closer to the ceiling, and was painted to look as if the books provided knowledge all the way up into the heavens themselves.

Four men around the room dusted leather-bound spines while a pair of maids conversed beside an iron bust of King Suttung Tyrrane. The ancient Tyrranean king *gave* Greenshade to King Eggan Rance the First out of fear the wily and unstoppable Rance might decide to ride northward instead of relaxing in the warmer middle lands of Andos.

It was a fitting spot for this little drama.

"Oh hello, sweeties," she said to the maids. Hulda did not know how far to push the farce, so she decided to entertain herself with it. "You two must be the delegation from Tyrrane, here to tell me how wonderful a ruler I am and how much all my subjects adore me."

Surprise, fear, and anger flitted across the faces of the two women as Hulda approached. They awkwardly pulled kitchen knives from their aprons and stalked forward.

"Now!" shouted one of the dusters, and all four of them dropped their rags for daggers or short swords.

"Oh my." Hulda flung up her arms and backed away but was unable to keep the smile off her face. "What a shock. I am genuinely distressed by this unexpected development."

Hulda's escort leaped forward and handily skewered the first maid but was no match for the four men who jumped into her place. He went down with a wet scream.

"Drat." Already the big rug was soiled. Hulda backed well away from the carpet. If they wanted to kill her, they would have to do it on the hardwood.

The men and woman formed a semicircle around Hulda and

brandished their weaponry. Their leather-soled feet made hard noises on the wood as they left the carpet behind.

They were *so* easy to maneuver. She almost cackled.

"How did you get in here dressed like that?" Hulda asked one of the men.

He was older, and his face said that he'd rather be tending his plants. His dirty shirt and pants repeated the idea.

Hulda put her hands on her hips. "You could have at least made the effort to look the part. No castle staff dresses like that. This is a very slapdash assassination attempt." She wondered how many more might have shown up if they knew she planned on feeding the city to Tyrrane.

"I am too staff," the older man said indignantly. "I keeps the garden."

"Shut it, Rol." A burly young man in a footman's uniform pushed the gardener in the shoulder. "We're here to put this wicked slattern down before she can do any more damage. No one's interested in listening to you talk about your damn garden."

Ah. This one was the leader.

"And what's your name, cutie pie?" Hulda let her hips slide to one side, and she pushed her chest out. "I like to get to know all the big strong men who kill me."

The maid, tears streaming down her face, tried to run forward and put an end to the encounter, but the footman held her back. He actually smiled at Hulda.

It took all her self-control not to roll her eyes at the sight.

"I'm Miko," he said. "And you've been a very bad little queen. I'm afraid I'm going to have to punish you."

Hulda shook her head. This was the person the castle staff put in charge of her assassination? This was how little they thought of her?

"Oh, just get it over with." Hulda waved a hand over her head.

The dozen soldiers who had hidden themselves against the floor of the walkway an hour ago, and who had risen and trained cross-bows on the would-be killers when the encounter began, let fly. By a weird coincidence, several of his conspirators were hit numerous times while Rol the gardener was left unharmed.

Blood spread across the polished wooden floor.

The soldiers above reloaded, and Hulda leaned forward and spoke softly. "Quick now, sweetie, if you can think of anything to say that might save your life, now is certainly the time. My soldiers are eager to cover their mistake and kill you."

"Um—" Rol responded, just before getting hit with a half dozen crossbow bolts.

"*Um*?" Hulda turned her head and looked sideways down at Rol's bleeding body. "No, that wasn't it." She smiled fetchingly and waved up at her soldiers.

Really, Roselle was the only one who could have organized this. Or would have. There were a few others with the brains to know about her dustup with the Tyrraneans and to use it this way and loads more with the courage to hold a dagger.

But the baroness was the only one with both.

Hulda went to the brocade wingback and settled in, crossing her feet on her escort's corpse. This sort of thing was expected and, given that, easy to avoid. It made her feel warm, excited, and more than justified in sacrificing this onerous place to her personal happiness.

She just needed to decide which cell to throw Roselle into.

HULDA'S SUCCESS buoyed her steps to the Lord's Hall entryway. Part of the Forest Castle Keep, the Lord's Hall was smaller and less ostentatious than the central grand Welcome Hall but finer and warmer than the plain and practical Peasant's Hall. It was also more private and secure, which suited Hulda's needs.

She had already dispatched a cadre of soldiers to apprehend Baroness Roselle and toss her in the cell next to Lady Ravenstok. The two could keep each other company in the dark and the stinking wet.

After all, Hulda was no monster.

With now *two* ducal guards trailing her, Hulda nodded to the chamberlain and allowed him to open the steel-shod door to the carriageway outside.

The royal carriage of the Hubrane family, riding between two military guard coaches, appeared around the corner as Hulda stepped into place beneath the broad stone overhang.

Cold sunlight lit the cobblestones and reflected off the melted snow. The carriages pulled up to the overhang and provided welcome shade from the bright ground to those within.

Behind Hulda, another score of wine-red-tabarded soldiers filed in and stood silent against the greenish walls.

The old chamberlain went to the central carriage and opened the door. After he checked to ensure the occupants were ready, he took a step back and announced the Ducal Prince Reid Hubrane and his mother Duchess Sigga Hubrane.

Hulda brightened the dark shadows of the overhang with a brilliant smile and reached out her hands to Reid and Sigga. She would have sooner boiled herself in pig urine than display her pique at listening to the chamberlain address Duchess Sigga with Hulda's title.

But then, that was the very issue the pair had been summoned from Castle March to rectify.

The boy was an assemblage of sticks, wan and brown haired, with an aspect of kindness and sadness like his father. Five years old? She did not know how tall children were supposed to be. The mother, on the other hand, while attractive in a sturdy farm-hand sort of way, stared at Hulda with narrowed eyes and open suspicion.

Both were pulled into Hulda's hug as the soldiers in the military coaches were led to their new billet and Hulda's hand-picked men replaced them.

"I trust your journey was uneventful?" Hulda released the pair.

"I caught a butterfly," Reid said. "But Mom made me let it go."

Hulda's smile faltered as she sorted out how to respond to this. She had little facility with children.

Sigga put a protective hand over Reid's chest. "The journey was fair, but we are tired. Let us rest, and you and I will discuss our business after dinner."

The dazzling smile returned to Hulda's lips. She leaned over, hands on her knees, to look Reid in the face. "Hey, Reid, I have a surprise for you if you're not too tired."

"Really? I like surprises."

"Later, Reid." Sigga pulled the boy to her side. "We must retire and bathe first. It has been quite a journey, and your mother is tired."

"Pleeeease?" The boy danced and pulled at his mother's arm.

"Won't take a minute," Hulda said, eyes a-twinkle.

Realizing she had been outmaneuvered, Sigga slumped, then straightened her back and set her shoulders.

Hulda shook her head an almost imperceptible *no* to the ducal guard creeping up behind Sigga.

He backed away.

"Very well," Sigga said. "We will see the surprise your aunt has kindly planned. Then it is into the water with you. You smell like a tongueless cat. Did I say something funny?"

"No, no." Hulda waved a hand to cover her grin. I was merely thinking about what a wonderful day today has been."

WIDE STEPS of green-gray stone curled the external wall of the Monarch's Tower, lit by intermittent windows in the day and by whatever light a person might bring with them at night. Officially, this stair was for anyone *but* royalty, but Hulda loved seeing the shock on people's faces when they realized she was on the stair and the alacrity with which they leaped to press themselves against the walls and not be a bother.

Today she possessed the added terrifying surprise of not being dead. Hulda imagined that every servant, staff, and courtier must have been aware of the attempt, and now they would all be panic-stricken with the thought that she might know of their complicity.

As well, she had now eliminated the last official glimmers of royalty—other than herself—that the people of Greenshade might rally around. This was all going so perfectly. The Ebon Host still fought Coldspine on the Paras Plains and was about to overextend itself invading Greenshade. Her uncle, King Wagnersen of Mirrik, would sweep across Tyrrane, a wildfire blown by a vengeful hurricane. Norrik, ever divided between its five competing kingdoms, would do nothing but watch and wait for the day when her uncle turned his attention back on them.

Life in a castle was a game of chess, and Hulda was its master. The March Castle and her time running the Hubrane Merchant House had prepared her for of all this. She would be glad to move the criminal enterprise to Mirrik when all this was over.

What she wasn't prepared for was a woman ahead on the stairs who fell backward in a gout of red.

"Eeeeee!" Hulda screamed, both frightened and embarrassed at the sound she made. That was not like her at *all*.

A man ran down the stairs with a short wide-bladed dagger in one hand and a hook on a chain in the other. He was bald and bare chested, and his skin was soot black. Not the warm brown of some superior Darrish noble, but more like he had been tattooed black over every inch of him.

His face held no expression, not even interest for the people he cut down on his way to Hulda.

Fair enough. She wasn't all that interested in them either.

She fled back down the stair as her two ducal guards ran up to meet the dark man. Perhaps they could kill him or maybe just slow him down long enough for her to duck into a door and bar it behind herself.

It was times like these she was happy she never bothered to learn anyone's names.

The body of one of her guards slammed into her shoulder, and she went sprawling down the steps. Pain made her want to scream again, but it also froze the air in her lungs and kept her from it.

She rolled outward to where the steps were two feet deep and stopped her bruising descent. Her head came up, white hair pointed in every direction at once, to try and spot her killer. Instead, she had to duck back down as long Darrish legs flew over her from below, and breezy linen clothing fluttered in the wind of its passing.

Tynos hit the dark man in the stomach and jaw, arresting his forward motion and forcing him to take two steps back up the stairs. Without a pause, he dove ahead with his short dagger and pushed Tynos back a step. But he had already cast his hook where Tynos's leg *would be*, and as she lowered her foot, he yanked back on the chain and jerked the foot into the air.

As if this was what she had planned all along, Tynos flew to the dark man and kicked him just under the chin with her other foot.

His head snapped back, and he lunged again as it came down. A straight slash crossed Tynos's ribcage just below her breasts, and the linen shirt soaked up blood.

But her foot was free.

Hulda would have been more worried, but she never did care for Tynos's wardrobe choices.

Tynos bounced away and drew a pair of long curved daggers. As she charged the dark man, she kicked the body of a curled-up hall boy who bled from a leg wound. With a *whoomp* and a cracking noise, the boy flew through the air, Tynos right behind him.

The dark man ducked and allowed the boy to crash into the stone wall. Then he flipped his chain at her foot again. At the same instant, he struck out at her eye with the dagger.

This time, Tynos lifted her foot and kneed his knife hand in the elbow to throw his aim. Her arms slashed down and out, and she jumped up, vaulting off one hardened soot-black shoulder.

She landed with only one curved dagger in her hand.

The dark man, who faced Hulda once more, reached up behind his head for something, but the motion fully opened the deep cuts that ran up either side of his neck. Blood bathed his inked skin, and he fell to his knees. He reached up again but could not really lift his arm.

"Are you harmed?" Tynos asked Hulda. Her thick Egren accent surprised Hulda every time she heard it.

"I forgot you could talk." Hulda pulled herself up on Tynos's strong hands. She nodded toward the dark man. "Is he dead?"

"We need to see if there is anuzzer of thems." Tynos's neck twisted as she scanned the frightened crowd.

The dark man slumped, fell sideways, and slid down several steps. The pommel of Tynos's other dagger protruded from the back of his skull, the blade neatly curved into his brain.

"I have to . . . I'm going down . . . upstairs." Hulda took a step down and turned to run upstairs. Her knee shouted in pain where she had banged it on the stone steps, but she fled on.

The dagger the dark man had carried was the emblem of Tyrrane.

Emperor Brannok had answered the death of his men and the question of allowing a woman to sit a throne in his empire.

Not that it mattered, but Hulda felt she already knew the answer to the second part already.

"Hello, boys." Hulda entered the war room to find General Roen over the large map of Andos, scowling and pushing painted wooden figures around in a line between Dismon and Treaty Hill. On the floor in the far corner, huddled in the dark, Major Talon watched fearfully. Blood smeared his forehead and hands.

"My queen." General Roen concentrated on the map. "How went your assassination—" He looked up and stopped speaking. Even his mustache paused as if in mid-breath.

He rushed to her side and turned her about as he inspected her for injury.

"The attempt on my life went a little better than planned." Hulda tried again to push her hair back into some kind of shape and again gave up. "The second one, anyway."

"Issta's dance. The staff planned a second attempt we didn't hear about?" General Roen's jaw set a determined line that promised pain and death for the staff of the Forest Castle.

"No, sweetie." Hulda fell, exasperated, into one of the tall-backed chairs that ringed the outer walls. She stared out of the one huge window in the northern face of the room. It provided all the light and looked over most of Treaty Hill below.

From where she sat, all she could see was blue sky.

"It was an actual assassin." Now that she had the time to think on it, Hulda realized just how rattled the encounter left her. "Tynos was barely able to stop him."

General Roen's brow lifted at that.

"What did he look like?" Major Talon asked.

A cane appeared in General Roen's hand, and he lifted it with a snarl. "I warned you about speaking out of turn."

"Roen." Hulda reached over and put a hand on the angry general's elbow.

He stopped as if suddenly cast in iron.

"The man was bald and painted black. Or tattooed black. Does it really matter?" Hulda stood and moved to the end of the table. There was considerable empty space in the long stone room at the end where Major Talon cowered, and the light from the window barely made it there. "He carried one of those daggers like you have on your chest." She tapped a forefinger to her left breast. How did a man covered in black ink make it into the innermost workings of the Forest Castle? What exactly was she dealing with here?

Major Talon's already hopeless face lost even more life. "That was a burned man. From a house of assassins that live in the mountains north of the Paras Plains. Or that's what the legends say, anyway."

"And if the legends are true?" Hulda asked.

"They'll come in numbers next." Major Talon lowered his battered head. "They'll kill us all. Especially me. They'll know I helped you. We're all going to die."

This information perked Hulda up. "Has he really helped?" she asked General Roen.

"After a bit of inducement, I'd say yes," the general answered.

"What was your name again?" Hulda asked Major Talon.

"Karel Talon, Your Grace." Major Talon kept his gaze on the floor.

Hulda had a grip on fear's neck now. She throttled it tight and felt it die. Anger of her own filled the space it had lived. Anger that warmed her bones and made her feel powerful and complete.

"Roen, Karel, I want a way to strike back at the emperor." Hulda took General Roen's cane out of his hand and smacked it on the map table. "I want a way to hit him that won't put us at risk, uses minimal manpower, but will *hurt* him."

General Roen and Major Talon exchanged glances. Talon spoke first.

"The Host is terrifying. I've killed more than my share alongside them. But they share any army's weaknesses. They all have to eat." Major Talon pushed himself to his feet and limped to the table.

"In a foreign country, the Host might spend as much as a third of their strength just guarding supply lines. But *within* Tyrrane? Almost nothing."

General Roen leaned over the table and pointed just north of the Greenshade River. "If we can sneak a small force in *behind* the Host, we can disrupt their supplies from Dismon. With some careful timing, we might even be able to stop them just *after* they have obliterated the Baron's Council but before they get to Treaty Hill."

The Host would still decimate Treaty Hill when they arrived, but they would have to spend extra time and manpower stripping the rest of Greenshade of food and resources along the way. They'd be constantly fighting, be at reduced strength once they arrived, *and* give Hulda more time to clean house here and get out before things got dangerous.

"Boys," Hulda said with a dirty-faced smile, "That is *exactly* the kind of thing I was looking for. I may not murder anyone else today at all."

22

KEANE IS A DOLL

SARAH

Sarah stepped up through the passageway in the floor and into Magda's enormous stone chambers. Having broken through her fear of intruding on a god's private time once already, she felt easier about doing it again. Reassuringly, Magda seemed to welcome the company.

Instead of staring out the window, Magda stood in the middle of the room, some forty feet tall, and examined a larger-than-life nude man, who floated in the air in front of her. As Sarah crept forward, both goddess and man shrank until Magda was less than ten feet high and the man about three.

Once she walked close enough to see the front of the man who hung in the air, Sarah gasped, and raised a hand to her mouth.

Keane's tiny face stared forward at the goddess.

"I do not understand," Magda said. "It is no more than a man, yet its presence in your mind is a powerful block. It keeps you from your destiny. I must discover why."

"What?" Sarah blurted out. Anger popped to the front of her brain. First Harden, then Finnagel, now Magda—what was their fixation on Keane?

Harden thought himself some twisted approximation of a father to Sarah, and considered Keane as a distraction to her. Her sorcerous teacher Finnagel felt that Keane was little more than a pet and that Sarah's nature as a sorceress was above such considerations.

Neither of those frightened her as much as this. Magda was a goddess. Her mind was impenetrable. What did she want?

Magda turned her face to regard Sarah, one eyebrow raised slightly.

Sarah swallowed.

"You are not what you are. This human stops you. It makes you something else. Something less."

"He's my friend." This had been a mistake. Sarah never should have come here. At this point, she was certain that if she were to butter a slice of bread, that butter would somehow want to see Keane dead.

Cassius was right all along.

Ugh. That hurt to admit.

Also, despite Magda's presence, a slice of buttered bread sounded like heaven.

"Do not fear, button. I do not desire to take your human from you. Time will do that. Time will ensure that you become who you are. For time cannot touch *you* but sweeps humans away as if they were dust."

"What does that mean? What am I?" Finnagel told her once that sorcerers were immortal, but she had witnessed his death firsthand.

Magda's eyes rolled heavenward in a very human expression. "You are my granddaughter, button. You are a sorceress, and the blood of gods runs through your veins. Your destiny is to rule the outside world, not to be friends with it. This"—Magda gestured toward Keane—"is nothing."

Sarah grew angrier. She was tired of having this conversation. She was her own person, not whatever some old mercenary, sorcerer, or even goddess wanted of her. She would be friends with whomever she liked, and anyone who disagreed could take it up with the edge of her broadsword.

However, Sarah was not so angry as to get into a shouting match with the goddess of insanity and obsessiveness. So, she deflected.

"Well then, Grandmother, should I assume that you will help me in my struggle against Tyrrane? You know, so I can become *me* and all that."

"Your battle is not with Tyrrane," Magda said, "but with the Son of the Serpent, consort of demons."

The sobriquet made no sense to Sarah. Still, she took a shot in the dark. "Are you talking about Angrim? The Anger Under the Mountain? Because if so, then yes. My battle is definitely with that guy. My battle is with him right through the heart, assuming he has one."

A long pause dropped over the room while Magda regarded Sarah. "Yes, button." She closed her eyes and lifted her face toward the unseen ceiling above. "I will aid you, and I accept your gift."

Again with the gift. What gift?

Magda vanished, and the light from her presence winked out. The three-foot-tall Keane fell bonelessly to the floor and lay there, quivering like jelly.

Magda would help them. Sarah needed to go find Grohann and get ready, not that there was much to do. They could leave immediately, and Sarah was eager to be on the move. Ever since they'd entered the valley, a sense of not being in the real world had bothered Sarah. It felt unsafe, as if the ground might open a toothy maw and chew them all to pieces.

From outside the window on the far side of the huge chamber, Cassius screamed, again, and again, and again.

ONCE OUT OF the horrible striped sands, Grohann led the trio through the sheltered mountain pass west of the Tower of Chains, opposite the way they had arrived. The pass lay only a few hours' walk from the tower, and the certain knowledge that they would never return there gave him and Sarah the fortitude to withstand the awful noises of the sand with—if not a smile—at least a grim satisfaction.

Surrounded by high rocks and sharp formations, the pass ran smooth and easy to traverse. Cut steps in the stone helped them climb first up, then back down the other side. They went between peaks, where the air blew bitter-cold, but not so high as to reach the snowcaps. No glimpses of the glittering sands to the east or the flat tundra of Coldspine to the west revealed where they or their path lay.

A mountain goat fell to Grohann's bow the second day out. They carried no wood to cook it with and ate the meat raw instead.

Cassius walked behind and in a strange double voice, both his own and Magda's, taught Sarah about magic. Or tried, anyway. There were quite a few interruptions.

"No, no, I still don't understand. The only way for you to escape your prison in the tower was to possess one of us, right?" Sarah's hair was held back by a pair of braids once more, which ran through a leather sleeve pinned with a wooden rod. Now though, one of the dark braids was shot through with silver where the scar across her forehead entered her hair.

"Correct," said Cassius and Magda's voice. "Although this vessel is not truly possessed. I have placed a splinter—"

"Right. You put a splinter of yourself into Cass. I guess that's different somehow."

"As Anger Under Mountain did vith Old Stone," Grohann said in reference to the time the evil sorcerer had taken control of Grohann's father. "Seems like an evil plan to me. Ven Sarah chopped Old Stone's head off, that vas good."

Cassius looked at Grohann, one brow raised.

"Don't fret. We are almost certainly not going to chop off your head." Sarah thought for a moment as they walked. "But what's going to happen here? To Cassius, I mean. We go to Tyrrane and sneak into the capital. Once we're there in Dismon, you attack the Fell Citadel, kill Angrim and the royals, and then what? Can you leave Cassius as he was? Is he your slave forever?"

Cassius stopped in the path, his gaze intent on Sarah. "This is not what will happen, my button. You came looking for a weapon to use against the Son of the Serpent, and you have found one. But the weapon is not me. The weapon is you."

"But Magda-Cassioos, ve already had Sarah vith us. Ve did not find her in your tower. I am thinking maybe Magda-Cassioos is as broken-brained as just-Cassioos. Yes?"

"I think I agree, Gro." Sarah walked closer to Cassius and returned his stare. "You're the goddess here; how are you not the weapon? The only magic I can do is blowing out candles. That hardly qualifies me to take on Angrim." Sarah's frustration over her lack of understanding pushed her to demand answers, but her terror that this had all been for nothing made her want to throw up.

"But yoo can also blow tundra cats all over the place," Grohann added helpfully. "This is big fun, yes?"

"You have misunderstood," Cassius said in his and Magda's voices. "I will try to explain it to you." Cassius opened his arms and sat in the air. And floated.

"I am presently trapped within the tower and prevented from leaving by the magic of Oldam himself. Close your eyes."

Sarah saw the tower in her mind, while Magda stared out of the window. It was strange, like being in a dream she could not wake from, even as she felt the pathway through the mountains beneath her feet and heard the icy wind blow between the stones.

"Although his magic is proof against my escape, it does not prevent others from carrying out tiny splinters of my mind within their own as this human has done." The voice that spoke in her mind carried no trace of Cassius within it. It was the splinter who guided this tour.

The picture changed to the rampway in front of the tower where Cassius sat. Abruptly, he pitched back, his body arched and supported on his toes and the top of his head. He screamed, over and over, and Sarah felt as though she were observing a horrible viola-tion, made only slightly less awful by the fact that it was happening to Cassius.

The picture changed again, and the three of them walked away from the tower into the mountains, Cassius with a serene smile on his face.

"I have placed knowledge of certain spells into this splinter," said Cassius/Magda, "and into the mind of this human. However, the brains of humans were not meant to carry the mind of a god. It will degrade. If we can be finished before the experience burns the mind out of this human, the splinter will return to me. If the degradation causes the human mind to wither fully, killing the body, the splinter will be unable to escape, and I shall lose it."

"You're killing him?" Sarah asked. "Why not put the splinter in my brain instead? I'm a sorceress. Wouldn't that make us more . . . compatible?"

"It would indeed. Too much so. The magic of Oldam would have perceived you as me and left you trapped in the tower. Grandmother and granddaughter, forever.

"Instead, I placed the splinter into the mind of your gift to me, and we shall use it to teach you the magic you will need to defeat the Son of the Serpent. Magic that would destroy the gift and the splinter to use itself."

"No, wait," Sarah said. "Angrim has had hundreds and hundreds of years to become what he is."

"Tens of thousands," Cassius responded.

"What? That's even worse. It's maybe a thousand miles to the capital of Tyrrane from here. Even if we walk *really* slow, I don't think we'll have time to even us out."

"Ve should be valking very fast, yes? Ve must get to Dismon and kill Anger Under the Mountain before he kills everyone all over the place. The Anger vants to kill everyone in Sarah's home, then everywhere else. This is no good."

"There is no time to instruct you properly in the underpinnings of the magic you will need to learn," said Cassius. "You must learn the magic by rote. Memorize the forms and words and constructions, without the true understanding of them that can only be learned by decades, centuries, or eons of experience."

Sarah's palms went clammy. There was a reason it had taken Finnagel two months to teach her to blow out a candle, and even then, he'd praised her as being his fastest apprentice ever.

"I know I'm the student here, but that's really stupid, right? Like diving off a bridge and flapping your arms stupid."

"Yes," answered Cassius. "Assuming you are a human and cannot fly, and the bridge is a thousand feet above sharp and rocky terrain, then the stupidity is comparable." Cassius smiled. "That is a keen observation. You are a bright button."

"Apparently not. Why is this all on me? I'm not scared—other than being terrified and all—but why am I learning these spells? Why aren't we just carting you out there and letting you explode Angrim's face?"

"As I have said, there is no assurance that this human would last the duration." Cassius gazed into Sarah's eyes with calm and assured serenity. "This body is not made for using magic. The probability is high that our efforts would be thwarted before the battle was truly joined."

Although she had not yet learned to read Magda's expressions, which lagged behind her words long enough to frequently appear random, Sarah got the definite impression the goddess was, if not lying, at least not telling the whole truth.

"You seem different, Magda." Sarah reached out and placed her hands on Cassius's shoulders. She turned the weapons merchant from one side to the other. "You certainly don't sound like Cass, but you don't really sound like you either."

"I am not me. This is only a piece. A splinter of my knowledge. A shard of my personality. It is as much as I could fit into the human, but it should be enough to suit our needs."

"Well, it isn't enough to keep me from feeling hungry or thirsty," Sarah said.

"Vould yoo like some goats?" Grohann pulled the bloody carcass off his back and held it out to her. "It is very good."

Sarah rolled her eyes and sighed. She could think of nothing in the entire world she wanted to eat less than another bite of raw mountain goat.

She reached out and tore a strip off of the leg.

"Thanks, Gro. This is just . . . the best."

23

SARAH LEARNS MANY DELIGHTFUL WAYS TO ACCIDENTALLY COMMIT SUICIDE

SARAH

As the travelers left the mountains for the foothills, they found several streams that ran downslope and plenty of brush for fires. The stream water, cloudy and mineral-laden from its trip through the rock above, was nevertheless safe to drink and home to a variety of life. While they could not see through it well enough to fish—without poles or nets, any fishing would have to be done with arrows—Grohann knew how to find clusters of black mollusks he called sharps, which could be cooked simply by tossing them into the fire. They popped open when done, and the troll showed Sarah how to fetch them back without burning herself.

Eaten one small hot bite at a time, they were the most delicious meal Sarah ever experienced. Watching Cassius/Magda eat was another treat all by itself. Magda was familiar with eating, but human tastes were apparently entirely different from those of the gods. She detested even the things he loved, and the two would make strange faces at one another as they ate. Though disconcerting at first, Sarah had come to look forward to it as a kind of silent dinner theatre.

The Bitter Heights mountain range ran away to the east of them and marked the northern border of both Coldspine and Tyrrane further to the west. North of the range the Troll Coast snaked between the mountains and the ocean, and was where Grohann's people originally came from. The coast was a forbidding place of ice and mist, populated by cruel raiding tribes, trolls, and most fearsome of all, the salt-blood giants. Or so Sarah had heard—she never intended to find out otherwise.

The vast tundra of Coldspine spread south to Oulan and east to the coastal fjords. That land would kill anyone not prepared for it, even when not covered in snow—as it was now—for the tundra forgave few mistakes. Sarah doubted her own ability to survive there. She had no such qualms about Grohann's.

Sarah looked back east at the forks of the mountain range that surrounded the Tower of Chains on three sides and estimated they were a week's climb from the point at which they had first entered the pass. Yet, they had been on the steps for no more than two days. Magda somehow sped their journey.

It was not easy to wrap one's head around the idea of a journey with a goddess. Sarah always believed in the gods—her Pavinn gods, at any rate. But that was not the same as taking an overland jaunt with one, sharing food and fire and sleeping space. Not that Magda slept. She just watched Sarah while *she* did.

Or while she tried to, at any rate.

To keep everyone straight in her head, Sarah resolved to try and think of the amalgamated person as whichever of them seemed dominant at the time. It was better than calling them Massius. Or Cagda.

Ugh.

The three—four?—of them made camp that night at the base of a low escarpment at the end of the foothills. After a meal of sharps, mushrooms, and milky water, Magda continued to teach Sarah her first god spell in the dwindling light. It had not been going great.

"You did that wrong. This casting would have turned your bones to sand and set your bowels aflame."

"You know"—Sarah balled her fist up against her increasing frustration—"before we began this, I had no idea all of the creative ways there were for me to magically murder myself."

"It does seem you have some capacity for it," answered Magda. "Try again."

They moved into the tundra and stayed close to an unnamed tributary of the Chillroad River for food and water. Their routine stayed much the same for the next days; Grohann caught food while Magda taught sorcery, and Sarah tried to turn her own brain into a lump of explosive manure.

Now two weeks in, Cassius's personality had relaxed. Magda's control on the reins of his mind had loosened as she realized the value of allowing some of his experience through. After all, Magda might have known the entire history of the world, but she had no idea how to maneuver through an environment in which she was not effectively invulnerable. She was hopeless when it came time for Cassius to defecate.

Apparently, gods did not poop.

This period also bore witness to the birth of a sickness in Cassius. He grew thinner, and the hollows of his eyes darkened. He ate and drank, but the food did not touch him, just passed him by. Sarah did not like the idea of him being eaten away by Magda, but she had the goddess's assurance he would survive if they could accomplish their task.

Not that it mattered. Once they were safely back in Treaty Hill, Cassius would be formally executed as a double agent and enemy spy. The thought no longer filled Sarah with the sense of comfortable closure it once had.

Ever serene, Magda shook her head. "That casting would have turned the air around you to stone and all your teeth to bees. You're getting better. Now try again."

Sarah tried the spell again. She spoke in Metzoferran, the magical language of the Alir. More powerful by far than the other languages of magic, the words rippled the air in front of her, and the stones beneath her bled. As she spoke, Sarah massaged the air with her hands in uncomfortable gestures, precursors to the Ghost Hand language which guided and modified most sorcerous spells but unknown to any sorcerer living today.

At the end of the casting, as before, a resistance came. The very air pushed against the advancing tide of magical energy. Sarah lowered her head against it and shoved back. She shouted out the words. This time she would not be—

Sarah fell forward as the resistance gave way with a snap. She looked up. The world looked different. What had she done wrong?

"Congratulations, button." Pride from Magda's voice overlaid Cassius's own. "You have success."

"No, I don't think so." Sarah looked around herself. Desperation gave her movements an unaccustomed furtiveness. "Something is wrong with my eyes. Everything looks wrong. It's wrong."

Behind her, Grohann rubbed at his own eyes. He peered out at the grass around him. His alarm grew as Sarah's did.

"Nothing is amiss with your eyes, granddaughter," Magda said, a wispy ghost of Cassius's old easy smile on his face. "It is not your eyes that have changed, it is this world."

"What in the fiery entrails of Bizzith-non does that mean?" Sarah's eyes stung, and she ground her knuckles into them to relieve the pain.

Grohann growled and stabbed his huge two-handed sword into the frozen ground. His mail jingled too loud.

"Please, calm yourselves," Magda opened Cassius's arms.

Sarah and Grohann's visions were mystically replaced once again, this time with a vast mountain whose snow-covered flanks gleamed like fiery silver. The mountain floated in an ocean of stars and held grand palaces and castles along its many peaks and valleys.

"I shall answer your questions and teach you about the foe we face." Magda's voice, and hers alone, spoke inside their minds.

Together, Sarah realized she was witnessing the Alireon, palace of the gods, before the creation of the world. Though she had heard it described in Andoshi legends, she now confronted something no other mortal ever had.

"I believe yoo might have killed us. I am not angry—but if yoo vere to tell us first, maybe ve vould have stood further away from the magics, no?"

Sarah laughed despite herself. "We're not dead, Grohann," she said. "This is a story. Like back up in the pass when Magda showed us how she put the splinter in Cassius."

"If yoo are saying so."

The vision closed with the mountain, dispersed, and came back into focus in a grand throne room of white stone shot through with veins that pulsed in a red glow. Cascades of stars made the walls, and columns of multicolored water cavorted between the floor and ceiling.

The room filled with the figures of gods and monsters who laughed, shouted, and feasted. Sarah wept for their beauty. She knew her mind could not hold their image for long.

Keane would shit himself if he saw this.

Above it all, on thrones of gold and cloud, sat the king and queen of gods. The king was powerfully built, bare chested, with a close-cropped white beard. His eyes flashed with tremendous intensity over his subjects and filled them with his light. The queen regarded the room with cool appraisal, as if she assessed each of the assembled for possible threats.

"The Alireon, home of the Alir," Magda said. "King Oldam watches from his throne and his first Queen, the goddess Issta, protects him. But who was there to protect her?"

The scene shifted to a craggy plain made of nightmares, huge rents torn in the ground held unknown perils. And among the upthrust rocks, under a sky of mustard-colored smoke, walked a goddess. Her skin glowed pale blue, and she approached a large tear in the ground, beyond which there was nothing but black.

"Yoo should be getting out of there, lady god!" Grohann shouted. "This is not a safe place for yoo. Vat is in your vay? Are your ears broken?"

"Hedra, goddess of storms, desired Oldam's heart. So, she jour-neyed to the Undergates and called forth the serpent, Sigundr."

Sarah watched as the goddess, a figure of incomprehensible beauty, pushed off the shoulder straps of her shift and allowed the garment to fall to the ground. She reached up and removed the pin from her hair, and it tumbled down around her shoulders in a glittering cascade of color and reflection.

Then she lay upon the ground.

A cold rattle came from within the black.

"I have told her." Grohann touched the tip of one of his backward-curving ram's horns. "I vish her vell, but there is nothing more I can do. I vash my hands on her."

"Sigundr, the Serpent of Hell, came forth from the gate and accepted Hedra's offering. The Serpent lay with Hedra and got the goddess with child before it returned to the dark from whence it came."

The last of the serpent's lengthy black tail rasped back into the ragged cave mouth, and Hedra, covered in dark translucent slime, stood. Her triumphant smile gleamed through the effluvia.

"Oh no," Sarah said. "I should not have seen that. Humans should not see that. Please don't let that be the thing I remember out of all of this."

"Trolls do not sex that vay."

"Hedra gave birth to Angrim, most beautiful of all the monsters on the Alireon. When he was ripe, Hedra presented the Son of the Serpent to Queen Issta who fell instantly in love with him, as Hedra had known she would."

So Angrim was the product of a god and a monster from the Undergates? How was Sarah supposed to beat something like that? Magda's spells had better deliver the way she said they would.

In the image, Grohann and Sarah watched as Hedra led young Angrim, straight backed and long limbed, to the airy sleeping chamber of Queen Issta. The queen opened her bed to the striking young monster in the form of a man who removed his clothing in an odd echo of his mother before the Undergates and entered.

"Angrim is truly the most beautiful?" Grohann asked. "He looks too much like a human for me to tell."

"Yeah," Sarah replied, her voice low and husky. "He's all right."

"Soon after, Hedra led King Oldam to his wife's bedchambers on pretext, so as to allow the King of the Alir to witness his wife's infidelity. Oldam shook the Alireon with his rage and struck off the head of Queen Issta on the spot. But Hedra interceded before Oldam could slay the Son of the Serpent, seducing the king and allowing her favored son to escape."

"They are having more sex? Did not Oldam *just* kill his vife a minute ago? This is vy humans are so stupid about the sex. They learn it from their gods."

"So typical." Sarah shook her head and watched Angrim slink off to the Undergates and be welcomed home by the snake Sigundr. "The woman gets decapitated, and the guy gets away to tell stories about it. Tell me how that's fair."

"The Serpent's Son learned much of sorcerous lore at the feet of demons during his stay in hell, including the forbidden lore that even the Alir do not practice. And all the while he waited and watched."

King Oldam now stood at the side of a regal and proud Queen Hedra, and spun land from the ocean of stars, making all the world out of the star stuff.

"When the time came for King Oldam to make the world, the Son of the Serpent snuck in, settling in the land which would become Tyrrane. His home became the seat of that nation, and he lent those people who would live there his power and wisdom."

Sarah watched the first Tyrraneans, savages with wooden weapons and a burning need to use them, discover the Fell Citadel. Angrim, now grown truly monstrous from his time in hell, with long dead-white arms and a hooded face, welcomed them inside.

"Oh, that's a shame," Sarah said.

"Throughout history, only the combined intercession of sorcerers from all the nations of Andos, time and again, has kept the Serpent's Son from attaining his goals," Magda said as the vision faded away. Sarah immediately noticed that over her time in the vision, her sense of wrongness with the world had dissipated. Whether it was her eyes or the world around her that had changed, it all looked normal now.

"Trolls believe that the Anger Under the Mountain vants to take all the humans to live on the ice, far north of Troll Coast. Give the vorld back to trolls, yes? It is vy so many tribes vorship him. Trolls do not like humans. Mostly."

"The Serpent's Son wishes to take all of humanity for himself to do with as he wishes," replied Magda. "He feels it would be the best vengeance upon King Oldam to wrest control of the King's favorite creations. I imagine he is right."

"Wait. Finnagel told me that Angrim was a sorcerer. The most powerful in history, but a sorcerer, like me." Sarah ran a fingertip over the scars on her forehead. "This isn't the story of a regular sorcerer."

"No, it is not." Magda paused to cough and spit. "This situation is far more complicated and the foe many times more dangerous than if we faced one of my own grandchildren. The son's hardening will be absolute, and he will not leave it."

Sarah assumed that by "hardening," Magda meant Angrim's place of power, the phenomena that caused the long-term residence of a sorcerer to become more conducive to his own power while at the same time inhibiting the magic of others.

"So how did your story explain the spell you had me cast?" asked Sarah. "What happened to our eyes, and what did you do to fix it?"

"I did nothing," Magda said. "Your sight was never impaired. The spell you cast changed the world. You've simply had time to get used to it."

"Come again?"

"Some mortals have the ability to catch glimpses of the future. They become leaders or villains, using their Sight for good or ill."

"Like Ghost Eye," Grohann said, referring to the shaman of his tribe that he, Sarah, and Finnagel had rescued from Grohann's father. Ghost Eye had known just where and when to send Grohann to intercept Sarah and keep her from falling into Old Stone's trap.

"The Serpent's Son is similar, except that he sees constantly into the future and is always aware of how to step to thwart his enemies. Such a creature is nearly impossible to outmaneuver without powerful allies and decades of planning."

"Well, I feel better about our chances already," Sarah said. "Gro, we have any celebration wines?"

"Maybe I do not understand. Are ve having more allies yoo have not told us about?"

Magda smiled. "The spell you cast, little button, unmoored this world from its future. The Serpent's Son will be unable to See. Everyone will be unable to See. The table is leveled."

Sarah's mouth fell open. She rocked back, stood up from her place next to the campfire, and found a good ten-foot stretch to pace. She wasn't normally a pacer, but she wasn't normally on a mission to learn fatally volatile god magics and use them to slay a monster older than the world itself.

Grohann watched her for a bit. "If Cassioos Lady God can change the whole vorld over sharps and mushrooms, vy can't yoo make us a door to Anger Under Mountain's bathtub and squash him like a tomato ven he is not looking for it?"

"Because I am but a splinter," Magda reminded the troll. "And because any magic I do runs the risk of attracting the attention of certain powers that might be listening, powers none of us wish to attract. We are all much safer if Sarah learns and casts the spells."

"So, if Magda the goddess casts the big magic, then Oldam or some other god will know you are out of jail and swoop down to destroy us all." Sarah waved her arms as she paced. "But if *I* do it, I'll probably kill myself, but at least I'll do it beneath the attention of any other Alir. Is that about the size of it?"

Magda watched Sarah walk back and forth and considered. "That is essentially correct."

"No offense, but that sounds like an excuse to me." Grohann frowned and crossed his big rock-like arms.

"Perhaps you would like to squash the Son of the Serpent like a tomato while we watch, then?" Magda smiled serenely.

Grohann's frown deepened. "I think Cassioos is a bad influence on lady god."

Sarah stopped pacing and glared at Magda, eyes narrowed and jaw set. "Why am I not surprised about that?"

24

THE ANGER STAYS
UNDER THE MOUNTAIN
BRANNOK

Emperor Brannok II, despot of the Second Tyrranean Empire —who no longer answered to "king"—slammed open the doors to his war room. His advisors and sons jumped in alarm.

Prince Brannok, a younger version of the emperor with thick arms, red hair, and a deep scowl, gave a snarl at the unexpected interruption.

Prince Cantil just sighed and stroked his pointed little beard.

Cantil was smart, and ruthless as well, the emperor thought, but he would never make a warrior. He even dressed as if he thought he might drop everything and run off to a ball somewhere.

Damn Jasmayre for being born a woman. She might as well have been born without a head as a prick. She was so much stronger than any of her brothers. Her injuries barely slowed her down, and then only because he had forced the issue.

He relied on her assistance now more than ever, which was why he had sent her to negotiate with Norrik for troops. But he would have enjoyed watching her kick Cantil around the room.

Brannok's mail jingled beneath his heavy bear cloak as he strode to the head of the huge blackoak table, bare save for the obligatory statue of holy Angrim. This one just looked like a swirling black cloak, but Brannok hated it anyway. The miserable Soul of Tyrrane could see and hear out of properly consecrated statues, such as this one, if his attention were so directed.

It bothered Brannok that he couldn't tell which way the cursed thing was supposed to be looking.

The war room, like the rest of the Fell Citadel, was sparse and drafty. Walls of cold gray stone, almost black, contained only the occasional uncomfortable chair or militant tapestry to break the monotony. It was the same everywhere in the citadel. Ceilings loomed low and oppressive, whispered conversations hushed as others passed, and the entire populace huddled in the shadows, furtive and pliable.

Rebellion, while common, immediately attracted attention and was easy enough to quash. All of Tyrrane had been built with an eye toward effectively pressing the desires of the monarchy onto the throats of the citizens. It was the perfect society.

Brannok pulled his bearskin cloak tighter around his big shoulders and sat in the black wooden chair at the head of the table. He nodded to his most senior advisors.

"What news of Greenshade, my imperial highness?" asked General Dutard, the elderly steward of the Ebon Host's home command. The reedlike man blinked, his bushy mustache twitched, and dirty lamplight reflected from his liver-spotted scalp. "Has the woman sent you news yet?" The general wore the gray dress uniform of the Ebon Host, embroidered in black and silver. A silver emblem of an upraised fist holding a short-bladed dagger gleamed on his chest.

"In fact," the emperor said, satisfied for once, "Songham's widow has sent several birds. She has assumed her husband's conquest of the Forest Castle and the throne and awaits our armies to secure the rest of the country from a few outlaw barons—and from her." He looked to Brannok Jr., who smiled back at him as a feral dog eying a crippled cat might. "She has proven herself to be both backbiting and treacherous, though I doubt it's anything we cannot handle."

Junior's savage smile grew wider. "Finally." The prince slammed a meaty fist down on the table. "When I arrive at Treaty Hill, it will be my hand that claims vengeance for my fallen brothers."

"As if you cared." Cantil waved a hand and looked away. "You despised Despin. You only want to kill this Keane person because you think father wants it." Cantil looked the emperor in the eye. "And he doesn't give a shit either."

Prince Brannok roared and stood from the table, huge fists ready to beat an apology out of his insolent younger brother. Cantil rolled his eyes and sighed, as if the junior Brannok's explosion were too boring for words.

The emperor held out a hand, and Prince Brannok quieted and sat back down, still glaring at Cantil who paid him no mind whatsoever. His eldest son was a brutish thug and would make a horrifying tyrant over Greenshade. That was why he was being sent there. After a few years under his rule, Greenshade would be completely cowed and accommodating to anyone Brannok sent as a more permanent monarch.

"Our love, or lack thereof, for Princes Tobin and Despin is immaterial," Emperor Brannok stated. "It was the mercenary Keane who murdered King Songham in the battle—*as well* as your brothers—and the criminal is presumed to have fled to Sedrios."

"Whoops," said Cantil.

"The Pavinn dog," Prince Brannok said in a low growl "Hiding amongst the rest of his filthy kind. We should slaughter them all and plant assassin flowers over their bones."

Assassin flowers were used to make baker's tar, the drug of choice amongst Tyrrane's elites and were grown and sold by the Royal—now Imperial—House. The tar was baked into pastries and eaten, resulting in euphoric hallucinations. Prince Brannok had developed a significant habit for black sweets ever since he had returned from a scouting expedition to Coldspine. Something there had unsettled him badly. The emperor did not press his eldest on the matter. Not because the tar wasn't potentially deadly—it was—but because it left the bullying brute more tractable.

Jasmayre would not touch the stuff. He wondered where she was now. Had she browbeat the five kings of Norrik into uniting under her banner yet?

"Junior," Emperor Brannok said to his eldest son, "you will take the Expansion Host into Greenshade, along with a contingent from Norrik and Mirrik each." Brannok had been careful not to tip Mirrik's King Wagnersen to his knowledge of the foreign ruler's involvement in the rebellious plots. Wagnersen would assuredly play along with his agreement to provide troops against Greenshade for now. "Go first to Treaty Hill and secure it. Then force Songham's widow's troops into the field against the rebel barons. Attack with the Host only after the widow's men are depleted, and put the Norrik and Mirrik raiders in the vanguard. That is what they are there for."

Brannok, on the other hand, was under no obligation to ensure that Wagnersen's men came home alive.

The elder prince scowled but said nothing. Brannok knew his son would make a bloody ruin of the assignment. Cantil, ever the clever one, likely knew it too. It was not important though. The Ebon Host was a mighty hammer, and Greenshade was a tiny house made of spun glass. Prince Brannok's overly aggressive nature might result in incalculable innocent deaths, but that would only make the point more forcefully.

The next job required more finesse.

"Cantil." Emperor Brannok straightened in his tall, hard chair. "You will drive the Plains Host, along with the bulk of the cavalry, to the far border of the Paras Plains. High King Ivarr has pressed forward and is driving Tyrranean settlers out of their lands." Prince Cantil's brow shot up, but he said nothing to betray his surprise at having been given so important a job. "You must be careful but decisive. Ivarr is a wily opponent, and he will not be defeated easily. But General Dutard assures me that you are ready for this. You will be leaving on the morrow."

Dutard gave Prince Cantil a tight smile across the table. The young man nodded and sank back in his chair—the only seat in the room with cushions—and stroked his beard. For once, he was silent.

A feeling of ill fortune settled on Brannok. There was no cause for it. Both his sons would carry vastly superior forces into the field with them. They could make a hundred mistakes and still carry the day. What bothered him so?

"Father," Prince Brannok said, "what of Angrim? Am I intended to run off with a third of our armies without receiving his blessing?" For the past two weeks, Angrim had not called for Brannok, and the emperor had been glad for the reprieve.

Reflexively the emperor glanced at the statue on the table.

Two feet high of spiraled black stone, glossy and enigmatic, stared back at him. Or possibly away from him.

It was infuriatingly impossible to tell.

Since the first Tyrraneans had come to Dismon and found the Fell Citadel already there, no Tyrranean army had marched to war without Angrim's blessing. It seemed an inauspicious start to the enterprise.

"You will not have Angrim's blessing, boy," came the stentorian voice of a short thick-bodied man from behind Prince Brannok. Everyone, the emperor included, jumped at the sudden and alarming intrusion. The only door stood shut on the other side of the room.

It was Valafar, Angrim's apprentice, and Brannok hated him more than anyone else. The apprentice shook his lengthy mane of black hair and glanced sternly at the emperor. He wore a black shirt, cloak, and pants to match his hair and beard. Acting, as always, as if he were the actual authority in Tyrrane, the Pavinn sorcerer cleared his throat and spoke to Prince Brannok.

"Angrim is involved in matters beyond your ken, Princeling. But he feels, as do I, that you require someone to watch over you during this venture. Therefore, I will be accompanying you to ensure that you do as instructed."

Emperor Brannok felt his pale face redden even before the next words came.

"Instructed by *me*, that is."

Prince Cantil laughed into his hand and provoked a glare from Prince Brannok, though the elder prince said nothing aloud.

Valafar's announcement scuttled Emperor Brannok's plans to allow his eldest to raze Greenshade and then install a more moderate-seeming ruler. He wanted nothing more than to pull his sword off of his hip and chop the Pavinn demon's head in half. But Brannok had seen Valafar fight before, and he knew he'd never live to carry such an action through. Instead, he redirected.

As his daughter would have done.

"General Lake." Brannok addressed the brooding man at the foot of the table. Lake was Dutard's opposite in many ways: tall, bushy bearded, with thick black hair and broad shoulders. He wore the same uniform as his frail and elderly peer, though it fit more tightly on him.

The widow had murdered his father at the negotiation table in Treaty Hill.

"Yes, My Imperial Highness?"

"You are the only one here with nothing so far to say," Brannok told him. "Have you reviewed the troops from Mirrik and Norrik? Will they be ready to accompany Prince Brannok come the dawn?"

"They . . . will, sire," Lake said hesitantly. "But you should know that the raiders have only sent us five hundred men apiece."

"What?" Emperor Brannok shouted, his voice thunder in the bare, stone room. "They promised us ten times as many. What are those bastards playing at?" He expected this sort of thing from Wagnersen but not the five kings. Did they truly plan treachery? And Jasmayre was now among them.

"I told you they were planning a double cross," said Prince Cantil. "The Norrikmen will never ally with Tyrrane, not for real, and Mirrik wants only to fight Norrik. Those troops are just for show." Cantil inspected his fingernails. "I doubt very much either would be willing to side with any nation that would have the other as an ally."

"It hardly matters." Valafar's deep voice stopped all other conversation. "One thousand raiders or ten thousand, the outcome will be the same."

"Then why not simply ride out and defeat all of Greenshade

alone?" Emperor Brannok's voice flew ahead of his sense. "I assume you require no troops at all, given the extent of your prowess."

Valafar turned to the emperor with narrowed eyes. Brannok felt a pressure in the right side of his head, just before his vision in that eye clouded over a misty black.

Prince Brannok gasped, and even Prince Cantil looked a bit pale.

The emperor had seen Valafar perform this trick before, bursting the blood vessels in a man's eyes to rob him of his sight for a time. He knew what it looked like from the other side. Having it happen to him was a terrifying experience. He knew that with just a flick of his sorcerous finger, it would be Brannok's brain filling with blood instead of his eye.

As usual, Brannok's fear turned immediately to anger, though this time he leaned on his recent experience in Dismon's sewers and refused to allow his anger to force his hand.

"Learn to respect your betters, Emperor," Valafar said. "I am happy to repeat the lesson as many times as necessary, though I suspect you would run out of eyes soon."

"Is it too late for me to withdraw my request for an angry sorcerer to accompany me to the Paras Plains?" Cantil asked. Although he had suffered more *rebukes* than any member of the Tyrranean royalty, the young prince seemed the most determined not to be afraid of Valafar and Angrim. He and Despin had been the only royals never to attend chapel, where Angrim was worshiped as the god and soul of their nation.

Though Jasmayre, by some unknown trick of her own or a failing of Valafar's, was the only one of his children who could, and often did, mock the sorcerer to his face and receive no retribution. Valafar seemed at all times entirely unaware of her presence.

The emperor of Tyrrane had just suffered an assault on his person, in the witness of family and military, and no one in the room were going to do a damn thing about it.

But then, neither was he.

Brannok grew up in the Fell Citadel, and things were the same today as they had ever been. His own uncle Fongr had been flayed alive not ten feet from where Brannok now sat for crossing Valafar—and by extension, Angrim—his skin rolled up in strips by unseen hands while he floated in the air and shrieked.

Emperor Brannok sat back in his uncomfortable chair and lowered his head. That would not happen to him.

But he would not play the obedient pet forever.

25

THE FREE HAND MEETS SOME FANS

KEANE

Keane held Megan's hand as they dodged down the rain-washed alleyways of Dahnt, shadows still stark in the morning sun. Angry shouts pursued them and inspired them to greater speed.

"You're sure you didn't do anything to set them off?" Red-faced with exertion, Megan spun around a bleached crate and shoved off of the orange stoned wall.

"Not recently." Keane sprinted across a narrow street into another alleyway, his diminutive wife in tow.

Other than being the site of the only remaining Temple of the Sky in the known world, the town of Dahnt, on the western coast of Rousland and close to the country of Arlea to the south, was a more or less unremarkable fishing community. Its docks made it a regular stop between Rousea to the north and everything south, including the Paradisal Islands and the mouth of the Beacon Sea, which led to all of the middle and lower nations of Andos without having to sail around the whole continent. Keane had been here once before with Sarah, though he did not recall too much of the experience.

Salt wind blew through the alley, and Keane spotted the opening he was after. The sound of gulls grew louder in front of them, even as the sounds of pursuit did the same from behind.

Megan's thick mane flew out behind her like a chestnut-colored cloud as she ran. "It isn't like I don't appreciate the excitement, but if you're just trying to keep me interested, you should know that I find cheese pastry every bit as exciting as being chased by angry townsfolk."

She puffed out her cheeks with the exertion. "Pastries are a lot more in line with a pregnant woman's needs than footraces, too."

Keane flashed her a quick grin over his shoulder. "*Now* you tell me."

Like the rest of Rousland, Dahnt had suffered its share of disasters, most of which had come at the hands of invaders from the north, south, and east. The population shared Rousland's general attitude about strangers. Leave your money, then leave.

They weren't usually this vigorous about it though.

Ahead of them, Keane saw the boardwalk. Their objective almost in sight, he and Megan bore down even harder.

Sparse business along the wharf conducted itself quietly among even-tempered and efficient men and women, who moved people and goods in and out of plain sight. Well-maintained wooden buildings fronted against the boardwalk. Over the tops of the low warehouses, fishermen's homes, a tavern, and the rounded stone façade of the temple could be seen in the strengthening morning sunlight—ancient blocks rounded with weathering and blueish in cast.

From between these sedate, fading buildings ran Marshall Harden Grayspring, accompanied by the squat Darrishman Mahu and his lanky partner Sabni. Harden paused for an instant, during which distant shouting could be heard from the streets behind, and bolted toward the lone ship that floated at dock. Keane and Megan followed, the wizard Morholt and his black-garbed sister Raven after them, and finally Loffa, who held hands and ran with Eli.

The shouting grew louder as the desperate band legged it for the ship.

Harden leaped aboard as an angry crowd spilled onto the wharf.

The vessel's captain, a barrel-shaped man with short gray stubble on his face and head, stomped over with a pronounced limp and yelled, "Who the blazes d'ye think ye are? Get the hell offa my ship, ye loon."

Harden ignored the grizzled captain in his sweat-stained clothes and helped Sabni pull Mahu up onto the deck. Keane and Megan ran past them on the dock and scrambled up the gangplank.

"We gotta get the fuck outta here," Keane yelled. "Cast off, now!"

"And just who the fiery hell are ye now?" The captain rounded on Keane, who turned his back on the man and reached down to help Loffa essay the narrow plank.

"No, thank you," Loffa told him. Beside her, Eli glanced between Loffa and the oncoming crowd indecisively.

From the boardwalk, the red-faced crowd spotted the group and ran toward the dock.

Loffa smiled fetchingly. "Eli will help me."

"Oldam's snug and sandy armpit," Keane said desperate, "we do *not* have time for this now. Give me your hand."

Harden and Sabni pulled Morholt and Raven over the prow while Eli made up his mind and snatched Loffa up in one arm, dancing nimbly up the gangplank with her.

Loffa winked at Keane as she passed.

As the captain was just about to release another bellow of outrage, Eli threw a bag of coins at him with his free hand, which the captain caught.

"How 'bout we get movin'?" Eli said.

The captain weighed his choices, as well as the coins in his hand. As he did, tentacles as big around as a cow's belly reached up out of the water and wrapped around the dock in front of the oncoming crowd of townsfolk. There was a loud cracking noise, and the dock ruptured. Large pieces of it disappeared beneath the water.

The townsfolk's angry cries turned to terrified screams. The captain's indignation followed a similar trajectory. "Cut and run, boys! Cut and run!" He sprinted down the length of the deck, chopping tie lines apart as he flew.

Sailors grabbed poles and shoved at the dock, slowly pushing the slim two-masted sailing ship into the ocean. Everywhere ragged men crawled over deck and rigging, clambered up masts, and untied sails. The light breeze carried them slowly away from Dahnt, where people still fretted and shouted—and kept well away from the tentacled beast that continued to tear at the dock and boardwalk.

"I imagine that's enough of that," Harden said to Morholt, who nodded.

The runecrafter massaged one wrist as the tentacles slipped beneath the waves without sound, and the broken portion of the dock reasserted itself, growing back into place. The townsfolk, now a comfortable distance away, shook their fists and shouted impotently.

"What happened?" Megan stepped up onto the foredeck. "Were Hulda's men in the town?"

"I guess someone recognized us," Keane replied. "Was everyone wearing their hoods up? I knew we should have gone around town instead of through it."

This earned him a sidelong look from Megan.

Loffa pointed to Harden. "He stole a doll. The shopkeeper saw him take it. That's when everyone started yelling at us."

"You stole what?" Eli asked Harden, chuckling. "A doll? I think you're mebbe a couple decades off."

Harden's gaze went flinty.

"I don't understand," Megan said. "Those people were enraged. That wasn't about a child's doll. Someone recognized us. How did that happen? What went on last time you were here?"

Keane lowered his head and looked up at Megan sheepishly. "We sort of sacked this town once. Wallace's Company did. Apparently, they're still angry."

"Once?" asked Megan. "How long ago?"

"Forever ago," Keane answered.

"Four years an' three months, give or take," Eli said. "They do seem kinda sore about it, though."

"And you came back?" Megan sounded exasperated.

"Well now, it was dark last time." Harden took off his wide-brimmed hat and scratched the back of his head. Stringy dust-colored hair blew in the breeze. "I believe it was dark. Didn't think they'd recognize me, anyway. I didn't recognize any of them."

He snapped his fingers.

"Eli," Harden asked, "was that the week we got paid in head dust?"

"That it were. Truth to tell, I barely recollect bein' in Dahnt at all."

Harden rubbed his chin. "Hm. Hope we didn't do anything especially horrible."

"You hope we didn't do anything especially horrible?" Keane leaned back against a railing and hitched his shoulder where the leathers pulled tight. "Harden, you *ate* a guy. Some local lord or something. You were mad because he asked you not to burn down his house. You burned it down anyway, cooked him in it, and gave his daughters to the soldiers."

Harden shrugged. "Well, *that's* not especially horrible."

Sabni and Megan both wore the same expression of shocked horror, and even Morholt looked taken aback.

"You really are a monster," Megan said.

"We all have our strengths," replied Harden.

"I ain't hearing none of this." The ship's captain approached from aft of the group. "Just wanna know where yer goin' is all. Ship's headed for Steed and parts south."

"Skip Steed an' take us straight to Port Placid," said Eli, "an' you can keep that bag o' money I know you already counted. Deal?"

"Aye," said the captain. "Just keep t'yerselves. We don't need t'be friends. Don't tell me no names, and I ain't gotta lie t'no one if they come askin' after ye."

"Not sure that's how lying works," said Keane after the captain had taken his leave, "but if it's good for him, I'm all right with it." So saying, Keane rounded on Eli.

"Now as for you, you are gonna stop this shit with the queen mother right now. That's an innocent woman, and she doesn't deserve to be defiled by the likes of you."

Eli laughed. "Don't know how you think you got the standin' to have a say in who I plan to be defilin'." He cast a meaningful glance at

Queen Megan, who found something more interesting in the featureless blue sky to stare at.

"The standing?" Keane came forward until he stood nose to nose with the old mercenary. "I'm the king of goatfucking Greenshade. That's my standing."

"No, you *were* the king o' goatfuckin' Greenshade. Today you're some kid I didn't quite manage to kill once." Eli poked Keane in the arm where he had once thrown a dagger into it. "Get back to me when yer a king again."

Megan grabbed Keane by the arm and led him, with some difficulty, to the opposite side of the foredeck. The wind picked up, and Megan shook out her hair, which blew about her like a dark, shining cloak.

Keane's eyes wandered over his wife, the way she filled out the plain brown traveling dress she wore, already a little tight in the belly. They would have to get her new clothing in Port Placid.

"Hey, up here."

He *had* been staring at her chest, which was also beginning to test the limits of the dress.

"Sorry. Have you ever been to the Paradisals? Sarah and I always wanted to go, but . . ." He trailed off, his transient mind now on Sarah. He realized that he had stopped worrying so much about her recently, and that came with its own crushing piece of guilt.

"Absolutely not." Megan leaned her head back to catch the sun. "That would have been entirely inappropriate for a princess of Greenshade. There are pirates there, you know." Eyes closed, she smiled into the warmth.

Although Megan teased him, Keane worried about exactly that. She was still shocked at Harden, but the *thousands* of pirates in the Paradisals had a similar reputation. Keane hoped that Harden's contact there was good enough to keep them safe. It would be a shame to have survived Wallace's Company, King Rance and his evil Secretary Hubrane, as well as that bastard Songham with all his soldiers, only to be killed because he walked up to the wrong people now and asked them for help.

26

NOT SO PLAIN PLAINS FISH

SARAH

From the top of the hillock where they made camp, Sarah and Grohann stared openmouthed in the night at the lines of multicolored fire that stretched across the Paras Plains. Cassius stared at Sarah.

They were four days west and past the Chillroad, the river that separated the Paras Plains from Coldspine, and had been obliged to turn a bit more southerly to skirt the pine woods that surrounded the southern feet of the Bitter Heights. Streams and ponds crisscrossed the northern plains with the runoff out of the mountains, and these were now the spawning grounds of adult flickerfish come home to breed.

Flickerfish were known as duns around much of the world and were big, tasty, and numerous, as well as easy to catch. In all the oceans of the world, they were ordinary fish. But once a year, the duns would swim back up into the freshwater streams of their birth to spawn. Something in the fish's bodies reacted to the milky mineral-laden waters coming off the Heights and created a bright glow, blue for females and green for males. This was how the flickerfish found each other in the opaque water to mate, and they lit the streams and ponds of the Paras Plains in a brilliant display known as the fire runs.

Everywhere across the night ran streaks of bright blue-green water, shimmering and moving under a star-filled sky. Sarah leaned against the troll, and they both stood and watched.

"It's amazing," Sarah whispered.

Grohann nodded. "This is a very beautiful thing."

"You know, in Tyrrane, everyone stays indoors during the runs. They think the nights are evil, and the dead walk." While Sarah had never spent any real time in Tyrrane, she had served for years in Wallace's Company with men from every corner of the Thirteen Kingdoms. An attentive and curious woman, she reckoned she knew plenty about her world.

It wasn't the same as seeing it though.

"Hm," responded Grohann.

"But in Coldspine, the runs are the first night of Bedwinter. They feast and drink and have lots of sex for an entire week. So, they're pretty happy to see the runs come."

"I think I like Coldspine's holiday better. Though maybe it is more similar than not, yes? Vat do yoo think Tyrraneans are up to ven they are hiding in their houses for a week?"

"I hate to disturb this reverie," Cassius said, "but we are not alone out here."

Sarah dropped into a crouch, her muscular legs ready to spring. Soundlessly she pulled her broadsword from its sheath. Beside her, Grohann strung his huge troll bow, lifted it, and nocked an arrow.

"There is no need for yoo to kill us, I think," shouted a voice from the dark. It was a troll's voice, like Grohann's but softer. "Ve are here to help. Ghost Eye has sent us."

Grohann lowered his bow and grinned wide to display a fearsome set of sharp teeth. "Finnlaug? Is that yoo?"

A big shape stepped up out of the dark to the top of the little hill. A troll, bound in thick furs and carrying most of a medium-sized tree as a spear, spread her arms toward Grohann who responded in kind. The newcomer was equal in height to Grohann but thinner, with obviously female curves. She wore her greenish hair in long well-cared-for mats, out of which sprouted short sturdy points that curved upward in contrast to Grohann's big ram's horns. Sarah found her pretty, in a rough-and-tumble, barroom fight kind of way.

"Yes, it is me." Finnlaug pushed Grohann out to arm's length and held him there. She looked him over from top to bottom. "You have not been eating, I think. Yoo need troll food."

"Vy did Ghost Eye send you to this place?" asked Grohann. "Do yoo have vord from home? Are trolls in danger?"

Finnlaug rested one hand on Grohann's solid chest. Sarah smiled to herself. This lady knew what she wanted, though Grohann was oblivious.

"The Kyrrvatin people are good. Not in danger. Ghost Eye sends us because yoo are in danger. The three of yoo need troll help."

"Ghost eye sends *us*?" said Sarah.

Finnlaug took a step to the side and swung an arm out to encompass the night.

Her other hand remained in contact with Grohann.

"Warriors of the tundra tribes," shouted Finnlaug, "come and say your hello to Var-Chief Grohann!"

There came a loud many-throated bellow from the bottom of the hillock below Sarah's sight lines to the fire runs. With a small gasp, she realized that she had overlooked what now appeared to be hundreds of trolls maybe a thousand feet below her. With the wind blowing down from the Heights and the fire runs spoiling her night vision, they had been undetectable. Thank Slago they were friendly.

The hill became a woodland of big folk who all laughed, back slapped, and pledged allegiance to Grohann. They welcomed him as their new chieftain now that his father Old Stone was dead and buried, and Ghost Eye had given his official blessing.

Sarah made her way to Cassius, who sat beside their campfire and watched the trolls with amused interest. He smiled at her and patted the ground next to himself, offering her a spot to sit.

She hesitated a moment before sitting. The ongoing process of carrying a splinter of Magda's mind in Cassius's head seemed to be blending the two personalities into one. It was practical since no one had to show the goddess how to pee anymore, but it also worried

Sarah since she felt certain that the longer it went on, the less of Cassius there would be at the end. The physical toll continued as well, and his once-snug blue jacket and pants hung on his limbs like limp flags.

"We seem to have allies," Cassius said. "Big ones."

Sarah no longer even thought of the strange voice as being from two distinct throats. "Ghost Eye sent us five hundred and thirty-four troll warriors. I appreciate the assist, but given that he's a Seer, it makes me nervous, too."

"Was a Seer," Cassius replied.

"That's right. How did he know to send these trolls to us? Did your spell not work?"

"I believe it did." Cassius tapped the side of his chin in an entirely human gesture. "I have been listening to the trolls talking. Apparently, Ghost Eye began gathering the tribes immediately after we left the Kyrrvatin village. As soon as he had enough fighters, he sent them here to wait on us. That was months past. The spell you cast to sever the future from Seers was barely two weeks ago."

"They've been waiting here for months?" Sarah asked.

"Such is the power of faith." Cassius smiled serenely.

Grohann and Finnlaug, hand in hand, strode out of the press of big folk and moved beside the fire. Grohann turned to the throng and bellowed, "Trolls of the tundra tribes. Give your faces to me."

Sarah clapped her hands over her ears. Grohann's stone-against-stone voice battered her. Who knew anyone could make a sound that loud?

The trolls quieted and turned to Grohann, expressions happy and expectant.

"As chief of the Kyrrvatin tribe," Grohann yelled, "I accept your request!"

The trolls as one shouted "Hurrah!" up the hill. This time, Sarah pressed both hands against her ears with force.

"But as *var-chief* of the tundra tribes, yoo do not need me. Yoo vill have Finnlaug, smartest of all the troll warriors."

"Hurrah!"

"Vise trolls have their dream of victory against the Anger Under the Mountain who uses trolls against each other. Trolls are for trolls. It is good, yes?"

"Hurrah! Hurrah! Hurrah!"

"That was certainly to the point." Cassius pressed his fingers against one temple.

The trolls broke off and headed back down the hill in ones and twos. Finnlaug and Grohann stood and faced one another, sly smiles on their faces.

Finnlaug noticed Sarah and Cassius staring at them. She coughed into her fist.

"Grohann." She took a step back from him. "Yoo and I are needing to discuss strategy. And things. Over here behind this hill is good for talking. And things."

Finnlaug led a grinning Grohann by the hand past the campfire and down the other side of the hill. Cassius watched them, interested, but Sarah matched Grohann's grin with one of her own.

"Have yoo ever heard," Sarah heard Grohann say to Finnlaug as he was led away into the dark, "of how the Coldspiners celebrate the fire runs?"

27

THREATS, OBJECTIFICATIONS, AND BUTT-TROLLS

SARAH

They had traveled for two days since Sarah and her companions met with the big folk contingent, and she thought them easy company to march with, if a bit long-legged and fast. A dwindling Cassius found himself passed along from troll to troll during the trek, not that any of them seemed to mind.

Frozen tundra had evolved into grassland, and Magda continued to teach Sarah god spells. Without understanding how they worked, it was hard going, and she was all too quick to point out her failures.

"You did that wrong. You would have turned every molecule of air in your lungs into a short sword made of hardened peanuts."

"You did that wrong. You would have grown your enemies into giants and made them sing arias as they killed you."

"You did that wrong. You would have transported every living creature inside of ten miles to the beach. That one wouldn't actually have killed you. I think maybe you're improving again."

A shout rang through the encampment.

"Riders!" bellowed one of the trolls who watched the horizon while the others ate. Sarah jumped up and ran to the outer edge of the camp along with Grohann, Finnlaug, and a large number of trolls.

Sarah stood against the wind, braids holding back her twirling hair and keeping it from hitting her in the face. Below her, perhaps fifty windibou riders, men and women in bound furs and mail, charged up the dale. Sarah recognized the lead rider, smiled, and sheathed her broadsword. She walked a dozen steps in front of the trolls, and went to one knee, her head lowered.

High King Ivarr stopped his steed a hundred feet from Sarah and jumped heavily to the ground. He was as she remembered him, a big burly man, larger than life with huge rounded shoulders and just as big a stomach. His teeth shone through his bushy blond beard, and his fur-wrapped mail glinted where it peeked out at the sun. Not for the first time, Sarah found herself thinking of Ivarr as some kind of storybook king of legend.

"Do my eyes deceive me?" Ivarr's booming voice rolled happily over the grass. "Could that be Sarah of Greenshade?"

Sarah stood and smiled. "High King Ivarr, it is my pleasure and honor."

Ivarr closed the distance between them quickly and gathered Sarah up in a big hug. "The pleasure is entirely mine," he said and set her down. The High King was one of two men Sarah had ever met capable of lifting her so easily.

She had broken the other man's arm and left him unconscious in a jail cell.

"Your wounds where the cats clawed you"—Ivarr ran his finger-tips over her forehead, his eyes round with amazement—"healed. How can this be? Has it even been a whole month since I saw you last? You are no mere apprentice sorcerer; you are now a healer too." He grinned again. "The new color in your hair is quite fetching as well."

Sarah ran her hand over the silver-and-black braid. "I'm just happy to have survived the experience," she said. "How goes the campaign for the plains?"

Ivarr scowled and motioned for one of his riders to come and take his windibou.

Sarah felt a sharp stab of guilt over the animals she had killed heading into the striped sands of the Tower of Chains. She shoved it down and concentrated on Ivarr instead.

"Bah." High King Ivarr indicated that Sarah should walk with him away from the two groups of warriors. "We were scouting for the main army when we came across you. The damn Tyrraneans showed up with far more men and horses than we expected. The whole affair has turned into a stalemate. One side jabs, and the other flees, again and again. That is why I am so happy to see you and your trolls. I believe they may be the wedge I need to turn the tide of this offensive and retake the Paras Plains once and for all." He paused. "Or just take it. You know, I've never been all that clear on who actually owned it first anyway. Not that it matters now. What?"

Sarah stopped dead in the grass. They hadn't gotten far and still stood between the two forces.

"I'm afraid that isn't going to happen, sire. My own mission for Greenshade is ongoing. I still have a lot of people to save in Treaty Hill."

For the first time, Ivarr appeared on the edge of being truly angry. Sarah squared her shoulders and met the king's gaze.

"This is a centuries-old conflict, and I have it within my grasp to end it once and for all." Ivarr ground his teeth. "Thousands of men on both sides have thrown their lives into this land. Who are you to walk away from it now?"

"I wish you well, Your Highness. I truly do. But I am not going to stay and bleed for this utterly empty and abandoned stretch of grass when I have actual loved ones in need of protection. You will have to win this on your own." Sarah had no idea if she would truly be able to defeat Angrim once she reached him in Dismon. It seemed impossible. But a genuine goddess walked beside her and taught her spells created to do just that. Who was Sarah to call her a liar?

It seemed Sarah believed in Magda's magic more than she did Ivarr's war in the Paras Plains, at any rate.

There was rustling on both sides as men and trolls unlimbered weapons and readied themselves.

"You have no more loved ones to defend in Treaty Hill, Sarah." King Ivarr looked sad for her. "You are too late. Songham the Usurper took the throne in Greenshade. Your king is missing, and your capital is lost." Ivarr glanced down at Sarah's hand, white-knuckled on the grip of her broadsword. "Though if it eases your heart, King Keane killed the usurper as he fled. Greenshade is now ruled by the villain's wife, Queen Hulda Hubrane."

That was no better in Sarah's mind and possibly a great deal worse. Sarah and Keane had met Hulda Hubrane in the alleyways of the Harrows, Treaty Hill's poorest sector, and both of them had considered themselves lucky to have gotten away alive.

As Keane had again, Al-Dagos guide his steps.

Ivarr spoke with unusual earnestness. "Come with me instead, and strike a blow against Tyrrane they will never forget. Once Coldspine holds the plains, we may strike even further into the heart of Dismon itself."

That had been the plan before Treaty Hill fell. Sarah stared at Ivarr and tried to decide what to do. He was probably lying about carrying the fight to Dismon. He certainly had not been interested in that sort of thing the last time they talked. She needed to be smart about this, think like Keane. He always came up with some bold, unexpected idea that left his opponents confused.

And all she could think to do was chop off Ivarr's head.

"Fuck you." If she couldn't think like Keane, she would at least talk like him. "Treaty Hill wouldn't have fallen at all if you'd have been willing to get up off your hairy ass and do something about it." She felt her control melting away. Now that she had started this, it was hard to stop.

She didn't want to stop.

"And now that it *has* fallen, you ask me to risk my fucking neck, the very thing you weren't willing to do for me, to come pull your fucking sac out of the fire? Fuck you again." Sarah's heart beat like a green hare. Part of her original mission had been to secure the aid of

Coldspine, and this rant didn't seem like it was going to accomplish that. But her mouth had a mind of its own, and there was no stopping the rush.

Was this what Keane felt like all the time?

"So let me ask you this, High King Ivarr. If you think you're having a hard time fighting the Tyrranean cavalry now, how well do you think you'd fare with five hundred pissed-off trolls up your fucking ass? Because I'm having trouble thinking of a better place to put them right now."

Silence blanketed the two sides. Even the wind did not rustle the grass. Sarah stared forward into Ivarr's scowl, his shaggy blond brows gathered together like thunderheads, wondering if she had accomplished anything more than adding another enemy to Greenshade's long list. The quiet stretched out until Sarah thought she would either call the attack herself or just start screaming.

And then Ivarr laughed.

He threw back his head and let out a grand bellowing guffaw. The rich howling belly laughs rolled out of him. Uncertain, Sarah looked between High King Ivarr and his riders and tried to smile.

"Oh Sarah!" Ivarr wiped tears from his eyes. "I wish you well on your journey. Had I a half thousand such as you, I would take the Paras Plains and the rest of the world besides. May your vengeance be bloody and full, for he who lives, is right." Ivarr turned to go, still laughing to himself. For an instant, Sarah wondered if she should speak, but long before the thought concluded, she already was.

"You could never have someone like me, King Ivarr," Sarah said to the king's back. He stopped and turned around, cheeks red and smiling. She had just threatened him, and he was laughing about it? Was that a measure of how seriously he took her?

"A man who ignores the desperate peril of friends and allies to take gain for himself is not a fit man to rule over real women." At this, some of the men among Ivarr's riders sniggered, and a few of the women broke into open laughter. But it only took one look at the king's darkening face to tell Sarah that she had taken things a step too far.

Ivarr burned at the laughter of his riders and glared at Sarah. "Get out of my sight, witch, before I feel forced to remind you of your place when addressing a king."

Sarah felt loose and ready. Fighting, at least, she understood. Beside her, Grohann stepped forward and crossed his arms.

Ivarr looked from Sarah to Grohann and back. "Bah!" He threw up his arm, turned, and stalked away, back to his windibou amongst his riders who tried not to laugh. He climbed up and signaled the run, and the Coldspiners quit the field.

With a hand on Grohann's forearm, Sarah said, "Thank you," and ran off to look for Cassius. She found him at the rear of the trolls, smiling at her. It was not his old, characteristic, easy grin, but at least it was friendly.

"That went sideways in a hurry," Cassius said. "Do we think it was worth it?"

"I need to talk to Keane, now. Ivarr mentioned that the king in Greenshade was missing. Not captured, not dead. *Fled* was the word he used. I need you to teach me a spell that will let me talk to him. I have to find out if he's okay."

Cassius's face became serene which Sarah thought meant that Magda was asserting herself.

"There is no time to waste learning spells just to talk to mortals, little button," she said. "You have yet to learn how to cast any of the spells I have been teaching you without killing yourself or your allies. No. I will not teach it."

"Then I guess I don't need you anymore. Or did you forget whose party this was?"

"I suppose that I did," Magda replied. "I have very little experience being an instrument in someone else's machinations. Though I still believe it to be a waste of time."

"Use some of Cassius's experience." Sarah sat down. "He's spent lots of time being a tool. Now, let's learn how to talk to someone who might be thousands of miles away. That sounds like fun."

28

PUNCHING UP

BRANNOK

Emperor Brannok II sat in his ebon and gold throne, a handful of yellow pages crushed in his fist. The messages sent by orven and transcribed by keepers told him that Angrim, who had not spoken to Brannok for weeks now, had instructed his bastard apprentice Valafar to hold Prince Brannok's armies at the border just north of the Greenshade River, where they continued to sit even now.

Brannok scowled upward and glared at the gigantic sculpture of Angrim that hung by thick chains from the ceiling. From most angles, it appeared as a swirling cloud of steel and smoky glass, but from the throne, it was a malevolent figure in a dark robe and hood that watched over the room.

Brannok knew that this representation was the one Angrim used the most often, looking through its eyes as if he were in the room. The statue's presence was a constant reminder throughout the centuries to the kings of Tyrrane that their power extended exactly as far as the Anger Under the Mountain wished it to.

Another of the messages crumpled in Emperor Brannok's fist said that Mirrik held their ambassador from Tyrrane for ransom. King Wagnersen was no longer hiding behind diplomacy.

Of the five kingdoms of Norrik, there was news as well. An emissary to Summervatn had been killed, and the Sund and Horrikvik were agitating for war. Jasmayre was in the Grengards where things were safe, though thinking about her in that blighted land made Brannok anxious.

He did not care for the feeling.

Adding to the bad news, the final missive told him that the Barons' Conclave in Greenshade had attacked the Forest Castle under cover of darkness and freed the war prisoners Songham's widow kept in the camps outside of the city. Baron Tralgar, the widow's ally—and thus Tyrrane's as well—had been assassinated and his troops assimilated into the conclave's. The emperor squeezed his fist and looked out across the huge chamber. If Angrim had not ordered the halt of Prince Brannok's forces, this would never have occurred.

The throne room in the Fell Citadel contained all of the height that the rest of its rooms lacked and was built like a cathedral. The acoustics in the dark gray chamber with its wide glossy stone floor and double row of huge columns were designed so that the utterances of the emperor on his throne could be easily heard by anyone anywhere within the enormous space. Thus it was that nearly a hundred people jumped, startled, when Brannok screamed his rage and rose from his huge ornate throne.

Brannok glared murderously ahead and prompted one young courtier to run from the room as the burly ruler stalked out and into the halls. The rest of the people in the chamber he left frozen like frightened deer.

While functionaries fell aside and doors slammed behind him, Brannok played out the oncoming encounter in his mind. He hated talking to the ancient creature under the citadel, but the damned thing was fucking up his war, and Brannok would not stand for that. He descended a flight of stairs as he imagined himself finally chopping the old monster down with the blade of his father, which bounced on his hip.

For a moment he even smiled to himself as he imagined his

daughter's pride in him, confronting the ancient thing. He pictured her smile and her disdain for Angrim and Valafar.

They gave him strength.

Cold air and a faint smell of rot greeted the emperor as he unlocked and opened a door to yet another staircase leading down into the dark. He paused there and looked down the stairs, a sudden panic halting his forward motion. With a deep breath he mastered himself and continued, grabbing a torch from the wall outside.

The doorway to the final flight of stairs lay open, and Brannok's breath steamed ahead of him in the frigid, stinking air.

There should have been a guard with a torch here.

Ah.

The guard's corpse lay across the threshold, little more than dried skin pulled tight across a skeleton. Brannok had heard of Angrim's hunger, of course, but others cleaned away this sort of thing. He had never witnessed its results for himself.

This was why he was here. He despised the creature, but more than that, he realized with no small amount of surprise, he hated the thought of his children existing in the same world with it. The same *house*. And after he was gone, who would protect them from it?

Who would protect Jasmayre?

What a ridiculous thought. Jasmayre needed far less protection than he did himself, especially considering what he intended to do.

Somewhat more timidly than when his journey had begun, Emperor Brannok stepped over the desiccated guard and continued into the dark. His guttering torch lit the way.

A rustle carried through the next room and caused Brannok to stop and listen. The chamber was circular, perhaps thirty feet across, and functioned as a mezzanine for Angrim's audience floor below. A banister ran all the way around, save one spot, where it opened for a spiral stairway that led down.

To Brannok's knowledge, no human person had ever willingly climbed down those stairs.

The emperor forced himself to the edge and looked down. The round, stone chamber—he was well into the bedrock beneath the citadel now—was empty save for a table to one side. The table supported a wooden stand which held several bottles of milky glass that contained unknown liquids. Brannok gasped as a large white-limbed figure covered in a dirty black cloak and hood glided into the room from an unseen doorway beneath him and, muttering to itself, gazed intently at the bottles. With a noise that sounded almost like a sob, it spun and exited the way it had come in. The cloak rustled as it did so.

Rooted to the spot, Brannok tried to imagine what he should do next. The sight of Angrim's distress left his brain as paralyzed as his feet.

The Anger Under the Mountain was a monster, yes, but he was also the motivating Soul of Tyrrane. He was its spine, its heart, and its god. As many times as Brannok and every king before him had wished for the creature's death, the reality of seeing him so distraught filled Brannok with terror. Terror and . . . something else. Was it opportunity? If he left here alive, he would go and visit the Soaring Pikes and speak to the Orven Master.

Perhaps the time had come for men to rule Tyrrane.

Stock still, Brannok waited above as Angrim repeated the action —once, then again. This was a mystery that the emperor did not want to solve, though he knew he must. He waited for the creature below to repeat its circuit and went to the stairs to climb down as quietly as a man of his bulk could. His mail jingled cacophonously in his ears.

He went to the table and peered into the bottles. There were six of them, of various sizes and shapes, and they all held varying amounts of black liquid. But Brannok could detect nothing remarkable about any of them. He shied away to one side and avoided his spectral god who moved once more to the table and stand and examined the bottles.

"*Blind, I am blind.*" The creature's horrid voice scratched the words on the inside of Brannok's skull. "*I must talk to Valafar. What does he know? Blind . . .*" Its whisperings faded as it swept from the room.

Noises from beyond the lightless doorway indicated that Angrim's search continued inside. With a deep breath and his hand on his sword hilt, Brannok entered.

His fitful torch revealed a small square room, filth strewn in piles all about. The stench and the cold were hellish, but fear kept him from dwelling on them. A bony arm that ended in skeletal fingers extended from one of the piles, and opposite that, a small round mirror adorned one wall. Two open doorways led into black.

Brannok's need for answers competed with his desire not to be noticed by the creature, but if he turned and left, what would this trip have been for?

"Angrim," Brannok said as the monster blew into the room and stood in front of the mirror. Its head swayed side to side as if it searched for something in the corroded silver plate. "Soul of Tyrrane. Your king—your *emperor*—requires answers of you."

Angrim muttered and swirled past Brannok into the round outer room. Brannok crept to the doorway Angrim had just exited from and peered within. This room was huge, at least sixty by eighty feet, with a high vaulted ceiling. Skeletons of every size and description, from rats to humans to beasts much too large to have been brought here through the corridors above, filled the majority of the room, their meat rotted on the bone.

Had any living man ever witnessed this place before?

Brannok jumped aside as Angrim swept past and moved to a small pool of fetid water amongst the bones. The hooded form gazed into it, murmured and stroked the water until it looked up and came back for the doorway. In the light of his torch, Brannok could just see a chin and a bit of mouth from underneath Angrim's hood.

Even that much he found horrifying.

The need to leave this place screamed within Brannok, triggering his default fear response: anger. He stepped into the doorway directly in front of Angrim and shouted, "Attend me, beast!" As he did, he punched the figure in the midsection which shattered his hand and knocked Angrim to the floor.

Pain exploded in Brannok's broken hand and dashed cold water on his temper. Angrim stood, and the emperor knew he had breathed his last.

Hood fallen off his head, Angrim looked at Tyrrane's supine ruler. Brannok, unable to move or even breathe, held the monster's gaze. The creature's face was beautiful and despairing.

Angrim's features could only have been sculpted by the gods, and inside Brannok's soul, he cried out in thanks that he might have lived to see such a thing before his life was snuffed out. Foul-smelling tears ran down Angrim's ideal cheeks, and every flawless curve bespoke wretched suffering.

With his other hand, Brannok reached forward and touched the face of perfection. The skin felt cold and unclean beneath his hand, like some rotting disease that left the surface unblemished but tainted everything it touched.

And that, too, was perfect.

"*I cannot see*," Angrim hissed the words and grasped Brannok by the upper arms, lifting him from the floor. "*The future is—gone.*"

"I don't understand." The pain from Brannok's broken hand pushed all other thoughts out of his head. "You are looking right at me."

With a cry, Angrim threw the burly emperor into a wall. The creature ran after Brannok, who lay dazed on the floor. It grabbed him up by the collar and shouted, "*There* is *no more future. It is severed. Gone. Destiny is* lost."

Brannok said nothing, hoping that if he remained silent, Angrim might forget about him and drop him again. It was not, he reflected, his proudest moment. Horrified, he realized that his body was aroused. What was happening to him?

"*This is High Magic.*" Angrim cast his gaze, terrible to behold in both its anger and its fear, up into the black stone. "*Such power has not moved across the face of Andos since—no. No, that is not possible. This must be the effect of events so momentous that history has no mark for them. Events so important the glare of them blinds our Sight.*" Angrim walked in circles as he spoke and gestured wildly while Brannok flopped about in his fist like a child's doll.

"*Yes, that must be the answer.*" Angrim dropped Brannok to the floor. He landed on his hand and bit cruelly into the side of his cheek to keep from crying out. Instead, Brannok lay still, just another pile of trash in the lair of the beast.

"*We must proceed with caution. Valafar may know something. I must talk to him.*" Angrim resumed his earlier wanderings from bottles, to mirror, to pool, and back again to the bottles. Brannok crawled toward the steps out of the pit any time Angrim wasn't in the room and lay as a corpse when he was.

He had entered the lair of a monster with the intent of taking control of himself, his war, and his home. Failing that, he would put it to the sword or die in the attempt. For the future of Tyrrane and for Jasmayre. But once his eyes beheld the face of his god, beheld the truth there, all he could manage was to crawl away, his courage as shattered as the bones of his broken fist.

Brannok's good hand closed on the biting chill of the stair's rail, and he froze in terror when Angrim's claws-on-bones voice sounded just behind him, cold polluted breath on his ear.

"*The button brings ruin to Tyrrane. Find the button and smash it. Kill it, burn it, and mix salt into the ashes. It is death to us all.*" At this, Angrim spun and swept away, his misery a wailing cloud floating behind him.

"*Button, button . . . Who is the button?*"

29

LIVING UNDER BIRDS,
AND ALL THAT ENTAILS

BRANNOK

Brannok cursed as he strode the low halls of the citadel and held his broken hand in his good one. He would have his surgeons tend to it presently, but first he had some orvens of his own to put on the wing. He swayed sideways to rest his shoulder against the wall. The pain threatened to block out everything else. If Jasmayre were in the castle, she could have handled this next task for him.

He hoped the orven keepers would be able to help.

After all, Brannok couldn't allow this moment to pass. With or without the demon, he would take control of his empire himself as an actual emperor would.

And every time he stopped, that face loomed up in his mind, a dark-winged eagle scattering his thoughts like so many crows.

He stumbled onto the wide flat roof of the citadel and spied the Soaring Pikes, the home of the imperial orvens and their keepers. The black stone tower had been added generations ago to the citadel rooftop by some previous king of Tyrrane. On the southeast corner of the massive castle, the squat tower looked out over the city of Dismon and, just beyond it, to the meeting of the mighty Blackwood River and the smaller Bitterwater. To either side of the door, individual guardhouses stood and sheltered the man inside from the freezing wind.

As he entered the Pikes, Brannok stepped into a round room that accounted for the entire first floor of the tower. Three men stood, conversed by a fireplace, and ignored the constant shouting above them. They dressed in long white robes, and while two of them were quite young, the third was gray haired and held wisdom in his eyes. This one also wore a brown woolen overcoat that reached his ankles. As one, the three men saw the face of their visitor and fell to their knees.

Brannok took in the room around him. Unlike the rest of the citadel, the Soaring Pikes had warmth, even coziness. Probably because it had been constructed by people who were otherwise forced to reside in the fortress below them. Jasmayre had liked the place as a child.

After the bitter chill of the roof, the heat set his hand to throbbing again.

The interior walls were coated in plaster, and the fireplace and lamps created more than enough light to read and write messages by. Several tables and numerous chairs filled the floor, and bookcases against the walls held books, yes, but also stacks of yellow writing paper, pens and ink, and recorded volumes of previously sent messages. It was this last that necessitated keeping the Pikes under constant guard.

"Why do they shout so?" Emperor Brannok asked the three orven keepers. The din of the birds, who screeched at each other in the chamber above in their squawking voices, would have driven him mad.

The eldest keeper looked up and said, "To be heard, Lord Emperor. They have our speech but not our intelligence. They do not understand the value of a quiet moment."

Brannok tried to remember the last time he had enjoyed a quiet moment, but the effort broke his concentration on his task, and that let the pain from his hand slide in. He grimaced and slipped sideways into a chair.

That face . . .

"Lord Emperor." The gray-haired old keeper rose to his feet. "You are injured. Bendle, go fetch a surgeon immediately. Hax, alert the guards."

"Both of you leave here," Brannok commanded, "but do not bring the surgeon nor alert anyone. Go."

Bendle and Hax looked fearfully over their shoulders at their master and exited the Pikes.

The elder keeper walked to Brannok's side and placed a weathered hand on the emperor's large shoulder. He smiled.

"You really ought to have that hand looked at." The creases and lines of his aged face showed equal parts warmth and concern. "It looks like a horse stepped on it."

"Feels like it too." Brannok sighed and sat up straighter in the wooden chair. Firelight played with his face. It stole away some of the years and worry but left the pain. "I wish one had."

The keeper pulled another chair from the side of the table and sat in it. He waited, without speaking, for Brannok to continue.

Instead, the emperor eyed the old keeper. He looked for something in his face—maybe his posture. A hint of subterfuge. Ulterior motive.

Not finding it, he returned a bleak smile of his own.

"I punched Angrim," Brannok said. At the keeper's look of alarm, he continued, "I don't think he noticed, and I doubt he'll be after me about it." Brannok's gaze picked slowly over a bookcase in the far corner of the room. On the next to top shelf, flanked by a pair of candles, sat a statuette of twirling black iron trailing metal ribbons like razor-sharp streamers of smoke.

Panic gripped him.

"Don't worry about that," the keeper said, a wry grin on his face. "It's not consecrated. I replaced the real one with that rubbish decades ago. I just leave it there to keep the apprentices honest."

Brannok laughed, the sound peculiar in his own ears. He was coming to understand where Jasmayre had gotten her sense of impiety. Cantil, too.

"So how is it that you engage in fisticuffs with the Soul of Tyrrane and yet I speak with you here, now, instead of with some page come to tell me about my nephew's recent and gruesome death?"

Brannok's lips stretched back across his teeth somewhere between a grin and a grimace, and he shook his head. "Angrim has taken leave of his senses, Uncle Moli. He spoke to me, but it was as if he could not see me."

"Really." Moli leaned back in his chair and crossed his legs. He rubbed one finger against his cheek.

In that movement, Brannok saw reflected his son Tobin, who had been murdered by Greenshade's pretender king, as had Despin. Tobin always enjoyed his granduncle's company. It was as if all his family were reflected in the old man.

Except for Junior. That one was in every respect Brannok.

Moli met his nephew's look. "Does anyone else know?"

"We have to assume Valafar knows, though I cannot imagine him having told anyone else."

"No," answered Moli. "That could weaken his position here. The people worship the Anger, not the Anger's understudy. And that means you have something worth holding over the old bastard's head."

"Then that is how I will get Junior's army moving south again," Brannok said with a fierce growl. His hand throbbed, but the realization that he was about to outflank Valafar made the pain suddenly worth it. "By threatening to expose Angrim's vulnerability and undermine Valafar's place here, I can make him do as I wish. And as I wish includes letting Junior chop the widow from crown to twat so he can take the throne of Greenshade—and burn the blasted place to the ground."

"Which boy will you replace him with? After he burns it down. Cantil or Jason?"

This was why Brannok came up here in times of trouble. Most of the world thought Moli dead, as were both of the man's brothers. But Brannok knew the old bird was not only very much alive, but he was as canny as they came and had a habit of seeing straight through to the crux of any problem.

"Depends on how Cantil does in the Paras Plains against Ivarr," Brannok said. Jason was the more dependable son, but Cantil was undoubtedly more competent. Junior's uncrowning would be softened by placing the savage prince at the head of yet another army and pointing him at the west coast. No land from Norrik to Arlea would be safe.

No matter how absurd the notion, he simply could not help thinking that his *true* heir was in Norrik right now negotiating for an alliance with Tove the Mountain, Queen of the Grendals. Somehow, he knew she would succeed, though how much it would help with the *rest* of Norrik falling apart around her ears was anyone's guess.

It truly was not fair.

Moli stood and went to the bookcase that held the paper and ink and returned to the table with them. "Let's prepare your responses."

Brannok's hand had purpled in the last hour, and the swelling pushed against the skin. The ghastly sausage of blood and shattered bone hung from the end of his arm and tormented him. The pain was intolerable, and Brannok pulled his breath in shallow gasps. He would have to hurry on this.

The face looked at him—into him.

"Quickly." Moli sensed his nephew's distress. "You're going into shock, and we don't want to lose our window to your convalescence."

"Send birds to all five kings in Norrik and Wagnersen in Mirrik. Tell them their choices are these: They may put aside their differences and join the Second Tyrranean Empire of their own accord, or I will burn their lands to ash and gift it to the bonewheels. Be fair with Queen Tove. Jasmayre is with her in her court."

Moli scratched the message onto the yellow paper, pausing when he finished. "Shall I add troop numbers for them to send and a date by which to send them? Best not to leave anything open to interpretation."

Sweat broke out on Brannok's forehead, and he nodded.

"To Prince Brannok, say that he is to ignore any further messages from Angrim to Valafar and is to proceed as I have ordered. Tell him that I have commanded that he verify this order with Valafar himself."

At this, Moli's eyebrow went up. "That is quite brilliant, nephew. By so saying, you convey to Valafar that you are aware of Angrim's predicament, while at the same time keeping it from your son. Your father would have been proud."

"I doubt that." The set of Brannok's mouth was that of a man eating salted lemons, though even he was unsure if it were the thought of his own father or the screaming pain in his hand that caused it. They were much the same.

"Tell the boy to march on the Barons' Conclave," he continued, "and run them toward Treaty Hill. When he gets there, he can break their backs over the widow's forces."

A dark thought slid into the back of Brannok's brain. This empire. Dominating all of Andos. To make such a mark on the world as could never be forgotten. Was this his dream, or had it been Angrim's?

Why was he doing this? And did it even matter anymore?

Would this make his children's lives better or provide the whole of Andos to them as enemies?

That face, so close.

The old keeper finished writing and looked up. The orvens above continued their shouting matches with one another, but now Brannok viewed it less as nuisance and more as cover. Nothing he said to his uncle could possibly be overheard.

Orvens were related to crows but dark brown instead of black, with a deep orange breast and the black eyes, beak, and legs of their brethren. They were even more intelligent, however, and could understand—and speak— quite a bit of human speech. While for the most part that speech was confined to yelling at food, about food, or demands for sex.

Breeding season at the Soaring Pikes was a source of surprising and often amusing vulgarity.

The birds also had a particular talent for memorizing short passages and carrying them to their destinations. With a passphrase, the memorized communications were far more secure than written messages, as orvens were famous for carrying their reports to their graves should they be captured.

"Thank you for your assistance, Uncle." Brannok's face shone pale and slick.

"You are always welcome, Nephew. Now allow me to help you to the guards, and we can send Bendle for the surgeon before you make your eldest son an emperor for real."

Brannok grinned and only grit his teeth a little at the thought of handing that malicious thug the keys to the kingdom over such a simple thing as a broken hand. Junior was his favorite, but he did not deserve to rule. That was for her.

No, that was not right.

"Uncle," Brannok asked as they reached the door, "why didn't you press your own claim for the crown when my father was murdered? Surely you know you could have had it if you'd wanted it." The emperor asked his uncle this question every time he saw him, though the old keeper always refused him an answer. This time, however, he surprised Brannok with a reply.

"Because it wouldn't have made me happy, lad," he said, looking wistful.

The smile faded from Brannok's face as he realized just how wise the old man truly was.

30

SEX ON THE SECOND DATE
KEANE

The biggest land mass in the Paradisal archipelago, Storm Flower Island, stretched out its arms in a huge semicircle to form the caldera of an enormous—and extinct—volcano. Exposed to the ocean from the southeast, the resultant bay opened into a peaceful and permanently tropical paradise, sheltered from storms and remote from both Andosh and Darrish peoples.

Which made it the perfect spot for a mostly Pavinn pirate city. Port Placid clung to the gentle inside slope of Storm Flower's caldera, a colorful cluster of painted barnacles just out of reach of the ocean. The wooden buildings gripped the angled ground, some large, some tiny, and some built on top of others and connected by woven bridges. Once garishly tinted whitewash covered all of them, now muted by the sun into a field of pleasant pastels.

At the top of the city, the palace stared sternly out over the taverns, brothels, and shanties of Port Placid, as well as the vessel-choked dockways and glimmering bay beyond. One of the very few sandstone buildings here, the palace was wide, square, and boasted a series of rounded crenellations around the roofline. It did not match any of the other construction in the city, save the odd inn or boucan house. But it was the biggest, and it was at the top, so it was the palace.

The Free Hand were led into the palace by a laughing and cantankerous bunch of half-drunk pirates who carried well-worn and cared-for blades at their hips. Keane was familiar enough with the look of a professional killer not to give them any excuses. He wasn't here to fight in any case.

The pirates brought the group into an open courtyard filled with flowers, brightly colored birds, and banana trees. The courtyard was small enough to be intimate and big enough to hide plenty of combatants, should someone feel the need. Windows opened into individual palace rooms in the walls. At the center of their blank regard was a round clear space with sandstone benches. To Keane it felt like the bullseye of a carefully planted and manicured archery target. The thought made him smile and squeeze Megan's hand.

She looked up at him and smiled back. His queen had changed since he'd met her, in ways delightful and intimidating. While she'd always been strong-willed, the tests of the last six months tempered her. Left her harder and stronger, though still soft and feminine. This was a riddle to Keane that he was delighted to spend the rest of his life puzzling out. She fought, and she loved more fiercely than ever.

The child that grew inside her cemented the two of them together in a way he had never understood before. Being honest, he still did not understand. But understanding was not required.

Only being there for her. Beside her. Forever.

"Wait here," said one of the pirates, a lean-limbed brown-skinned man with rangy muscles and an ugly scar that ran down from his neck to beneath his ratty vest. He wore no shirt, as was common here. "If'n the Daughters want t'be seein' ye, they'll come presently."

"An' if they don't?" asked Eli. His voice sounded pleasant enough, but Keane knew the old man. He'd as soon gut this bunch and run as say hello.

"Depends." The pirate hung back as his friends wandered away. "Any of you worth any ransom?"

No one answered, and the pirate sucked his teeth, shrugged and left, closing the door behind himself.

"Oh, Eli, look at the birds." Loffa made cooing noises as she danced toward wooden cages at the far side of the yard. "They're delightful, don't you think?"

The old mercenary went to her side to ogle the twittering birds with the queen mother, a most un-murderous expression on his face.

Megan slid her hand up to squeeze Keane by the forearm, forestalling any commentary from him.

"Who are the Daughters?" Mahu asked Harden. His wide, serious face betrayed a hint of real concern, and his short, thickly muscled body was tense as a compressed spring. His head swiveled as he tried to see all the windows surrounding the small courtyard at once.

The Darrish fighter made Keane nervous.

"We are happy to follow your lead, Marshal Harden." Sabni stepped up and put a long arm around his partner Mahu. "But as Mother Love teaches us in the tale of *Nephret and the Widow*, 'Open your eyes and you will not only witness wonders, you will also not trip on the stairs.'" He smiled. "We wish only to know the plan, sir, and our part in it. We have been respectful to this point, but it is time."

Harden fidgeted and looked uncomfortable. His gaze flicked down to the doll in his hand, then up at his companions.

"Hey, don't look at me," Raven said. "I don't give a shit. Everyone's got baggage."

"Hush now," Morholt told his sister. "I'd like to know Harden's dirty little secrets."

That was one candy box of cat turds Keane had zero interest in opening. He suspected even Morholt might get more than he was bargaining for with Harden's secrets.

At that moment the doors on the opposite side of the courtyard opened, and a man and woman walked out. The man looked every inch a pirate king. He wore a fitted leather vest and pants, a blousy white shirt, and numerous gold chains, bracelets, and earrings. His bald head shone in the noonday sun, and his scruffy white beard jutted out over an especially insolent jawline. Bright blue eyes regarded them all with a twinkle.

"Halloo, ye bastards," stated the pirate. "Who the fuck are ye?"

Harden bowed, followed by Mahu and Sabni, as well as Keane and Megan. Eli and Loffa remained at the bird cages, and Morholt and Raven stood to one side and practiced looking sardonic.

Keane felt a stab of panic. Harden was supposed to know these people.

"My name is Harden Grayspring, and I am the leader of this band of free men. I am escorting—"

"Orri," said the woman beside the old pirate king, "you know Harden."

"I do?"

"You have told me stories about drinking with him."

Keane thought perhaps he recognized the woman. Maybe. He'd never been to the Paradisals before. Maybe they'd met somewhere else? She looked barely thirty with curly sun-bleached hair, tanned Pavinn skin, and freckled cheeks. Her formal looking blue-gray robes were tailored into a long coat with black leather trim and big brass buttons.

She put her hands on her hips. "Are you going to tell me after all this time and all those tales that you don't remember the face of my father?"

Keane gasped aloud, and Megan gripped his fingers until it hurt. All eyes snapped to the woman's face, even Loffa's.

"Well now," she said with an eerily familiar lupine grin, "that seems to have gotten everyone's attention."

She crossed to Harden, who stood rigid, and gathered him in a wild hug. He sniffled and held her back.

"Bennah." Harden choked on the name.

"Can't believe I fergot me own pappy-in-law," Orri said.

More women dressed similarly to Bennah filed into the courtyard. They were mostly Pavinn women, but there were a few paler Andosh and several darker Darrish. All were younger than Bennah, and all had curly hair.

"It is difficult to imagine you forgetting him, you old drunk," said one of the girls, a grinning redhead with a round face and a huge thick-lipped smile. "Especially since he's the only one who lived."

"Harden!" shouted Orri. "O'course I remember ye, lad. The boy onna beach. O'course." At that the pirate king hopped down from the steps, crossed to Harden, and slapped him on the back.

Keane's mouth hung open. It was no great thing for a mercenary to have a few fatherless children scattered about the Thirteen King-doms, but this one appeared to be *royalty*.

Megan reached out and tapped the redheaded girl on the arm.

"Excuse me," Megan said as the girl turned and directed her smile at the queen, "I don't mean to be impolite, but I feel as if I've just been dropped into a dream. Can you explain to me what is going on here?"

The young woman laughed. "I'd be delighted to help you, Your Grace." At Megan and Keane's startled looks, she laughed again and swept her arm, indicating the other girls in blue gray. "It's hard to keep secrets from a coven of witches."

"Of course." Megan's face lit up with recognition. One hand absently covered the small swell of her belly. "You're the Daughters' Coven. I just didn't realize you were a *real* coven."

"That's all right," the girl said with a grin. "We're also real daugh-ters, and Bennah is our *waywoman*. Our leader. I'm Ameli, by the way, and you were asking about how Harden fits into all of this?"

Megan nodded.

"The Deep Witch lives beneath the waves of the archipelago, granting favors to sailors brave enough to pay her price."

Megan looked at Keane, who shrugged. This was pirate lore, and he was strictly a land-type mercenary.

"The price is always the same; give a daughter to the Deep Witch to help rule over her people. We are the Daughters' Coven and every one of us is a child of the Deep Witch. The eldest of us marries the pirate king and rules at his side. Harden Grayspring is the only one of our fathers ever to survive the price for his wish."

"I wonder what he wished for," Megan whispered.

"Great Oldam love a badger hole, she fucks them to death?"

Keane asked. Several of the surrounding daughters, listening in, laughed at this. "What kind of wish is worth that?"

"Oh, you know," Ameli answered, canting her head to one side, "heal my plague-stricken wife, gold for my poor kids, sink the ship of my enemy. Typical pirate stuff." Her head popped upright and she tried to assume a more serious expression. "I think being willing to die for a wish kinda weeds out the people who might wish for something really good or clever."

In the middle of the courtyard, Harden presented the stolen doll to Bennah.

"I know it isn't much . . ." Harden trailed off. "I just—I'm not the kind of daddy a little girl dreams about. I've never been here, and now that I am, it's just because I need something. But I've never forgotten about you, girl. And I always wanted to be—"

Bennah threw a lightning punch at Harden's mouth that snapped his head back and up again. She showed him his own wolfish grin once more.

A laugh broke free from Keane. He tried to stifle it but not hard.

"Feel better now?" she asked.

"Yeah." Harden spat blood into a bush. "I kinda do. Thanks." He shook his head. "Nice punch."

Bennah shrugged. "Grow up with pirates, you learn how to fight. So what is it you're here for?" As she asked the question, she turned to look at the others around the courtyard. Keane noticed that Morholt was nowhere in evidence. Even Raven seemed concerned, craning her neck as she searched about for him.

Ameli pushed on Keane. "She already knows why you're here." She shoved Keane to the middle of the courtyard, toward Harden, Bennah, and the pirate king. "But it's your request. It's formal. It has to come from you."

"Oh." Of *course* it did. Keane stepped forward to Bennah. He looked into her knowing light-brown eyes, so much like her father's. "I have come to request the aid of the pirate navy of the Paradisal Islands, to combat and repel the Oulani navy which seeks to cut off Greenshade from the Beacon Sea, and to help me retake the Forest

Castle from the usurper widow, *Queen* Hulda Hubrane. We will not fight alone but will have the strong arm of the Barons' Conclave at our side.

"With your help," he continued, "we will fuck Hulda Hubrane right in the—"

Megan cleared her throat, and Keane looked over at her, confused. Her drawn brows and downturned mouth told him everything he needed to know.

"Ah, excuse me. That is, with your help, we will defeat Hulda soundly with minimal loss of life. Without your help, we are doomed."

"How many?" asked Bennah.

Keane winced and looked away. This was the sticking point. He knew from general briefings that the entire Oulani mobile army could all be on those ships. What he did not know was how many more Coldspiners would be with them.

"Enough to crush what's left of Greenshade if they're allowed to make it," Keane said. "At least twenty thousand, more if Coldspine joins them."

"Hee, hee," said Orri. "This sounds like a real scrap."

"Orri Stoneprow," said Bennah. "Can you at least wait until the decision is given?"

Sarah told Keane about an Orri Stoneprow a few years ago. Orri was a raider from Norrik who somehow became governor of Port Placid and beat the old competing pirate lords into line with his bare fists. There would be no kingdom here to ask aid of without him. But that man would be ninety, at least. This Orri looked barely sixty, and a spry sixty at that. This must have been that man's son—although these islands obviously contained some deep mysteries.

With a sidelong look at her husband, Bennah continued, "King Keane of Greenshade, you ask for our blood and sacrifice. Our treaty with your nation obliges us to no such actions. We're compelled only to avoid taking Greenshade cargoes whenever possible, which we've always done."

"Are you telling us no, Bennah of the Daughters' Coven?" Megan asked.

"We're unwilling to commit our men to the retaking of the Forest Castle," Bennah said. "While I wish it weren't so, our fighters aren't infantrymen and lack the organization and discipline to do anything other than die in a massive land battle."

Keane felt gut punched. They had come *so* far for a no.

"This is disappointing," Megan said. "Is there nothing at all you would be willing to do to aid us?"

Bennah looked tense. She glanced around at her sisters who, one by one, nodded back at her. The last glance was for Orri, who merely stood and grinned at her.

"I'm up fer it," he said.

"The possibility exists that we may be able to remove the threat of the Oulani navy," Bennah said to Megan and Keane, "and give you all safe transport to Fish Hill. You need to be aware that such a gift is not lightly given and can only be provided with the Deep Witch's aid and consent."

A glimmer of hope preceded the sinking feeling in the pit of Keane's stomach. The Deep Witch only asked for one thing. Ameli had only just finished telling them.

"Do you agree to her price?"

Keane and Megan looked at one another. He wouldn't let the tears out in front of her, even though he was terrified.

A lesser woman would have said no. A lesser woman would have cried and wheedled and tried to bargain, but that was not the woman he married. Her first and foremost obligation, before Keane's life and before even her own, was to the people of Greenshade. It always had been, and Keane knew that walking in the door. If she had to rule alone, if she had to raise their child without a father, that was a sacrifice she would make.

Keane would not. Not by a long shot. Not for Greenshade anyway. But for Megan?

Anything.

But really, fucking a witch couldn't be all that deadly. He needed to look at this logically. Sarah could be intimidating, but under all the armor and strength, she was just as much a woman as anyone else. Keane was willing to bet that this Deep Witch was the same.

Harden survived it.

Everything said, he wasn't afraid. He just had to answer the question in the next two seconds before he had time to think rationally.

Maybe he would cry and wheedle and bargain later.

"I agree." Job done.

Fuck me.

31

PLEASE REMOVE YOUR CLOTHES AND GET READY TO DIE

KEANE

The twenty or so members of the Daughters' Coven clapped and smiled, nodding and laughing to each other. They would have a new sister soon.

Bennah was more reserved.

"That's wonderful." Ameli took Keane's hand. "Say goodbye to everyone, and we'll take you to Quiet Beach. There's no real ceremony or anything. You can just take off your clothes, and the Deep Witch will come take you to the bottom of the ocean and have sex with you until you drown."

"Wait, what?" Keane said. "The bottom of the ocean? Nobody said anything about the bottom of the ocean."

Megan threw her arms around Keane, holding him tight. Tears poured down her cheeks. "There has to be another way. I've changed my mind. We'll find another way to save Greenshade. We've barely had any time together at all. I don't want to raise our child alone. What if I forget your face?"

"Forget me?" Keane said, off-balance and panicky.

"It's been an honor, Your Majesty." Sabni extended a hand to Keane. Behind him, Mahu nodded a silent farewell.

"Hold on, hold on." Harden came forward with his hands raised.

"Let's not make a spectacle. No sense sending a boy to do a man's job. I'll go in the king's place."

"Yes," Megan said, her eyes wide and her voice breaking. "Harden can go. He's done it before. He'll be fine."

Keane had faced death, but he had never agreed to sacrifice himself before. There had not been anything worth the sacrifice anyway except Sarah, and her job was to make sure that such stupidity was not necessary. The near-debilitating relief at Harden's offer surprised him.

Bennah held her doll in one hand, reached out, and took her father's shoulder with the other. "You've already received your gift and have not yet made use of it. Why throw your life away on another?"

"He'll be fine," Megan repeated. "Let him go."

Harden looked sidelong at his daughter. "I'd love to tell you now that we've met that I'm over being a shitty dad. I'll come visit more often, maybe even move here, and start up a business. But we both know it'd be a lie. I'll take another go at your mom. Maybe save some lives and whatnot. What's the saying here in the islands?"

"A dagger a drink." Eli raised his flask from the far side of the courtyard.

"That's the one. A dagger a drink. When something is worth more than your life. Besides, I survived once. I reckon I can do it again."

Through his relief, Keane considered Harden's proposal. The two of them had been getting along better, true, but that did not seem like a good enough reason for the man to volunteer his life in Keane's stead. The only thing that made any sense was—Oldam's abandoned stone daughter.

This explained *everything*. Harden actually felt *guilt*.

Since Keane and Sarah joined Wallace's Company all those years ago, Harden had acted like a sort of really shitty overprotective father toward her. But it wasn't *about* Sarah; it was about Bennah. It was about his feelings of shame for having left his daughter here to be raised by pirates without knowing her true father. And now that he had the opportunity to be all noble and crap in front of her, he was going to show her that he was not the terrible person everyone assumed he was.

For an instant, Keane almost said something. He almost told Harden that staying alive and actually *being* there for his daughter was the better way to be a decent father.

But he didn't.

He wanted to be there for his own wife and child.

As if listening to Keane's thoughts, Bennah stared at Harden, then turned away. "The terms are acceptable." She opened the doors to the palace interior. One by one, her sisters entered while she remained with the mercenaries. Orri clapped Harden on the back and followed the women inside.

"Don't look like I'm gettin' lucky t'night," Orri said to the mercenary as Bennah, who remained in the courtyard, closed the doors behind him. Through the door he yelled, "But you will, ye poor bastard."

32

DO IT TO ME ONE MORE TIME
KEANE

The members of the Free Hand stared in silence at Harden. Eli just frowned at the flask in his hand.

"That was stupid," Keane said to the graying mercenary, "but I appreciate it."

"You know I didn't do it for you," Harden replied. "I made a promise to myself. That's all. It isn't for any to hear."

"I know." Keane put a hand on Harden's gray-coated shoulder.

Bennah and the mercenaries stood in silence for a moment. Orri Stoneprow and the Daughters' departure stole all the energy from the beautiful little courtyard.

"Piss on that." Harden stormed up to Eli and snatched the flask from him. "I haven't had a good morning if I haven't broken thirty promises by lunch." He downed the contents of the flask, handed it back to Eli, and slapped his second on the chest with the back of his hand. He crossed the courtyard to the steps where Bennah stood. "Truth is, I just want to be the only man in the history of bugger all to fuck her twice."

Harden stood in front of his daughter and waited to be let into the palace.

She leaned sideways and spoke directly to Eli. "See to it that should my father survive a second time, he comes to the islands to visit his daughter more than once every twenty-eight years."

"Don't know why you think I got any pull." Eli shook his head with a wry smile.

Bennah nodded, put her arm around her father's shoulders, and led him inside.

"Just when you think you've seen everything," Keane said, "the world goes and throws you a three-dicked walrus like that."

Green armor slid out from behind green leaves, and Morholt popped into view. "Sounds uncomfortable for the *girl* walruses."

Keane and Megan both jumped.

"Well, if he doesn't come back, I'm taking over the gang and renaming us the Three-Dicked Walruses in honor of Harden's stupidest decision."

"Just where the arch fuck have you been?" demanded Raven. "I thought you'd been stolen and murdered, and I was about to go all bloody vengeance on these fish-molesting water bandits."

"For me?" Morholt spread his hands. "I was here. I simply thought it best to hide with all the witches about. Witch is just another name for sorceress, and I don't mix well with that type."

"Eli," Megan said, "do you know how it is that Harden survived his first encounter with the Deep Witch? Do you think he can do it again?"

Eli raised an arm filled with hard strength and gristle and scratched the back of his stubbled head. "Last time, they left him onna beach," Eli said. "He were naked an' all that, but no one figgered to check up in his armpits. He snuck a dagger under one arm. So everybody skedaddles an' leaves him there, an' when the Deep Witch shows up to drag him off, he bops her one onna noggin with the butt o' that dagger. Knocks her cold." Eli stuck one thumb behind his sword belt. "Then he just drags her up a bit inna sand, and fucks her onna beach. She don't really have to be inna deep water; she just likes it better." He rubbed his chin. "Can't imagine they'd let him sneak in another dagger though."

Morholt laughed while Mahu shook his head. Keane, on the

other hand, felt a growing sense of unease. Not about Harden's actions on that beach. The Deep Witch was there for sex and another daughter. That was going to happen anyway. While he went about it in the most horrible way possible, Harden had simply been struggling to survive the encounter.

"Dishonorable, but practical," Sabni said. "Much like Harden himself. He is the fox that kills the cow's tick in *The Tale of*"—Sabni read the room—"perhaps later."

"What's wrong?" Megan asked Keane. She stood close, gazing up into his eyes. As always, he felt the heat of her as if she were a fire, and the smell of flowers from her hair filled his nostrils even though it had been more than two months since she had bathed with her scented waters. Just a memory, but the smell was a part of her in his brain.

"I don't think I can hate him anymore," said Keane.

"Harden?"

"Yeah," Keane answered. "I don't like it."

"Why not?" Megan touched Keane on the chest and stroked him there. "You're not a hateful person. Why would you want to hate him?"

"I—" How could he say it? "I guess I always considered that Harden was the man I would have turned into if I had remained a mercenary. As long as he was just the villain—as long as I *hated* him —it was easy to tell myself that I've always made the right choices. Now, seeing him act like some kind of actual human being? I just don't know."

"Fuck that guy." Megan's eyebrows knitted together in mock seriousness.

"What?" Keane couldn't help the grin that took over his face.

"You heard me. Fuck that guy. Look, Harden has only ever been a shit to you your whole life because you were Sarah's friend, and she, apparently, was a stand-in for the daughter he abandoned. Wow." Megan put her other hand over her mouth. "You people are starting to make so much more sense now." She shook her head, brown curls waving, and continued. "See, Harden isn't doing this to be noble. He isn't even doing it to be useful, or heroic, or even practical." Megan grew intense, and Keane could see the pieces swirl in her brain. "It's the same old story as always. He's doing this for Sarah. And it's not even really for her because Sarah just represents his guilt over Bennah."

"I had the same thought. But I like the way you said it better."

"I wonder if he even knows why he's doing it. I wonder if it would have mattered." She moved her hand up to Keane's shoulder. "Imagine how much easier your life would have been if Harden had just visited his own daughter once in a while."

For some reason, the thought made Keane angrier than ever.

33

A ONE-SIDED CONVERSATION

SARAH

After a hasty day of travel away from High King Ivarr and his wild fighters, Magda spent most of the next one teaching Sarah how to cast the spell that would allow her to reach across the miles and communicate with someone she knew well. Unlike the other spells the goddess was teaching her, this one was almost within her grasp, so she learned much of the true workings of it. This meant that it would be safe to cast on her own after a bit more study, which would be handy.

She only almost transformed her skin into frozen dung once.

"I believe you are prepared enough," Magda said. "Picture your subject's face in your thoughts, but concentrate more on his mind. The way he thinks. When you feel ready, cast the spell."

Sarah did as she was bid. She pictured, concentrated, and cast. Unlike the future-sundering spell, this casting offered no resistance. It seemed to want to be cast, though that might have been her own eagerness.

She would have to keep the message short and would be unable to follow up on it afterward. Magda warned her that Angrim would likely realize that a communication was happening and, once he was aware, would be able to listen in. The goddess estimated they would have but a few seconds of safe talking time.

A gray wall greeted Sarah's thoughts, but Magda had prepared her for this. She probed at the wall with her images of Keane and, in a twinkling, was rewarded with his presence. No sight, nor smell, nor sound of him, but she could feel him with her. It was like looking into a tiny portal that existed in her mind, so she was only able to see through it with her own imagination—except that everything was real.

And he was alive.

Grohann watched the one-sided exchange, one craggy brow raised and a half frown over his fangs.

"Keane, this is Sarah," she said into the air. "I'm fine and on my way to attack Dismon. I've got five hundred trolls and a plan." She paused. "Magic, dumbass. We only have a few seconds. Where are you?" Another pause. "Oh, uh, all right. See you there!" She returned to her surroundings, looked at Grohann and Magda, and her crooked half smile shone.

Angrim was going to have to wait. Keane was far more important, and he was going to need her.

"New plans, everyone." Sarah clapped her hands together. "We're headed to Treaty Hill!"

34

GOTTA SEE A MAN
ABOUT A CARRIAGE

KEANE

The streets of Port Placid sang their cacophony to the clear blue sky, loud and boisterous. Crowds tumbled up and down the throughways, a tide of human waves that ebbed and flowed, and all the while tried to sell you something. Color abounded, from the pastel buildings to the overflowing bins of the fruit sellers, bolts of cloth and barrels of bright spices, right down to the clothing of the people in the street. Everything was designed to stimulate as much as possible.

Keane recalled a conversation he and Sarah had once about selling Prince Despin's carriage here in the Paradisals. He wished he had that carriage now. The fancy fucker would command a fair sack of crowns in the pirate markets.

Maybe. Did sea rats even use carriages?

Mahu and Sabni, as well as Morholt and Raven, wandered off into the city in search of drink or other diversion. Probably to discuss what was next for them in the very likely event of Harden's death. The rest decided to see the city, find something to eat, and discuss their own next steps.

Loffa giggled. "Your beard is so scratchy," she said to Eli, who seemed incapable of doing more than stare back at her. He nuzzled her ear which set her off again.

Keane watched them play, a faint smile on his face.

"Over your manly, protective phase?" Megan asked.

"No. I guess I just realized you were right. There's no telling how much longer any of us have, and who the fuck am I to say we don't all deserve a little happiness?"

"What I deserve is a new dress." Megan held out her unraveling skirt. The stomach and the bust had been let out to accommodate Megan's pregnancy with a pale blue fabric that did not match the faded brown garment she wore, making stripes at the sides. "Hello? Keane?"

Keane stared up into the sky and laughed. It was an honest, happy, and relieved sound. "Oldam's granite cock, Sarah! How are we talking?"

He spoke to nothing but blue sky, but Eli and Megan stood suddenly rapt.

"Collecting allies." Keane smiled from ear to ear. "Forget about Dismon and meet me in Treaty Hill. We're taking it back." He shook his head and grinned down at Megan. "Don't ask me how, but I just spoke to Sarah. She's going to meet us in Treaty Hill, and she says she has *trolls*."

"That's the best news we've had inna while." Eli clapped Keane on the shoulder.

Megan sighed, visibly relieved. She had never admitted to being worried for Sarah, but Keane knew she was.

"Sarah?" Loffa asked Megan. "Isn't that your handmaid from back in the castle?" She lifted one of Megan's hands and patted it. "I'm so happy for you that she's well."

"Food." Keane pointed at an open-air restaurant where a tall and very round cook worked at an even bigger and rounder fry pot, making food for the people who sat at the tables behind him. Everything was covered by a roof of thatched fronds supported by skinny poles every ten feet or so. The roof looked as if it might collapse at any moment, but the smell from the fry pot made up Keane's mind that the danger would be worth it.

Keane thought he might never leave when he tasted the food brought to him by a large Pavinn woman who smiled at them with a sort of maternal knowing. Her name, appropriately, was Mama Bou, and she ran the dining room, such as it was, with efficiency and authority. Even the drunkest of pirates gave her a wide berth.

"Travelers' rolls." Keane held up one of the fat fried rolls for inspection. "I'm home." He bit into it and sighed.

Travelers' rolls were ubiquitous throughout the Thirteen Kingdoms, but the manner of their making differed regionally. Here, a heavy starchy plantain bread had been stuffed with smoked pork strips in a sweet and spicy fruit sauce, along with soft tart goat cheese, then fried in pig fat and sprinkled with salt. The results brought tears to the King of Greenshade's eyes.

"Very flavorful," said Loffa, biting off a corner of hers.

Megan was lost for the next several minutes as she wolfed down three of the plump rolls in a row.

"That's gonna be a strong baby," Eli said with a wink, mirroring Keane's own thoughts.

"Yeah." Keane licked his fingers. "Um, I had something I wanted to tell you three."

"Those were amazing," Megan said. "Why don't we have those in the castle?"

"I've been told—repeatedly—that travelers' rolls aren't refined enough for the palates of royalty. You'd think being the goddamn king would be enough to get the food you wanted for dinner." Keane pushed his plate away. "But that wasn't what I wanted to talk about. Megan, Loffa"—he looked at each of the women in turn—"you're gonna stay behind here on the island while Eli and I, and as many of the others who come back, go try to retake our home. I have given this a lot of thought, and I'm afraid my mind is made up."

All three of them began speaking at once, raising Mama Bou's brow and causing several other patrons to turn and see what all the fuss was about.

"I can't lose Eli." Loffa clung to the grizzled old mercenary's arm. "I simply can't."

Keane couldn't help but notice how, over the past couple of months, the pair had begun to look less and less mismatched. Loffa remained half—or less—of Eli's age, and she moved with the grace of a dance-trained swan, but without the glamor of court, she simply looked happy. And Keane had seen a side of Eli recently that he never would have imagined existed before.

"And you shouldn't need to," Keane told the queen mother. "With fast boats and a little luck, I'll bring this old fucker back to you safe and sound."

Loffa looked far from mollified, and Eli spoke up. "Don't matter, far as I see it. Unless Harden comes back, an' that don't look likely, I ain't goin' off with you anyway. An' that's assumin' he wants to go his own self."

"But the conclave," Keane said. "You took their money."

"Did at that. But that money were to find allies here on the island—which we done—an' nothin' more. Nobody said nothin' about attacking no castles."

"The simple fact is, my king"—Megan turned Keane's chin so he faced her with a forefinger—"I *am* going. You do not get a say. I have earned the right, as much as anyone and miles more than most. While it's cute that you think you get to tell me no, I'd really prefer not to have to embarrass you about it."

Keane looked helplessly across the table.

Oldam shit a mud bath.

Clearing his throat, Eli held up a finger. "Let's assume that somehow Harden makes it out of this alive. Don't know how, but the sonuvabitch is a survivor, no doubt about that." He held up a second finger. "Then let's assume that he does want to sail off to Treaty Hill an' attack Hulda. That one's a little easier to believe since he's done already lost his mind, what with volunteerin' to fuck the Deep Witch again. So given alla that, do it sound like the best idea to you to leave your pregnant young wife an' her beautiful, almost-the-same-age mother-in-law here amongst them what count rapin' an' pillagin' as an honest day's work?" Eli dropped his hand to the table. "An' before you go mentionin' that woulda been us a couple years ago, I want you to really settle on *exactly* what that means."

Keane considered Eli's words. While he had been more a fan of the pillaging than the raping, that put him in the minority. The thought of leaving Megan with the men he used to call friends flashed through his mind.

"Nope." Keane stood. "You are right; I was wrong. I take it back. Everyone comes with us. Eli, Loffa, you too. Even if we're just dropping you off somewhere along the way."

"Wonderful." Megan bounced from her seat. "It's settled. Come along, Loffa, let's go find something more appropriate to wear to a naval battle."

Keane grabbed the uneaten roll from Loffa's plate and ran to join the others.

35

THIS ONE HAS CATS

HULDA HUBRANE

Although food continued to be brought and sheets continued to be cleaned, Hulda almost never caught sight of her staff anymore. Her spies told her that the botched assassination attempt in the library had thoroughly disheartened the others, and they now pinned their hopes on someone from Tyrrane doing the job.

It seemed that without their ringleader, they were all out of ideas. She'd have to go down and say hello to Baroness Roselle in the dungeons soon. Very convenient it was to have her right next to Lady Ravenstok.

This led her to thinking of the chancellor Tynos and General Roen had shelved down there. Finnagel. That was his name. He was much further down than the women and happily out of earshot. Hulda visited him once, curious to see what the arrangements actually looked like. She did not return. Some things need only be witnessed once.

At least the chancellor was still alive.

Off and on.

The ancient chamberlain announced himself at the door of her sitting room. He alone did not appear terrified of her and had appeared when her lady's maid from the March Castle vanished. This too was worthy of investigation. The woman—whatever her name was —had been with Hulda over a decade and knew all of Hulda's likes and dislikes. But, as with so much, there simply was not time for it.

She had a lot of preparations to make and a nation to run into the ground.

"Come in, sweetie," she called out to the chamberlain. Hulda was alone in this space of creature comforts. Lace and pillows and girlish trivialities surrounded her. The trappings of her disguise.

The elderly man, now wearing the livery of the Hubranes, brought a pair of letters on a small silver tray. Despite his age and apparent infirmity, that tray was steady as the bedrock the Forest Castle was built into.

She snatched the first letter from the tray and pried the wax seal away. Flipping the page open, she flopped back on the overstuffed sofa and scanned it.

The letter had been transcribed by the castle orven keeper from several birds and sealed with his own wax. The keepers had a rigid code of ethics regarding the privacy of their customers. All the same, it made Hulda itch to think of letting someone else's keeper go and read her messages unmurdered.

"Our dearest friend, Queen Hulda Hubrane, safe reign and good health. Have you found a suitable replacement yet?"

Really?

"The Host hastens on its way to you to destroy your foes and relieve your burdens."

This just won't do.

"Happily, we have encountered no difficulties or adversity along the way. Prince Brannok looks forward to making your acquaintance."

No difficulties. That meant the skirmishers she sent to disrupt the Host's supply lines had not been successful. Probably captured and spilled their guts as to where they had come from, too.

"Well that's too awful to contemplate." Hulda held the letter out to the chamberlain. "Swap me out."

The servant took the letter from Tyrrane and replaced it with the second one.

Hulda stopped when she saw the seal. The letter was from Mirrik, from King Baldrik Wagnersen himself.

Hulda sat up and turned the letter over. Why had her uncle, who had never once written her since marrying her off to the Hubranes, sent her this message? Could he be angry with her? Perhaps he wanted to warn her or advise her of the best manner to defeat Brannok? She had not informed him of her plans; perhaps he had figured them out himself.

Of course, she *could* simply open the damnable thing.

The dark orange seal cracked under Hulda's gentle pressure, and she unfolded the letter.

"*Dearest Niece,*

News has reached me that you intend to stand at odds with the new Tyrranean Empire. I applaud your fervor in assailing our enemy thusly.

While I naturally fear for the blood of my kinswoman . . ."

Her uncle always talked like a king from one of the grand tales. Like King Jokr from *The Second Husband.*

"*While I naturally fear for the blood of my kinswoman, it is your home that I fear will most feel the emperor's wrath. Brannok seeks the strength of Mirrik's strong spears, and when he cannot have them, he will take the wild rage of Norrik in its stead.*

I would have Mirrik stand apart from Brannok's empire and crush Norrik in the teeth of our justice once they have sent their warriors to proclaim allegiance to that quick-tempered fool."

Hulda laughed at this. The teeth of our justice. Please.

"*But the headmen of Mirrik are not so sure. They see one of their own, you, my niece, set openly against Tyrrane and wonder if we should cleave to an ally who would place our true goals on such public display.*

As I hope you see, the only recourse is for us to maintain pretense of, if not friendship, then at least not hostility with the empire, until such time as Brannok drains Norrik of its ability to defend itself. As a result, for the good

of Mirrik and in defiance of my own heart, I must disown you and disavow
you as a daughter of our nation.

With love for your mettle and hope for your audacity,
King Baldrik Wagnersen of Mirrik"

"Huh." Hulda set the letter down in her lap.

She waved the chamberlain off. "You can go, honey."

As he closed the sitting room door behind himself, Hulda considered the letter. Obviously, she was now more set than ever to oppose Tyrrane, at least up to the point where she might be killed for it. But she and Lady Ravenstok had devised a clever way to keep that from happening *and* make an astounding profit at the same time.

Her uncle might be disowning her formally, but he had all but kissed her on the head and patted her on the butt as she left to go and murder some Tyrranean soldiers. It made sense. The more fight the Host encountered in Greenshade, the more troops they would try to pull from Norrik. Mirrik just needed to play it cool until that happened.

A noise from the bedroom door brought her to her feet. The ivory-painted door stood slightly ajar, and she could hear rustling from within.

Rhythmic rustling accompanied by heavy breathing.

Hulda rolled her eyes as she approached the opening, ready to pronounce death on whoever was so inconceivably crass as to use her bed for their fornication. But her indignant anger died in her throat when she caught sight of General Roen atop Tynos, a master farmer working a willing and luxuriant field.

With a soft click, Hulda closed the door. Her feelings were muddled, so she left to check on the preparations for her departure.

The idea was to accumulate as much of Treaty Hill's wealth as could be carted away and leave in secret just before Prince Brannok and the Host arrived. It was not really a complicated idea, but the window for her departure would be narrow. She did not want to leave far enough in advance that anyone would realize she was gone before the battle. Someone might be sent after her. Nor, obviously, did she want to be caught out by the Host.

The King's Swords and her own ducal guard would be left behind to fight and weaken the Ebon Host, and they obviously did not need money for that. She would turn her star toward Mirrik, and its capital city of Knarrax, relying on her criminal contacts in the Hubrane Merchant House along the way. And once there, back in the loving arms of king and country, she would use all of her ill-gotten gains to become the most powerful Mirrikwoman ever.

Queen Maarika was an idiot. Perhaps her uncle would be glad to be rid of her should an accident befall—as was almost certain to happen.

King Wagnersen would look *so* good on her arm. And such children they would have!

~

SEVERAL WAGONS heavily built to haul extreme weight, like gold coins, waited for her in the Thirteen Markets. She and a dozen ducal guard left the castle walls to check on the progress. The day before the Host would appear, the wagons, filled with all the most precious things in the capital city, would ride down to Fish Hill, *not* along the Cattle Streets where they might be spotted, and board a ship bound for the Beacon River and the Western Marches.

According to Hulda's scouts, she needed to leave very soon. The wagons should be almost ready to go.

The Thirteen Markets were ordinarily a bustling center of activity in the Quarters. Shops and restaurants from every corner of Andos operated here, and money and goods changed hands at a bewildering speed. A blustery winter day did little to keep eager shoppers and avaricious merchants apart.

Especially compared to an oncoming army.

Hulda had ordered all the gates closed and the citizens locked within. If there was a great press to escape when she left, all the better, more cover for her.

She spotted the red and green tent that held her wagons and headed that way. As she did, shouts came from the top of the Country

Gate, and soldiers bellowed reports up and down the walls. It only took a moment for Hulda to interpret what they were saying.

The Barons' Conclave was surrounding the city, a full day ahead of the Host. Damn.

Her window had already closed.

"Boys," Hulda said to her little troop of guards, "our market adventure is over. We're going back inside."

An overstuffed chair with painted oranges and leaves on the upholstery rested in the dungeon hallway between Lady Ravenstok's and Baroness Roselle's doors. Hulda sat deep within it, beneath the lamp she'd had installed high on the wall.

"I am accustomed to cutting my losses and running," Hulda said to the bars in Lady Ravenstok's door. "No proper criminal enterprise survives to affluence and fame without that, and the Hubrane Merchant House has more than enough of both." She lifted an arm and let it drop again. "But this is just depressing."

The dungeon corridor had been cleaned and scoured and now smelled more of soured milk and urine than the horrifying stink it previously possessed.

"If you want to escape, you're going to have to dye your hair." Lady Ravenstok's voice took on a motherly tone. "It's too distinctive. Especially in a woman as young as you are. And no, a hat isn't going to work."

Hulda, about to interrupt, closed her mouth.

"If you surrendered to the barons and let them in the walls, they might very well allow you to flee," Roselle added from behind her own little barred window. "Wouldn't that aid your plans of battering the Host as much as possible?"

"It would," Hulda admitted. "But I can't be certain they'd let me go. And, even if the Host took all of Greenshade without a fight, they'd still need all the forces they could spare to keep it. Letting the barons in is a risk I don't need to take."

Lady Ravenstok's shadow moved behind the bars. "I trust you still have confederates in the Harrows who would hide you until you could get out of Treaty Hill?"

"Yes." Hulda thought of a few nefarious men on her payroll. "You didn't kill all of them. I'd still have to get past the walls though."

"If there are any walls left by then," Lady Ravenstok said. "It's too bad the Barons' Conclave wants you dead. Otherwise, they'd make fine allies."

Hulda nodded agreement. "Yeah. Too bad."

"I heard that you summoned Prince Reid back from March Castle," Lady Ravenstok said.

"How do you hear anything down here?" Hulda looked left and right. There was no one other than her guard, who stood a discreet distance up the hall.

"That would have been me," the baroness said.

"Sorry, sweetie." Hulda waved a hand neither of her captives could see. "I should have known that." Baroness Roselle was infamous for her knowledge of goings-on in the castle.

"If I might be so bold," Roselle asked, "why did you kill Branch's son Reid? He was such a dear, sweet boy."

"Reid is dead?" Lady Ravenstok asked.

Although she felt no need to explain herself to these two old hens, Hulda found herself wanting to prolong the contact. Sadly, she realized, these two women she had thrown into the dark were the closest people she had to friends.

"Even if he was too young to be a competent duke like his father," Hulda answered, "Reid would still have been a rallying point in the Western Marches, and the March Castle is at least as powerful as this one, if not more so. Killing the boy just seemed like the right thing to do."

This conversation was leaving Hulda feeling glum.

"How did the child die?" Lady Ravenstok asked.

"The water dragons with his mother," Roselle answered. "They went to see them first thing, when they arrived."

"I'm surprised either of them wanted to see the horrid beasts at all," Lady Ravenstok said.

"They really didn't," Hulda answered. "It wasn't exactly voluntary."

"I'm sorry, Aerith," Baroness Roselle said to Lady Ravenstok. "I didn't want to burden you."

"That's all right," Lady Ravenstok answered. "I've more than enough burdens already. One more won't make much difference. I'd never met the child anyway, though I did respect his father."

Roselle's door creaked as she leaned up against the other side and gave a great sigh. "This is all so horrible. Hulda my dear, how is it you've come to this?"

Feeling the chill, Hulda pulled an ornate pair of red leather gloves off her belt and pushed her fingers into them. "Sold as a child to a distant and wicked man, made a well-to-do merchant house into a thriving criminal enterprise to keep myself entertained, did anything necessary to stay atop it, and then found myself caught by the murder of that same distant and wicked husband into this awful place. Now I just want to go home and run my smuggling empire from afar."

"Won't Brannok want to take that from you, too?" Lady Ravenstok asked. "Or have you grown a penis you've kept hidden from me?"

Hulda gave the door a tight-lipped smile. "One disaster at a time. Though if I *had* grown one, you'd be the first person I'd share it with." She picked up the page in her lap and smiled. "Hey, Aerith, do you want to hear some more of the ways the council came up with to kill you?"

Warm laughter came out of both cells. "Of course. You'd be surprised how little there is to do down here. I'm starting to think of it as a punishment."

"Before we start," Baroness Roselle said, "is there any more wine?"

Hulda got up, filled the two women's cups, and returned to her seat. It made her feel good to do something nice for them. She tried not to think about the fact that she put both of them here to begin with.

"Let's see." Hulda peered over the list. "Here's a good one. Lord

Farwall wants to feed your arms and legs to his dogs and then smother you with the arm-and-leg poop the next day."

"Why do so many of these have to do with excrement?" Baroness Roselle asked.

"It's hardly dignified," Lady Ravenstok observed.

"I guess that's just where everyone's head is at. Here's a better one. Suspended by the feet over a barrel full of . . . no. That's poop again. I think you're right."

"Keep reading until you find one that isn't about me drowning in feces."

Hulda's finger ran down the page. "All right. Here we go. You'll like this one. There's cats. You're tied down to the floor with dozens of hooks through your skin, all attached by strings to the biggest rats that can be found."

"This sounds promising," Lady Ravenstok said.

"You're awful," Baroness Roselle said, chuckling.

"Then twice as many feral cats as there are rats are thrown in to chase the rats and fight over the dead ones. You get torn up by hooks and either bleed out or are eaten by cats. I'm not sure which." Hulda whistled. "Sweetie, this boy does not like you."

"Who is it?"

"Guildmaster Sorrent."

"*No!*" Lady Ravenstok exclaimed.

Hulda raised her face toward the bars. "Do you know him?"

"I've *slept* with him," Lady Ravenstok said. "I can't believe he wrote that."

Laughter came from Baroness Roselle's door.

"To be fair," Hulda offered, "I did threaten to cut off a foot of anyone who didn't participate."

"I suppose it's understandable then." Lady Ravenstok let out a sigh of her own from within the dark cell.

"Um, there's something I want to tell you, but I feel a little weird about it." Hulda realized she was nervous. Almost jittery.

"What is it, dear?"

"I've, uh—" The words resisted her desire to speak them. So she pushed and forced them all out in a torrent. "I've really enjoyed having you down here to talk to, and I'm leaving soon, and I'm afraid that if you stay down here, you'll be forgotten or worse; so I'm moving you to the diplomats' cells which are basically fancy hotel rooms you can't leave, and I'm just so appreciative of everything you've shared with me, and I care about what happens to you; so please be safe when I'm gone."

A momentary silence blanketed the hallway as Hulda caught her breath. She only hoped that Aerith understood what she had tried to communicate in all that mishmash.

"Me too?" Baroness Roselle asked.

"*Yes*, you too," Hulda answered.

Lady Ravenstok moved to her door and slipped her fingers around the bars in its window. "Thank *you*, my dear. Now you really must go. Hopefully, the next time we see one another, we'll be trying to murder each other properly over someone else's riches."

Hulda nodded, grinned, and quickly walked back up the hall.

Lady Ravenstok had understood perfectly.

36

THAT'S NOT A GRASSHOPPER

SARAH

You did that wrong," said Magda. "You would have caused a rain of grasshoppers to fall over this entire region."

"Comparatively," Sarah observed, "that one seems pretty mild."

"The grasshoppers would have been seven hundred feet long and exploded on impact," Magda said, a hint of a smile creeping in at the corner of her mouth. "But I can see why you might think them mild in comparison to your previous mistakes."

Sarah, Magda, Grohann, and five hundred thirty-four troll warriors crossed the eastern bend of the Greenshade River two days ago and now crept through Three Sisters Wood, southeast of the town of Fenrath. Advance scouts told them that the western edge of the wood was not far off.

Cassius looked like hell. He continued to lose weight as the trip dragged on, and there was now no distinction between him and Magda when they spoke. It was like the goddess was pushing out everything that had once been Cassius, and no safe reserve of him was left. Everything was them, not him and her. What would that do to Cassius when Magda left him?

Sarah resolved to think of the two entwined beings as the

goddess. It made it easier not to think about what was happening to the disappearing man if she only acknowledged the dominant goddess.

Although Sarah was more than half competent with the spells Magda taught her, she still could not cast any of them all the way through. Even when she did practice a piece of one correctly, the next part would be a horrific botch. The situation frightened her more than a little.

She could only hope that Keane was doing better than she was.

The wood in this area was thick overhead, which meant little undergrowth down where Sarah and her allies moved. Huge oak boles stared at them as they passed, and fallen trees required navigation. Still, the going was steady and smooth and continued to be hastened by whatever subtle magic the goddess possessed.

Close ahead, a female troll warrior stepped out of the perpetual twilight and called to the group.

"Var-chief Finnlaug. You have got scouting reports."

Finnlaug stepped forward. Her greenish matted hair and bound furs rendered her invisible amongst the trees, even at eight feet tall.

"Please tell them to us," Finnlaug commanded the scout.

"The end of Three Sisters is close." The scout's eyes flashed gray as an errant beam of sunlight broke through the canopy above. "Hooman soldiers march south on the other side. Many captives. Heavy vith loot."

"Soldiers?" asked Sarah. "What color do they wear?"

"Gray chests, vith black fists, holding daggers," answered the scout. "Many, many of them."

"The Ebon Host," Sarah said. "They've gotten ahead of us then."

"If they march on Greenshade, there are certainly more of them than we can handle by a long shot," Magda said. "But we can likely slow them down a bit. Give Keane a chance to do whatever it is he has planned before they arrive to bust up the party."

Sarah looked away from Cassius's body, suffering an unexpected stab of guilt. She thought he might be losing his hair.

"I have an idea." A slow grin spread across Grohann's face. "It is good to slow down the Host, yes? Killing lots of the Anger's soldiers, even better."

THE NEXT MORNING, well before the sun rose, the company of trolls advanced to the tree line and watched from behind the brush. The big creatures were quieter than humans despite their size, and they blended into everything.

Not fifty yards distant, the vast expanse of the Ebon Host were rousted from their slumber with loud horn blasts. Sarah took a few experimental tugs on the big hunting bow that High King Ivarr gave her back when she left his hall, well before their most recent and less pleasant encounter.

To either side of her, through the trees, trolls waited with bows eight and nine feet long and as thick as Sarah's wrist.

Far into the middle of the camp, well away from any chance of escape and therefore away from any chance of friendly fire, people with their arms bound behind them sat around a central group of bonfires. There had to be nearly a thousand of them. Given the army's present location and direction, they could only have come from Fenrath.

Sarah and the trolls waited as the Host ate breakfast and began breaking camp.

Magda waited a safer distance into the wood.

The sea of small campfires extended to the limits of her vision north and south and hundreds of yards west. Behind her, Sarah knew the sky would be paling but not enough to help. As the tents fell, Sarah raised her bow.

Her arrow took the first one in the throat, the feathered shaft no more than a sliver of darkness that stretched out its kiss from the black wood. The soldier coughed, made a squeak, and fell.

This was the signal, and the trolls who, along with Sarah, could see much better than the human soldiers in the dark—even without the campfires both blinding the Host and illuminating them like targets—filled the starry morning with huge whirring arrows.

Men fell left and right, a tiny number compared to the whole but continuous and without an obvious enemy to defend against. Finnlaug had instructed the trolls to remain silent, and they did so, firing arrow after arrow into the flat coverless camp. Shields were no protection. The heavy troll projectiles flew with such force that they punched through them and through the man behind as well.

One side of Sarah's mouth quirked up.

As they had known would happen, horn calls rang out, and men organized to respond to the threat. Within minutes, the charge toward the wood sounded, though those minutes had cost the Ebon Host dearly.

The trolls broke rank and fled, half north, half south, in response to the soldiers' charge. Men ran into the trees, some actually running *into* trees, swords flailing, their vision unable to compensate in the gloom.

Sarah, in the twisted arms of a wild great oak, watched over two thousand men enter the wood. Once she was certain that all who would come were among the trees, she sounded her own horn. North and south, trolls quietly returned back the way they had come.

When they reached the Host, the real slaughter started.

In the branches above, Sarah emptied her quiver, then dropped into the middle of the terrified soldiers. Her broadsword spun a circle of death, and she used the one spell she knew well enough to cast on her own to send the enemy flying through the air whenever they got too close. It was the Blow Out the Candle spell Finnagel taught her, but—with just a little adjustment and far away from the debilitating effects of another sorcerer's place of power—it became a hurricane she could direct with a pointed finger.

While the fighting went on in earnest in the wood, Finnlaug led a small team of her most aggressive warriors to liberate the captives. They were a flung brick smashing through a stack of black and gray sugar eggs. The Host flew to pieces, and before the scattered

Tyrraneans could regroup, the trolls *and* the captives were gone, back into the Three Sisters and killing more soldiers there.

In less than an hour, the first skirmish against the Ebon Host was over. The trolls had killed thousands and lost less than twenty of their own. Sarah considered it a spectacular victory.

By the time the fighting was over and the trolls had regrouped, the rest of the Host had moved on.

"They don't even care whether they lost those men or not," Magda said. "That shows admirable resolve, if not humanity."

"You care about humanity now?" Sarah fished through bodies for arrows. Finnlaug had ordered them all into the field to recover what ammunition they could before assigning a small contingent of trolls to escort the beaten and underfed captives east. "I didn't think that was something Cass *or* Magda really had much use for."

"It seems like the combination has awoken some new feelings. Or perhaps other events are to blame. I honestly don't know. This does seem like a sizable waste of human beings though."

"No vorries," Grohann said. "There are lots more. Trolls vill never use up all the humans."

Sarah laughed. "Just this once, Gro, it's all right if we use them up."

"Perhaps," said Magda, "but I'd like to sound a note of caution. You, Sarah, are the only member of this group we cannot afford to lose. Perhaps you should stay further back in the woods and direct the trolls from there."

Sarah furrowed her brow. "You're pushing it a little far, Cass. I don't like it when you act like you care. It's creepy."

"I feel as if I do not have very much longer to be able to care. Maybe I should take advantage of it while I still can."

FURTHER RAIDS WERE HALTED when Magda announced that Angrim's apprentice was personally monitoring the eastern flank. Finnlaug was eager to try her trolls against the sorcerer, but Sarah knew better.

Valafar learned his magics at the foot of a godmonster, and he would be surrounded by wary Host anyway.

They concentrated on running instead.

Even hindered by the trees of the wood, the trolls still moved faster than the Ebon Host. But there were so many of them. Their lines went on out of sight. Even with at least eighty miles of woodland between themselves and Treaty Hill, which force reached there first would be a close thing.

"Hey, Magda." Sarah jogged behind Grohann who held the goddess over a huge shoulder.

"Yes?"

"Remember that thing where you made us go faster? Can you do that now?" She ducked a tree branch that whipped from Grohann's passing at her face.

"I am."

"Oh." Sarah grimaced. Her feet ached like hell. "Well, good. Keep doing that then."

Magda rolled her eyes in a very Cassius-like expression. "I will continue to do my part. Now try the spell again. I am impressed you managed not to kill anyone last time, but turning oak trees into mounds of angry custards is not going to help us defend the Forest Castle from Valafar or his army."

"Treaty Hill is Finnagel's place of power. Won't that dampen or whatever, you know, my sorcery?" They were already getting close enough that her Blow Out the Candle had begun to encounter resistance.

"The spells I am teaching you are far too powerful to be held by the hardening of one grandchild. They do not draw power in the same manner as your innate sorcery. It is more deliberate than that." Magda lifted an eyebrow and bounced along on Grohann's shoulder. "Try it again. Make the trees terrified of you."

Sarah ran through the woods on sore feet and dodged roots while she learned the magic of the gods. As she rounded the first stanza in Metzoferran, the ground beneath her turned to bitter smelling mud and ran in great globs up into the tops of the trees. The trees, now lacking any earth beneath them to support their bulk, fell in a massive cacophony of toots, honks, and chimes.

Miraculously, Grohann leaped ahead and avoided most of the wretched mess, but Sarah fell straight down into the gigantic bowl of foul mud and crashing trees. She was not injured, though she had about a pint of slimy stink-mud up her nose.

Whatever Keane was doing, it had to be better than this.

37

TRANSCENDENCE AND MASS MURDER TASTE GREAT TOGETHER

KEANE

From the main deck, Keane and Eli watched Megan and Loffa up on the ornamentally crafted forecastle of *The Pirate's Wit*, the flagship of the fleet and Orri Stoneprow's personal vessel. Unique among the hundred or so craft in the water sailing hard for Treaty Hill, *The Pirate's Wit* was a true warship, large, fast, and deadly. It held four elevated and crenellated positions from which archers could rain death and fire.

A dozen iron-hinged and sharp-spiked boarding beams stood along the thickly lapped wales. These heavy drop bridges could be cast down onto the decks of another craft to catch the enemy vessel fast and crush its sailors and decking, as well as provide a gangway for armed and bloody-minded boarders.

The ends of the boarding beams had been fashioned into the heads of frightening dragons, and the spikes to grab enemy vessels were long and curved teeth.

Finally, a dozen oversized ballista, ridiculously made to resemble cranes with wings outstretched, were fastened to the decks and fitted with not only the huge bolts common to such weapons but a lethal variety of anti-ship ammunition as well. *The Pirate's Wit* had obviously once been the property of a wealthy and important captain before falling into pirate hands, as every surface was artfully—and wastefully—carved with swooping lines, waves, and decorative animals. Keane, down on the main deck, kept one eye on Megan and Loffa up on the forecastle, even as he thought about the ego of the man who had constructed this floating art museum.

"I do like it," Megan said to Loffa. "But yours is prettier. It's the roses."

Loffa held out her arms and bowed, her silvery pink frock coat reflected the morning sun. Darker roses were stitched into the fabric, the same color as her tricorn hat. With a white ruffled shirt and dusty-rose-colored pants stuffed into knee-high black boots, she looked like an adventurous lady preparing to attend a pirate-themed masquerade. Similarly attired, Queen Megan's color palette trended more conservative, with a dark blue coat and hat and pale-yellow pants. The coat hid her bulge in the middle.

"I'll trade, if you'd like," Loffa said to the shorter queen. "Is there a seamstress aboard to lengthen your pants for me?"

"I rather doubt it." Megan hid her smile. "Besides, yours suits you better." She eyed the wide platform suspended at least twenty feet up the forward mast. There were four-foot crenels to hide behind, and each bore a different kind of carved bird on the front, as well as barrels of arrows bolted to the floor. It would be an excellent place for her to shoot from when the fighting finally started.

Megan reached over her shoulder and ran a hand over Leafy, the bow that Baroness Fenrath had given her.

A magnificent weapon. A terrible name.

"Seriously." Harden walked beside Keane and Eli up the wave-carved steps to the top of the forecastle. "I met him thirty years ago." The moonlike mark of a woman's bite was still fresh on the side of his neck from his experience with the Deep Witch. He had not wanted to explain it, or his survival for that matter, while still on the islands. But now that they were well at sea, Keane intended to find out.

Loffa's face lit up as she ran to Eli, and she flung an arm around him to hold the old mercenary tight.

"Fuck that." Keane topped the stair. He pulled on one of the armguards of his leather armor and shifted it back into place. "He can't be older than Eli."

"Watch yer tongue, lad." Eli slid an arm around Loffa's waist. "Orri Stoneprow's north of ninety an' pushin' twice my age. I just look older 'cause I ain't fuckin' no witches."

"He's right there at the wheel." Harden pointed back to the aft castle where Orri Stoneprow growled orders at the wheelman. "Why don't you go ask him yourself?"

"As long as he can lead his men in battle, I don't care how old he is," said Megan, "or who he takes to his bed."

Keane grinned at Harden. "You might if it were your daughter."

Harden pulled back his dusty long coat and let the sun shine on the fancy gold basket hilt of his cutlass. Keane's grin fell.

"There's no man livin' this side o' hell as adept at leadin' his fellow humans to violence an' mayhem," said Eli. "An' that's a fact." At Harden's sour look, he added, "Present comp'ny excepted, o' course."

"Anyone else think this tub is a bit much?" Harden asked, changing the subject. "Killing folks is one thing, but killing them with a ballista that looks like a bird in a ship that's decorated like some little lord's bedroom is just uncomfortable."

"I guess we can agree on that." Keane's own tastes were plainer, and he wondered how many spears and shields could have been bought with the money spent to carve frolicking horses and dolphins on the inside of the forecastle's crenels.

"Where are the others?" Megan asked. Contrary to Keane's expectations, when Harden elected to follow Keane and Megan to Treaty Hill, the remaining mercenaries stayed on. Back when Harden led Wallace's Company, that kind of move with no sure money at the other end of it, would have resulted in a major walkout—at best.

"Mahu and Sabni left on the *Fat Gull* because it had the widest hull and Mahu is afraid of drowning, apparently," answered Harden, "and Holt and Raven are belowdecks on this boat with us. Holt needs his beauty sleep, I guess."

"All right, Harden," Keane said, "you said you'd tell us as soon as we were comfortably away from Port Placid, and now we are." Harden said nothing, so Keane continued, "Eli told us about the dagger you used the first time you met the Deep Witch, but I also know they checked you a lot more thoroughly this go-round."

Harden winced. He held his face as if he had a mouthful of dirty feet in it.

Keane pressed on. "So, no weapons, yet here you stand. How'd you do it?"

Harden shrugged. "First, I wish to stress to you that this entire navy and the salvation of your nation—should that happen—is owed entirely to my erotic magnificence. It's not that I object to whoring myself out on principle, but this particular adventure carried a significant danger of death, so I expect to see some hazard pay. As to the other matter, I was naked on a beach and . . . I hit her with a rock."

Eli guffawed which set Loffa to laughing. Megan drew her brows together and frowned while Keane smiled. He knew Harden well, and he knew when the evil bastard was lying. Something had gone wrong for him, and he didn't want to admit it. Something that did not go wrong the first time around. Whatever it was, Keane felt certain that the one thing that did *not* happen was Harden knocking the Deep Witch in the head with a rock.

"Has anyone noticed that the sails are blowing the wrong way?" Megan pointed one finger up.

Everyone stopped and held still. The sounds of wind, full sails, and the pirate king berating some poor unfortunate filled the air.

"Sails don't blow." Harden followed the line of Megan's finger. "Wind blows . . . Well, how about that."

Every craft in the fleet crashed through the waves under full sail, yet the wind that filled those sails came from ahead of them rather than behind. The fleet moved fast *against* that wind and pounded broad wakes out of the waves.

"That don't seem right," Eli observed.

"Hello, all." Morholt hopped up the last steps to the forecastle. "I see you've noticed the efforts of the Daughters' Brothel to speed our way. As I understand it, the Deep Bitch is doing basically the same thing to the Oulani fleet but in reverse. We should catch up to them in no time."

"Deep Bitch?" asked Megan. "Isn't that a little beneath you?"

Morholt bent over in a ridiculous approximation of a very fancy bow. "I assure you, Your Grace, nothing is beneath me."

"Had any luck with the imp?" Harden reached up and pulled his gray hat tight down over his skull. The wide leather brim fluttered in the wind.

"She's talking to me again. But she's lost her Sight. Says the future is gone. I have the feeling if she were more than paint on pasteboard, she'd have eaten my nuts and be wearing the end of my dick as a fishing cap. She's pretty pissed."

Keane raised an eyebrow.

"A really *tall* fishing cap," Morholt added.

Megan poked Keane in the ribs. "He's dirtier than you."

"It's not a contest," Keane said, irritated. "Do you hear that?"

Women whispered unintelligible phrases across the water. Their voices carried as if they spilled secrets directly into Keane's ear, though he didn't see anyone.

From the faces of the little group, he knew they heard it too.

At the aftmost point of their ship, Bennah stood with her arms outstretched and brown hair blowing behind her. She spoke into the wind, voice coiled into those of the other Daughters, and her fingers twisted into unnatural shapes.

"What's that?" Loffa pointed ahead of the fleet.

A puff of white swirled and danced five hundred yards ahead of *The Pirate's Wit*. It blew looped tendrils and towering whorls of vapor in every direction. As they watched, it doubled in volume, then doubled again. The crew of *The Pirate's Wit*, as well as those of the other ships, sent up a cheer at the sight.

"It's fog," Harden said as the first wisps reached them. "This is the Daughters' doing. We must be getting close."

Soon, they were fully obscured in the all-enveloping fog bank. Vision extended the length of the ship, but no further. They could hear all the other vessels around them, louder than normal, as well as the murmurings of dozens of hushed conversations.

Orri commanded a sailor to help Bennah to her cabin.

"Does it seem to anyone else," Keane whispered, "that the Deep Witch doesn't really need any of us here?"

"What do you mean?" Megan's curly hair dripped where it hung beneath her tricorn hat. Keane found it adorable.

"She and the Daughters can speed one fleet while they hinder the other, whip up fog banks a mile wide, and still have time for tea." Keane felt less and less assured as he gave voice to his concerns. "Why don't they just spin up a maelstrom big enough to sink the Oulani and be done with it?"

"Transcendence," Morholt answered.

"Transwhat?"

"Transcendence. The Deep Witch was once just a sorceress who lived on an island. Her place of power was an old shack somewhere." Morholt winked at Megan. "Thankfully, runecrafters don't have to put up with any of that crap."

"What's a place o' power?" asked Eli.

"Never ask a runecrafter to go back and explain when he's being inscrutable," answered Morholt. "The point is, she was just some native islander who ran around with her tits out shaking rattles all day."

Loffa giggled.

"But look at how these people treat her now. Like she was a goddess. Like she's transcended. Near as I can figure, her place of power these days is the whole damn ocean."

Eli shot a glance over at Keane, who shrugged back at him.

"How did that happen? How does a bare-assed sorceress go from cursing someone's banana tree and healing pink eye to shoving around fleets of ships like she was knocking over blindfolded six-year-olds?" At Megan's dark look, Morholt grinned. "Don't tell me you've never done it. It's hysterical.

"The point is, these people worship her. In some way, because of what she was, that worship has caused her to transcend into whatever godlike thing she is now. But she has to keep these people worshiping her in order to stay that way."

"I still don't get it," Keane said. "Any of it, really, but specifically the part about not wiping up the Oulani herself. Why doesn't that make everyone happy and even more worshippy than before?"

"Because, helping the pirates to vanquish their foes assures her their worship. They get to be there to see her do her thing and be a part of it. They toast her for the rest of their lives and sing songs about her and put their kids to bed with stories of how amazing she is and how fantastic her boobs still look after a thousand years." Morholt raised a finger. "But if she drowns twenty thousand men all by her lonesome in under a minute, people just shit their pants and hide under the bed."

"Makes sense to me," Eli said.

38

KNOCK KNOCK

KEANE

Most of an hour later, Keane could hear the sounds of Oulani sailors as they shouted in Darrish. *The Pirate's Wit* slowed to a drift, water and wind all gone quietly flat. The enemy fleet's crews were angry. They cursed the fog and the calm.

Megan had already climbed into the archer's nest, and Loffa was belowdecks. To port, Keane saw the shadows of masts in the white fog ease toward them. He wiped an oiled cloth once more over his sword blade, clear oil with just a hint of clove, and coated the edges of his stolen sword like silk. Frightened anticipation of combat lit his veins with adrenaline. Scary, yes, but he had to admit he liked it. That might make him a bad person if he ever gave himself permission to stop and think about it, which he certainly did not.

Bennah stood against the mast of their ship, her mouth a grim line and her eyes narrow and determined. Keane suspected that the rest of the Daughters were arrayed similarly throughout the fleet.

The Oulani troop carrier, a menacing hulk of a ship, drifted closer. It was big, bigger than the carrack warship Keane rode, although *The Pirate's Wit's* fore and aft castles rose well above the transport's broad decks. Gold-and-red-garbed Oulani sailors ran about the craft, stopping only to peer into the water on the other side. Because of this—and possibly because of some other workings of the Deep Witch or her Daughters—they failed to notice *The Pirate's Wit* until the two vessels physically bumped up against one another, and Orri Stoneprow howled the attack with a voice like briny thunder.

"Hey, Eli," Keane said as the old mercenary drew his sword, "I just wanted to let you know that Loffa really seems to love you."

"Really?" Eli's face opened up in a rare earnest smile. It made him look like a different person, a person you might have a pint with and not even think a bit about him throwing a dagger into you.

Keane nodded and tucked the oilcloth in his belt. "Yep. And *if you live,* I'll perform the fucking marriage myself *if you live,* and afterwards *if you live* the two of you will be happy as a frost-cocked Norrikman with a yard full of crippled sheep *if you live,* but then you probably won't live now that you know how happy you would have been."

Eli's face fell into a scowl, but whatever he said back to Keane was lost beneath the dragon-headed boarding beams that fell on the Oulanis with a horrendous crash. Men screamed. The pirates swarmed across like a starving pack of wild hogs after a felled deer, and Keane crossed with them—only slightly behind Harden and an angry Eli.

The Oulani hulk held two hundred and fifty trained and well-armed soldiers, while *The Pirate's Wit,* the best manned vessel in the fleet, carried half that number of half-naked drunks with knives and belaying pins. It was almost too easy.

Orri called the combat, and the mercenaries, for once, followed orders. First, the pirates cut down those Oulani sailors who failed to abandon their weapons, which was most of them. Not well armed, they went down quickly to the pirates' and the mercenaries' blades. Keane felt eager to avoid coming to grips with anything approaching a fair fight, but the enemy acted as if they could barely see him.

A fair fight it was not.

As well, everyone he did face had a tendency to sprout arrow feathers from one eye or the other—Keane's guardian queen watched out for him from the archer's nest.

All of the Oulani real combat troops had been sent belowdecks to keep them out of the way of the sailors when the carriers hit the dense fog. As the fighting raged above them, these men pressed to escape the three huge transport decks of the hulk, all of which shared but two exits on the main deck, one fore and one aft.

By the time the initial battle was done, other pirates had hammered these doorways shut with planks and long thick nails and were busy soaking everything in oil.

"Withdraw, ye bastards!" bellowed the pirate king. His long years had done little to diminish his vigor. He shouted like an avalanche, and the tip of his blade to his shoulder was covered in Oulani blood.

All around him, Keane watched the same scenario play out again and again. While the fog lifted, ship after Oulani ship burst into flame, and the screams of the soldiers caught belowdecks filled the morning air. It was only then, as he stood on the deck of the enemy transport hulk, that Keane realized that while the fog had left the pirate vessels wet and sodden, the Oulani ships were dry as tinder.

He ran back to *The Pirate's Wit.*

The pirates hauled on ropes attached to the dragon ends of the boarding beams and jerked them back into the air. Their curved spikes pulled loose of the Oulani decks easily. *The Pirate's Wit* came free and headed toward one of the Oulani vanguard, a cluster of identical hulks that rode much higher in the water.

These ships were intended to ferry the Coldspiners who had declined the trip. Instead, they brought extra provisions and plenty of empty cargo space for whatever might be looted from Greenshade. As pirate ships and boats pulled alongside, the sailors threw away their weapons and went down on hands and knees. All were spared, and at the end of the day, the pirates boasted twenty new Oulani hulks to add to their fleet. Keane couldn't help but think that they might have considered this more appropriate compensation than Harden's erotic magnificence.

39

GETTING THE BAND
BACK TOGETHER

KEANE

The afternoon fog, while sudden, was not unusual in the winter months at Fish Hill. All the same, the appearance of masts at the end of the docks and the sounds of oar drums alarmed the Hubrane soldiers who stood guard there.

The shuttered dockside community, a mishmash of sturdy new and teetering old docks, faded clapboard warehouses, and impressive stone company billets, had officially refused all ships until the Oulani navy arrived. The constant presence of Queen Hulda's new Royal Army, dressed in wine-red tabards instead of Greenshade's green on yellow, kept the locals indoors as well.

In the yellow-gray fog, weathered storehouses and whitewashed business fronts huddled against the quay, to drip quiet and still notes on the stones. The scene was a depressing contrast to Fish Hill's normal buzz of activity and commerce.

～

"I SEE IT." Keane stood with Harden, Eli, and Bennah on the main deck of *The Pirate's Wit*. Images of rolling waves carved into the decking lent the warship a festive air. Most of the rest of Keane's group were in the galley, hastily grabbing a final meal before leaving the ship.

"That's Fish Hill, all right." Eli peered through the sunlit murk at the shadows of buildings. "Hulda ought to have the place locked up tight. They might buy we's Oulani or mebbe not. Let's see what sorta reception we're gonna get before we—"

A cheer went up from across the water. Smaller silhouettes ran about the quay, headed for the docks to shout their greetings.

That *was* the plan, but Keane hadn't thought it would work so readily.

Eli frowned, and Harden grinned. "Don't you ever get tired of this trick?" Eli asked. "What if one of Tralgar's boys had blabbed how you beat him the same way?"

"I'll get tired of it the instant it stops working." Harden smiled and waved to the wine-colored soldiers who ran down the docks. An arrow flew through that hand and splattered both him and Eli with blood.

Keane ducked behind the mast only to find Bennah already there. They nodded to one another and ran behind the port wale.

"Hedra's tits." Harden grabbed his hand and fell to his ass. "Mother of frogshit, that hurts."

"Toldja they'd tell the difference between Darrish sailors an' Pavinn pirates." Eli tightened his jaw against his grin, and he tore the arm off of his shirt for Harden's bandage. On the docks, Hubrane's men raised the alarm, and more arrows flew overhead.

"I am officially tired of that trick," Harden said. The two of them scooted behind the mast that Keane and Bennah had just vacated.

"Bennah," Keane whispered, hunkered down against the fancifully carved wale, "you have to stay and fight. At least take and hold Fish Hill. We can't even land without your help."

"My mother told me you would try to change my mind." Bennah leaned her head against a prancing wooden mare. "And while you have all my sympathies, you cannot have my men. They are, as I believe I have mentioned before, not made for land battles."

"They're not fucking fish." Keane grew desperate. "They're men.

Are you planning to leave us here to our deaths? Is that what the Paradisals do for their allies?"

"If you have changed your mind, you can always come back to the islands with us. I am certain we could find you someplace where you would be comfortable." An arrow hit the railing atop the carved wale they hid behind, cracking it and sending splinters flying. Keane flinched away, but Bennah's dark eyes did not waver.

For a moment, Keane considered going back to the Paradisals with the Daughters. But Megan would never be happy there. Not while a Hubrane ruled her country.

"Oldam lick my ass and call it a barstool, this is goddamn ridiculous." Keane turned to see how Harden and Eli were doing.

A short distance away, the two old mercenaries sat behind the mainmast. The decorative bark carved into it made the ancient fir trunk look like an ancient oak. Eli tied off the sleeve of his shirt around Harden's hand and inspected his work. All around them, pirates shouted, ran up into the protected fore and aft castles, and returned arcing arrows. They had already sent most of the attackers, caught out in the open on the docks, back on their booted feet.

"Looks like our time to run for it," Eli said. "You gonna be okay?"

"I'll be fine." Harden scowled down at his hand. "It's not my sword hand. I—"

"Hello, Harden Grayspring," came a buttery female voice from the water. Streams, then rivers of bubbles, came bursting to the surface of the ocean alongside *The Pirate's Wit*. The noise of it shook the ship. *"You look well for a man in your condition."*

Keane spun and raised his blade. Megan ran to him, then stood and loosed several arrows at the retreating soldiers.

"I do?" Harden asked the bubble fountain. "I suppose I do at that. Wait, what do you mean, 'in my condition?'"

"It has been a long time since I walked among men," came the answer, *"but as I recall, most would be resting."*

Her voice vibrated the boards under Keane's feet and loosened the vertebrae in his back. If he judged by no more than the instinctual terror he felt, this must be the Deep Witch.

"Well," Harden raised one brow, "I guess I'm not most men."

"*Indeed, you are not,*" the voice said. "*Fare you well, Harden Grayspring. Return to me should you tire of the world of men.*"

The fountain, which had reached a dozen feet above the waves, collapsed, and the water went still in its absence.

"That sounded a trifle ominous," Eli said.

Harden nodded agreement and let his old friend help him to his feet.

To starboard, squat Mahu rowed *The Fat Gull's* dinghy alongside *The Pirate's Wit.* "Come along my friends," he shouted. "We must go now. The difference between a hero and a corpse is the timing of his retreat."

"*The Immortal Queen Nefret and the Fallow Orchard,*" Megan shouted.

Sabni grinned at her while Morholt and Raven climbed down into the dinghy.

"You are correct as always, my queen. Now come, let us go while we have the opportunity. The enemy will be—"

"Quiet," Mahu said to Sabni. "Let's go," he said to everyone else.

Harden looked at Bennah. He stood shifting his weight between his two feet, feeling awkward.

"Just go." Bennah rolled her eyes. "I'll be fine."

Harden nodded, turned, and was almost knocked over by Loffa who accidentally struck him in her eagerness to get to Eli. When she reached him, she flung her arms around him and kissed him, deeply and at length.

Eli's eyes opened wide in surprise before they closed, and he returned her fire with a little of his own.

"Um," Harden said.

The two broke, and Eli staggered back a step. Loffa, a new glimmer in her eyes, said, "Was that right? You're supposed to have something to fight for, I think."

Keane, one leg over the wale on his way to the dinghy, looked up just as Megan rushed over to kiss him, too. Their front teeth clacked together, and they both jumped back and shouted. Megan moaned and held her hands over her mouth, and Keane fell off the deck and into the ocean.

He floundered for a painfully cold moment before Morholt and Raven pulled him into the boat.

"I'm pretty sure you did that wrong." Morholt's red hair was damp and stuck to the sides of his face. "But then I'm not a king, so I might not be up on all the latest fashions in royal kissing."

"Just do the thing," Raven said to her brother. "I'm sure Keane'd be happy to teach you to kiss later."

As soon as the rest of the party swarmed into the small boat, they were underway. Keane seated himself at the oars. It was only right that it be the king's back that pulled them this final leg of the journey home.

He almost laughed at the sentiment. Megan had been a corrupting influence on his unprincipled life. The one silver lining he could think of was that no matter what, even if the Thirteen Kingdoms all flung their skirts up over their heads and screamed for salvation, Harden would never lift a finger to help without being paid for it. Honor, as unlikely as it seemed, was the difference between them.

"We're going to need a minute as soon as we get ashore," Harden said to Keane. "Keep everyone in the tree line and wait for us. There's a friend nearby, and Eli needs to stash Loffa there for safety."

"Good idea. Megan can . . ." Keane's voice trailed off as he caught the queen's glare. She pulled meaningfully on the string of her ornate bow. "She can come with us while you do that."

He was never going to like it, but it was also a fight he was never going to win. The best he could do would be to keep Megan in sight and make sure she stayed unharmed. His feet were way out over the edge of the cliff here. He risked not only his own life but Megan's and his child's as well.

There simply weren't any better options. It was their lives against all of Greenshade.

Fuck honor right in the cherryhole.

Irritated, he recalled Eli's words about keeping Loffa close-by during the fighting. Those two weren't turning out anything like Keane had feared. Eli's constant presence and support pushed Loffa to flower and grow in ways Keane thought dead to her. It was sort of miraculous.

Well, he needed to stop imagining that just being the goddamn king made him in charge of anything more important than oars. That would probably be for the best anyway.

Pointing at a pair of Hulda's soldiers who stood at the base of a dock just off the quay, Loffa whispered, "Why aren't they shooting at us?"

The fog, while still present, burned away quickly.

"They're watching the ships leave," Morholt whispered back. "Also, to them we look like a cluster of driftwood and trash floating up to the beach."

"We do?" Loffa looked around at the boat.

"Yeah," Raven said. "Holt just waves his magic cock in the air and all the bad guys go blind."

"Really?" Loffa stared into Morholt's crotch. "That's amazing."

"Let's all please shut the fuck up now," said Keane, "before the guards with the bows notice how chatty this pile of trash is."

Everyone shut the fuck up, and Keane slowly rowed the boat into a slight curve in the narrow spit of sand, just deep enough for the woods behind it to cover their landing. They moved into the trees, such as they were, scrubby and stiff with tiny leaves that formed a solid canopy about twelve feet up.

"Good. You lot wait here, an' me an' the marshal'll be back afore you can shit," said Eli. He, Loffa, and Harden moved off through the sparse undergrowth toward the small town.

"I must be getting tired," Keane said. "I can't believe it took me this long to consider that those two might be double-crossing us."

Sabni put a powerful long-fingered hand on Keane's shoulder. The ropes of muscle under his skin rippled its surface. "You have a suspicious nature, sire," he said with a gentle smile. "I think you would be happier allowing people the space to be worthy of your trust. No king could be richer but that he has good friends."

"You're a weird mercenary, Sabni. I suppose it says something about all that trust and friendship stuff in one of your fables?"

At this, Sabni's smile spread into a grin. "Nearly all of them, sire. For instance, in *The Opal Woman*, Nefret says that—"

"He wasn't asking for a lesson," Mahu said, sourly.

"Do you really think they would turn us in?" Megan reclined against one of the twisted little trees, dashing in her pirate gear. Keane pushed off of the tree he leaned against and went to her, his heart aching. He couldn't figure out why his love for his tiny queen always felt like pain, as if the happiness were unbearable. Probably because he had no right to this happiness and always felt as if she would come to her senses and run away screaming.

"No, I don't," Keane replied. "I don't know why I think that, but . . ." He paused and thought. "I just wish you would let me keep you somewhere safer while this was going on." He put his hand, rough and calloused, over the swell of her belly, bigger every day. "Both of you."

"I know." She reached up and pushed a bit of dark, windblown hair down on his head. "And I know why, and I love you for it. But I can still fight, and I'm going to. The cause is worth my life. It's worth both our lives."

This time, when Keane pulled his wife to him, they melted together as if their cores were aflame. As they kissed, Keane thought there could not be in the world another woman so warm, so passionate, and so deadly as the one he held in his arms. No woman at all so suited to him. Even if the coming fight swept them both into history, he would go happy for having experienced her in his life.

Of course, that wasn't the *plan*.

They separated, with everyone but Morholt finding something else in the surrounding foliage to interest them. The runecrafter stared at his card, a little bigger than an outstretched hand.

Keane snuck a peek over Morholt's green leathered shoulder.

What he had once seen as an image of an ugly red-and-gray dog now revealed itself to be far more disquieting. Beady black eyes stared out of a snouted face, red rimmed with patchy gray fur. A wormlike tongue flickered over black and pointed teeth, red lips, and a wet chin. But the worst part was the yellow dress covered in blue and white flowers that made the creature appear as a little girl.

Morholt had called the imp *April*. Like the wolf in that story.

April's eyes snapped upward. Morholt turned the card and put it away.

"Holt." Keane spoke quickly to disguise his racing heartbeat. "Can you make us look like Hulda's men?" He only hoped they didn't run into Sarah while under disguise. He was giddy thinking about seeing her again.

"Sure. I can even make you look like Hulda herself if you suck in your gut a bit."

"What?" Keane looked down at his flat stomach. "No, just soldiers will do. We wouldn't want me to be so pretty that someone got the wrong idea, and I had to kill you for it."

"Touchy."

"So, we sneak up to Treaty Hill," Keane said, putting the image of the imp out of his mind, "and figure out our next move there. A lot will depend on what the Barons' Conclave has been able to accomplish while we were gone."

40

IF YOU ASSAULT A CASTLE AND NO ONE SEES IT, ARE YOU STILL A HERO?

KEANE

"Well this is a shitshow." Harden stared out across the barons' lines. He and Eli had returned from stashing Loffa, and the rest of the group—now disguised by Morholt's magic—made their way up the Cattle Streets to the corner of Storage Road and the Way of Cherries, along the southern edge of town.

Keane felt Harden had a point.

The barons' troops were staged in companies outside the city to the east, which provided as little target for Hulda's men to reach them as possible. The whole of the city stretched between them and the outer wall that ringed the Quarters and the castle walls within. Unfortunately, this left them with no opportunity for offense either, and with the Ebon Host from Tyrrane stalking closer up their asses every day, each second spent here in the field was a second closer to death for them all.

As it stood, the barons' forces lay directly between Hulda and the Tyrraneans, their necks waiting on the block.

The one and only bright spot was that a quarter of the troops on the barons' side wore the green on yellow of the King's Swords. When Songham took Treaty Hill and the Forest Castle, he'd created prisoner camps just outside the city. As preparation for this battle, the barons attacked those camps and freed the captives. There weren't many of them, but those men had been through hell and back and would be ready to fight.

And just maybe, some of those *inside* the walls wouldn't.

Keane led his band south of the main city through the small wood on the north side of Tall Hall Road. They crept around the wall enclosing the Stone Houses and into the fields, avoiding Pocket Way altogether. Around here, Keane asked Morholt to disperse their disguises, and they soon found themselves picked up by one of Baron Orrikson's patrols. The baron wasted no time bringing them to the rest of the conclave.

There was no word of Sarah's arrival. Yet.

The barons convened in a large canvas pavilion in the very middle of their sprawling encampment. Inside, they sat at three long tables arranged like a square-cornered 'U,' mirroring the grand chamber in Fenrath Hall. They even sat in all the same positions.

As Keane entered, a shouting match was taking place between the silver-haired Baron Rollins, in his customary red leather jacket, and Baron Hapstan, the elderly hunter, whose white mustaches shook in indignation.

"You'll break this army on those walls, Rollins," Hapstan yelled, "and when the Tyrraneans get here, they'll smash what's left like roaches under their boots. You're just not talking reason."

"And if you leave us here to fight them," Rollins retorted, his voice louder even than Hapstan's, "Hulda Hubrane will roll right out of the castle and crush us between them. Have some damn sense!"

Hapstan's face said he hadn't considered that as a realistic possibility, and the old man grew afraid.

"While listening to all the ways we may be broken, smashed, and crushed is both diverting and morale building," said Lady Fenrath from her seat in the center of the far table, her even voice silencing the others, "I see we are honored by the royal couple once more, as well as Marshal Grayspring and company. Your Majesty, do we have good news?"

"Yes and no," Keane replied. "The Oulani navy is destroyed. I'm calling that a win. On the other hand, your army is sitting in a field waiting to be decapitated and fucked in the neck by the Ebon Host. So overall, you tell me."

"We are trying to devise the most effective strategy, sire," said Baron Drake, layers of purple velvet covering his balding bulk. "There has been some disagreement."

"Well that's what a fucking king is for." Keane's voice gained a ragged, field captain's edge. "And I'm about to *tell* you what your fucking strategy is."

Maybe he really was in charge.

IN KEANE'S ABSENCE, Hulda had repaired the broken walls with huge timbers, sandwiching the breaks and filling them with sand. Once Morholt made Keane, Megan, Baron Orrikson, and the Free Hand invisible to everyone except each other, most of them crept to the outer wall and climbed the broad beams that held the break in it together while Megan and Orrikson made their way to the rooftop of a nearby abandoned townhouse.

"Hey," Keane asked Morholt, "how is it we're invisible to everyone else, but we can see each other?"

"No offense, Your Highness," Morholt said, "but you have about as much chance of understanding that explanation as a cow does of understanding . . ." He trailed off. "Sorry, I'm just trying to think of something you know how to do that couldn't be explained to a cow."

"I know how to make friends I didn't paint on a piece of board."

"Now that's just hurtful." Morholt's face set in a deep frown. "April can hear you, you know."

As they reached the top, they huddled together between the timbers and crouched in the sand.

Megan stood, invisible to anyone else, on the roof of a nobleman's home just below and a few hundred feet east of them, well within sight of Morholt. She looked grim with her graven bow in one hand.

Beside her loomed Baron Orrikson, his fur cape blowing in the cold wind. He also carried a large bow, but—more importantly to Keane—Orrikson was famous for his swordsmanship and the defense of his charges, which right now included Megan. The big-shouldered man's appearance practically screamed hero. Or it would have had anyone else been able to see him.

"All right," Keane whispered. "You stay here, Holt. And don't anyone else forget, as soon as you leave Holt's sight, you become visible. Right?"

"Yup," Morholt said. "Ass in the wind."

"Everyone know their job?" Keane asked. They nodded. "Then let's go."

ONCE THEY PASSED the timbered portion and got to the top of the greenish stone wall, the small group easily skulked behind the soldiers who stood between the crenellations and watched the barons' troops. Out in the fields, those troops marched and drilled to repeated and lengthy horn blasts—more than sufficient to distract Hulda's men and cover the sounds of Keane and company's passage.

They made their way across the wall top to the Country Gate, which watched over the central run of Coach Street like an obsessive parent. Sabni and Raven stole past the guard at the door and climbed the exterior steps to its roof. Sabni put his back against one of the crenels at the front, and Raven tiptoed to the back, both of them on the northern edge where Morholt could see them.

Mahu, Eli, Harden, and Keane went to the door and the guard standing in front of it. Eli shoved his short sword into the man's ribcage while Harden and Mahu held him up, Harden with a hand over the soldier's mouth. Keane reached around behind and opened the metal door into the gatehouse, and they all crossed inside.

Inside the gatehouse, a lone guard stood from his wooden stool and said, "What?" as his fellow was dragged in and thrown to the floor. But then Harden was on him, shoving him to the ground and cutting his throat.

The guard said nothing more.

Keane closed the door and barred it. He hefted a solid iron rod nearly two inches thick and six feet long down from the wall and dropped one end into a depression in the floor and the other against one of the metal door's steel braces. This door had been designed to be impenetrable once the alarm was sounded in order to keep people from doing exactly what Keane was about to do.

The room ran the whole top floor of the gatehouse, although there were a few interior walls that held a variety of gear works. To either side of the floor, the handles of a huge winch jutted up out of wide slots in the stone. Only the top portion was visible, the rest of the beastly thing being hidden in the gatehouse structure below them.

"Remove the locks." Keane pointed in the lamplight. Megan had briefed him on what he would find here, and she did not disappoint. If they had relied on Keane's knowledge alone to get them through this, the entire project would be little more than a mass suicide.

Damn Sarah for not being here.

Keane hoped she would connect with him again magically, but she had not. Although his understanding of sorcery was limited, maybe her silence was a good thing. Maybe she was too close to him —and to Finnagel's place of power—to cast the spell.

After the large blocks were removed, the four men took their positions, Mahu and Eli on one wheel and Harden and Keane on the other, and waited. Outside, the drill horns from the barons' armies continued, and the sounds of fighting began above them.

Someone screamed.

Keane pulled the winch handle, itself as tall as he was, to the limit of his strength. Harden pulled with him, grunting and straining, but nothing moved.

"This ain't working," Eli said between grunts. Above them, all four could hear the melee as Sabni and Raven cleared the top of the gatehouse.

"We should go help them," Mahu said. "Bring them down to raise the gate faster."

The distant and constant horns of the Barons' Conclave ceased, and a chilling silence rushed in the fill the space they left.

"Shit." Keane stood straight and stared at the barred door. "They're about to—"

The long blast of dozens of war horns cut him off, calling the barons' charge.

As one, all four men bent once more to strain against the stubborn winches. None so much as raised a head when a steady banging arose from the door.

"Hey, assholes!" Raven shouted from the other side of the reinforced door. "Open the fucking door!"

41

A GOOD DAY FOR A BARBEQUE
HULDA HUBRANE

I s everything good and soaked through?" Hulda Hubrane stood beside an enormous pile of meat, bread, grains, as well as smoked and pickled foodstuffs, in the middle of the wide avenue between the Legation of Kos and their recreation of the Colossus of Ippo.

At a quarter the size of the real thing, the maned and fanged statue glared down hatefully on the street below. A dark sky glowered down on the flames in the bitter statue's head, which lit its eyes an unstable orange.

"Good enough to see from Dismon once you drop that torch, my queen," answered Major Talon. Once he had committed enough sins against Tyrrane to ensure his death should he be captured, the major had become a useful, if occasionally despondent, tool.

Hulda wore her wine-red winter dress with the white panel down the front and matching red leather long coat. Everyone would see her here, torch in hand, before she vanished into the Harrows.

The barons set up their camps in the fields in front of Three Sisters Wood. Even now Hulda could hear them blowing their horns and running about the field. But this left an opportunity for her to slip away into the city proper where her allies could hide her underground in the old town district known as the Harrows. She already had a wagonload of the best foods sent ahead of her.

She dropped the torch and stepped back.

The food in front of her represented half of everything her ducal guard could prise out of the population with any speed. It was twice her height and fifty feet across. Its loss would not starve anyone today, but it might tomorrow, and it would certainly cause a problem for any army who took the city next.

Flames spread over the piled provisions and shot up into the air as the oil took. Hulda turned away and ran to the curved legation building to escape the heat.

The other half of the city larder had been redistributed to the wealthiest families in Treaty Hill. This had been done in full view of the populace to encourage fighting once people became truly hungry and desperate.

Hulda was not one to miss an opportunity to sow confusion behind herself and cover her tracks.

The cloud smelled of roasting meat and cinnamon.

"My queen!"

General Roen ran up to Hulda from around the corner of the legation house. Out of breath, the red blotches on his cheeks and dark waxed mustache made his face look all the paler by comparison.

He gathered himself and took Hulda by the elbow. "There is fighting atop the Country Gate. We have to get you into the castle now."

They ran.

Damn the barons. They had left no time for her to finish her preparations to hide in the Harrows, just as they prevented her escape with the Forest Castle's treasure. At every turn, they closed off a piece of her world.

Behind the Rousland Embassy, almost at the inner gate, Hulda gasped and nearly fell.

Could this have been Aerith Ravenstok's plan all along? Did she know I could never escape in time?

That fucking WHORE.

"Please, ma'am," General Roen beseeched. "We're almost inside."

Hulda could hear the fighting atop the walls as she entered the castle gate, though she could not make out who her soldiers fought against. The machinery of the gate clanked, and the Country Gate portcullis lifted several inches.

They ran again.

Behind them the portcullis raised several more inches and stopped. Through the bars in the distance, she could see the barons' troops running in toward her. She ought to do something about the gatehouse. Someone was obviously trying to take the Country Gate, but she needed to get away.

No matter what Lady Ravenstok or Baroness Roselle's plans for her might be, she wouldn't be slaughtered out here like a *soldier*.

It did not seem fair, but in Hulda's experience, very little ever did. She was simply more used to being on the other side of the table.

Tynos waited for them in the entryway of the Welcome Hall, backed up by twin rows of twenty-five-foot-tall statues of all of Greenshade's kings. The trio fled down the middle of the hall as prior kings looked on in judgment from their plinths.

She would have sworn the last one, the mercenary king, smirked at her as she ran past.

They bowled past frightened servants and shoved men and women alike to the ground in their hurry to find a suitable place to hide. Outside the kitchens, General Roen leaned in to shoulder a scullery maid into the wall but screamed and fell to the floor instead.

The maid's knife clattered to the floor when Tynos smacked the woman's head against the wall, but it was too late. The damage was done.

General Roen rolled on his back and clutched his knee where the scullery maid's blade had bitten deep. His flight was over.

With the maid's own knife, Hulda stabbed her in the chest. The maid's eyes flew open and closed again. She sighed and went limp.

A nod passed between the general and the assassin, and Hulda and Tynos continued their pell-mell run while General Roen pushed himself up against a wall and unscabbarded his cutlass.

Tynos skidded to a halt in front of one of the wide Flying Halls. People hurried in both directions. "It iz not safe for you here. Theze peoples are allies of the barons. They will feel emboldened to take actions."

"What are we doing?" Hulda tried to stand behind Tynos's broad back. Even in the cold, the assassin wore just that loose-fitted linen shirt and pants.

"The Tall Garden is that way in the Stone Tower." Tynos spoke to Hulda in her thickly accented voice over her shoulder while she kept an eye on the crowd. "There iz the hidden passage there we could hide in. Follow me."

I guess you need to know about hidden passages when you're an assassin.

The two of them almost made it to the end of the hall when Tynos slowed, stopped, and drew her curved daggers. Ahead of her, three gray-haired men, veteran soldiers by the look of them, drew knives of their own and spread out around the pair.

"Back away," Tynos said.

For once, Hulda did as she was told, only to discover another two armed men behind them.

"Sweeties," she said, "I really have someplace I need to be. But I think we can take a minute to kill you all."

42

NEVER FORGIVE A HEDGEHOG

SARAH

Across the city and a short stretch of farmland from the outer walls, Sarah, Cassius, and close to five hundred troll warriors broke from the Three Sisters Wood. A line of Tyrranean troops was already ahead of them, having traveled Woods Road instead of through the trees. This fragment of the Host was so intent on pursuing fleeing soldiers of the Barons' Conclave that they failed to notice the trolls until it was far too late to do anything about it.

Earlier that day, Sarah and Finnlaug had worried that *both* sides might take the sudden appearance of that many charging trolls amiss and attack on sight. Instead, the conclave greeted them with cheers.

As both the conclave and the trolls fled through the city toward the Country Gate, they chopped down the Host soldiers that suddenly found themselves between two enemy forces. The victory died fast when the rest of the Host came pouring out of the trees and the Woods Road behind Sarah.

Now they just ran. Past the conclave soldiers, past even the Host who bolted pell-mell, faces white and terrified.

"Is the gate open?" Sarah shouted. "I can't see from here."

"Just run," Finnlaug yelled back in her gravelly voice. Her long greenish mats were bound behind her head with a bit of black ribbon and flopped side to side.

Sarah ran. The frigid wind lifted her mane of dark hair behind her, barely held in place with her twin braids. The half-silver one flashed in the chilly sun. Her broadsword sang a dirge for the Tyrranean soldiers who happened across her path. Sarah's blood-soaked furs covered her chainmail hauberk, and the Host fighters fled until there was no place left to go.

Most of them never even drew their weapons.

Soon there was only them and the conclave and the wind. Their enemies were behind them, the wall before. The trolls picked up Coach Street at the corner of Eggan Square and bore down. Ahead, Greenshade's armies—standing at the Country Gate—parted for them revealing the still closed portcullises within.

"Not open," Finnlaug said.

Sarah spared a quick scowl for the troll.

"Thanks."

Keane

"PULL!" Keane's voice was little more than a grunt. This was no use. The winch was obviously meant to be operated by twenty men or more at a time. Even with the addition of Sabni, Raven, and Morholt, there was no way the seven of them could—"PULL!"—do it alone. The huge winch wouldn't budge. It was like they weren't even there. Keane couldn't tell if—"PULL!"—he was pulling at all. The—

CRUNK.

It moved. It moved!

"PULL!" Every muscle in Keane's body tensed against the long handle in his arms.

CRUNK. CRUNK. CRUNKCRUNKCRUNKCRUNK.

They were doing it. The winch spun. Every clank of the chains below was a victory, every inch the handles spun was a triumph. Keane was going to lord this over the conclave *so* much.

The winch stopped, unwilling to give any more ground. "Replace the locks." Keane held the long handle still.

Harden jumped away from the wheel and grabbed the wooden blocks, sliding them back into place. Keane wanted nothing more than to fall exhausted to the floor, but instead he removed the bar once again from the door and stepped out onto the wall top. He ran to the side and looked out into a nightmare.

The Ebon Host held the city from the Three Sisters almost to the wall, tens and tens of thousands of them. Directly below him, the conclave's forces pressed against the wall. Their lines bulged out into the surrounding streets closest to the gatehouse where they ran through the raised portcullises.

The conclave soldiers were being protected by—trolls? Sarah was finally here! He cast about to try and spot her.

Keane glanced up toward the rooftops and saw his worst fears realized.

43

CAN YOU SMELL THAT?

SARAH

Several hundred yards away, Sarah spotted Megan and a tall broad-shouldered man on a manor roof close to the Country Gate, surrounded by Host. Megan turned her back and moved to the other side, a white ash bow in her hands. How could Keane have allowed the queen to be trapped on top of a manor house in the exact middle of a war?

Sounded like a Keane plan to her.

The portcullises had not been constructed to lift from the ground, but when the trolls tried, gears and chains clanked above, and the gates unexpectedly raised a good five feet above the ground and held there. Sarah and Grohann ran to cover their allies' retreat outside through the buildings to the gate. Inside, the Swords took point when they rushed through the gate and tore into Hulda's now numerically inferior army.

What was that smell? Burning cinnamon?

On the outside of the gate, every place Tyrranean soldiers faced trolls, the Host held back and allowed a space to form between the two forces.

One side of Sarah's mouth went up. She would not have wanted to be the first one to run into a wall of angry and armed trolls either. She was being given a window of opportunity here, and for Megan's sake, she would not squander it.

The situation was still perilous. She and Grohann ran through alleyways and side streets toward the manor house with Megan atop it. Clusters of Ebon Host moved along the larger avenues, and there was no telling when they might round a corner into a pitched battle.

Sarah tried to bring one of the spells Cassius/Magda had taught her to mind, but her thoughts churned with combat, and she could only grasp at the edges of the magic. The one spell she knew well enough to cast in this state was Blow Out the Candle, which here at Finnagel's place of power was only strong enough to blow out an actual candle.

Cassius, carried here by Grohann and passed off to another troll, was already down and through the Country Gate with the King's Swords.

Out of the corner of her eye, Sarah saw Megan's face peer over the roof of the tall house, fully surrounded by Tyrraneans and as yet unaware of her presence. Long curly brown hair blew sideways in the wind.

Sarah and Grohann stepped into the open in front of the Country Gate. In the very middle of Coach Street, with the open portcullis behind her, they stared hundreds of Ebon Host in the face. Ahead and to her left, Megan and the unidentified man peeped over the edge of the roof.

"Kyrrvatin warriors, to me!" Sarah commanded in her loudest voice.

Trolls marched up, twenty at least, to hunch in a protective cluster around her.

The Host backed away.

"We're going to secure the front of that building." She tipped her head toward the manor so as not to give away their objective to the opposing army just thirty feet ahead of her. "We'll have to fight through to get to it, but we should only have to hold for a minute, maybe two. The Queen of Greenshade is in there, and she's my friend. Are we ready?" As one, the Kyrrvatin trolls stamped their feet in agreement.

The Host soldiers directly across from them grew pale.

Sarah led the charge to the manor. Above, the face disappeared, while below, two trolls fell. The Tyrraneans had used their time to shift a squad of pikemen to the front, hoping to utilize the extra reach to kill anyone who covered the conclave's retreat through the gate.

Sarah led the trolls left away from the pikemen, then right again to the front of the manor. Then she turned to face the Ebon Host.

Several soldiers, never having witnessed trolls in combat and emboldened by the numbers at their back, fell immediately to troll spears and axes. Behind those, however, the pikemen turned and lined up for what would soon be a devastating charge. There was a crash behind Sarah at the manor's door, but Sarah ignored it, readying herself for the pikes.

"Try to knock the blades aside," Sarah shouted, "but be ready for another line just behind those. If you can get inside the blades, kill them all." It sounded tough, but Sarah knew it was just talk. She should have thought this through a little better. She hadn't seen the pikemen march up behind the lines. They were all going to die here.

Sorry, Megan.

Really sorry, Keane. In her guilt she imagined she could hear Keane screaming at her to do something, but she couldn't make out what it was.

Sarah watched the pikemen line up and saw the captain give the command to charge. The blades went down, and she wondered for an instant why Grohann hadn't at least shot one of the bastards with that giant bow of his. Then a shadow passed over her head.

A long, elegant, and golden-colored sofa crashed into the squad, shattering both pikes and the men who held them.

A fusillade of matching chairs, footstools, and tables, as well as a fainting couch followed the sofa, all thrown with bone-splintering force by Grohann and his fellow Kyrrvatin trolls. Sarah spared a glance over her back to see that the trolls had removed the front doors—as well as a portion of the surrounding stonework—and gained entrance to the inside of the manor, from whence came the expensively upholstered ammunition.

Grohann appeared in the former doorway, Queen Megan tucked behind him. He paused just long enough to lift one of the oversized doors from the ground when Sarah called the retreat.

"Hey!" Megan tried to wave at Sarah. "I like your trolls."

The tall Andosh man Sarah saw accompanying Megan, all broad shoulders and piercing eyes, broody dark cloak and fur trim, stepped out from behind Grohann. He flashed Sarah a brilliant smile from within a dark close-cropped beard, and waved as well.

"I'm Baron Orrikson. Thank you for the rescue." His confident baritone rumbled against Sarah's ribs.

Megan dashed behind the front rank of trolls. She stopped and fired her bow upward, eliciting a scream from an arrow slit within the outer wall.

"Shut up and follow the queen," Sarah ordered the baron.

Orrikson followed.

Trolls carried doors and tables against the Tyrranean archers who fired at them from a distance, all of which sprouted a forest of feathered shafts. Grohann found some additional use for his door as he bashed Tyrraneans out of his way.

As he passed, he stomped on a few more who fell in front of him.

They reached the Country Gate just as the last of the conclave's men ducked beneath the twin portcullises. Sarah and the Kyrrvatin set themselves to guard the open gateway as the Host ran in. Behind her in the Quarters, Sarah heard a lot of shouting and commotion, and then her world narrowed to blades, blood, and speed.

Keane

UNABLE TO HELP, Keane shouted and watched Megan's frantic escape with his heart in his throat and finally threw up over the side of the wall when both his wife and his best friend made it to relative safety. He ran down the broad stone steps, intending to rush into Megan's arms, but he couldn't get through the crowd. Soldiers were hugging trolls, and the trolls laughed and sang to one another.

Keane thought he might pass out. Their stupid plan had succeeded, and everyone was still alive. Sarah made it back in the last instants, and they were only surrounded by a zillion enemy troops.

That part, at least, he was pretty familiar with.

All around Keane, Hulda's defenses collapsed as poor morale and strained conditions caught up to them. They threw down their weapons rather than fight once more against their countrymen.

Keane almost felt like he could breathe again, though the acrid smell of burnt cinnamon discouraged it. What was left of the Hubrane force would almost certainly join them against the Tyrraneans on the other side of the wall.

Especially if he turned any dissenters over to the menagerie as animal food.

Even as Keane had the thought, the huge double doors of the castle flung open, and Baron Sins, at the head of a squad of his own black-on-white-liveried soldiers, stalked out, wide grins on every face.

Keane told Sins where to find the secret passageway that he, Megan, and Loffa used to escape Songham a few months ago. He probably shouldn't have done it, but he could always collapse the tunnel and have another one dug.

Startled, Keane noticed that someone below was shouting at him. Casting about, he realized that nearly everyone inside the wall was shouting at him.

"Shut the gate!"

Keane whirled and ran past members of the Free Hand who just now came out of the gatehouse and bolted back inside. Standing between the two great winch wheels, he grabbed the dark ropes attached to the locking blocks and pulled them both together. His arms cried out, having spent so much of their strength already, and he fell to the floor.

One of the blocks shifted slightly.

Then Mahu and Sabni were there. Each took hold of one of the ropes and yanked the blocks from the mechanism.

The huge wheels spun swift and loud and came to an abrupt halt with a bang that shook the entire gatehouse. Keane heard something tear below and clatter as it fell. But the Country Gate held, and a cheer rose from outside.

This time, Keane did let himself fall on the floor, and he grinned up at the dark stone ceiling.

Megan was fine. Sarah was fine. Everyone would be fine.

Sarah

SARAH CONTINUED to scan the torchlit wall top. Others wandered there, smiling and relieved.

But not Keane.

The man possessed a near-infinite capacity for getting himself in trouble. Sarah would relax when she held him in her own grip and not a second before. While she would neither leave Megan until the situation was officially under control nor bring her into potential danger to go look for Keane, the whole situation left her feeling antsy and dangerous.

Grohann stood to one side of the pair. He glanced from Sarah to Megan and back again. At length, he leaned forward and whispered to Sarah, "This is yoor queen? For true? She is still a baby, yes?"

They stood in front of the castle in the middle of Coach Street just south of the Rousland Embassy. The sun was set, and the street lit with torches. Outside the outer wall, the Ebon Host slowly encircled the entire city.

Nothing in and nothing out.

Along the south side of the street, Barons Sins and Rollins inspected the assembled troops of Hulda Hubrane. They took turns speaking to them about duty to country and how to choose the honorable side of a fight. Sins offered to let any of Hulda's men who wished to leave and join the Tyrranean forces the opportunity to do so. No one volunteered.

The traitor Hulda had yet to be found.

"Don't kill me." Harden raised his hands and grinned, wolflike, as he sauntered up to Sarah. "I know I promised you'd never see me again, but I had to keep your boy alive."

Sarah scowled down at Harden, mouth a hard line. "Is that true, Eli? Did he keep Keane alive?"

"On more'n one occasion, lass. To my surprise an' considerable befuddlement."

Sarah's smile broke free, and she swung a brawny arm around Harden's head, jerking him into a hug.

"Good," she said. "I'm so glad I don't have to kill you."

"I'm glad not to be killed." Harden pushed against her to try and regain his breath.

Then Keane was hugging her.

A million questions faded from her mind, and she hugged him back.

Keane squeaked.

Sergeant Stath and his small squad of royal bodyguards caught up to Keane, alarmed, but the rangy old soldier held out a hand to stay the others. They faded back to allow the two friends their reunion.

When they did pull apart, both of them sniffled and wiped their cheeks.

"What *is* that smell?" Keane asked.

"The Hulda woman set fire to the city's stores," Sergeant Stath answered. "A goodbye present, I'd imagine."

"Bitch," Sarah and Keane said together.

Keane sat up on the street and regarded Sarah. He ran a hand across her brow and traced the claw marks there. He raised an eyebrow in query.

"Tundra cats," she said.

"You've lost weight," he told her.

She knew there were new hollows in her face. Her typically bulky frame now looked hard. Spare.

"The north not have any food?"

"No. They eat slugs."

Keane's eyes widened. "I-I missed . . ." He lowered his head and held a hand over his face, and Sarah pulled him to her once more.

This time she leaned down and whispered in his ear, "I know. Me too. But you need to be good now. You're still king."

She did know, seeing Keane again, touching him. They had been inseparable since early childhood, for nearly twenty years now. Each one's weaknesses were the other's strengths. But to save Greenshade, they had been apart for so long, in constant worry that the other was dead. To see each other now was an inexpressible relief.

Keane

KEANE NODDED AND PULLED AWAY. He stood and glanced around him to see who had noticed his brief moment of weakness. Satisfied that it was pretty much everyone in the whole fucking kingdom, he brushed himself off, nodded again to Sarah, and limped to his tiny wife, who stood with a knowing smirk on her young face.

Cassius—thin, bedraggled, and haunted—stood beside her.

"Sorry," Keane said to his queen. "Should have known better. I got excited."

Keane concentrated on Cassius. The man was a skeleton. His gray skin hung limp and lifeless from his bones, a rotted sail too loosely wrapped by the wind around a broken spar.

Keane hoped he would look better than that when he died. And Cassius probably wasn't even dead.

Probably.

Cassius's face worked itself in strange ways, appearing alternately confused, sad, and intensely angry. His eyes bored into Keane's in a way that sent Keane's hand drifting toward the hilt of his sword.

"This is the one?" Cassius pointed at Keane and thrust his bony jaw at Sarah. "This is the one you have forsaken your destiny for?"

Soldiers in the street, both Swords and conclave, paled and gave Cassius a wide berth at the sound of him, and the light in the Quarters dimmed.

Keane had no idea what Cassius was on about, but the instant he heard that voice, his blade whispered out of its sheath almost of its own accord. Stath and his men's drawn blades ringed the wasted figure as well.

"Now that's a bit creepy." Stath worked his craggy face and spat sideways. "And I can't even properly say why. But I feel I'd like to kill it."

Keane shrugged. "Wanting to kill him is normal, but the voice thing is new." He sheathed his sword, and the others followed suit.

Sarah walked up to Cassius and looked down into his gray-stubbled face. "It seems to me that you severed us all from our destinies when you sundered the world from its future. We all belong to ourselves now, *including* me." Sarah put her hands on her hips and frowned. "I am grateful for everything you've done for us, goddess, but don't talk to me about your plans for my life. You won't appreciate the answer."

Goddess?

"I can attest to that." Harden raised his hand from behind Megan.

"But he has ruined you, my button. You should be mighty, but he makes you human. You love him, but he is not even yours." He let his arm fall, open hand indicating Megan. "He belongs to that one. Even Cassius didn't understand this."

A warm flush crept up Keane's neck. There was something cockeyed going on here. He exchanged glances with Stath. The wily sergeant scratched his cropped gray head in a way that said to Keane, *I dunno either. But I'd feel a lot more comfortable with that thing chopped to bits. Then we'll go grab a pint and some travelers' rolls.*

Sarah leaned in. "It doesn't matter what Cassius understands, or you either, for that matter. There are many kinds of love, and mine for Keane keeps me sane and good, despite what you and every other sorcerer tries to make me into. And that makes me love him all the more."

Defeated, Cassius shrank back. To Keane, he resembled a bunch of dried sticks tied together with a dirty and tattered blue cloth.

"Sarah's gonna be who Sarah's gonna be," Keane said. "I don't really know what all this is about, but if your interest is in turning her into what *you* want instead of what *she* wants—goddess or not—you are out of your league."

The very faintest trace of a crooked half smile played about Sarah's lips.

"I'll say," Megan agreed with a chuckle.

"Your Majesty."

Keane saw the speaker and sighed.

This guy.

"Baron Orrikson." Keane faced the broad-chested man. He really wished he could like this baron, but he was too good-looking, too unmarried, *and* he had taken it upon himself to protect Megan on top of the manor house. Keane *had* been grateful, but now he instinctively wanted to throttle the man.

He'd keep that to himself. "What can I do for you?"

"The enemy is pitching a parlay tent up the road," Orrikson said. "Shall we inform them that you'll be on your way?"

"Oldam's twisted granite turds. I hate this part. Frankly, I'm surprised they're bothering. Yeah, tell 'em I'm coming. Any volunteers to come with me and listen to the stupid people act stupid?"

Sarah's eyes glinted as her lips pulled back from her teeth. "I think I'd be up for that."

44

SING-ALONG WITH THE ENEMY
KEANE

There are so many more assholes out here than when Songham did this." Keane stared out at Treaty Hill. Campfires surrounded the entire city. It was a proper siege, and there seemed to be no end to them. "How many you think we're looking at?"

"They this deep all the way around?" Harden asked.

Keane, Harden, Sarah, and Cassius walked east on Coach Street past the abandoned shops to the north and the empty homes to the south. Twenty hand-picked members of the King's Swords followed close behind led by Sergeant Stath and his squad. The city—bright in patches from all of the reconstruction following Wallace's Company's fires and looting—was quiet as a graveyard.

A chill wind whistled through the streets. It smelled of salt and smoke.

"There are close to thirty thousand Tyrraneans out there." Sarah flexed her hands and made the muscles jump. "We had plenty of opportunities to observe them while we chased them south from Fenrath."

Keane winced. He hated thinking of the Ebon Host destroying that beautiful town by the waterfall. There was guilt as well, for

Baroness Fenrath had taken her troops away from home—where they could have been protecting their families—and marched them to the capital. He shoved the thought away. Plenty of time to be miserable later.

It started to snow. Keane rolled his eyes. He hated snow. It seemed arbitrarily cruel to him for it to be snowing now, as he risked his neck walking out to parley with an evil and conquest-minded foe.

Again.

Keane tried to ignore the flakes and eyed the parley tent. "Why didn't we bring that big folk fella of yours, with the horns? That big-horned fucker'd be a handy deterrent to any violence here."

Sarah focused on the parley tent as she walked. "Grohann and Finnlaug have asked for a bit of privacy ahead of the battle. There is some sort of ritual for them to undertake to ensure good fortune in war."

"Does this 'ritual' have anything to do with Secreed sending pages all over to find the sturdiest bed in the castle?" Keane asked.

"I did not ask." Sarah stared straight ahead.

Secreed, the Forest Castle's elder chamberlain, had weathered Hulda's occupation well and had immediately directed them to Keane's good friend Lady Roselle down in the dungeon. Thinking of the baroness, he had to smile. Keane should have brought her with him to the parley. By the end of that talk, the curvy and highly intelligent Roselle would have added Prince Brannok to her 'harem,' and Greenshade would have another thirty thousand troops to defend herself with. He chuckled.

He left Lady Ravenstok where he found her. No need to let himself be flanked by his enemies this early in the fight.

There was still no sign of Hulda Hubrane, nor of Finnagel.

"There is power ahead." Cassius peered forward at the large tent. Several campfires were lit around it, and the white canvas glowed dully with the light of interior lamps. "It is not Angrim, but it is nearly his equal."

"Valafar," Sarah said. "He and I have met, sort of. How come you never said anything about him being so almighty powerful before?"

"He is different now," Cassius replied.

All three stopped to listen to Cassius's response. When it became clear that no more information was forthcoming, Sarah flung up her arms in irritation and walked on. The rest followed.

More than one of the Swords that flanked them threw black looks Harden's way. Keane hardly blamed them. Treaty Hill was still recovering from the mercenary attack a year and a half ago. Doubtless a lot of these people had lost family to Harden's sledgehammer tactics. It had to sit hard that the man was an ally now.

"So"—Keane edged closer to Sarah—"what happened to Cass? He looks worse than I feel."

"He betrayed us to the Tyrraneans, got possessed by a goddess, and treated me really shitty after I finally got drunk enough to have sex with him." She paused. "Not in that order."

Keane leaned back to look at Cassius around Sarah's shoulder. The worn-out merchant shuffled and swayed as he walked, as if something were eating his muscles away by the minute. A bit of grayed hair slipped off of his head.

"You want me to beat him up for you?"

Sarah grinned. "No, he's good. I think Magda finally burned the last of his brains over the past few days."

"Cuz I will, if you want."

"No. Please don't."

"Hey, Cass," Keane said. "C'mere. I wanna kick your ass."

"Gonna have to wait." Harden pointed ahead of them. The pale tent opened, and soldiers of the Host stepped smartly out. At least three dozen black-on-gray-liveried men held brutal looking halberds and moved to line the street.

When Keane met with Songham in a smaller tent in almost the same spot a few months ago, the little prick hadn't wanted to parley. He only wanted to rub Keane's face in the fact that he was going to take the castle away and then be the man to kill Keane. As the snow continued to fall, Keane couldn't help the feeling that this meeting wouldn't be as much fun.

The snow-capped city around him—filled with the Ebon Host—

seemed old and frail, a white-haired man whose fevered breath came in fits and starts while he slept.

Keane left Stath and the Swords behind, and the small group walked through the twin lines of the Ebon Host and entered the pavilion.

Unlike his previous experience, there was no table and chairs for everyone to sit at and deliberate. Prince Brannok, in glittering gold-and-black-lacquered plate armor, sat atop a high wooden throne decorated with graven images of swords and lightning. An enormous two-handed blade leaned against the side of the ostentatious chair. The prince's oiled red hair laid back on his head, and his beard projected forcefully forward.

His eyes blazed madly.

To either side of the throne stood a hulking soldier, each armed with a pair of thick-bladed short swords. Either of the men were the size of Burgen, who topped the chart as the biggest man Keane had ever met. And these two did not look as stupid as that poor soul had been.

In front of the prince and to the right, a short well-groomed Pavinn man stood with his arms folded in front of him and an arrogant smirk on his face. He was hard to look at in the eye. Some power pushed Keane's glance down at the man's feet.

This of course made Keane more determined to meet his gaze, and after a brief internal struggle, he managed to do so.

With his wide muscular body, shoulder-length black hair and close-cropped beard, and a smug twist of his lips to indicate his amusement at Keane's discomfiture, this had to be Valafar.

"I assume you're dressed all in black just in case someone forgets what an evil donkeyfucker you are," Keane said to Angrim's apprentice.

"You should be more friendly to your conquerors," Prince Brannok said from up on his throne, though there was no friendliness in his smile. "We are going to grind your nation into the mud. But that doesn't mean that we can't be civil. A little respect can take you a long way."

"I learned long ago that very few people who demand a man's respect are actually worthy of it." Harden circled around to stand at Keane's right. "But don't worry that you have lost ours. I promise that my opinion of you and your family remains unchanged."

"It better have." The growl in Prince Brannok's throat grew deeper.

Valafar looked pained and rubbed his forehead.

"I have known dozens of men in my father's courts like Songham," Prince Brannok said, "preening popinjays who feel that they are better than other men because of the accident of their birth. They fell into power. Money." He frowned down from his tall chair. "Killing him was no great feat. And besting a woman is not worth mention."

Keane felt, rather than saw, Sarah mark the prince for some education on that score.

Prince Brannok continued. "But you shouldn't make the mistake of thinking that is *my* philosophy. I don't expect your respect because of my station or wealth. These things say nothing about a man. I expect it because I have the strength to kill you where you stand and the willingness to do it."

"Oh. My pardon. I didn't realize you were a philosopher. Now I completely respect your insane, murderous rampage." Harden grinned. "Come to think of it, we have a lot more in common than I figured."

His frown deepening into a scowl. Brannok asked Harden, "Do I know you? You seem familiar."

"We met briefly," Harden said with a nod. "Harden Grayspring. I was marshal of Wallace's Company. Your father hired us to sack Gullhome and kill the demon."

"That was you?" The prince leaned forward. "You struck a mighty blow for Tyrrane that day. Why are you on the wrong side of this?"

"Your dad stiffed us. Didn't seem right to the men under me to keep doing business with him after that. They got mouths to feed too." Harden held out his hands and took a step forward. "'Course, if you saw fit to square up old debts and made me an offer, I imagine we could work out a deal."

"You gray-dicked son of a whore," Keane said. "That's why you asked to come along? You better hope Prince Redfuck accepts your offer 'cause you won't survive it if he doesn't."

Brannok grinned widely at the display of rancor between Keane and Harden. "It seems to me that by killing you all, I not only get Greenshade, but I also cancel my father's debt—for free."

"It had occurred to me you might see it that way, but I figured you might not be smart enough to puzzle it out so fast." Harden smiled. "Live and learn."

"In your case," Valafar said, low and menacing, "I doubt there's much danger of either. But you . . ." he trailed off, looking past the two men at Sarah.

She stepped forward into the middle of the pavilion.

Valafar walked around Sarah and eyed her up and down.

Behind her, Keane stood and fumed while Sarah put her hands on her hips and glared at Valafar.

Angrim's apprentice slithered, eellike, once more to his place to the right of the prince.

"So, Finnagel claimed you for his apprentice," Valafar said, "and Kadir tried to steal you away. I can see why. Good lines, strong stock. You would last a long time."

"Excuse me?" Sarah said.

"It takes a sturdy woman to share my bed. Most don't make it through the night." Valafar smiled and stroked his beard. "I bet you would last a week at least."

"Slago's teeth." Sarah shook her head. "I cannot believe what typical, self-important assholes you two are. At least I don't have to feel guilty for killing you anymore. And as for you, the only sexual experience I'd share with you is to tie you down naked and watch you be danced on by a herd of fat oxen. You'd have more luck getting a blowjob from Bizzith-non than having me actually share your bed."

Bizzith-non was a Pavinn goddess whose body was composed entirely of roaches, each one of which was the transformed and tortured soul of a wicked man. Keane shivered as Sarah's imagery came, unbidden, to his head.

"Your permission is not at issue," Valafar replied. "I never have sex with anything that isn't screaming."

A wind from outside flapped at the sides of the tall tent, and a swirl of snow blew into the space.

"Nope. There is no way I can get beaten by people who suck as hard as you two. That just can't happen." The prince and his sorcerer revolted Keane. They were the shittiest sort of persons possible, brought to the highest station there was. Even a murderer and sell-sword like Keane had more morals than these two horrible beasts.

"Hey." Keane grinned up at Prince Brannok as a thought popped into his head. "It just occurred to me how much better I am than you."

The prince stood out of his chair and screamed, "You will respect me!"

"Kinda doubt it," Harden muttered. "Not really in his wheelhouse."

"You know, Songham had a lot to say about respect, too," Keane answered. "But in the end, all he really gave a fuck about was showing me up. And that blew up in his face, just like it did Hulda's, and just like it will yours."

Brannok's face reddened, and he reached for his huge sword. Valafar raised a hand, and the prince lowered his arm to his side. That arm trembled with rage. Good to know who the real boss in the room was.

"Speaking of our dear Widow Hulda, where is the true Queen of Greenshade?" asked Valafar. "Bring her to us at once, and you will be formally executed as befits a king. Failure will result in railing. That is when we tie your intestines to a wagon with you behind it, and then spook the—"

Valafar stopped speaking as both Harden and Keane burst out in laughter.

"Something amusing?"

"I was gonna do the same thing to him," Harden said with a chuckle. "It's just funny how things come full circle sometimes."

Keane laughed and nudged Harden in the ribs. "I don't get it.

There are more ways to kill a person than I'll ever know. Is there just something about me that says, 'Hey, I wanna tie that fucker's guts to a cart and watch him chase them all over the field?'"

Harden met Keane's gaze with utter seriousness. "Yup."

They both cracked up again.

45

THE SHOWDOWN

SARAH

Sarah's eyes rolled heavenward. She looked over her shoulder at Keane and Harden. "Idiots. It wasn't funny then, and it's not funny now." They quieted, and she returned her attention to Valafar. "Hulda is missing, presumed killed. No one has seen her. My bet is the slippery mot escaped and is somewhere between here and the Western Marches. If she's important, go there."

The prince opened his mouth, but before he got anything out, Valafar spoke with a doubled voice like steel nails scratching along the inside of a skull.

The two huge guards to either side of Prince Brannok broke and stared at Valafar.

"*Button.*" The voice rolled out of Valafar's opened and motionless mouth. "*Kill it.*"

Magda leaped forward and stared into Valafar's suddenly alien face. "Angrim is watching us," he said.

Damn. Sarah *really* was not ready for that kind of fight.

Valafar recoiled from Magda. "*What are you?*" he grated. "*I cannot see you.*"

"Cassius?" Brannok's eyes widened and his jaw fell slack. One hand gripped the arm of his wooden throne. "What have these bastards done to you? You are their captive no longer. Come here immediately. My surgeon can return you to health."

Magda smiled up at the prince and shook his head. "Cassius had a change of heart."

"It doesn't seem to have agreed with you." Brannok sat back and glowered at Magda. Disappointment and frustration poured from every inch of him.

"So, Angrim is here?" Sarah put a hand on Magda's shoulder and gently led her to the side.

She nodded.

"Good." Sarah stepped directly in front of Valafar, his eyes wide and staring. Within those dark pools waited terrors.

"I've got a message I want you to deliver to your boss right through your skull, apprentice," Sarah said.

She intoned the beginning words of a spell that would reach into Valafar's past and make a slight change—ah, there it was. Instead of being Angrim's apprentice, he would become Angrim's premier shoemaker and be murdered in his sleep by a vengeful cobbler who would blame Valafar for taking his job—and his wife.

Apparently, Valafar would be an asshole in any version of his history.

Sarah would have laughed if doing so would not have miscast her magic. Such mirth at this stage would have emptied her veins of blood and replaced it with desiccated fruit. But Magda had been right about one thing. The power of god magic was not touched by Finnagel's place of power.

She continued her spell.

"*Magda*?" Valafar screeched. With a shudder the grim presence vanished from Valafar, and as if waking from a daze, the sorcerer responded to Sarah's casting with a confident phrase in Metzoferran. He reached forward, arms rigid, his fingers twisted in some dialect of Ghost Hand Sarah did not recognize. Valafar's casting switched to Kirrokoan midstream, and Sarah felt the edges of her own spell begin to unravel.

Keane and Harden dove left, and even Magda shuffled right.

Sarah abandoned her cast and jumped sideways to roll into a crouch. Behind her the bricks where she just stood glowed and fused together—whether by Valafar's efforts or some accident of her own casting she didn't know.

Her mercenary instincts ordered her to attack again without delay, and Sarah fell back on the one spell she knew cold. The breeze she created blew snow and sand into Valafar's face. While it did not hurt him in the slightest, he did turn his head for just an instant.

The cobblestone Sarah ripped out of Coach Street knocked Valafar's head sideways, and Sarah's fist flew right behind it. She punched him in the back of the head and drove him to the ground.

Without hesitation she pounded him in the back, rib-cracking blow after blow, bouncing his skull off the stones.

Prince Brannok leaned to one side of his throne and rested his chin in one hand.

To her considerable distress, Sarah realized the man she should have killed by now was laughing. Despite her rain of punishment, Valafar pushed himself up and stood, as if Sarah's efforts were no more than a spring rain.

He waved a hand and spoke a single word, and black clouds bloomed in both of Sarah's eyes.

She gasped but blew it out when a sledgehammer punched her in the stomach and doubled her over.

"Stop it, boy," came Harden's voice. "You can't help. Just gonna get . . . killed yer own self."

"Let me go, you miserable old fuck!" Keane shouted.

The hammer struck her in the temple, and Sarah fell to the cold stone. White spots danced behind the black clouds.

"Learned a little magic after all?" Valafar sneered from the dark. "We'll have to discuss that later. I certainly am not going to let you go to waste here."

Sarah couldn't see to cast another spell. She needed to hold him in her mind. Take his full measure before daring the sorcery Magda taught her. There was no telling the damage she could cause if the forces she brought were not properly directed.

She concentrated on a mental picture of Valafar's face.

"Your suffering will be legendary. Truly, they will sing songs."

She thought of his cruelty. The way she had seen his mind work.

"Tell me, Sarah, which side of the bed do you like to sleep on? Spikes or hooks?"

She made a tiny portal. The communication spell Magda taught her to contact Keane.

"What?" Valafar shouted. Through the connection in their minds, Sarah *saw* Valafar leap back in sudden fear.

The next spell she threw was not so subtle.

Valafar screamed a sorcerous response and held his hands out as far as he could to his sides. His voice roared thunder, and his eyes blazed with white heat.

Speaking in a normal, even tone, Sarah lifted herself up on one elbow and inclined her head toward Valafar, *seeing* up into his face. Her syllables shook the air until she hovered over the ground. When her hands moved, a screeching, tearing sound rolled in from the distance, breaking pieces off the world that were not meant to be broken.

Exhilaration and exultation roared through Sarah's body. It lit her every cell with joy and wild, mad fire. Only now did she touch—did she begin to *comprehend*—what she was. What she was meant to be.

She was *more*.

The spell twisted danger and cacophony out of the universe around them and brought it screeching into the tent. She heard it rip the canvas roof over their heads, an enormous invisible screw concentrated on Valafar. He fought as hard as any creature before him—human or sorcerer—ever had against a force as inexorable as the making of the universe.

At the fringe of her expanded consciousness, Sarah *saw* Keane and Harden back away through the shredded walls of the pavilion.

Good.

In front of her, Valafar leaned left even as his legs leaned right. The sorcerer wove magic with his hands, with all the effect of an ant shaking an angry leg at an oncoming boot.

Then the sorcerer broke.

A stuttering crack erupted from the point where the apprentice stood, and all that had been Valafar splashed outward with such force that everyone in the pavilion—and most of the Host surrounding the tent—were knocked to the ground. Prince Brannok's throne flew back off its platform and sent the prince rolling out of the shredded pavilion.

Greasy blood and sour fluids covered everything.

For a long instant, no one spoke.

"That was fucking gross," Keane exclaimed. "Can you do it again?"

As if in response, Sarah slumped to her knees. Keane ran to her and grabbed a large lean-muscled shoulder. She looked up in his direction, a huge grin on her face.

"I did it. Take that, asshole."

Over Keane's shoulder, Sarah felt the contemplation of a presence. She thought she could see it in her mind but was unable to note any particular of its appearance: Pavinn, Andosh, or Darrish, male or female. With some alarm Sarah realized she could not even tell if it merely peeked over Keane's shoulder or filled the sky over all of Greenshade. It was foreign, yet she had known this presence all her life.

Was it herself?

She had almost certainly miscast the last spell and turned her brains into oatmeal-pepper stew.

"I just thought you were gonna, you know"—Keane wiped blood and effluvia off Sarah's face—"*tell* him a message to deliver. To Angrim?" There was a pause. "What's wrong with your *eyes*?"

The image faded, as did her impression of it. Sarah held out a hand for Keane to help her up. "I think I delivered exactly the message I wanted to."

46

HAVE YOU ALWAYS BEEN ABLE TO DO THAT?

KEANE

That's new, thought Keane. The sight of her eyes, entirely occluded by bright red blood, was alarming, but she seemed otherwise all right. Just wiped out.

And she had won.

Outside the remains of the tattered pavilion, soldiers retreated from the obvious threat of sorcery and shouted warnings to each other. Sergeant Stath called the charge. All around them, battle was joined.

Harden rubbed his ribs where Keane had elbowed him to get free when he ran to Sarah's side. While it might be possible he owed the mercenary his life yet again, he was in no mood to admit it.

Stath barked more orders, and his squad grabbed Keane and pulled him toward the gate.

Keane shouldered away from them and helped Sarah up with his sword hand as he watched Prince Brannok draw his big two-hander from its sheath. The enraged prince ran around the empty throne platform and leaped through the air at Sarah, his long blade whistling.

Keane pitched back his left arm, caught his hidden throwing

knife from his sleeve, and sent it spinning directly into Brannok's proud projecting red beard.

The prince crashed into Sarah, and they both fell to the cobbles beneath them. Brannok's sword clattered to the ground, and he rolled onto his back and sat up. Brannok reached under the wide beard and yanked Keane's knife free. A fountain of red poured down the front of his once-glittering armor.

Sarah spun to her feet.

"Oh," said Keane. "That does not look good. You know, they say you should just leave stuff like that in there until you can find a surgeon."

The younger Brannok's face became a white mask of pain and determination. He propped himself up on one elbow while the other hand gripped his throat. He glared up at Keane, fell forward into the dirt, and did not move again.

"Oldam sit on a stone fork, that asshole was *mad*." Keane shook his head and picked a bit of Valafar's brain out of his hair.

Keane, Sarah, and Harden clambered over torn canvas and the sorcerer's viscera to escape before Tyrrane's army fell on them. Stath's men guided them while the sergeant himself carried Cassius out of the carnage.

"Hey," Keane said as they reached an unobstructed road, "that knife trick worked way better than when I tried it on his brother, Tobin." Keane glanced back over his shoulder. "Shit. We gotta go."

Behind them, the two huge bodyguards had cleared the Valafar out of their eyes, untangled themselves from the whipping folds of white and red canvas, and drawn their blades. One for each meaty fist.

To either side, the King's Swords battled the Host who lined the road and surrounded the pavilion. And further out in front, the rest of the Tyrranean army drew weapons and ran toward the savaged tent.

"Take Cassius back to the castle." Sarah spoke to Sergeant Stath. "The rest of you men help the Swords against the Host."

Keane looked at Sarah's eyes. The red was already fading, though she moved with obvious pain. Black flowers rose under brown skin, and her shoulder was already swelling.

Stath obviously did not want to leave his charge on the field of battle, but did as he was bid anyway. As captain of the castle guard, Sarah was the only one who could force him to walk away from the king. Even Keane was not supposed to be able to order that.

"Now you two hold those big guys off until I say," Sarah said to Keane and Harden. "Then hit the ground and cover your ears." She closed her eyes, hummed, and waved her hands in big spiraling circles, only slightly wobbly from her injuries.

Breath panicky, Keane drew his stolen blade. His hand slid into the finger-worn grooves in the leather. Though he'd been using the sword for the past couple of months, those grooves still weren't from *his* fingers. They belonged to some soldier of the West Marches. Some Hubrane.

Sarah's new sorcery left him feeling as if he were in someone else's life. Someone in a really scary story. *I wasn't really relaxed yet with her blowing out candles from across the room, and now she can break a guy in half with some chanting? Maybe Tyrrane would give me a few days to chat with Sarah about it before we continue the battle.*

The two men stepped in front of Sarah. Keane held the longsword out in front of himself, trained on the bodyguard's eye. Harden cut the air with his cutlass. The gold basket hilt glinted in the nighttime firelight.

Added together, Keane and Harden did not weigh as much as either one of their assailants.

The guard's first swing knocked Keane's sword point to the dirt, and the second would have killed him had he not rolled forward with a shoulder into the huge man's stomach and thrown him off balance.

To Keane's right, Harden had already wounded his man in either arm, one of which dripped crimson down the blade of his own short sword while the other arm dangled uselessly. Remembering his duel with Harden in the ravaged Rousland Embassy, Keane once again thanked Oldam's great stone cock that his old boss had been extremely drunk.

Then Keane flew through the air with the wind knocked out of him.

47

ARE YOU CERTAIN YOU SHOULD BE TOUCHING THAT?

SARAH

Sarah centered herself and drew the power to her. Unlike typical sorcery, god magic did not use ambient magical energy created by metaphysical friction from the spin of the universe. Instead, it drew from a specific and powerful place and pulled rivers of force together to be twisted and manipulated—strung and knitted into the desired effects. Sarah had not had time to learn anything about the source of that power, but she really felt that she should have.

A misty black haze hung over her world. She could barely see. Her shoulder stiffened and tried to seize with pain. Something was definitely broken in there. Her breath hitched, and she felt as if she were moving underwater. Or underwater *and* made of sand.

Fear stabbed at her mind. She had botched these spells so any times, could she count on herself to do it correctly now? Valafar was dead at her hand, but could she believe she could do it again?

Her tongue continued, but her mind was no longer ahead of it. It seemed every word was conjured up by her memory as she spoke it. As she thought it. Her body threatened to freeze up with every gesture.

But she pressed on, regardless.

As she spoke one magical language aloud, she canted a second in her mind, and yet a third with her hands. As much as the spell that destroyed Valafar had drained her, the one she cast now might do her in for good. These magics were designed, as Magda had told her, to permanently kill.

Even an immortal sorcerer.

She went on.

It was almost time. She waited for the break between the eighteenth and nineteenth stanzas and, switching from Metzoferran to Pavinn, shouted, "Now!"

Harden twisted his head and yelled at the King's Swords who fought around them, and everyone dropped to the ground, hands clapped over their ears.

Sarah finished the spell. In a brief moment of glowing peace and weightlessness, she said but a single word.

"*Die.*"

The night sky rumpled as the word rolled across it. It emanated from Sarah as if she were an explosion without fire or heat. Everywhere the wave struck, men pitched back their heads and screamed. Shattering, incoherent screams, not of rage or fear, but of bodies in spasm. They sucked air into their lungs and sent it shrieking out as fast and as hard as possible.

The sound overwhelmed everything. Everything except, curiously, those who had dropped to the ground beneath it.

Blood flecked the lips of the Ebon Host as they fell, the strength in their legs stolen by their own bellowing, ripping lungs. The screams became harsh, choked coughs, no less horrible for the drop in volume. Sarah watched the giant man who had been about to stomp Keane's skull claw at his own bulging throat, his mouth filled with crimson.

All around her, as snow twirled to the ground, the men in gray tabards drowned in their own blood.

Sarah heard a tiny pop. There was a pressure in her eyes and an awful pain in her head. The ground rushed sideways, and she lost her balance and toppled over. Hands pushed her over onto her back, but by now, all she could see was a dim red.

"You did that wrong," the voice of Magda said. "You burst all of the blood vessels in your brain."

Red faded to black.

48

BEEN NICE KNOWING YA

KEANE

Keane and Harden hauled Sarah's unmoving form toward the Country Gate as fast as they could, surrounded by dead men on all sides. Thanks to Harden's shouted warning, most of the King's Swords were alive to accompany them.

The horrifying spell Sarah had cast killed as many as two thousand Tyrraneans which still left the defenders outnumbered five to one inside compromised walls.

Keane's brain reeled from what he had just seen. Had it actually happened? Were all those people really dead? His feet stumbled toward the open gate. His own soldiers screamed for him to hurry.

Denial undermined Keane's memories. Did *Sarah* really do that?

After a lengthy instant of hushed silence, horns blared all around the city, and the Host ran for the gate. The swath of dead extended in a circle around them, but more soldiers rushed into it, eager to claim vengeance for their felled comrades.

They wouldn't stop Keane and his companions from reaching the gate, but they left no time to waste.

What about Cassius? Did Stath get him inside? Keane spared a glance ahead and through the portcullis to look for him. Cassius lay slumped in the dirt and blood, just inside the gate. He looked dead to Keane.

No great loss there.

But Keane *knew* Sarah was unconscious. He wouldn't let *her* be dead.

The hooves of war horses clopped up behind the fleeing trio. Damn.

They weren't going to make it after all.

Arrows arced off of the wall in front of him, and horses shrieked.

"Defend the king!" shouted the Swords.

The surviving soldiers of Greenshade ran back the way they had come, past Harden and Keane, to face the horsemen. There were more shouts and whinnies in the direction of the hissing arrows.

Keane flinched at every noise, as if each shout brought the sword stroke or hoof fall that would end him. But none did, and together, he and Harden dragged Sarah's heavy weight through the twin portcullises held aloft by a dozen strong-backed trolls. Over half of his Swift Shields ran close behind them.

The trolls dropped the broken gate with a crash that made Keane jump.

Despite horror and unearthly powers, they had made it in.

"Great fucking Oldam fill his pants with clay."

Keane shifted Sarah's weight and tried to wipe his nose. The cold always made it run, and he didn't want to be seen having just run heroically back through the gates while snot dripped off his chin.

The big double doors slammed shut over the portcullis behind him, and Keane dropped to the ground beside Sarah. Her breathing came shallow, and a trickle of blood ran from her nose.

She would not wake, and her skin had a sallow greenish cast.

Panic grabbed his chest and squeezed.

The area inside the gate glowed with torchlight and activity. The Norrik Embassies were composed of six long houses. Five, currently occupied with a warlord or king currently in charge, lay to the right and the Thirteen Markets, their gardens covered in patches of white, sprawled to the left. The falling snow melted instantly on contact with the warmer cobbles, leaving them wet and slick.

Megan found Keane in the midst of it all and they embraced. He held her tight and breathed through her hair.

Flowers were still the first thing he thought of when he held her close.

"Where is Sarah hurt?" Megan brushed the bigger woman's hair out of her scarred face with a pale delicate hand. "I can't find a wound. She looks so bad."

"Just a sec." Keane leaned over and punched Harden solidly in the testicles.

"Haaagnn." Harden doubled over and dropped to his knees. "I'm —nngh—starting to get *real* tired of all this aggression, boy. Gaah—fuck." On the other side of Harden, Eli raised an eyebrow.

Keane pulled a dagger off his hip and pointed it at Harden. Eli shifted his weight and said nothing, but even out of the corner of his eye, Keane could tell the old bastard was ready to draw steel.

To Eli's right, Sergeant Stath already had a blade half out of its scabbard.

"I think you oughtta explain just what the stone fuck all that business was about you negotiating sides with Prince Brannok." Keane had experienced all the surprises today he was prepared to stomach and enough nightmares ready to keep him awake for weeks.

"Keane, stop." Megan held him by the shoulder. "This isn't the time. You're just worried about Sarah. We need to find Finnagel. He can help her."

Though he knew she was right, his anger was driving the wagon, not his brain. Pain and worry turned to anger and focused on Harden.

The gray mercenary held up a finger and dragged his legs around to sit on the cobblestones. Above them men shouted and horns clamored, and on the street around them, people rushed and made ready.

When Harden could speak, he raised his head.

"That was just me trying to figure out how desperate the prince might be. If he was worried enough, he would have tried to turn me against you." He inhaled and let out a shallow sigh.

"And just what do you think you learned?"

"He wasn't all that worried." Harden looked down at Sarah. "Might should have been, though."

That was the truth. When Sarah left the castle two months ago, the only magic she knew was a light breeze. What she had done—

"Your Majesty." Sergeant Stath held out a hand to Keane. "We should take Mistress Sarah to the surgeon and get you and Queen Megan out of harm's way."

"Yes, do that," Megan said. "And fetch Finnagel."

Stath's men lifted Sarah up.

"Sorry, Your Grace." Stath's face might have been made of granite. "Finnagel's been missing for months. We assume Queen . . . We assume the Hubrane woman killed him."

"That's not possible," Keane whispered. Beside him, Megan lifted a hand to her chest and took a step back.

Stath's men struggled with Sarah. Cassius gripped Sarah's wrist like death itself. The act of doing so apparently took everything the steel merchant-turned-spy had left in him. When Keane yanked his stiff hand off Sarah, the thin flesh was cold.

"Someone throw this in a hole." Keane was bitter and angry about Cassius, his lies and his treatment of Sarah. But he would get over it.

For now, anyway, the duplicitous merchant or goddess or whatever, was still alive, if only barely.

Keane let himself be hauled to his feet. "Thank you for being here, Stath."

"Where else would I be?"

Stath moved closer to Keane and glared at Eli who raised his hands and backed away.

Keane put away his dagger. Megan was right. This wasn't the time. "For the peace, and for Sarah, I'm letting it go." He really didn't want to, but he was so tired. "I've enemies enough already."

Sergeant Stath's reply was lost in the sudden commotion behind Keane.

Eli ran past.

An unknown voice shouted, "That's for my family, you murderer!" and Keane whirled to see Eli drag a man in Greenshade livery to the ground and pummel him in the stomach.

Next to the beating, Harden lay on his back, propped up eight inches or so by the pommel of a sword. The blade jutted out of his chest, wavering and steaming in the air. A pair of Swords attempted to haul Eli off of the soldier, the first of which immediately lost all of his front teeth while the second hit the ground and clutched his broken knee.

"Eli, stop," shouted Keane. "He's not going anywhere."

But Harden is.

Eli clambered off the Sword and stumbled to Harden.

Dismayed, Keane saw that the Sword was just a boy, no more than fifteen years old. Just a boy who got in a lucky shot. Harden led the mercenary army that almost destroyed Treaty Hill and Greenshade along with it nearly a year ago. Keane imagined he had been responsible for the murder of plenty of people's families. This boy must have seen it happen.

The only thing that upset Keane more than having been allied with the murderous bastard was having been the same kind of murderous bastard once himself. Looking at Harden's blood pooling in the street, he figured both things were over for good.

To one side of Harden, Eli held his oldest friend's head up so that he could see around him. Keane and Megan knelt on the mercenary's other side.

Harden looked at Keane and then at Eli. He coughed up some blood. Among other things, the sword blade had pierced a lung.

"Eli, don't talk. Just listen. Not much time." Harden smiled, his lips red.

"Take that Loffa . . . and get a boat. Go west past Port Placid. Past Rumfish. There's an"—he paused, coughed, breathed for a beat, and swallowed—"island with a tall peak in the middle. Orange flowers all over it. Only one. That's . . . my island. That's what I asked . . . the Deep Witch for the first time."

"You had an island alla this time?" Eli asked. "An' you never saw fit to tell no one?"

"Said don't talk. So shut up. Thought I'd retire there, but it never . . . happened. All my money is there. It's . . . It's a lot. You and the girl can live like kings. Build a fine house. All the slaves you want. Enjoy your lives. Stop all this . . . bullshit. I know you hate it."

"I will, Marshal." Eli's voice broke over the words. "I'll do it up proud."

"I would think the king should be consulted if you intend to run off with the queen mother. After all I . . ." Keane looked into Eli's black glare and forgot the rest of what he was saying. "Hey, whatever. Take her if she'll have you. I was just kidding."

"Thank you, Harden"—Megan leaned over him to make it easier for him to see her—"for helping us. It almost makes up for you trying to kill us all."

Harden grinned, his mouth bloody. "Thank you, my queen. Can someone roll me over? This is . . . killing my back."

Gently, Eli eased Harden over toward him. This elicited a gasp from first Harden, then Megan as she saw the volume of blood on the cobblestones.

"Take it out," came Harden's harsh whisper.

With a nod from Eli, Keane slid the sword blade free. "Ahhh." Harden rolled onto his back. "That's better."

And then he lay quiet and stared at the sky.

No one spoke as Keane, Eli, and Megan sat in a tight cluster around their friend and enemy. Megan reached down and took Harden's hand in hers. She squeezed it tight. Harden's eyes darted over to her and he smiled a bit.

Despite herself, Megan shrieked and dropped Harden's hand. "Sorry. I thought you . . . I mean—"

"I don't mean to rush this," Keane said, "but I do have king stuff to do. City under siege and all, you know."

Harden lifted his head and probed at the opening in his chest.

"I ain't complainin' myself," Eli said, "but that is a fairly life-endin' hole you got there. An' I'm pretty sure that's at least a whole person's worth o' blood on the street. Shouldn't you be flyin' with Slago to the happy beaches of Nedda or somewheres?"

Keane snorted. "As if."

"I don't really know. Truth is I kinda feel better." Harden stuck his finger further into the hole. "Well shove a fish up my bung and call it feast-day. *That's* what she meant. *Would be resting*, my ass."

"Does this make any sense to anyone here?" Megan asked.

Harden pushed himself up on one elbow. "I think I *am* dead, Eli. I think that fishy bitch fucked me to death and left me some kind of dead guy. But still handsome."

"That's, uh . . . Y'know, I ain't rightly sure how to respond to that."

"I can feel my heart. It isn't moving."

"Do I still get the island?" Eli asked.

"You know what?" Harden held out his hand to Eli. The old mercenary took it and pulled Harden to his feet. "Why not? I think I'm better at fighting than retiring anyway; otherwise, I'd have done it ages ago. Just promise me I can come visit if I've a mind."

Eli winked at him. "Maybe. I could be busy."

49

ON THE EDGE OF DEATH —SO BACK TO NORMAL

KEANE

Keane stood in the window of his private audience hall up in the heights of the Crow's Tower. A single candle picked out the mother-of-pearl inlays on the small dark table while the softer furniture around the walls faded into the dark. On the sofa lay Queen Megan, asleep, one hand curled protectively around her gently rounded stomach.

The intimate room gave him little solace tonight. More sounds rose up in the night than the hooting calls of the crag lion in the menagerie.

The Ebon Host's attack pulled back less than an hour later with little having been decided. Although it was not possible to see what was going on through the snow and dark, the sounds outside were unmistakable. The Host were building something, and that something was almost certainly siege engines. To the good, the missing Hulda had repaired the broken walls with timbers and sand while she led the castle and collapsed the sappers' tunnels used to bring them down. Also, the Host was out of sorcerers, so there would be no more reanimated dead creatures to worry about like those that had accompanied Songham's forces when he took the castle.

Except Harden, that was. Keane did not know how to even think about that, much less how to resolve his feelings about it. So much had changed since he'd been forced out of the castle. Even more since he'd just been a mercenary soldier.

It occurred to Keane that everything, every bit of it, could be traced back to Harden's dislike for him and the old man's decision to try and kill him.

Of course, some of that *could* be laid on Keane's problems with authority.

The Forest Castle had also depleted their sorcerers, which evened that score. Sarah slept on, and Finnagel had reportedly been dragged off and killed. Keane would have to look into that. Could Songham or his wife have killed Finnagel when Kadir couldn't?

Truth to tell, Keane had experienced more than his fill of all that bullshit anyway.

When Keane asked how much Morholt might be able to help, the ginger wizard shrugged and smiled. He was pretty sure his magic would be just enough for him and his sister to escape.

So other than being vastly outnumbered with no food, things seemed about even.

He gazed out into the black. There were doubtless a few generals left out there ready to carry out orders from Dismon. Keane hung his head. This was such a waste.

A light knock came at the door.

"Hello, Secreed." Keane felt nothing but relief at the familiar sight of his chamberlain.

"Your Majesty, the Barons' Conclave is in the primary audience hall. They asked that I see if you were still awake and invite you, should you wish to attend."

Keane looked over at Megan. "Yes, Secreed. Tell them I would like that very much. Just give me a few minutes to walk the queen to bed."

"Very good, sire. I expect they will be pleased to hear you say so."

After the chamberlain left, Keane lifted Megan in his arms. She had bathed and smelled like flowers once more. For real. It was the best, most reassuring thing he had ever smelled. He could almost forget the world outside the tower windows.

"No." She pushed sleepily against his chest. "I can walk."

"I know you can, I just want to." Keane toed the door open and carefully walked down the stairs.

"Don't drop me. I'm the queen. Can't drop queens down stairs."

Though he didn't say it aloud, Keane would sooner have pitched himself into hell than let his pregnant wife go rolling down those steps. He *wanted* to save Treaty Hill and Greenshade because it was important to Megan. But what he *needed* was to figure out a way to save *her*. The tunnel that he'd used to spirit himself, Megan, and Loffa away from Songham was useless. There were so many Tyrraneans out there that they would come up right in the middle of them. In any event, he knew he couldn't leave Treaty Hill to the Ebon Host.

For all their evils, Songham and Hulda Hubrane were at least *of* Greenshade. They wanted to rule. Songham did, anyway. Keane didn't know what Hulda was doing. All of her actions seemed engineered toward maximizing casualties.

The Host was only here to destroy.

KEANE HEADED to the Royal Audience Chamber in the Flying Halls, where he typically met with the nation's various councils.

Darkness claimed most of the chamber as the king entered. The only light came from a quartet of oil lamps arranged on portable stands. The heavy velvet draperies were down across the row of windows to the east and west sides of the long room to keep the bitterness out of the chill.

The Barons' Conclave sat in high-backed, upholstered chairs brought in for them and arranged in their usual fashion, with a single exception. At her deceased husband's spot sat Baroness Roselle Tralgar.

She smiled and winked at him as he passed and put to rest his concerns over Horace's execution.

Keane walked up the steps to his throne and, on a whim, grabbed the big gold-coated chair and dragged it thumping down the steps, even with the barons. He situated it and sat, observing several looks of approval.

"Before anyone says anything," Keane began, "I want to tell you thanks for coming to Treaty Hill's aid. Without all of you, Hulda Hubrane and Prince Brannok would be sitting here right now, frying Hedra's farts in a stolen pan over our murdered corpses."

Next time there was food, Keane would ask Cook to make some farts. He was starving.

"And Lady Fenrath, I can't tell you how sorry I am at what happened to your home. That town—those families—were Greenshade. Every one of us was wounded by the Ebon Host's march through Fenrath. It's one more reason to break Tyrrane's fucking legs and send their Host hobbling back home."

The Baroness Lady Fenrath stood and nodded to Keane. Face sallow, she moved uncertainly. But her voice was steady and true.

"Had we stayed behind to defend our homes, we would be dead along with all others who opposed the Ebon Host. Our chances here, bad as they might seem, are the best we could have done. We are trusting you now to lead and save us."

Keane sat speechless. The Barons' Conclave was a collection of the proudest men and women Keane had ever met. To cede their fate to him was inconceivable.

"And we would like to thank Your Majesty in turn," Baron Sins said, the relentless, wry smile on his long face turned up at one corner, "for engineering the defeat at sea of the Oulani Navy, for personally climbing the wall and opening the Country Gate which allowed our troops to safety, and for alerting me to the tunnel that made it possible for me to lead my soldiers into the castle and take it almost bloodlessly."

Put like that, maybe it didn't sound so inconceivable that these stubborn people would look to Keane for leadership. It still seemed crazy, though.

"Would it be at all possible for us to go ten full minutes without hearing about how you took the damn castle?" complained Baron

Rollins, his normally well-groomed appearance marred by his disheveled silver hair. "I'm tired, I'm angry, and I haven't had a proper shit in three days. And"—Rollins increased his volume—"everybody knows that you captured the castle. So, shut up about it."

Sins grinned, and Rollins shifted in his chair with a wince.

Lady Roselle stood.

"Our primary reason for asking you to attend, Your Majesty, was to pledge our fealty to the crown and to you personally. It is a tradition the conclave did not find opportunity for before now but one whose time has come."

The other Barons and Lady Fenrath stood.

"I am . . . overwhelmed. Should I take it, Lady Roselle, from your being here that you have decided to run the Tralgar lands as baroness?"

"As is my duty to the crown." Roselle's eyes twinkled. She favored the king with a curtsy. "As well, I have assumed my husband's former role as head of the conclave, for so long as they'll have me."

"Does that mean you'll be leaving us here?" Keane asked.

"Oh no." Her round face dimpled with the depth of her smile. "I could never do that to the good gentlemen of Treaty Hill. Assuming we survive."

"Right. So, do I stand for this or what?"

"Standing is appropriate, sire," Roselle said.

Each of the conclave members reached beneath their chairs and removed a small pillow, some round, some square. Keane recognized them from the antechamber just outside this hall. They placed these on the floor in front of themselves and slowly got to their knees. Baron Hapstan helped Lady Fenrath while Baron Orrikson trotted off to one of the darkened corners of the room. He returned with the stone image of the Father-King, Oldam, pinched from the chapel. On its pedestal, it was easily three feet tall and must have weighed a hundred pounds. Orrikson hefted it to the center of the assembly and left it there to face Keane.

He stood before them and wondered what he should do with his hands.

Formal worship of the Alir was not permitted in Greenshade since its inception when Eggan Rance the First threw down the Temple of the Sky. Private worship was tolerated, which was what the chapel was for. That Orrikson had brought Oldam's image here spoke to the age of this ceremony and the unbent natures of the barons.

The conclave spoke as one.

"Thus, do we take our oaths of fealty to our nation of Greenshade, and Keane, its king," they intoned.

"Before the Alir and in the sight of the Father-King, we the Barons' Conclave shall be ever faithful and true to King Keane of Greenshade. We shall hold dear all that he holds dear and turn our faces from all that he would shun. Never, by word or by action, shall we ever do that which is displeasing or injurious to him, on the conditions that he hold us to him as we deserve and keep our lands to us and our families in his service."

"Unless he needs his ass kicked for his own good," added Baron Rollins.

The conclave laughed at this, and as no one seemed inclined to retract it or add anything else, Keane raised his arms in his most kingly fashion.

"Thank you, one and all." No one moved.

"I, um, accept your fealty and will do all those things you said, and you'll do all those other things you said."

The conclave members looked around at each other. Some shrugged; others nodded their approval.

"And then the oath of fealty was done." Keane clapped his hands together as loud as he could manage.

The lords and ladies rose, and everyone agreed that had been good enough to do the trick. Keane thanked them all and left. He was so very tired, but there was still one more stop ahead of him before he went to bed.

~

THOUGH HE HAD INTENDED to talk to her in the long high-ceilinged hall that served as infirmary to the royal surgeon, in the end, Keane simply sat at Sarah's side and held her hand. There was nothing to say. According to the surgeon there was nothing wrong with her, and she could awaken at any time—though to Keane she looked horrible. So, he sat and said nothing and drew comfort from her presence. When he woke up a couple of hours later, his head in her lap, he stood, stretched, and went upstairs to his bed.

50

TARGETED PRACTICE

KEANE

Every time a boulder or part of someone's home struck the outer walls, Keane's muscles jerked taut. He really needed to strangle someone.

While two of the Tyrranean trebuchets stayed aimed at the spot on the outer wall where Songham had sapped, destroyed, and then his wife later repaired, a third, much larger device sat unused far down Coach Street beneath a cloudy sky, some distance from the Country Gate. The Host had painted it blood red and black and ornamented it with white skulls. On the front was painted the name they gave it, *Mekal*. It referred to a custom of the Alir for settling affairs, both practical and spiritual, when death was imminent.

If the Tyrraneans had built the thing for no purpose other than to unnerve the defenders in the castle, they had received more than enough return on their investment.

Sarah continued to sleep, which Keane found extremely lazy behavior. He'd been forced to devise tasks for all the barons and baronesses in order to keep them out of his ass. They were helpful, but they all wanted to help at once, and they very rarely agreed on anything.

At the moment, they were the least of Keane's worries.

Snow fell, as it had all day, from the dark afternoon sky. Keane stood outdoors with Captain Falt between the Mirrik and Tyrranean embassies and watched engineers examine the repaired outer wall. Keane took their extreme agitation every time a several hundred-pound portion of some city dweller's garden wall struck the other side as a bad sign.

The captain sneezed. "Sorry."

Falt was the captain of the Swift Shields, a contingent of the King's Swords that roamed the countryside providing the people with safety and arbitration. When Keane and Sarah first came to the Forest Castle as Prince Despin of Tyrrane and bodyguard, Falt had been the one to bring them.

Keane and Falt both wore chainmail armor beneath, and weapons above, their fur cloaks, heavy gloves, and boots. Falt stamped his feet and breathed into gloved hands.

The engineers on the wall, two old men, two young men, and a young woman, conferred, glancing nervously up at the repaired section. It was hard to tell much about them, given that everyone was bundled in wool clothes, outer clothes, and blankets. They wore the gray-green acorn caps common to Greenshade, hers peaked, the others domed.

Eventually one of the older men, a bushy-eyebrowed codger with a hooked nose, climbed down the ladder and walked over to Keane and Falt.

"Majesty. Cap'n. That wall's comin' down."

"We assumed as much," Captain Falt answered. "That's why you were called. We were hoping you could give us an idea as to when."

When Keane first met Falt, he had deferred all he did to his surly sergeant, afraid of overstepping himself with every word. What a difference six months of hell could make. He stood straighter and spoke with confidence. His always tall frame had gone from gawky to somewhere in the vicinity of brawny, if still chinless.

"Bein' honest, sirs," the engineer said as he removed his cap to scratch at his bald head, "I'd be surprised if she were still standin' by the end o' this conversation."

Falt nodded. "Get your men in the castle. Sire, you should go with them. Stath and his men are waiting for you. Baron Orrikson is seeing to the outer walls. I'll deliver the message myself."

"Don't get caught up there." Keane gave Falt a grim smile. It was the only kind he had left. "I still need you."

Keane let him go, but instead of going back to the castle, he went past the entryway to the extensive gardens surrounding the Thirteen Markets, where the conclave's troops had chosen to set up their snow-encrusted camps.

Sergeant Stath appeared at Keane's side. Though he was not always obvious, he was always around and always had an eye out for Keane.

The man took his bodyguarding seriously.

"Looks like we're finally gonna die here." Keane flinched as another hunk of masonry struck the other side. A muffled crack accompanied the loud *thud*, and sand spilled down the inside of the barrier.

Stath scratched the back of his neck. "Well, I don't know about all that, but I *would* say that wall is right shitted out."

"I never did ask how you survived Songham and the bitch."

"Me and the Elbows"—Stath referred to his squad of bodyguards by their nickname—"we were trying to ferry some of the castle staff out of the big wall. Got ourselves pinched and ended up in the prisoner camp. Orrikson rescued us."

"Oldam sit on my head and call it a hat." Keane felt unreasonably irate at his friend and protector's good fortune. "I am never going to be free of that damnable, heroic fuckwit." Orrikson had just pledged undying fealty to Keane. Maybe it was time to let the one-sided rivalry go.

"You know, I don't want to be telling you how to king, but maybe we oughtta be getting outta here."

"I was coming to the same conclusion." Keane gazed around thoughtfully at the ordered rows of tents and campfires. "I don't think we're gonna win, but I don't see any reason to make it easy for the fuckers."

Keane climbed up on a statue of some Arlean hero on horseback and shouted for attention. Soon, five hundred men surrounded him, and more came every minute.

"Soldiers of Greenshade," shouted Keane, his fingers cold through the furry leather gloves he wore, "the outer wall will fall within the hour." Alarm spread on the faces of the men. "When it does, the Quarters are gonna fill with Tyrraneans." Alarm turned to worry. "We need to bolster the men on the outer wall, put more people who can shoot a bow up there, and catch as many of the frost-cocks down here in the crossfire between the inner and outer walls."

Something unexpected happened then. Keane realized he was still used to talking to mercenaries. Men who fought for money were typically cowardly and brutish, with as much use for a fair fight as they had for a bucket of snot. But these men weren't mercenaries. They fought for their country, for their families, and even for their king.

Worry turned to resolve.

"This is probably a suicide mission." Keane wondered where his sudden honesty was coming from. "We'll do everything we can to get you back off that wall, but there are going to be a lot more of them than there will be of us. That's why this has to be on a volunteer basis."

All around Keane, a sea of hands went up into the air. These men already knew they were going to die. Keane was offering them a chance to make the Host pay for it first.

For the first time, he was glad Sarah was out of commission. He would not have been able to handle it if she had volunteered for the wall.

"Go quickly." Keane struggled to keep his emotions in check. "Find Captain Falt or Baron Orrikson. They'll be chopping down the stairs soon."

The soldiers, dressed in a variety of tabards, both of the individual barons and of Greenshade, rushed toward what was almost certainly their deaths. Keane watched them go. After a moment, he climbed down the statue and followed the rest of the troops through the inner castle gate and into the broad courtyard where the final defenses were being set up. He walked past it all and into the castle keep to find Megan and a good place to watch.

EXCEPT FOR A FEW rooms such as the one Keane and Megan observed the battle from—that might be used for some other, more strategic purpose—the castle's keep was filled from rooftop to dungeons with the citizens of Treaty Hill seeking refuge. In most places there was barely room to sit. Keane reckoned there might be enough food to give everyone a single meal, as long as it didn't take more than about a raisin to fill them up. The Host didn't have to attack anymore to win, they just had to sit there. Wouldn't take more than a few days, and no one else would have to die. But that wasn't how evil fucks like these worked.

Keane certainly knew better than to surrender to them.

The outer wall fell with a splintering crash. Sand collapsed inward and made a soft hill clogged with timbers. It would be impossible to traverse in armor.

The Tyrraneans charged it anyway. They pushed the sand with their shields even as their legs bogged down.

Baron Orrikson and his men fired arrow after arrow into the breach and sought to choke the gap with bodies. In the gray light and the air full of snow, arrows were invisible and harder to block with shields and cover. The black-and-gray-garbed Host, shields held hopefully over their heads, ran in, picked up rubble and bodies, and ran off again. Many were shot in the leg or foot, but many more succeeded. Soon, the Ebon Host flowed through the breach and into the Quarters.

Archers on the outer wall fired down on the Tyrraneans at Orrikson's command. Across the Quarters, atop the inner castle wall, Captain Falt barked his own orders to fire. Hundreds of Tyrranean soldiers died—and even more pressed forward to fill the gap.

Ladders by the dozen rose up on both sides of the outer wall, the only means to the top now that the wooden steps had been destroyed. The stone stair beside the Country Gatehouse had been covered in thick tarry grease and set aflame.

Polemen shoved the ladders away, and soldiers with sword and axe attacked those who made it to the top. But there were too many. Every clash allowed three more ladders to stand in place, and the fighting spread. Soon it was everywhere along the wall top, and it slowly stopped as the Tyrraneans overtook the wall.

Keane's fear for Megan was almost debilitating. He had to think about something else.

Eventually, the only fighting that remained was a small knot just south of the gatehouse. Orrikson and a band of defenders were determined to bring three of the Host to hell for every man of Greenshade who went down. With two of his men still battling, Orrikson was shoved from the wall. He twisted and clutched the man who pushed him, and they both fell, the baron stabbing his attacker repeatedly on the way down.

The asshole couldn't even die like a regular man, Keane thought. Always gotta be the hero. The thought brought to mind one of Eli's favorite sayings: *Murderers kill men; heroes kill everyone.*

Keane guessed he had finally become a real hero.

51

YOU PROBABLY COULD TAKE IT WITH YOU, BUT YOU SHOULDN'T

KEANE

Time for you to go," Keane said to Megan. They held each other and watched the slaughter outside from one of the keep's forward windows. He felt numb, as if to touch his own emotions would burst a huge dam of boiling water and simply kill him where he stood.

The royal couple procrastinated in the small spare room with Sergeant Stath and his five-man squad behind them. Neither Keane nor Megan wanted to leave the other, though they both knew they must.

Keane had assigned the soldiers to guard the queen, though he had been forced to resort to threats and dishonor to convince Stath to leave him. In the end, he pointed out that against all the armies of Tyrrane, it would not matter if Stath were with him or not; Keane would not survive. But there was a very slim chance that if Megan could be kept alive, she might be allowed to live in banishment, and then Stath could continue to guard the welfare of Greenshade's ruler-in-exile.

It was a lie, and they both knew it. Megan would not be allowed to live with Keane's child in her belly. But Stath was kind enough not to mention it and simply agreed.

Megan nodded to Keane and lifted her bow. She once again wore the pleated green skirts and shining silver breastplate she'd worn when they fought against Valafar's reanimated *fallen men*.

Her quick thinking had saved that grim day. But there would be no clever ploys this go-round. The Host was a huge hammer falling on them from the sky. It couldn't be bargained with or outsmarted. Sarah was unconscious, and Finnagel was gone or dead.

And still Megan refused to give up hope. Keane envied her that.

She sighed. "Time to save the city. Again."

Keane raised an eyebrow and held the tiny queen out at arms' length. "I don't think so." He shook his head. "It's my turn. You got to save the city last time."

She smiled up at him, more than a hint of sadness in her eyes. "I'll race you."

They embraced, and Megan left for her tower perch above the battleground, Stath and his Elbows in tow.

～

ONCE THE TYRRANEANS captured the outer wall, the portcullises of the Country Gate were raised, and ordered rows of the Ebon Host marched through. They filled the Quarters and stomped snow into slush as they hid behind embassy and merchant buildings—out of sight of Greenshade archers atop the inner wall.

Frightened by the combat noise and scent of blood on the air, every animal in the menagerie capable of making a sound did so, and the air filled with honks, hoots, roars, and croaking cries of panic.

Watching from his window, Keane sympathized.

This frenzied fear transferred to the Host, who had never imagined such noises and were not prepared for it. Some appeared to Keane to think themselves under attack by monsters, and they broke ranks and ran from the strange and terrifying cacophony. Tyrranean officers ordered bowmen to fire on the panicked soldiers and brought a swift halt to the desertions. Keane sympathized with the deserters even more than the animals. The racket was both thunderous and chaotic.

And in general, Keane more closely identified with deserters anyway.

Out in the city, the sound of drums rolled in and competed with the menagerie for the most bowel-loosening din.

Mekal was on the move.

Keane, alone in his little observation post, watched the gargantuan trebuchet roll forward to the sound of the drums. Huge stacks of masonry and stone debris showed where they intended to haul it— well outside of bowshot even from the outer walls.

The slow crawl continued for the better part of an hour, during which time the Host vacated the outer wall sections close to the Country Gate. When it stopped, the drums changed tempo and gained speed.

Keane realized he was holding his breath.

Lines of horses pulled the winches that ratcheted the huge tree trunk into place. A wagon was used to ferry ammunition from the stacks to the sling beneath the main body of the device. The drums went silent, and Mekal dropped its enormous counterweight, drawing the sling—filled with a huge piece of some nobleman's home —back, up and over, and then hurtled it through the snow and wind toward the Forest Castle.

Unable to do anything else, Keane followed the flight path over the outer wall and bit his lower lip until the missile, as high as a man, struck the castle gatehouse not ten feet from where Captain Falt stood. The gatehouse cracked, and pieces of it fell to the ground below. Falt ran from one end of the gatehouse roof to the other, checking on his men and issuing orders.

Outside the walls, the drums beat again. The clangor boomed like the knocking of Oldam's great granite testicles.

Mekal threw death at the Forest Castle a second time. Captain Falt and his Swords fled to either side of the inner gate as the squarish corner of stone and lime cleared the outer wall, though they needn't have bothered. The huge piece dropped just below them, flew through the castle gate portcullis, and crashed into the doors of the gate behind them. Steel-riveted wooden doors exploded inward to send debris hundreds of feet into the courtyard.

"And that's me." Keane left the tiny room at a trot and headed for the stairs leading down.

52

NO ONE TEACHES GEOMETRY IN WICKED NOBLE'S CLASS

HULDA HUBRANE

A shudder rattled Hulda as she shimmied sideways in the dark. The fighting outside must be getting serious.

"I mean *really*, sweetheart, you haven't been in this place any longer than I have." Hulda picked at something soft and cold and sticky in her hair. She had lost the capacity for squeamishness, if she had ever possessed it. "How is it you know all these hidden rooms and corridors and miserable little spaces like this one when the people who lived here their whole lives have never seen them?"

The passageway was barely a foot wide, and Hulda spoke to keep her claustrophobia at bay. The past few days had not been pleasant for her.

She tried to ignore the cold of the frozen stone, the disheveled state of her clothes, and the smell of her unwashed body, inescapable in the close confines.

"Is geometry."

There was a gray light coming up, and fresh cold air blew into the suffocating space, relieving Hulda's suffering. She closed her eyes and smiled, thinking of the glory of an open window while the sounds of combat and screaming men played outside.

"Geometry." Hulda curled her tongue around the unfamiliar word. "Is that some kind of sorcery?" She knew a sorceress. The Red Lady in Rousland. Hulda did not suffer from the rest of Greenshade's superstitious view toward magic.

"Is science." Tynos leaned heavily against a wall. She had been wounded badly in their flight, and her leg did not work the way it was supposed to. "Look at the wall. Look at the uzzer wall. Is too much space, so the chamber hides between."

"And you can tell all that by glancing at a wall?" Hulda watched Tynos come upon the face-height window, look out, take a breath, and slide back into the darkness on the other side. Hulda's mouth watered at the thought of fresh air. She ached for it.

Tynos did not answer, but Hulda did not care. Hulda stopped in front of the window, perhaps ten by ten inches and nocked on the outside as an arrow loop would be—and just breathed. Three days of living in walls with Tynos's stinky leg wound had affected her more deeply than she expected.

Set in the face of the castle keep, the window looked out on the main courtyard and walls. Hulda could see the Host charging in through the shattered gate while a lanky, chinless captain of the King's Swords on the damaged gatehouse above exhorted his men to fill them with arrows.

What was his name? Falk? Falt? Why did she remember that? Ah yes. This man had represented the Swords during General Roen's efforts to integrate them with her ducal guard.

"We should move," Tynos said, her face invisible in the dark but her linen clothes a paler shade of black. "We have no way of leaving here. When Prince Brannok comes, we are less safe than now."

"What's the rush?" Hulda leaned forward—barely—and inhaled deeply. This was a perfect vantage to watch the battle rage a hundred feet below her. "One wall is as good as another."

From somewhere beneath her, a force of soldiers in orange and brown—doubtless one of the Barons' Conclave—rushed forward to attack the encroaching Tyrraneans. With about three hundred men, they bottled up the Host in the corridor under the castle gatehouse, where Captain Chinless rained boiling water and stones down on their heads.

The pile of bodies accumulating in the entryway grew impressive. Behind it out in the Quarters, Hulda could see through the gate to the Host soldiers that refused to step in and the pileup that gathered there. Those in front were unable to move. Pressed tight by the thousands behind them, they buckled and fell forward.

Captain Chinless saw it too.

"What's he up to?" Though she still couldn't see Tynos, Hulda felt her impatience. "Relax, wouldja? We're in a *wall*. No one knows we're here. I can't imagine anyone even knows *here* is here." She stared out the window across the courtyard to the valiant captain on the gatehouse.

"Oh my."

The captain had taken an iron bar that was as long as he was and pushed it into a vast crack along the outside facing of the gatehouse's crenellated wall. Several more Swords joined him, and with a bit of manly heaving, the crack expanded.

Hulda clapped her hands when she saw the expressions on the faces of the Host through the entryway. An instant later, the protective fronting fell off the other side of the gatehouse and crushed nearly a hundred Tyrraneans flat.

Laughter escaped Hulda and she covered her mouth with a dirty hand. She did not think anyone could hear them, but there was no reason to be stupid about it.

Tynos leaned out of the dark to share Hulda's view.

Hulda wrinkled her nose.

"The Swords are very brave. But see out past the castle gate. Past the Country Gate too. The Ebon Host still fills all of Treaty Hill. This castle is the lonely rock in the Ebon Sea, and the tide rises. Their heroics are for nuzzing."

Ladders popped up on the far side of Chinless's position, and his Swords threw hooks attached to chains over the ends of them. They shouted to drovers in the courtyard below who ran big farm horses and oxen Hulda had not previously noticed—that were attached to the other ends of those chains—toward the castle.

The ladders came clattering up and over the walls and gatehouse, sending more than a few Host flying high into the sky as they were catapulted over the eighty-foot inner wall.

Even Tynos smirked. Just a little.

But a few Tyrraneans did make the top, and where they gave battle, more followed behind them. Beneath, with nothing left to discourage them, more Tyrraneans cleared the bodies and came charging out at the brown and orange baron.

The end for the brave Captain Chinless grew close.

From above and to Hulda's right, an arrow whizzed in an arcing path into the stumbling steps of a Tyrranean soldier. Hulda saw him catch the missile in his chest and fall backward.

It was an amazing shot.

"Place the barrel there, Sergeant Stath," a young woman's voice said from the source of the arrow.

Who is that? Hulda wondered.

"Yes, my queen," a man, presumably Stath, answered.

Hulda grabbed Tynos's face in both hands—awkwardly in the tiny space—and kissed her full on the lips. "Tynos my sweet, I just found us a way out. Go"—she pointed diagonally up—"that way."

53

TOLD YOU SO

SARAH

Everything was black. It took a moment for Sarah to realize it was because her eyes were closed. She thought about opening them, but it seemed far too much effort.

Soft. She was in a bed. And pain. That brought memories. There had been fighting, and she had killed someone.

No.

Lots of someones.

Even her thoughts exerted her. They came slow and brought more pain. She had injured herself. And then a face in the sky looked down on her and said . . . What did it say?

Was she going to die?

Someone told her she would never die. Finnagel. Because she was a sorceress, like he was a sorcerer. But now Finnagel was dead, so maybe he was not the most reliable source of knowledge. Was she trained enough as a sorceress to be immortal yet anyway? Did she count? Was there a ritual or something?

She just didn't know.

The sound of a door. Breathing. A shuffling gait. Someone was in here with her. If she could just get her eyes open, but no. It would be easier just to be killed. She was so tired.

"We warned you this was not your path."

Magda stood beside her bed. Of course. Cass *would* be here to gloat, and Magda delighted in expounding on Sarah's failures.

"By the time we reached Angrim, you would have been able to destroy him as you did his apprentice."

Go fall down a butt. That was terrible. Was she really this bad at cursing? No wonder she needed Keane so badly.

Where was Keane? Hadn't she just seen him?

"That was impressive by the way. We didn't think you'd be able to do it. Valafar was a frightening talent."

Well, Sarah did not expect to be praised. But there was something else. Something wrong. Magda sounded ragged. Used up.

Old.

"We doubt you will believe this, but we truly do hope this will have been worth it somehow. The Forest Castle is falling to the Ebon Host, and Angrim remains in Dismon, safe to hatch his plots against the Thirteen Kingdoms." There came a ratty sigh. "But against this, you hold our love."

What the butt? *Get off the butts.* What was he or she saying? Love? Cassius never loved anything besides himself, and Sarah wasn't sure if Magda was familiar with the concept.

"This piece of us will die here. It is unavoidable. But you should know that even if this path did not end the way you wished it to, it has been worth it to us, and we would do the same a thousand times over."

No no no nononono.

Magda's breathing grew more and more labored. She pitched forward and fell across Sarah.

It hurt quite a lot more than she thought it would.

54

ALL I EVER WANTED

KEANE

I wonder if they'd wait while we make more arrows?" Keane peered out of the crack between the tall double doors. A line of gray light fell in with the snow and failed to illuminate the dark hall.

"The Host appear to have plenty." Sabni twisted his neck and looked through a tiny glass window to Keane's left. He smiled at Keane. "Perhaps they would share?"

"They've been sharing their damn arrows with us all day," came Eli's voice from the darkness somewhere behind. "That's more or less the problem, innit?"

"You ready with the horn, Mahu?" Harden asked. "I don't wanna jump out there with my ass hanging in the wind."

By way of answer, Mahu blew a loud *blat* that set several hundred men in the hall to laughing. Behind them, the great stone kings of Greenshade waited in the shadows.

"I want you to know, Harden," Keane whispered, unable to keep the smile off his own face, "that I am pissed the fuck off that I am going to die fighting side by side with you and your goddamn mercenaries. All I ever wanted was you out of my ass. By every god who ever raped a cow, how was that too much to ask?"

Harden's teeth flashed in the dark, wolflike. "Me too, kid."

"If we're all finished kissing and playing with each other's dicks in the dark," Morholt said from somewhere, "I'm getting hungry. And if I have to wait for all of you to get killed before I eat anyway, I'd like to go ahead and get this ridiculous shitshow started."

"Nobody is playing with anyone's dicks, Holt," Raven said. "If someone were, it would by damn be me."

"Then what am I holding?" asked Morholt.

Keane chuckled and flung open the broad front doors of the castle keep. "For Greenshade!" he shouted and charged into the surprised Ebon Host. A teeth-rattling horn blast sounded from the entryway, and behind the Free Hand, hundreds of Kings Swords stormed out, shouting battle cries and waving their blades in the air.

At the sound of the horn, Baron Drake and Baron Hapstan, both of whom led contingents of their own troops, flew out of the royal stables on horseback and lay about themselves like crazed woodsmen, chopping down frightened Tyrraneans.

From the north wall, Baroness Fenrath, full of wrath and more impressive than ever, directed her brave soldiers in an assault down the wide stairs. They shoved the big barrels of sand they'd been hiding behind down to crush the Host below.

From the south wall, Baron Rollins, silver hair shining and red coat dusted with snow, bellowed the attack as he and his men followed their own barrels down into the courtyard.

The conclave entered the battle in earnest.

Outside the courtyard on the other side of the castle wall, an ocean of black and gray waited to join the fight.

55

OPENING A CAN OF TROLLS

KEANE

The double doors of all three barracks exploded outward, and more trolls than Keane thought would fit surged out with great swords and axes taken from the Forest Castle armory. They bellowed their terrifying war cries and sliced across the ranks of the Tyrraneans as if men were no more than long grass. The Host surrounded them in the huge courtyard, and the trolls formed wide circles, shoulder to shoulder. They cut down all comers who threatened them.

The Host withdrew from the circle, leaving a ring empty of anything but bodies and red- and-white slush between themselves and the savage trolls. The Tyrranean horns blew, and another battery of pikemen made their way through the press at the gate.

"Didn't you kill that guy?" Harden breathed heavily and pointed with his chin. Keane and the Free Hand formed a small knot of steel edges that danced from point to point on the battlefield, wherever Harden thought they could do the most good.

"Oldam fuck my uncle."

At the front of a group of fresh pikemen, surrounded by gray-and-silver-clad soldiers in plate armor, Prince Brannok strode into the courtyard. His red hair flew out in a disheveled mess on his head, blood smeared his otherwise shiny black lacquer and gold plate armor, and his face shone with a deathly pale pallor.

Keane watched that horrid face laugh as the prince's honor guard disarmed Baron Drake and threw the fat lord to the ground at Prince Brannok's feet. Brannok thrust his sword into Drake's shoulder, which brought an alarmed cry from the baron. He stabbed again, though not to kill him, and several more times before he grew bored and walked past, allowing some other soldier the honor of the killing blow.

"I'm gonna kill him better this time," Keane shouted as he started off in Brannok's direction.

He was also going to throw that fucking wrist knife away.

"Form up!" he barked. Only then did he wonder if there were some kind of horrible magic at play here.

The Free Hand clung to Keane, Harden, and Eli and cut a path through the Host. Mahu and Sabni held the flanks, while behind, a curious open space invited attackers to rush in and be stabbed several times in the space of an instant, apparently by the wind, before falling dead and making room for the next bold Tyrranean.

"Just follow the rest, Raven," Morholt's voice said from the empty air. "If they get killed, we'll be closer to the door. No heroics."

"You know I can hear you," Harden yelled. "If I need some bloody damned heroics, I expect to see you up here performing them."

Raven dispatched another Tyrranean. Her invisible daggers punch-punch-punched into the back of his neck.

"If it's all the same," she yelled back, "I—look out!"

A sudden rush of gray-and-black soldiers shoved in from the left. They clustered and fled from trolls. One of them turned and shoved his sword at Keane while another sidestepped Eli and tripped. The thrust blade entered Keane's left hip, and the weight of the falling Tyrranean pushed him into it. Keane heard his pelvis crack under the pressure and screamed. He fell to the ground with the blade protruding from one buttock. More Host fell over him, and the mercenaries counterattacked, trying to clear their way back to Keane.

There were a hundred times too many gray and blacks.

Outside the walls in the distance, horns blew. Other, closer horns blew in response, which prompted more of the further, longer notes. It was as if a musical conversation discussed the best way to fall on a city and crush the life out of it.

Keane went a little crazy. He cut with his sword and screamed and stabbed with his boot dagger until all of the Tyrraneans that lay atop him were at least mostly dead. He felt as if the pain in his hip lanced out at everyone around him.

"Sounds like the rest of them are coming into the city, Eli," Harden said between swings. "At least we know *I* won't die, eh? Sorry about you and the girl though. That's hard luck."

"Fuck off," Eli grunted in reply.

56

NOT THE RESPECT YOU DESERVE, BUT THE RESPECT YOU NEED

KEANE

Horns and drums continued to sound outside the walls. The distant calls of the war horns grew louder and more urgent as they closed the distance to the castle.

Across the courtyard and just inside the castle wall gate, Prince Brannok grew alarmed and shouted orders at his men.

Keane gripped Mahu around the neck and swung his sword with his other hand. They hustled behind the rest of the Hand while Sabni made long strikes with the point of a Tyrranean pike he picked up. Every step felt like daggers grinding his hip bone, but he was the king, and by Oldam's merry granite danglies, he was going to pretend to act like it.

"You should be in shock." Mahu lifted Keane over a pile of corpses to continue their shuffling run on the other side.

"The king defends his people to his last breath," Sabni shouted, a grand grin spread across his blood-spattered face. "For the worth of the king be judged in the House of the Gods by the last breath of the least worthy in his kingdom."

Mahu rolled his eyes and shared a conspiratorial whisper with Keane. "*Parable of the Angry Wind.* Don't tell him I knew it."

Eli laughed and batted a sword stroke aside, only to jab his own short-bladed weapon into a Tyrranean armpit. They were closing in on Prince Brannok's position.

"Fight, you bastards," Eli screamed to the Hand. "Fight for all yer bleedin' worth. Those are Coldspiner horns—"

"High King Ivarr is attacking the fuckin' Ebon Host!"

Fighting within the courtyard paused as everyone took a moment to stare at the gate. Beyond, Keane saw terrified Tyrraneans looking north, some trying to flee. Brannok and his guard ran to the right of the gate and jumped out of the way as the first warriors of Coldspine, mounted on leather-barded windibou, cut their way into view on the other side of the castle gate.

Laughter erupted from Keane and chased the pain in his hip and the clouds in his head away. He had stopped considering the possibility that they might win long ago. He just wanted Prince Brannok to choke on the victory.

He might live. Megan—and his baby—*might live*!

An armored mount lowered its head and charged into one of the Host, while its laughing rider plunged his lance into another before being dragged from his saddle by Tyrranean pikes.

A crowd of windibou-mounted fighters broke through into the courtyard, and the embattled defenders sent up a ragged cheer, redoubling their efforts against the Ebon Host.

Outside the inner gate, Keane saw a huge man that could only be High King Ivarr, accompanied by a mounted army of motivated and extremely violent-minded northmen, charge through the Tyrranean ranks, whooping and killing. Formerly rigid lines of soldiers scattered, leaving themselves easy prey for the howling Coldspiners.

Keane fought down his delirium and hopped with the rest of the Hand toward the Tyrranean Prince. He still had a job to do, and part of that included staying alive long enough to hold Megan again.

Most of the prince's gray-and-silver guard lay at his feet, and the embattled tyrant fought against three Greenshade defenders. He not only held them at bay but launched swift and devastating attacks of his own.

Eli and Harden were out front and looked as if they intended to take on the prince themselves. If they could kill Brannok now, this would all be over with.

"Hey, Eli, let's kill that short-changing bastard," Harden said.

"Aye, Marshal. An' then I'm fuckin' retirin'."

"Go get him, you old fucks," Keane yelled. "We'll keep you clear."

A black and gray fell in front of Keane, clutching his bloody face and making a *huk-huk* noise. Keane shoved him down and stabbed him in the stomach.

The two mercenary men stepped out of the melee as Brannok gutted one of his assailants. The prince maneuvered to the south stair that lead to the top of the wall and fought on the broad landing half-way up.

With Mahu supporting him, Keane called the defense. Sabni whirled his new pike in sharp steel arcs that slung blood in the faces of the oncoming Host. To Keane's surprise, a battered-looking Captain Falt ran up with a dozen Swords to help hold the base of the stair.

"C'mon, Mahu," Keane said. "Carry me up this stair, and throw me in that redheaded bastard's face. It'll be the *Tale of the Bastard Invaders and the Idiot King*."

Mahu shrugged and dragged Keane up the stairs.

Ahead of them, Eli and Harden ran the steps two at a time.

The remaining two soldiers on Prince Brannok, one a King's Sword and the other a man of Fenrath, were at this point merely trying to stay alive. Brannok was faster, stronger, better armored, and longer reached, and obviously adept at fighting more than one enemy at a time.

Eli and Harden paused several steps below the landing and watched the prince fight.

Keane wanted to shout at them to help, but his pain had returned tenfold, and he was mostly just trying to remain conscious.

Even in his plate armor, Brannok danced around his opponents. He flowed in and out—but mostly in. When the Sword came at him high, he leaned back and swung low, clipping the other man in the shin. Then Brannok reversed himself, bobbed inside the Fenrath soldier's thrust, and with the blade of his big weapon in both hands, smashed the pommel into that soldier's mouth.

The soldier from Fenrath fell off of the landing to the ground twenty feet below. The Sword blinked and bled from his broken shin and staggered nervously, his blade in front of him.

Breathing like a bellows, with sweat streaming off his frozen face, Keane tried to get his good foot under him and help Mahu shove his useless bulk up the stairs before his Sword died.

Prince Brannok charged the remaining soldier, enraged and screaming. The Sword yelped and drew back, misjudged his distance to the edge, and fell off the other side.

Keane's scream of rage came out a strangled yelp.

Brannok walked to the middle of the landing and grinned down at Eli and Harden. Filth and blood covered his armor, and his face still seemed much too pale.

It was incomprehensible that the brutish man was still even on his feet.

"You get anything useful out of that?" Harden asked.

"Well," Eli replied, "he's aggressive as hell an' moves good, but I think he's more about speed an' force than proper tactics."

Brannok's grin faded as he registered the conversation.

Keane stopped and remembered the fight he had against Eli and a drunken Harden.

"Not that I blame him," Eli said. "He does well enough with it."

"So, handle him like that old bandit master we found in Hide Wood?"

"It's your choice," answered Eli. "You're the boss. But if I'm pickin', I'd say treat him like that pig Ferri in Vastard."

The prince's brows drew together. He lifted his big blade.

A slow smile came to Keane's face. He tapped Mahu on the shoulder, and the two of them stopped on the steps, well below the fight.

"Who?" asked Harden.

"Big guy, scar from here to here." At Harden's head shake, Eli looked down and rubbed his chin. "You 'member his sister? Sharina? Black hair and—"

"I got it," Harden said, nodding. "Yeah, that'll work."

Out of patience, Brannok bellowed a challenge and bolted forward. He flung out a long mid-level swing that forced both mercenaries back a step and followed it with a hop toward Harden, a huge armored elbow aimed at his face.

Eli aimed a quick jab at Brannok's shoulder, but the red-haired prince saw him and batted the blade away with a gauntleted glove. Instead of pressing his advantage with Eli, Prince Brannok stomped forward and caught Harden with a steel-shod knee in the face that pushed the gray mercenary down two steps.

"Careful, Red," Keane shouted. "I know you Tyrraneans love a good sheephole, but Eli and Harden are both jealous types. They're not gonna appreciate you sniffin' around each other's butts."

Eli jumped in and banged his short blade against Brannok's forearm, not to hurt him but to keep him from killing Harden. Unfortunately, Eli now had the prince's full attention.

The big Tyrranean grabbed Eli's sword wrist and spun him. He wrenched Eli's recently wounded shoulder and brought a howl of pain.

The balding mercenary awkwardly punched at Brannok's face, but the blows that connected were weak and failed to do any harm.

"Hey, Prince." Keane was getting the flow now. "Does Angrim really ride your dad around the citadel at night? I heard your sister spends every morning washing emperor poop off his dick."

Prince Brannok growled, and his cheeks went a blotchy red. He pulled Eli's arm, eliciting a moan and causing Eli to drop his blade.

"Can ya please—*arrgh*—shut the fuck up?" Eli snarled at Keane.

Harden came in low and wrapped his arms around both of the prince's legs, pulling the bigger man's knees together. Brannok roared and swung Eli down. The mercenaries crashed sideways and rolled across the steps.

The prince turned to Keane.

"Whoops." Keane showed Prince Brannok his teeth in a defiant grin. "I think the frostcocked, father-fucking, cat-raping, baby-dicked, shit-licking, tunny-cunted *momma's boy* has finally noticed us!"

"Are you certain this is a good idea?" Mahu asked as the prince hefted his huge blade and came toward them. The Darrishman took position on the step above Keane, sword up, with Keane's hand on his other arm for support.

"I've never met anyone more likely to dress a pig in satin, feed it an eighteen-course meal of nothing but cheese, and then spend all night sniffing the chair it sat in. And, Junior, I know the Swifthart dynasty has never included any real intellectual giants, but in your case, I think all of Angrim's skull fucking has left some truly debilitating holes in your brain. Oh, and while we're at it, is it true that a man who carries a giant sword to battle is compensating for his mom being a lousy fuck?"

Brannok raised his blade above his head and charged down the stair.

"Oops!" Keane shouted. "*That* one hit a nerve!"

"*Shut your—*" was all the enraged Brannok managed to scream before Harden's dagger stabbed up between his right leg and balls. Blood pumped in great gouts down the prince's leg. Eli stabbed repeatedly into the side of the Prince's neck with his good arm, his own dagger splashing crimson with each wet cleaving.

Prince Brannok roared and dragged the two mercenaries another ten feet, within easy striking distance of Keane. He stood, and he swayed, while Harden and Eli carved death into his body.

Then the First Prince of Tyrrane fell. He tumbled over and rolled down the steps.

"See?" said Eli after the rolling corpse. "That's tactics."

"Can someone make sure that bastard is really dead?" Keane called out.

As if appearing from nowhere, Raven stepped over Prince Brannok's body and stabbed it several times through the face.

"That ought to do it." Harden observed. "Thanks for the distraction, you foul-mouthed little shit," he said to Keane.

"We all play to our strengths." Keane was about to fall over, but he wouldn't do it in front of the whole kingdom. Well he probably would, but he didn't *want* to.

A hush fell over the battlefield. The Forest Castle's defenders waited to see if it was over or if the Tyrraneans were going to howl for bloody vengeance.

They needn't have worried.

Everywhere in the courtyard, soldiers of the Ebon Host threw down their weapons and pled for their lives. A growing cheer drowned out all other sound as the soldiers of Greenshade, and Coldspine too, realized that they had won. The impossible had been accomplished.

Treaty Hill would live.

The front doors of the castle keep flew open, and Megan—a thick-bladed curved dagger like one of Raven's in her fist—stepped out, dragging a bound and miserable-looking Hulda Hubrane behind her. The once-pretty usurper queen's flesh was festooned with bruises and abrasions from being dragged down so many stairs by her feet. Megan, blood streaks across her face and neck, grabbed Hulda by her silky white hair and held her up.

"Throw down your arms this instant or—" she began. "Or—Did we win? Is it over? Did I just drag this stupid sow down all those steps for nothing?"

57

WHAT HAPPENED WHEN WE WERE LOOKING ELSEWHERE

SARAH

Sarah awoke in her own room in the castle. Sunlight streamed in through the many-paned windows. She had chosen the small room for its cozy intimacy, its single easily-defensible door in and out, and because it had already been decorated. The previous occupant, some highly ranked military lord, liked dark greens and red, eschewed lamps in favor of candles, and left a single painting of a fox slinking through a field that looked as if it had been painted at dusk.

There was a bed, a chest of drawers, a table, and a heavy wooden chair in which slept a familiar troll with big backward-curving ram's horns.

Sarah yawned, slipped out of bed, and considered her chamber pot. She had relieved herself in front of the troll before, but this didn't seem quite the same as out tramping through the woods.

"Grohann?" Sarah said from the other side of the small room. "Wake up. I gotta pee."

The troll's breathing quieted, and one eye opened a slit. A sharp-toothed grin spread across his face, and he stood, arms stretched out toward the arched ceiling. Grohann bounded around the foot of the bed and gathered Sarah in his powerful arms.

"Yoo are going to live!" He lifted her off the wooden floor. The fourth reason she'd chosen these quarters, wood felt warmer than stone on her bare feet. "Yoo are not even dead a little bit." The troll set her down at arm's length. "Stay here. King says to find him ven yoo are vaking up. Yes? I vill be back."

And with that, the happy troll ran from the room.

Sarah rolled her arms around to get the blood flowing and utilized the pot. She woke in a simple white shift, so she changed into some more practical clothes: a thick linen shirt, loose dark-blue pants, and boots. Her hair hung loose, and big black waves fell over her shoulders and down her back.

She had not realized how long it had gotten.

A knock came at the door. Before she could answer, Keane hobbled in, his left leg and hip splinted and wrapped and the fingers of his left hand bound together. Bandages barely covered green and yellow bruises on most of his face.

His grin ran from ear to ear.

"C'mon, ya big ox," Keane said.

Megan reached into the room and held the door to keep it from knocking Keane over.

"Don't wanna miss breakfast," he said.

"I guess we must have won?" Sarah asked

"Hi—*oof*—Sarah." Megan tried to stand out of the way while Keane thumped backward. Even the queen had a small bandage on her brow. "Keane, stop it."

The three of them walked the halls of the Forest Castle and caught Sarah up on the battle.

"So, after you went down, Cassius maybe healed you?" Megan related the events. "But I guess he was weakened from that goddess or whatever, and he died pretty much on the spot."

The mention of Cassius triggered a memory of a dream Sarah had. Cassius—or maybe Magda—standing beside her bed talking to her. She couldn't remember more than vague impressions.

"No big loss there," Keane chuckled. "I'm just surprised he was able to be useful at all. Did you know he killed those people who adopted him back when we were kids?"

"I did," Sarah said. "And he was cruel to me as well. Still, I'm not certain if anyone deserved to go the way he did. Magda burned his mind out of his head."

Megan whistled. "That goddess stuff was serious? I thought maybe you'd taught him some sorcery or something."

"Sorcery doesn't work like that," Sarah said as the three of them stepped into a wider busier hall. From here, they could smell the oncoming meal.

Sarah's stomach groaned audibly. "Sorry. Guess I'm hungry."

"You've been asleep four days." Keane grinned like the only man with money in a townful of brothels. "The only thing we could feed you was herbed chicken broth."

"Guess I'm delicious now, too." Sarah recalled Keane's convalescence the better part of a year ago. The castle surgeon must have thought herbed chicken broth cured everything.

They turned the final corner and walked—or hobbled—into the dining hall.

The entire far east wall, made of small glass panes, shone brilliantly. A long table dominated the room, at which sat Grohann, Harden, Eli, and Loffa, Captain Falt, High King Ivarr—what was *he* doing here?—Lady Roselle, and, to Sarah's stunned shock, Finnagel, who looked as if he'd aged two hundred years since she'd seen him last.

Everyone waved and welcomed Sarah, but she barely heard them. "Finn?" She walked to him and knelt beside his chair. He seemed so *frail.* "Is it really you?"

"Sit down and eat. I'll tell you everything you need to know."

Sarah sat in front of the colorful fruits, sausages, and pastries and picked up a strawberry. The instant it hit her tongue, all other considerations fell by the wayside. She became an engine of eating, loading and firing fistfuls of amazing, delicious food into her face as fast as she could chew, swallow, and open it again.

"Slow down, dear," said Lady Roselle. "You'll make yourself sick."

Instead of slowing, Sarah hunkered over her plate and grabbed her glass. She drained it of cool sweet water in one go before she returned to the cheese-stuffed pastries.

Everyone else stopped what they were doing and stared, amazed. Ivarr smiled, his face lit with a different kind of hunger altogether.

Eventually, Sarah did slow down and glanced up self-consciously at the attention she was receiving. She smiled and covered her mouth with a napkin.

"I told you I was hungry." There was some laughter at that, and the table chatted once again.

"So, Old Man Finn," Sarah said across the table, eager to start a new subject, "I saw you die."

Finnagel grimaced as if Sarah's ignorance pained him physically. "I told you that I am immortal. Death is little more than an inconvenience." His skin, once a lustrous near-black, hung ashen and wrinkled from his bones. Where his hair had neatly fallen to his shoulders, a few white wisps now hung matching the scrabbly and patchy beard. His typical gold-colored kaftan only accentuated the old sorcerer's gaunt and aged appearance.

"Well, sure, but I thought that meant you could survive getting stabbed or something like that. I saw you"—she waved a hand back and forth—"all sliced into bits. We got splashed on."

"That is right." Grohann nodded his big head. "Kadir killed yoo all over the place. All over us."

Staring flatly at the troll, Finnagel said, "That's not how it works." He glanced around the room and waved the servants out. Once they left, he continued. "A sword stroke will kill me just as dead as any other man. I told you that I had died more than once. But when I do, I am reborn here in the Forest Castle, drained and temporarily powerless."

"Like when we found you after you were killed by Kadir in Agran-ti," Megan said. "You looked older then, too. But nothing like this."

"It'll pass," Finnagel said, that pained expression on his face again. "When Songham took the castle, I had yet to recover my abilities. He caught and killed me easily. Unfortunately, when I was reborn, I was spotted."

"They killed you again?" Sarah reached across the table to take Finnagel's hand. He withdrew it before she reached him.

"At first, yes. But when the snakes realized what was going on, Hulda's people had a cross erected and tied me to it." He raised his hands in an 'X' shape. "They ordered a spear thrust through my heart and into the wood beneath. That way, every time I died and was reborn, I would come back in the same place, with a spear already thrust through my heart."

"How many times . . .?" Sarah's fingers covered her mouth.

"I don't know. Thousands? Tens of thousands? More? I don't know, and I don't want to."

"You told us before that dying made you more powerful," Megan said. "So maybe something good can come of your experience."

"I'm afraid it still isn't worth it, Your Grace," Finnagel replied. "But as I said, I'll get over it."

"So, what are you doing here, High King?" Sarah asked High King Ivarr, who sat quietly to her left. "The last time we met, things didn't end . . . quietly."

Ivarr chuckled, the sound making Sarah think of distantly rumbling thunder. It was the first time Sarah had ever seen the larger-than-life king in normal clothes. His loose shirt, brown vest, and pants made him look like an entirely different person.

"That was just a friendly disagreement. There was no harm in it." His face fell, and he looked serious. "But that's not—that is—" Ivarr took a deep breath and looked Sarah in the eye. "I realized, after your scolding . . ."

Sarah started and glanced around at the others, feeling embarrassed.

"You were right," Ivarr continued. "I was not being a worthy ally. And perhaps not a worthy suitor as well."

"You gotta be shitting me," Keane said, shattering the mood. "Learn to pick your moment. Oldam fuck a stone pig in the eye."

Sarah patted the reddening High King on the hand while the table laughed.

"Maybe we can be friends first," she said. "Let's see if we can just not kill each other for a while."

The High King smiled at that and, before long, led the table in laughter.

"Harden," asked Megan, "where are the rest of the Free Hand? We'd like to give them our royal thanks."

"Sorry, Your Grace," Harden replied. "I sent them along with the Baroness Fenrath. Her guard was looking a little light, and I figured the company might be worth something to the old battle-ax. You can give their share of the thanks to me, and I'll see it gets distributed fairly."

He and Eli both wore fine clothes of silk and fur, rich garments for the pair who ended Prince Brannok's attack.

Eli frowned and fidgeted as if the clothes were made of live river kraits, while Harden appeared entirely at ease—though still somehow oily. There would be no public declarations of gratitude, however. Not for these two.

"You missed Hulda's trial," Keane said to Sarah. He sat at the head of the table next to Megan who looked radiant in a pale green dress that showed off her growing belly. "It wasn't that long though."

"It would tend not to be when you commit the bulk of your crimes in the presence of the entire castle staff," Captain Falt observed. "And, Your Majesty, I have checked in on Sergeant Stath as you asked. His spirits are low. He lost his squad to Hulda's assassin right in front of him. But physically he is—he will recover."

Sarah looked down the table at Falt. He had certainly changed quite a bit since they'd met.

"I thought we were dead when Hulda and that woman attacked us." Megan's voice was barely audible. "I was looking out the arrow loop and"—she swallowed—"if Sergeant Stath hadn't called out . . ."

Keane took Megan's hand. "We'll go and visit him when we're through here."

The table sat in silence for a moment.

"Well then, Captain Falt," Sarah said, "how did you execute Hulda?"

Keane popped back up at that. "Haven't yet. We figured we needed something special, and it took a bit to set up. She's scheduled for this afternoon, though. You woke up just in time."

Sarah frowned and turned to Finnagel again. "I wanted to ask you about that, Finn."

He raised an eyebrow, prompting her to continue.

"When Magda put the splinter of herself into Cass, she said that when it was done, she would just leave. She wasn't sure how much of him would be left when she did, but if she hadn't burned him out of his own skull before she left, he was supposed to live."

Despite everything Cassius had put her through, Sarah found herself angry at Magda's casual use of the man. The way she took his body, seared his brain from within, and then left him to die.

"What is the last thing you remember before you fell?" Finnagel asked.

Sarah thought about it. "I remember Cass—Magda, I guess— telling me that I'd done the spell wrong, burst all of the blood vessels inside my brain."

"That can't be right," Lady Roselle said. "You'd be dead right now, not inhaling half of a baked ham before noon."

"True." Finnagel tapped an arthritic finger against his chin. "In fact, I believe you were."

Just past Ivarr, Harden pushed his chair away from the table and stared at Sarah behind the High King's back. She lifted her chin and widened her eyes in a "What?" gesture. Harden narrowed his own eyes and said nothing.

"I guess this must be hell, then," Sarah said. "I like the little cheese pies."

Finnagel snorted. "Obviously you are not currently dead. I believe that Magda expended the splinter of herself that she placed into Cassius when she returned you to life."

Sarah shook her head. "No, that doesn't make any sense. Why would she do that? I mean she didn't hate me or anything, but she made it pretty clear where I fell on the god-sorcerer-human scale. It was somewhere around pet rat."

"It wouldn't make any sense," Finnagel said, as he leaned back in his chair, "unless Magda had become infected with Cassius's sentimentality. Perhaps his affection for you rubbed off on her. Altered her ability to make decisions."

"Why would he do that? If I'm a sorceress, aren't I immortal too? Why would Cass have to sacrifice himself? I mean Magda. Why would anyone have to die for me?"

"You are certainly a sorceress," Finnagel agreed, "but you are not yet immortal. Not until you have a place of power of your own or your soul aligned and enslaved to another so you might use his. As Valafar was to Angrim."

Somehow the idea that Sarah was not an immortal like Finnagel or Angrim gave her some peace. She was not afraid to be a sorceress, but knowing she was still her own person, capable of love and friendship and all the other joys and foibles of her humanness, came as a relief.

She was still mad at Cassius though. He likely only let himself die for her just to make her feel bad about the way she treated him *after* he betrayed her.

"Cassius was a self-interested ass," Keane said. "He didn't give a stone fuck about Sarah. Not really."

"I must beg to differ, Your Majesty," Finnagel said. "The bonding process between splinter and host is a particular and troublesome one. It is simply not possible unless the inhabited party is fully aware of what is happening *and* is entirely willing. If Cassius agreed to become Magda's host, with knowledge of what his sacrifice truly entailed, I'd say that his affections must have run very deep indeed."

Sarah's anger deflated like a punctured wine skin. Magda sacrificed a piece of her mind to save Sarah when she had no need to. And she did it because Cassius convinced her to. Poor, stupid, desperately flawed Cassius who only wanted to make things right with Sarah again. Maybe it was the glittering sands that changed him or maybe not.

It didn't matter anymore. He died a hero.

Sarah thought that perhaps Cassius had avoided his destiny to die alone and reviled. Maybe they had all escaped destiny when Sarah unmoored the world from its future. She was no longer bound to her destiny of becoming a cold and heartless monster, like Kadir. Or like . . .

Finnagel. She glanced over at him.

He was already watching her.

"If I may, King Keane," said High King Ivarr, "might I offer you another neck for your block this afternoon? Just prior to our decision to head to your aid, my fighters raided behind Tyrranean lines on the Paras Plains and captured Prince Cantil, King Brannok's second son. Since you have already taken three of his sons now—"

"Hey," said Harden, "one of those was mine, uh, Your Highness."

"You and Eli would've been tossed off the stair to your miserable deaths if I hadn't been there to help," Keane's voice rose.

"Aye," Eli interjected. "You gave the brute a right proper yelling at."

Keane's head dropped. He inhaled, held it, and breathed out. "*Anyway*, I didn't really kill any of them. Finnagel pushed Tobin off a wall, Harden and Eli skewered Brannok Junior, and Despin just fell out of a carriage. I'm kind of a bystander in all this."

"Regardless," Ivarr said, "We have brought Cantil with us. He is my gift to you."

"Thank you, High King, but I don't know Cantil, and while I am really looking forward to Hulda's execution, if it's all the same to you, maybe we should just send Cantil home in disgrace. Maybe make a space to start from with King Brannok."

Ivarr sat up straight, one brow raised in confusion. "Why would you give a prisoner away—for *nothing*?" He shook his head. "Please forget I made the offer. Cantil can serve me as a house slave. We did not capture him to give him a windibou and a pat on the head and send him back to his daddy."

"How did you decide to execute Hulda again?" Sarah asked. Keane began to reply, but Megan interrupted him.

"She doesn't know," the queen said.

Keane's face became somber, and Megan slid her hand into his. "Just after you left for Oulan, maybe even a little before, Songham killed his brother Branch. He wanted to make sure that there was no one in his way when he stole the crown. In order to *honor* her husband's memory, Hulda had Branch's son and wife sent for and killed the same way."

Sarah hadn't known Duke Branch long, but then it hadn't taken long to like him. The warm, generous man had known everything about who Sarah and Keane really were and, instead of throwing them in irons, had tried to make them the best people they could be for the sake of the kingdom. She would miss him dearly.

And she had never even met his family.

"Where are we killing her?" she asked.

58

A FITTING DINNER
SARAH

The menagerie wrapped around the northern inner wall into the Andosh and Darrish Quarters, jutting further north as it followed the curve of the Monarch's Tower. Low and flat except for the aviaries, it housed animals sent to Treaty Hill as diplomatic gifts as well as numerous other acquisitions made by the monarchy. Built of white stone that set it off from the rest of the castle, the building held little strategic significance and had suffered no damage during the recent battles.

It was a place Sarah found relaxing and diverting, despite her attempted murder there.

For now, though, it held the significance of spectacle.

A half-moon of stands had been suspended—by order of the king —from the roof of the menagerie. They partially surrounded the open top of the water dragon exhibit and gave all a good view inside.

In a front row seat, Sarah sat before thousands of Treaty Hill citizens. They hooted and laughed and jostled on the long wooden benches. She looked back at the sea of eager faces and gray-green acorn caps. These people wanted to see justice done for what happened to them. They wanted to close the book and move on.

Above the dragons, four enormous and curving beams rose from the cardinal points along the edges of the open roof and met in the middle to make a sort of open dome. A catwalk extended beneath the furthest beam to a circular platform in the middle. In the center of that platform, manacles attached to a heavy chain hung over an open hole. A large bucket rested on the planks alongside. Directly below the platform, some twenty feet down, the dragons' artificial crag jutted from foul-smelling green water. The two water dragons attempted to stay out of sight, although there was not any real place to hide.

"This is a right big bit of to-do," Eli said from Sarah's left. Harden sat beside her, and Eli just past him next to Loffa. "We killin' the murderous bint or watchin' some kind of magic trick?"

"Perhaps some of both," said Megan from Sarah's right. "Hulda's execution will remove the last obstacle to a peaceful Greenshade. I didn't think it could happen"—she placed her hand on Sarah's—"and it wouldn't have if I hadn't met all of you."

"I kinda thought you never would have been in this mess to begin with if it hadn't been for us," Sarah said, a sad half smile on her lips.

Megan shook her head. "No. It looked that way because of the timing, but everything that happened would have occurred without you except for the ending. That would have been far less pleasant. The wheels were already in motion."

"I guess it's good Harden was trying to kill us, then."

Across the open rooftop stood Finnagel, now just a wizened Darrish man in a gold kaftan. She recalled a conversation in Holshat with him about appearing weak and drawing out powerful enemies.

The wheels were already in motion.

"What are we doing?" asked Loffa, a cheerful smile on her beautiful face. Her golden hair had been made into a pair of braids in the front and fastened in the back through a leather sleeve to keep the rest of her hair out of her face. It was exactly the same as Sarah's.

"Feedin' the lizards." Eli waved his hand toward the huge beasts below. Water dragons resembled some terrestrial lizards but were as much as thirty-five feet long and lived in huge numbers on the cliffs of the Paradisals and Sedrios. They were excellent oceangoing hunters and had no real natural enemies. They were too big.

"I hope we're feeding them that miserable woman, Hulda Hubrane," Loffa said. "She is the sort of person that can absolutely ruin a kingdom."

Eli stared at Loffa, speechless.

Harden just grinned.

"Why are you looking at me like that?" Loffa asked. "Did I say something stupid?"

"No, girl." Eli leaned over to gather the queen mother in a hug, "I think them days is past."

The change in Loffa over the past few months startled Sarah. Keane grumbled about it, but even he had softened.

"Harden." Megan leaned forward.

Sarah leaned back to give her a more unobstructed view.

"Aye, Your Grace. What would you have of me?" Since the fighting ended, Harden had been using the proper forms of address with Keane and Megan. Sarah assumed it was his way of acknowledging Keane's victory.

Megan handed a dagger over to Harden. It was wide bladed and curved to a point, like a flat steel claw.

"I wanted to ask Raven about this," Megan said. "It looks just like one of hers, but I found it on the assassin Hulda had working with her when she attacked me. Her name is Tynos. She's in the dungeon now, recovering from her wounds, but she won't talk. I was hoping that you might be able to tell us something, since Raven's gone to Fenrath."

"Maybe." Harden flipped the dagger over in his hand. He handed it back to Megan. "Looks Egren. I don't know where Raven got hers though."

"Well, damn. That's not a whole lot to go on." Megan looked down at the dagger and put it away. "Raven certainly isn't Darrish; she's as Andosh as they come. I doubt she picked up her daggers in Egren."

Sarah did not know Raven, but unexplained connections between enemies and allies were always disquieting.

"Hmm. Raven's not Darrish, but I'm not sure if she and Holt are Andosh either. Listening to them talk, I don't think they're even from the Thirteen Kingdoms at all."

A rise in the volume of the spectators stopped any further questions from Megan.

Where could this Holt and Raven be from if not Andos? What else was there? The idea made no sense.

"I think they're getting started," Sarah said.

From the small knot of people on the far side of the enclosure roof, Keane stumped forward onto the catwalk to the roar of the crowd. He continued around the hole, manacles, and bucket to the closest edge of the hanging platform and raised his arms, crutches in hand.

After a moment, the shouting subsided, although Sarah could still hear the occasional "*Hail the War King!*" or "*Hero of Treaty Hill!*"

When they quieted to a reasonable degree, Keane spoke. Behind him, a pair of burly Swords wrestled a soiled Hulda Hubrane along the catwalk.

Below, the water dragons perked up and watched the proceedings with new interest.

"Citizens of Greenshade and survivors of the Siege of Empires!" Keane yelled.

Surprised, Sarah realized that Keane, in his green vest and pants, yellow shirt, and ermine cloak, actually looked like a king. The crown didn't hurt, either.

Behind him among the gathered nobility, Sarah saw High King Ivarr. Suitor, indeed. That was a ridiculous notion she would have to put an end to. The burly king flashed bright white teeth and waved at Sarah, who, not knowing what else to do, smiled and waved back.

With a start, Sarah registered that Hulda was being fastened into the manacles and that she was missing part of Keane's speech.

"—have been found guilty of treason against your country, your sovereign, and your kinsman," Keane shouted. "You have murdered your nephew, Duke Reid Hubrane of the Western Marches and his mother the *rightful* Duchess Sigga Hubrane, acted against the well-being of your fellow citizens, endangered the life of your king and queen, entered into conspiracies with our enemies, and threatened the throne of Greenshade *and* the lives of all her people—to say nothing of all of the innocents you actually *did* murder. You wrongfully assumed the position of King of Greenshade, acted like a complete dick in his home, assaulted the queen, and—Oldam's butthole—you fucking *killed* Reid."

Sarah thought that Keane might be deviating from the script a bit there at the end, but it played well with the crowd. From all the noise they made, you'd think that they were ready to eat the deposed queen themselves.

"You did that last one twice, sweetie," Hulda said with a wink. Despite her calm demeanor, a furious pink blush crept up her neck and face. This woman was cool under pressure.

Too bad it wouldn't do her any good here.

Keane waited again, his eyes closed. This time, when he spoke, Hulda was pulled to hang, upright and fully trussed, over the hole in the platform. Salted duns, the dragons' favorite food, had been tied in a big fishy garland around her neck.

The dragons eyed her swaying form above them and made no further attempt to hide.

"Your lands and titles shall revert immediately to the crown to be disbursed as your king sees fit. You shall be executed here by the same animals you murdered your nephew and sister-in-law with and your husband used to kill his brother. What say you to these people?" Keane finished his part and faced Hulda.

On the far side, Sarah saw a big man in a black-hooded mask grip a long handle attached to Hulda's chain. When Keane gave the signal, the villain would be dropped, and the dragons would have her.

"If you're looking for an apology," Hulda shouted so everyone could hear, "you're going to have to catch my next execution." Hulda stretched fetchingly in her tight gown. "In this moment of reflection, I find myself regretting the people I didn't kill rather than the ones I did." Hulda wiggled her body to face a tall mustachioed man in a Western Marches general's uniform and thick manacles.

"Roen honey, you ought to know your wife has been cheating on you with every officer under your command for the past twenty years."

The general's mouth dropped open.

Hulda slowly spun, and she winked one last time at Keane. "See ya when you make it to hell, babe."

Well, Sarah thought, she was certainly going out on her own terms.

The larger of the two water dragons ran up the side of the crag and leaped unexpectedly and spectacularly into the air. His gigantic head sailed through the hole in the platform, taking Hulda's dangling legs fully into its mouth and closing around her middle, just below the ribcage. The creature fell and bounced its weight against the chain as Hulda tore in half.

The platform jolted. One end careered into the air and threw Keane flat. His crutches fell into the water below with a thick, green splash.

Sarah gasped and stood, but there was nowhere for her to go. She couldn't help in time.

Keane pulled himself onto his good leg with one of the thick chains that held the wildly rocking platform. Captain Falt ran out, grabbed him, and walked Keane off onto the catwalk and away from the still gasping top portion of Hulda Hubrane.

Just as Falt and Keane made the walkway, the smaller dragon attempted to leap onto the platform. The twenty-foot creature ripped it free of its moorings and sent the whole affair crashing down into the enclosure.

Hulda's upper half dangled alone from the broad beams above, lifeless.

Sarah and Megan stood in their seats while across the roof Keane, one arm around Falt, patted the hooded man on the shoulder. The executioner stepped away from the lever, and Keane yanked back on it to send the rest of Hulda to the dragons.

Harden put his thumb and forefinger in his mouth and whistled loudly.

"Do it again!"

59

YOU KNEW THAT GUY?

KEANE

"Did you pick a sculptor, yet?" Keane asked Sarah.

They walked in the noonday sun, Keane hobbling on crutches and Finnagel following, up Elder Street toward Magda's Cross. The three of them traversed the city in common clothes which allowed Keane a street-level view of the damage caused by the Tyrraneans. Other than the stone buildings sacrificed for siege ammunition, there wasn't much. Prince Brannok, despite all of his bluster, obviously intended to rule the city after he took it.

Or perhaps Valafar had.

"Baroness Roselle has given me three to pick from," Sarah answered, "but I don't know anything about statues. I'm sure that Cass would have had an opinion about who would sculpt his memorial statue, but I'm clueless."

To their right, the Merchant's Triangle, a section of town dominated by shops and craftsmen, bustled with activity. To their left lay Dorin Park, mostly tenements sprinkled with a few businesses and shut up tight against the winter weather.

"Secretary Roselle," Finnagel said from behind.

Keane smiled at that and said, "Actually it's Royal Officer Roselle.

She didn't want to inspire any enmity with the remaining Hubranes by taking their title even though she's basically doing the same job."

"I'm not calling her that." Finnagel's gray and white brow pulled together, and his mouth rumpled down. "It's preposterous. It means nothing." His long black leather coat flapped in the breeze. Underneath, he wore the familiar gold kaftan and soft boots.

Keane rolled his eyes and waved the issue away while Sarah laughed. He looked up at the right side of her face, appraising her critically.

"That tundra cat came pretty close to taking your eye. Did you even think about using a bow instead of running up on a bunch of man-eaters like that?"

The scars, though healed, ran in parallel lines from her forehead to her cheek. They started just behind her eye and back up into the hairline where the hair now grew silver. The whole almost looked like some exotic tribal marking rather than cat claws.

Sarah rarely wore her armor anymore since the siege, favoring the kinds of blousy shirt, dark vest, pants, and cloak that she wore now. Keane had heard she'd adorned actual dresses in Agran-ti, but he hadn't gotten up the nerve to ask her about it.

"Those cats gave me a lot to think about," Sarah replied.

"Oh, right." Keane nodded as a grin spread across his face. "The High King. What are you gonna do about that?"

Sarah favored Keane with a flat glare. "Nothing. I have more than enough crap in my life to deal with without adding that kind of complication. And you're not going to do anything either. Your record at matchmaking sucks. You *liked* Cassius."

The bright sun was no match for the frigid wind that blew right through Keane. He couldn't wait to get to the Jolly Chicken. He was cold, and he was hungry. Also, his armpits were chafing from the crutches. Keane pulled the heavy brown cloak tighter around his shoulders and tried to tuck it under his arms.

"I just liked him. I didn't *like*-like him. He was supposed to be useful on the trip. I never told you to fuck him. *Ow!* Hey, it's bad enough when Megan hits me. You'll take my whole fucking arm off."

He rubbed his shoulder. Yes, it hurt, but Keane just had to laugh. Not even a whole year ago, he and Sarah had just been mercenaries. They fought for the money of men they didn't know and were cogs on a wheel they couldn't even see.

Look at them now.

A king, a husband, and a soon-to-be father walked down the street with a sorceress descended from the gods above. It didn't seem possible to him, and he had lived it.

"I, uh, I have something for you," Sarah said.

Keane stumbled to a stop and Finnagel scowled further, his ancient and gnarled face folding in on itself.

"It's nothing, really." She shrugged and opened the red leather pouch at her hip. "I just, well, *Grohann* didn't want to leave it behind."

Though Finnlaug and the rest had departed immediately after the battle, Grohann waited until last week to return to his people. Nearly everyone who wasn't in charge of feeding him had been sad to see him go.

Sarah reached into the pouch and withdrew a sort of teardrop-shaped piece of light brown wood, flattish at the small end and bisected at the big one. Two stumps poked out of the pitted and notched length at odd angles and different lengths.

She held it out to him.

"What's that supposed to be?" Finnagel leaned over to inspect the strange creation with one milky eye.

"It's a walrus." Keane took the carving and held it up reverentially. "And I love it."

"It's stupid. I'm terrible at whittling."

"This is my best and most-favorite non-wife treasure," Keane said. "At least until the baby is born. Thank you."

Finnagel scowled. "Hmph. How far to this bar of yours? I'm thirsty."

"Not long now." Keane placed the walrus-ish piece of wood in his shirt pocket.

The trio resumed their walk. Patches of snow stood in the shadows along the street, and Keane had to be careful not to slip with the crutches. Though healing, the place where the Tyrranean sword broke his pelvis hurt like mighty Oldam shitting fire into his bones, and the last thing Keane wanted to do was fall and make it worse.

"Hey. Do you still remember any of those spells that Magda taught you? Can we make a volcano swallow up a city or sink an island or anything like that?"

"I do." Sarah's brow creased thoughtfully. "But I don't think they're safe to use. Not for a few years, anyway. I wrote them down but even Finn doesn't understand them."

Finnagel looked off to the left at a shop selling travelers' rolls, revealing no indication of having heard the conversation.

"You know I met a guy, one of Harden's Free Hand. Magic guy like you two. Said he was a runecrafter."

"You mean a sorcerer," Sarah corrected.

"Oh no," Keane said. "Not a sorcerer. He was very clear on that point. He said that sorcery was in your blood, but what he did could be learned by anyone. Apparently, he's taught quite a few—Whatthefuck?"

Keane's crutches flew as Finnagel snarled in rage, grabbed him, and spun him around. He held Keane up at arms' length.

The ancient sorcerer's desiccated arms gripped him with a strength like steel.

"Hey, fucker." Keane's breath hitched with the pain that flared from his hip. "That fucking . . . hurts."

"Who is this *runecrafter*?" Finnagel's intensity drew looks from people who walked by on the street. His eyes burned with ancient enmity, and his wrinkled lips pulled back over yellowed teeth. Sarah grabbed his arms but couldn't pull him off of Keane.

"Is he the red-haired Morholt? Where is he? Tell me now!"

60

DENOUEMENT AND OTHER FANCY WORDS

KEANE

Two weeks had passed since the climactic final battle. Keane's military men referred to it as the Country Gate Offensive, the final battle of the Occupation of Treaty Hill. Minstrels in the city taverns had taken to calling Keane the War King, which he liked much less than the Hero of Treaty Hill. But you did not get to choose how others saw you.

Words were funny things.

Keane's thoughts distracted him from his book. The healing hip bone prevented him from climbing all the stairs up to the top of the Crow's Tower, his favorite getaway spot. But the Royal Castle Library in the bottom of the Monarch's Tower served much the same purpose and, while bigger, was equally cozy with its rows and rows of books and statues of old kings from all over the Thirteen Kingdoms. The painted roof with books dwindling away into the heavens made him feel safe somehow.

Emberflies fluttered in their hourglass jars and lit the room, and a beautiful rug covered most of the floor. Keane's chair sat on a brown stain that it did not quite conceal, but he didn't mind. He liked lived-in things.

"It's a dry read." Megan sat curled up on a divan next to Keane's chair, sharing the light from his lantern. She smiled at him and stretched with a slow, languid curl.

Thoughts of longing and heartache rose in Keane. Even the few feet between them was too far away.

He closed the book on his forefinger to keep his place. *Stone on Stone* by Silas Hubrane. It was all about the most efficient ways to rebuild a nation after a devastating war. Keane felt it was his obligation to read the damn thing, but Silas had been a true intellectual, and Keane was new to reading. The book was an uphill climb.

Lots of fancy words.

"Did you know that Silas Hubrane was the one who stole the crown from the Rances?" Megan asked.

"He doesn't ever shut up about it. It's like he tied Oldam's colon in a knot and saved the whole world from being shat on to death. But the stuff about motivating folks to rebuild their own shit for free seems pretty relevant."

Megan stared at him.

"What?" Keane wiped at his face in case there was some breakfast still on it.

"You are going to make a fantastic king."

A knock at the door saved Keane from having to answer. Failure to live up to her needs was always his biggest fear. But recently there was some competition with failing to live up to Greenshade's needs as well.

"Come in," he called.

Sergeant Stath, who stood guard outside the door with one of his Elbows, opened it. "Royal Officer Baroness Roselle Tralgar and Lady Aerith Ravenstok."

The two women, one short and plump, the other tall and thin, stepped into the room and curtsied.

Roselle's mouth dropped open. "He's reading whole *books* now? My queen, did you know about this?"

"You taught him. You've no one to blame but yourself."

"Do you mean to say that the king couldn't read?" Lady Ravenstok said. "*This* is the man that outfoxed the most powerful army in the

Thirteen Kingdoms? Or at least stood by while High King Ivarr did." She shook her head. "I can only guess how much trouble we'll be in for now that he can simply walk in here and get *ideas*."

"I'm not reading a fucking thing with all this nattering going on. Oldam's crusty—"

"Language, my king." Baroness Roselle wagged a finger at Keane in an intimate and familiar gesture.

She had been an amazing tutor to him. Keane had always been confident that things like reading and table manners were simply beyond him. Roselle had shown him that wasn't true. She had gifted him with wings, and it was his responsibility to fly with them.

"—toenail," he finished. Keane canted his head to one side. "You do know, Lady Ravenstok, that you're here for me to decide what to do with you."

"Merely admiring your brilliance, Majesty." Lady Ravenstok bowed her head.

"I wanted to throw you into the water dragon exhibit along with Hulda, but the baroness here wouldn't hear of it." Keane waved an arm at Baroness Roselle. "*She* seems to think that it was *your* doing that kept Hulda in town long enough for mighty Queen Megan to beat her up and capture the evil woman."

Lady Ravenstok kept her head down and said nothing.

"But you aren't getting off for free." Keane put the ribbon in his book and placed it on the table beside his chair. He sat up and glared at Lady Ravenstok. "The treasury isn't just spread thin; it's been snapped in half, rolled up to the ends, and eaten by sharks. I have two towns that need to be put back together from the ground up, and I happen to know that you're sitting on a fortune that you've stolen from Greenshade's taxes over the years."

Lady Ravenstok's head slowly raised, and one eyebrow went up.

"You're gonna use that money to"—his eyes darted unconsciously to the cover of *Stone on Stone*—"reconstitute and modernize the town of Crosshouse. It will be bigger, more welcoming, and more easily audited." He thought he was using that word right. Lady Ravenstok's obvious irritation certainly indicated he was. "And Roselle? Since you were so interested in releasing Aerith back into the wild, I'm making it your project to check up on her. I know it seems like a punishment, but someone has to, and I don't have the time."

"Delighted to, sire," Roselle said. Her lips were pursed, and her gaze cut at Lady Ravenstok through narrowed eyes.

"Excuse me, dear," Lady Ravenstok said, "but what do I get for all this charity? I can't be expected to throw away my family money for nothing."

Keane's bloodless smile chilled the library. "You get to live above-ground, where you can see the sun and everything doesn't smell like your own piss."

Lady Ravenstok blinked. Once. Twice.

"That sounds fair."

"Also, you're changing the name of the town to *Keane's Crossing*."

Megan laughed, and Lady Ravenstok's eyes went wide. Even Baroness Roselle rolled her gaze heavenward.

"Now get to it." Keane waved them off. "But, Aerith, I want you to know something before you go. Roselle and Sarah have worked together for a while now and are very good friends. So good, I am told, that they're linked together, like with magic and stuff. If anything happens to Roselle while she's checking up on you, Sarah will know it—and she'll know who was responsible."

The color drained from Lady Ravenstok's already pallid cheeks.

"And whoever that is will have to deal with *her*."

Baroness Roselle backed a nervous Lady Ravenstok out of the room and shut the door behind them.

Megan arched a brow of her own. "That was . . . fanciful." She tried to conceal her amusement but could not. "If Sarah hears you're using her to scare the nobility into behaving themselves, she might start charging you."

"Money well spent." Keane leaned over and put his hand on Megan's knee. The warmth of her flooded his chest. Still not close enough.

"I just can't . . ." He did not have the words to express his feelings. Having the words to express himself was Keane's thing. But there had been little call for declarations of love and faith in a mercenary camp, and now his language failed him.

She moved her pale hand over his darker one and slid her fingers through his. "Your world has changed so much over the past two years. I can't imagine what that's been like." She looked down and shook her head, and loose brown curls fell over her face. "Maybe I can a bit. The point is you've risen to the task every time. I've known you were here for me for some time, but recently I've come to understand that you're here for my people too."

"*Our* people."

Keane did not trust himself to speak without tears, so he concentrated on her diminutive hand instead. So beautiful and so perfect.

Her other hand slipped beneath his, and she lifted it to her cheek. "That's how I know I made the right choice."

"Did we ever decide on names?" he asked in an effort to change the subject. He really was a different person now. His time with the Free Hand convinced him of that. He used to be happy amongst mercenaries. Relaxed. Yet his whole time with Harden's crowd was spent jittery and anxiety ridden.

Life had been easier when he had nothing more to worry about than his next meal, but it was a lot less fulfilling.

"Shayla if it's a girl, after Shayla Tyrrane, the first Queen of Greenshade," Megan answered, her gaze close on Keane's face, "and Volker if it's a boy, after Volker Rance III, who returned Greenshade to Rance rule from the Hubranes."

"And I liked both of those?"

"Oh yes. You love them."

"And did we give any consideration to Keane Junior and Sarah?"

Megan's face scrunched up in an adorable little frown. "Sarah isn't bad, but Keane Junior would be terribly bad luck. What if the child turned out just like you?"

"Hey." Keane pulled his hand away, "I'm a fantastic king."

"There is always room for improvement," Megan said. "Although, I really *am* impressed with the way you handled Lady Ravenstok. If she does as you ordered her and handles the reconstruction of Crosshouse—"

"Keane's Crossing," he corrected her.

She stared flatly at him. "*Keane's Crossing*—can we afford to take care of Fenrath? We owe the baroness and her people so much."

"We'll be lucky if we can make Treaty Hill whole, and that's mostly just trampled farmlands and a bunch of broken walls." Megan's face fell, and Keane hurriedly continued. "But I have a plan. It's working so far, and if it keeps up, we'll have enough to rebuild Fenrath twice over and three times as big."

"Are you going to ask the Hubranes?" Megan shifted on the divan to be closer to him. "The March Castle might have the cash, but all the ducal family is dead. Even if they could sort everything out, they might not be well disposed toward the crown."

"Roselle has already picked out a nephew we can count on to be loyal." Keane was grinning now. "I'm coronating him next month. But no, I'm not exactly *asking* them."

"Not exactly?"

"The throne is seizing all the dirty coins the Hubrane Merchant House made smuggling goods through Greenshade. Hulda Hubrane's operation has millions of crowns of crooked money. There's a legit front operation, and we'll return that to the Hubranes when we're done."

Megan's mouth dropped open. "You've been doing all of this while I was organizing the food shelters?"

Keane shrugged his shoulders "Well, that and sending out envoys. Sarah and I figure the balance of power has shifted in the world since we danced on Emperor Brannok's balls. We need some updated treaties that folks'll actually want to honor. Your dad was good at getting signatures but not so great at making actual allies. What?"

Megan continued to stare at him before her smile turned to laughter.

"What?" he asked. He ran his fingers over his face again. "What are you laughing at?"

"You, Your Majesty," Megan pronounced with as deep a bow as

her sitting position and swollen belly would allow, "are actually growing up. *Gawp!*"

The pillow Keane threw hit her in the face and knocked her backward on the divan. She rolled and laughed as he tickled her and smothered her face with his kisses.

He knew he would never deserve the life he had ended up with. He had been a bad person for a long time. The kind of bad not easily forgiven.

But that did not mean he would never stop *trying* to deserve this life.

And her.

61

GIVE THE KING A HAND

KING BRANNOK

A little over five hundred miles away in the dark city of Dismon, capital city of Tyrrane, King Brannok brooded in the throne room of the Fell Citadel, his dreams of empire as fractured as his ruined hand.

His eldest son, Prince Brannok Junior, was slain in battle after losing Greenshade to a vastly inferior force.

Prince Cantil, his next oldest son, had made some headway in the strategically inconsequential Paras Plains, and now reportedly served as a house slave in High King Ivarr's hall for his trouble.

His fourth and fifth sons, Princes Tobin and Despin, had been either killed or murdered by the new king in Treaty Hill. That left him only Jason, softhearted and soft-minded, and Jasmayre, a girl. Damn the gods for that one. The thought of marrying such an astounding mind as hers to the impotent son of some far-flung noble doubled his fury.

Never. He would live to see her rule.

Other than the quartet of black-armored guards in the corners of the chamber, Brannok sat alone—as alone as it was possible to be under a giant Angrim. The storm-like structure glared balefully down on him.

His shattered hand throbbed. It refused to heal at all, and the pain was a constant torment.

The real Angrim now refused to speak with him which suited the king fine. The devil could rot in his tomb.

At the far end of the chamber across the glossy black floor, a knock came at the tall double doors. A guard opened them and spoke to someone in the hall outside. He pulled the ironbound door further open to allow a messenger familiar to Brannok to enter.

The king thought between the pulses of pain, *Rodrim maybe*? The boy was recently married. What a thing to remember about such an insignificant person. As he watched the messenger approach in his black-on-gray livery, Brannok imagined different ways of murdering him and his new bride.

Anything to distract from the pain.

"Your Majesty, you have messages from both Norrik and Mirrik." Possibly Rodrim held up the yellow papers. "Would you like for me to read them to you?"

"Please. Just—don't read them all. Just tell me what they say." Brannok found that when his hand was true misery, like now, his span of attention grew too short for formalities. By the time the lad reached the end of the missive, he would have forgotten the beginning.

"Yes, sire." Rodrim scanned the two pages and cleared his throat.

Brannok twirled his good hand, indicating the boy should speak.

"Both the country of Mirrik as well as all five nation states of Norrik have pledged full support to Emperor Brannok II of the Second Great Tyrranean Empire. Although—" Rodrim looked puzzled at the page, one brow on his attractive young face rising quizzically.

"Yes?"

"Well, sire"—Rodrim flipped back and forth between the pages—"both Mirrik and Norrik seemed to believe that this was the First Great Tyrranean Empire, not the second."

King Brannok grimaced in an attempt to smile and waved his

hand again, this time to dismiss the messenger. His quiet laugh as the boy stalked toward the distant doors held no happiness in it.

Now that all was already lost, the two raider nations were finally ready to set aside their differences and help. They undoubtedly hoped that Tyrrane would be too weak to conduct war and defend itself at the same time. Brannok would have to recall Cantil's mounted troops from the Paras Plains and send them along the Mirrik and Norrik borders. He winced again, gripped his wrist just below the bandages, and squeezed.

The king of Tyrrane, emperor no longer, sat like that for a long time, while outside the feeble sun fell behind mountains, and snow rolled in from the foothills.

"Guard." From Brannok's left, one of the black-armored men stepped forward and snapped a salute.

"Yes, Your Majesty. What do you require?"

"That boy. The messenger."

"Rodrann, sire?"

"Yes. Have him and his wife brought to my chamber tonight. My hand . . ." Brannok let the rest fall off. It wasn't important.

"Yes, sire. It will be done."

Rodrim or Rodrann or whatever it was reached the doors and opened one of them to leave. Just outside the door, a woman smiled and leaned against the frame. She looked like Brannok's wife when younger but was tall and held a canniness Moru never possessed.

Jasmayre had returned.

"And send the castellan in," Brannok said to the guard, a tight grin on his face. He waved up at the huge shape of Angrim. It had been there forever, and Brannok was tired of being looked at by the malignant figure.

"We're taking that fucking thing down."

ACKNOWLEDGMENTS

As I write this at the tail end of 2020, I have to observe what anyone reading this must know—it's been a weird year. What I don't know is how much better or worse it will get from here. Certainly, there are things to be grateful for, and I *am*, but the cloud of oppression from this year has yet to clear.

Which makes those people who have aided me along the way all the more precious.

First and foremost, as always, is Lena. There are many things that had to fall into place, without which there would be no Misplaced Mercenaries, but Lena touches all of them. The truth is, without her, there would be no me. Certainly not the me sitting here now. And I like that guy. She made him better.

Second, but mostly only in proximity, is my publisher, Kelly Colby of Cursed Dragon Ship Publishing. I joke with her sometimes about teaching a cheerleading class for authors, but it's not really a joke. No matter how deep in the doldrums I can get (writing hits your brain in unexpected and jarring ways sometimes), or how stressed I can be about extraneous horseshit, she is *always* there with a supportive word or pat on the back, and I never fail to feel better after talking with her. She is an amazing collaborative partner, and I simply could not have gotten luckier than to end up with her on my team.

Beta and ARC readers Lena Shore, Lloyd Brown, Devin Rollyson, Rook Watterson, Douglas Oosting, Courtney Walker, Thomas Fowler, Brent Shore Jr., Nic Patchett, Jason Harris, Ryan Koch, Brian McCray, Kristin Shore, Adam Czechowski, Julio Rodriguez, Toby Santerelli,

David Drake, Justin Herzog, Mary Natwick, Murshida Va, L.A. Selby, Justin Herzog, David Moran, Doug Boggess, Susan Wilkerson, Kirsten Oliver, Maggie Schill, Adam Davis, Jennifer Taylor, Joseph Hayes, Jo Houghton, and everyone else I have forgotten. These are the Quality Control team that kicks my ass and makes sure that everything is up to snuff. They are the boom-bombiest.

Now my last acknowledgement is both the biggest and most important, and that's the readers. It sounds trite and hackneyed to say it, but you are the most necessary component of this entire endeavor. You are the person I am talking to, and you are the only one that can keep this whole operation afloat. So, thank *you*. Thank you for reading, and thank you for being there.

Maybe we'll get to say hi someday soon. I'd like that.

ABOUT THE AUTHOR

Kevin Pettway hails from Jacksonville Florida and is the author of the Misplaced Mercenaries books, a funny adult fantasy series that was awarded by the NYC Big Book Club, a finalist in the 2022 Imadjinn Awards, and has received several professional write-ups in Kirkus Magazine for which the author did not even have to pay. He has published a modest number of short stories, both within and without the Mercenaries world, with more on the way. Most excitingly, Kevin's publisher, Cursed Dragon Ship Publishing, has threatened encouraged him to open his world to other authors, creating the Misplaced Adventures Shared Universe. There are currently six authors toiling away to bring even more humor, fun, and backstabbing murder into the world, with plans to add even more in the next few years.

Although the old stereotype about writers just wanting to be locked away in a darkened room with a typewriter is as true of Kevin as it is anyone else, the other thing he enjoys tremendously is going to conventions and meeting new people. (In writing, two opposing motivations in the same person are often used to create tension and conflict and engage reader interest. Now that you know his conflicting motivations you understand just how deep and fascinating Kevin is!)

He regularly attends a large number of popular culture conventions, selling books and telling stories to people who haven't heard them before while his wife Lena tries to ignore him. Feel free to walk up and say hi. Nothing makes him happier. (You might also express condolences to Lena, who has heard all the stories.)

River and Book, Kevin and Lena's two dogs, also love meeting people, but hotels rarely love meeting dogs, so they stay behind at the puppy resort. Canine fan-mail will be accepted and forwarded to the appropriate addressee.

Kevin thinks Strange New Worlds is the best Trek series, nudging The Orville off that top spot, and is enjoying the Tolkeinesque comedy The Rings of Power more than he thought he would. His favorite new author is Tamsyn Muir, and his favorite old author is Roger Zelazny. (He may be dead, but he's still selling!) He is also developing an obsession for kayaking, having discovered it late in life and is unable to get enough.

Despite being from Florida, Kevin still has all his own teeth and has never had a restraining order placed against him.

Make sure to join Kevin's newsletter from his website: https://kevinpettway.com.

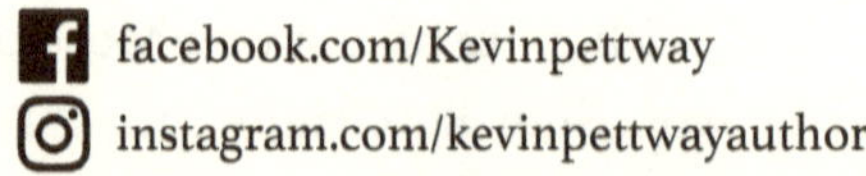

JOIN THE CURSED DRAGON SHIP NEWSLETTER

Want more just like this one? Sign up for our newsletter so you don't miss out on the adventure. You'll get:

- A free book for signing up
- Advanced notice of new releases
- First word of books on sale
- Opportunities for free books
- Most up-to-date information on author appearances.

We're busy and know you are too. We won't send more than one newsletter a month.

Register below.

ON TO BOOK FOUR

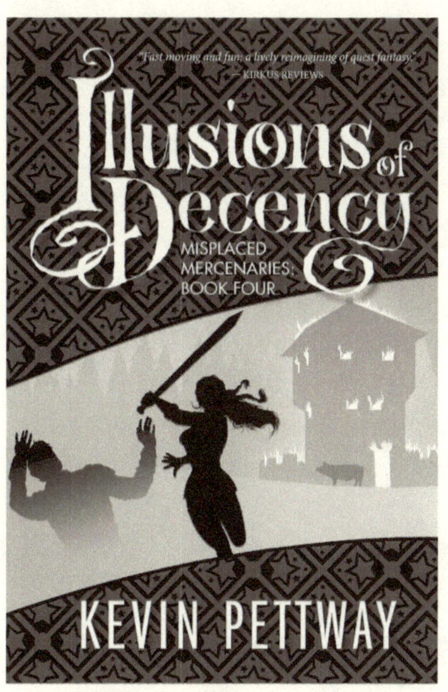

Will the forces of good and sorta-good come together before the forces of definitely not-good crush them, ruin their lands, and take all of their ex-girlfriends?

Not if history is any indication.